"Are you tempting me?" Ramsey asked.

"I CERTAINLY HOPE SO," Helena said.

What was she playing at? He was tired of games. He was impatient, frustrated, and the self-control he so carefully maintained did not hold nearly as well here in the dark, with her body under his.

"And how am I to respond?" he asked coolly, though his hands slipped beneath her shoulders.

"As a man," she answered breathlessly.

"Oh, I can assure you, on that count you will not be disappointed." He smiled into the darkness. "No, what I meant is, what mien would you have me adopt? Whom shall I be in this dark room? Do you prefer the polished swordsman, the sophisticated rake, the disreputable habitué of low places? Shall I be tender or careless? Rough? Interested only in my own pleasure? Shall I fill your ears with compliments? Or oaths?"

Her hands gripped his shoulders tightly. *"Love me,"* she whispered.

PRAISE FOR
CONNIE BROCKWAY

"Romance with strength, wit, and intelligence. Connie Brockway delivers!"

—New York Times bestselling author Tami Hoag

"Connie Brockway is truly an innovative, wonderful writer whose work belongs on every reader's shelf."

—Romantic Times

"If it's smart, sexy, and impossible to put down, it's a book by Connie Brockway."

—New York Times bestselling author Christina Dodd

"Connie Brockway's work brims with warmth, wit, sensuality, and intelligence."

—New York Times bestselling author Amanda Quick

"If you're looking for passion, tenderness, wit, and warmth, you need look no further. Connie Brockway is simply the best!"

—New York Times bestselling author Teresa Medeiros

THE BRIDAL SEASON

*RITA Award Winner for Best Historical Romance
and one of the Romance Writers of America's
Top Ten Favorite Books of 2001*

"This frothy literary confection sparkles with insouciant charm. Characters, setting, and plot are all handled with perfect aplomb by Brockway, who displays a true gift for humor. Witty and wonderful!"

—*Booklist*

MY DEAREST ENEMY

RITA Award Winner for Best Historical Romance

"Brockway's respect for her audience is apparent in her latest Victorian. The rare story introduces social issues without preaching, characters who are well developed, and enough passion, humor, and pathos to satisfy most readers."

—*Publishers Weekly*

AS YOU DESIRE

"Smart, sassy, sexy, and funny. . . . Wonderfully entertaining romance. Connie Brockway has a way with humor that not only makes you laugh, but touches your heart."

—*Romantic Times*

BRIDAL FAVORS

"A scrumptious literary treat . . . wonderfully engaging characters, superbly crafted plot, and prose rich in wit and humor."

—*Booklist*

McCLAIREN'S ISLE: THE PASSIONATE ONE

"An undercurrent of danger ripples through this exquisite romance, set in the 1700s, and Brockway's lush, lyrical writing style is a perfect match for her vivid characters, beautifully atmospheric settings, and sensuous love scenes."

—*Library Journal*

ALL THROUGH THE NIGHT

"Intricately plotted, with highly inventive lead characters, Brockway's latest is an intense and complicated romance. . . . There is excitement, chemistry, obsession, and best of all, a tortured romance."

—*Publishers Weekly* (starred review)

BOOKS BY CONNIE BROCKWAY

My Surrender

My Pleasure

My Seduction

Once upon a Pillow
(with Christina Dodd)

Published by Pocket Books

CONNIE BROCKWAY

My Pleasure

POCKET BOOKS

New York   London   Toronto   Sydney

An *Original* Publication of POCKET BOOKS

POCKET BOOKS, a division of Simon & Schuster, Inc.
1230 Avenue of the Americas, New York, NY 10020

ISBN-13: 978-1-4165-4090-8
ISBN-10:   1-4165-4090-3

This Pocket Books paperback edition January 2007

10 9 8 7 6 5 4 3 2 1

Cover illustration by Alan Ayers
Hand lettering by Ron Zinn

Manufactured in the United States of America

For information regarding special discounts for bulk purchases, please contact Simon & Schuster Special Sales at 1-800-456-6798 or business@simonandschuster.com

For Page Winebarger, whose talent, determination, and unswerving dedication has so well and so long served the Minnesota Wildlife Rehabilitation Center. On behalf of all the creatures who have benefited from her love and commitment, thank you, Page.

ONE

SALUTE:
a customary acknowledgement
of one's opponent

Vauxhall Garden, London
June 1805

"SOMEWHERE IN HEAVEN, Maestro Angelo weeps."

"Who said that?" Young Lord "Figgy" Figburt, demonstrating a parry for his teenage companions, wheeled about. He peered down Vauxhall Garden's dimly lit Lovers Walk to see who'd invoked the name of the last century's greatest swordsmaster.

"I did." A tall, graceful figure detached itself from the surrounding shadows, like darkness coalescing into form and substance, and glided toward them. "I tried to refrain from interfering; I meant to pass mutely by," the stranger purred in elegant Scottish accents. Teeth flashed white in the Scot's shadowed face. "But, as there is life in me, I cannot let a sport I hold dear be so blasphemed."

"What d'ya mean, 'Angelo weeps'?" Hulking Thom Bascomb, dressed for the evening's masquerade as a rather hirsute shepherdess, demanded tipsily. "Whadda ya implyin' 'bout Figgy's swordplay?"

"I imply nothing. I *say* his remiss is an abomination. Still . . . it's not beyond redemption."

The man glided nearer, and the muted light from the gas lanterns strung through the trees revealed one of the most extraordinarily handsome men Figgy had ever seen: a tall, whipcord-lean and athletic-looking fellow who'd eschewed the costumes worn by the other attendees of this night's revels. Instead, he wore dark trousers, a black frockcoat with a blue waistcoat beneath, and a simple white stock about his neck, pinned by the only ornamentation on his person, a small gold stickpin in the shape of a rose.

Everything about him made Figgy feel gauche and, therefore, rather surly. "This is a *costume ball*, sir! It means you have to be in *costume*," he pronounced irritably. "See Thom there? He ain't really a gel, and I ain't a rajah."

"You don't say."

Thom wobbled forward and glared at the Scot. "Just what is it you're rigged out as, mister?"

The Scotsman, nearly as tall as Thom but at least three stone lighter, let his gaze slide down the young man's thick, corseted trunk to the layers of pink flounced skirts below. "A gentleman?" he suggested mildly.

Guffaws erupted from the other lads as Thom's face turned brilliant red, but Thom did not demand satisfaction for the insult. Something about the Scot pierced the alcoholic haze clouding what little good sense he owned. Here was something dangerous. Something outside his experience. Something . . . lethal.

"Who're you?" he demanded.

"Ramsey Munro." The man inclined his head slightly.

"I am the owner of L' École de la Fleur. A small salle in White Friars. At your service, young sirs."

"*You're* a swordsman?" Thom sneered, handing Figgy the flask he'd produced from beneath his skirts.

"I am," Munro replied. "I chanced to be walking by when I overheard you young gentlemen discussing the forthcoming International Dueling Tournament. You are considering entering?"

"And what if we were?" Figgy asked. "What's it to you?"

"Nothing. But as an instructor of the art of swordplay, I was interested. I paused and saw you execute a *remiss* a child could counter."

"I s'pose you could do better?"

The man's shoulders lifted in an elegant gesture. "More to the point, I could teach you to do better."

Figgy, seeing a bit of sport to be had, grinned. He was by far the best swordsman of the lot of them. "Could you teach Thom to counter my remiss?"

Munro glanced over. "The milkmaid? Absolutely."

"Or any of these others?" Figgy waved at the rest of his companions, milling drunkenly about the periphery.

"Any of them."

He sounded far too sure of himself, and Figgy's confidence wavered. Perhaps the Scot had some secret *botte*, an uncounterable move that needed little practice but only a few whispered words of instruction?

Fiend seize it, he couldn't back down now. He only wished he wasn't quite so bosky. On that thought, he lifted the flask and emptied the remains into his mouth. As he did, he spied a movement at the end of the gravel path. A figure dressed in the fashion of a young footman from the previous century hurried toward them.

Figgy watched her gratefully. *Her*, because, despite the masculine attire, there could be no doubt that the figure beneath the ruby velvet pantaloons and tight-fitting surcoat was decidedly a "her"—a sweetly curving, luscious "her." She'd stuffed her hair beneath a black cap and a black silk mask covered her eyes, but nothing could disguise the sway of her hips or the bosom that made a mockery of whatever device she'd used to bind it.

Lady or ladybird, it made little difference. She was here, unattended at a Vauxhall Garden masquerade, on the infamous Lovers Walk. Which meant she was at best a barque of frailty looking for a shoal to wreck herself upon, or at worst a Haymarket scow seeking new passengers. Either way, she was fair game, and the game he had in mind would prove fair, indeed. He smiled.

"You could, in fact," he addressed Munro, "teach *anyone*?"

"Yes."

"Well then, how about her?" Figgy pointed at the woman.

Her pace slowed. A glint of lantern light caught the sapphire flash of her eyes behind the mask. Ah, he did fancy blue eyes.

Munro turned his head. "A woman?" he asked with a bored look of contempt. "No."

Figgy grinned with relief. Having shown the stranger up as a blowhard, he could now send him off and investigate the evening's suddenly more interesting prospects.

"Just as well," Figgy replied amiably. "I'd as soon teach her some skills she could put to better use."

His friends laughed while the woman, after a second's hesitation, veered off sharply, quickening her pace. Thom grabbed her, wrapping his great arm about her waist.

"Young man, take your hands off me." Her voice was low pitched, composed, and unexpectedly forceful. If Thom hadn't been quite so ale blown, he very probably would have dropped his hand and sidled sheepishly away. But Thom was drunk. Very drunk.

"Come now, sweetmeat," he crooned. "We're who you've been looking for."

"You most certainly are not." She did not struggle. She simply tipped her chin up above her lace-edged cravat and gazed calmly from behind her black silk mask into Thom's sloppily grinning face. "Come now," she continued in a voice just a shade above a whisper. "Haven't you better things to do? Night watchmen's boxes to tip? Lanterns to throw rocks at?"

"Did that last night," Thom confessed, pulling her into the light.

Figgy felt Munro tense and glanced at the Scot curiously. For a second, Figgy could have sworn Munro looked startled.

"Young sirs," the woman said, "you have obviously taken me for someone, or something, else."

A little color had developed in the visible part of her face, but she spoke without trepidation. Old hand at this sort of thing, was she? A habitué of pleasure gardens and lively entertainments? Lovely.

"No, we ain't." One of the lads shook his head. "We know'd you straight off. A bird of paradise looking for a roost."

She *looked* the part of a Cyprian, that was certain. Her legs were long and her bottom rounded, and the pantaloons encased them just tight enough that imagination provided what eyes did not. She had smooth skin, too, pale and cameo clear, and her mouth was deep pink, a short, bowed upper lip crowning a lush, full lower one.

"You are making a mistake," she repeated, pulling away.

"Not so soon!" Thom protested, tugging her back.

"This is ridiculous. I don't have time to play with little boys. Let me go." She jerked her hand free.

Little boys? Figgy stepped in front of her, blocking her way. Why, he'd be eighteen this very month! He'd teach her who was a man and who a boy! Marchioness or scullery maid, she had come here, they hadn't sought her out. If a girl didn't want to play at a bit of slap and tickle, why, then, she hadn't ought be out on Lovers Walk alone, ought she? Nor dressed in so indecent a manner, one that shouted for men to take note . . . and anything else they could get away with.

Besides, he'd let his sword fall to the gravel path, and it wasn't as if he was going to hurt her, just taste those incredible lips—

"I have changed my mind." Munro was suddenly between Figgy and the girl. "I can not only teach her to counter your *remiss*. I can teach her to disarm you."

"What?" Figgy blinked. He'd forgotten Munro. Forgotten everything but his intention of having a bit of sweetness off this uppity honeypot. And that was exactly what he meant to do.

"That is," the urbane voice continued, "if you're the neck-or-nothing fellow I take you to be."

Neck-or-nothing? Figgy, in the act of reaching for the girl, stopped. He had the unpleasant notion Munro had just questioned his mettle.

"What? Certainly I am," Figgy mumbled, frowning. Of course he was. Who could doubt it?

"*And* a betting man?"

Figgy promptly nodded. Like any Pink of the Ton, he considered himself a regular Captain Sharp, if a temporarily unlucky one.

"I have ten pounds," the Scotsman said, "that says with fifteen minutes of instruction this woman will be able to disarm you."

"And I have twenty pounds that says give him his ten and send him on his way!" Thom exclaimed, his eyes feasting on the girl.

"A hundred," Munro shot back.

At this Thom and the rest of Figgy's friends quieted. A wager of a hundred pounds sounded interesting. Especially when they knew that Figgy had been dished up proper the night before last and would be leaning heavily on his companions to finance tonight's play.

"Do it!" someone shouted.

A woman disarm him? A hundred pounds? Too easy by half.

"Done."

"This is absurd!" the girl declared. She turned around, and even though she still wore the mask, Figgy could tell the exact instant she saw, really *saw*, Munro. She stopped, trapped by his curst handsome vis like a dove in a net. For three heartbeats she stood frozen, and then she was pushing past Munro, declaring hotly, "I am not—"

Munro clasped her upper arm, drawing her effortlessly to him, abruptly stopping whatever she'd been about to say.

"I am afraid what you are or who makes no difference at this point, my dear," he said, tipping her back over his forearm. "Now, be a good girl and a better sport."

Even half drunk, Figgy could see the hot retort rising to her lips. But this, too, Munro halted by dipping her back even further.

"For luck," he said and kissed her.

TWO

<>

ALLER:
French for "to go"

IN HER TWENTY-FIVE YEARS of life, Helena Nash had never been kissed—not like this. Hard, expert, and impersonal. Insultingly impersonal. She might have been a mannequin or a prostitute.

Her sister Kate would have resisted, and her baby sister, Charlotte, would most certainly have fought, but that was not Helena's way. She had cultivated detachment to a fine art. She used that skill now, disassociating herself from the Scot's performance. And *that*, she had no doubt, was exactly what it was: a performance designed to impress an audience rather than its recipient.

She knew who he was, of course. Had from the moment she'd seen his refined face catch the half-light as he'd turned toward her approach. But then anyone who'd ever seen Ramsey Munro would remember him, just as any woman who'd ever imagined the Dark Angel in his most seductive guise would think him familiar. He was simply that beautiful.

He'd been just as beautiful nearly four years ago, when she'd first seen him, but time had imbued the classic features with jaded knowledge, hardening them into adamantine brilliance. Born in an earlier time, his face would have moved Michelangelo to genius: subtly Roman nose; firm, mobile lips; deep-set, almond-shaped eyes, and strong, angular jaw. Tall and lean, he reminded her of some emperor's hunting hound, an elegantly fashioned creature built for lethal speed and long-range endurance, his shoulders broad and his hips trim, his long legs muscled and his belly flat.

Even if long ago he hadn't stood in her mother's bare drawing room and pledged his service to her family, she still would have known his name. It was whispered in the corridors of opera houses by any number of matrons, hostesses, wives, and expensive courtesans, his physical attributes dissected by the doyennes dutifully watching their charges dance, his conquests speculated upon at afternoon teas, his acerbic wit and dissolute sophistication aped by would-be rakes.

Reminding herself of that reputation, Helena anchored her hands on Munro's broad shoulders to keep from tumbling to the ground, and prepared to suffer his affront as she had suffered so many since her family's fall from fortune: with clinical indifference, unruffled dignity, and cool . . . and cool . . .

His kiss had changed.

And with it, everything else.

His lips softened, growing persuasive. His mouth gentled, moving seamlessly over hers. A soft, seductive kiss. A cushiony melding of lips, an exchange of breath, a succulent invitation to sin as—dear God! His tongue touched her mouth, languidly tracing the contours of her lips, teasing them apart, easing in against the edge of her teeth.

She had never imagined such a thing!

She forgot everything: her reason for being there, the fear that someone was following her, the appointed meeting at the end of the lane, and the terrible sensation of being watched by malevolent eyes.

He wrapped his arm around her waist, pressing her closer. One hand slid up her throat and framed her jaw, the supplication inherent in that light touch transfixing her. Her careful defenses began to crumble, and there, on the point of collapsing utterly, something deep inside her awoke from a lifetime of slumber and recognized danger.

She tried to right herself, but he tipped her even further back and she clung, light-headed and weak-limbed. He took her breath away. He stole her modesty. He broke through her barricades. His kiss brought to life sensations only half-remembered from dark, heated dreams: erotic, eager, hungry.

She trembled and, in answer, for one brief instant, his arm lashed her more tightly against him. Then he was lifting her to her feet, and she knew that he was about to end the kiss, and God help her! Her fingers dug deeper into rock-solid muscle beneath his coat as she helplessly pursued his retreating lips.

"Jesu!" The ragged oath escaped his lips, and he crushed her to his body. His mouth opened over hers, and *this* time his focus was absolute, excluding everything outside of this kiss. His unchecked hunger poured over her, through her, a fiery ardor that eclipsed her own awakening desires, demanding and—

Around them, coarse laughter erupted.

His head lifted. Whatever the others saw in his bright eyes killed their laughter. She'd forgotten their audience.

" 'Pon my rep," someone snickered, "I didn't realize you meant to teach her about *that* sword!"

He lowered his mouth to hers. "If you wish to leave here unmolested, follow my lead."

And then she was on her feet, her head spinning, her heart thundering. Why was he doing this? Why trouble himself over the fate of an unknown woman? Because he couldn't possibly know who she was! She'd purposely kept her voice low and rid it of the Yorkish accents.

It was absurd. How could Munro possibly conceive that he was kissing Colonel Nash's preternaturally serene daughter, one of three daughters he'd sworn to protect (quite possibly from such insult as he had just offered) as repayment for her father's ransoming Ramsey's life with his own? It was a notion she could scarce believe herself! Though she did not, in truth, feel as insulted as she did . . . disturbed.

" 'Bout time, Munro! There's a wager at stake!"

"Quite right," he was saying. "Now the lesson. The *other* lesson."

More male laughter erupted, returning her to this appalling situation, the ridiculous wager, and her part in it. She couldn't do this. She had never even held a sword.

The drunken boys surrounding them would have to find some other amusement. "I cannot—"

Munro's gaze cut to hers and she bit back her protest. Seemingly, matters were a bit more complicated than she understood them to be.

The bullish young man in the bright pink skirts and curling wig crossed his arms over his corseted chest and stepped in front of her, barring the path ahead, while the one dressed like some rajah and whose features were obscured by black paint smiled nastily.

"Thank you." Munro took the center of the gravel path. "Pray, heed well what I am about to show you, miss. I will demonstrate a few simple maneuvers, which you will later emulate. Do you understand? Good.

"Now, if one of you lads would be so kind as to offer yourself for the purposes of a demonstration?"

"What is this about?" the turbaned youth, Figgy, protested. "You said you were going to teach her to disarm me!"

"And so I am. But the best way of learning a thing is to see it done first. Fear not, young valiant, you'll have your match." Munro looked around. "Who will aid me? Come now, you will be the one armed with a sword. All I ask is that you attack me. Is that so difficult?"

"No." A youngster staggered to his feet, tossing down the skin of wine he'd been drinking from. "No. I'll do it."

Munro hooked the toe of his boot beneath the blade of Figgy's abandoned sword and casually flicked it up into the air, catching it neatly and presenting it to the gapemouthed lad. "Here. Now, present and attack."

"Huh?"

Ramsey sighed. "Present . . . and . . . attack."

"Huh?"

"For God's sake, stab him!" Figgy yelled.

"Oh!" With a blaze of speed, if not grace, the youth lunged, driving the foil forward. Only, its target was not there. And the sword the boy had held was now in Munro's hand.

The lad stared in amazement. "What happened?"

"I disarmed you. That was the point, was it not?" Munro asked, holding out the foil. "If one finds oneself in a duel, a real duel, and his life depends upon his skill and he has none to speak of, then he ought to make certain he knows at least one thing very well and that, for such as you, young sir, would be to disarm your opponent."

"Ha!" the youngster blustered, snatching back his foil. "Well, we shall see about— Aha!"

He plunged forward again, but this time Helena was prepared to watch for what happened.

A slight adjustment of weight, a movement of Munro's outside arm, and the boy's foil shot beneath it. Munro caught the blade against his ribs and, with a serpent's striking speed, wrapped his forearm under it and over, curling his finger over the top of the bellguard and effortlessly plucking the weapon out of the young man's hand.

"Like so. Do you see, miss?" He turned his head, quizzing her calmly.

She nodded gravely, trying to look sanguine.

"Of course, this is simply the easiest way to disarm someone. There are other methods that require a bit more strength." He held up the confiscated foil. "Anyone else care to have a go?"

With a growl, the hairy man in the skirt and wig, the one they'd called Thom, stomped forward. "Me."

Munro shook his head. "Your skirts render you too easy to overcome." He turned to Figgy. "How about you, young sir? Here." Munro tossed him the sword. "For this, I require a weapon. Ah!" He'd spied Thom's shepherdess's crook. With a smile he lifted it up, testing its balance. "This will do nicely."

Figgy snickered. "Oh, aye. I would be able to disarm a man, too, if I'd a staff twice as long as his gut pricker."

Crack! Munro broke the stave against his knee, halving its length, thus making it a good deal shorter than the rajah's sword. "Present."

At the sharp command, the youth fell automatically into the proper stance.

"Your move," Munro said, resting nonchalantly against the crook, the broken tip buried in the ground.

Figgy licked his lips and made a tentative parry. With a faint expression of disgust, Munro slapped it aside with his hand.

"Come now," he admonished. "I have a piece of *wood. You* have steel."

The provocation worked. With a grunt, Figgy extended and lunged. The broken tip of Munro's crook flew up, whirled once around the gleaming steel blade, flashed towards the hilt, and suddenly the foil was flying into the night and the boy was shaking out his hand, cursing.

"Would you care to see that again, miss?" This time Munro didn't even bother to pretend to be addressing her. His eyes—lazy, amused, unutterably dangerous— stayed on the group of young bloods.

What good would it do for him to demonstrate it again? There was no possible way she could re-create that, and he knew it. "No. I think I have it."

"As I thought. However, you may want to try a more subtle means of disarming your oppon—"

"No!" Figgy interjected angrily, nursing his stinging fingers. "No more demonstrations! You've given enough instruction. The wager is that you could teach *her* to disarm me in fifteen minutes. Well, let *her* try."

Munro smiled. "Certainly. Retrieve your weapon."

One of the lads tossed Figgy his weapon. The rajah grabbed it out of the air and whipped it savagely about.

The tall Scotsman's expression changed to one of utterly unconvincing amazement. "But . . . this will never do."

"What?" demanded Figgy, still slashing at the air.

Munro lifted his hands, palms up. "She has no sword. No weapon. You can hardly ask her to use this stick."

The air left Helena's lungs in a rush of relief. So *that* was his plan.

Figgy's lips thinned in a nasty smile. "Not at all. Ed, give her your weapon."

A boy stepped forward, having produced a smallsword from somewhere, and held it out.

Oh, no. She edged backward, but before she could retreat any farther, Munro clasped her wrist and slapped the handle of the sword against her palm. His gloved hand covered hers, curling her fingers around the satin-wrapped hilt and pressing them closed.

This was insane. She felt like a character in an overwrought gothic novel, incapable of moving, incapable of retreat, swept along by dangerous currents.

Panic set needles in her thoughts. The sound of her own breathing filled her ears. She, Helena Nash, who never panicked, panicked. All she could think was that as drunk as the boy undoubtedly was, he would likely pierce her straight through the heart. Whether or not he meant to do so, the result would be the same— she would be dead. It would be so *stupid* to die thus, here, *now*.

"As soon as I say 'present,' drop the sword and fall back a step. Do you understand?" Munro said in a voice pitched for her ears alone.

Understand? She couldn't *breathe*. "No."

"You will be fine."

"Oh, yes. I'm certain the boy is well able to judge the depth at which he might impale me without pricking something vital!" she whispered back in a shaking voice. A shimmery ring had begun collecting at the edges of her vision.

Munro's hand clamped more tightly around hers, bringing her back to the present in a rush of pain. Her gaze flew to meet his, startled and injured. His bright eyes had darkened beneath the lush banks of sooty lashes. "You will be fine. *I swear it on my honor.*"

Amazingly, she believed him. He'd sworn. She recalled that other vow he'd made three and a half years ago. He'd stood before her family, beautiful and graceful, like sin itself come to make amends, and promised to come to their aid should it ever be required. And she'd believed him then just as she believed him now. Which was not, she supposed, saying much for her powers of discrimination. Still, she nodded.

He turned away, and she found herself facing a very drunk, very surly young buck, his turban askew above a black-painted face. With a mocking sneer, he raised his foil and saluted her. Awkwardly, she hefted her own blade and attempted to duplicate his action.

"Are you ready?" she heard Munro ask.

"Yes, yes," Figgy replied. " 'Twill be the easiest hundred pounds I have ever made. I almost feel guilty."

"Present."

It was easy to do as Munro had directed. The heavy blade tumbled from her nerveless fingers at the same time as his tall form glided between her and the young man. There was a shout, and she stumbled backward just as Munro grabbed her opponent's blade, blocking its flight. Casually, he wrested it from the youngster's grip.

She wasn't going to die. *She wasn't going to die!* The pure delight of not dying swept through her, making her giddy.

"That ain't fair!" the boy bleated. "She didn't even try."

"I did so!" she claimed, grinning idiotically.

Munro looked at her with exaggerated disappointment and shook his head. "No, miss. You did not. You disarmed yourself."

She hung her head, trying to look contrite. "I did. I disarmed myself. Terribly sorry."

Munro looked back at the boys and sighed heavily. "I am sorely disappointed that my initial assessment was correct. She is, after all, just a woman. Impossible to teach."

"I can barely read," she confessed dolefully.

Figgy's mouth opened and shut like a beached fish. Once. Twice. "But you—"

"Owe you a hundred pounds? Quite right." Munro reached into his pocket and peeled off several notes from the small roll he withdrew. Smiling, he pushed them into Figgy's hand.

"Fairly won," he said, and then, while the others were still staring at them in confusion, he took Helena's arm.

His smile found Figgy. "The only advantage you might have in a duel, young sir, is your apparent unfamiliarity with your weapon. No one who sees you with it could take you seriously. Now, should you ever decide to pursue the sport seriously, do look me up. White Friars."

"But . . . but . . . the *girl!*" Thom cried plaintively, ignoring the insult to his friend.

Munro shook his head sadly at the forlorn-looking group of youngsters. "Gentlemen—and you are, I presume, *gentlemen?*"

They glanced at each other to see what the group's current stand on that particular issue was before they all reluctantly nodded.

"You would not take the money *and* the girl, now would you?" Munro didn't wait for an answer. He turned, pulling Helena after him. "I thought not."

THREE

OPPOSITION PARRY:
defensive action with blade that deflects
opponent's offensive action without roughness
but while maintaining contact

THEY LEFT LOVERS WALK and entered the broader, though still dimly lit, South Walk. Here, finally removed from the boys' reproachful glares, Helena stopped, intent on thanking Munro for his aid.

She stared up into his eyes. They were hypnotic, the color of some fabled sea, too deeply blue to be fathomed.

"Yes?"

Or like the blue in a peacock's feathers, rich and exotic and regal.

"You were going to say something?"

"Yes." She blinked. "I was going to assure you that I was not going to provoke them further or say anything that would incite them to violence. I'm not a fool." With a wince, she realized that anxiety had allowed some round Yorkish syllables to creep into her voice. She must remember to keep her voice husky and London-accented.

It would be too, too lowering for Ramsey Munro to realize that the man he'd idolized as his savior had a daughter who haunted Vauxhall dressed like a boy. She couldn't do that to her father's memory, and she could not explain her presence.

Munro looked amused. "And you think that a woman dressed like you are would have to do something more in order to incite or . . . provoke hot-blooded young men to . . . violence?"

"No." She blushed hotly. "Yes. I meant I am not unaccustomed to fending off unwanted advances."

"Forgive me for doubting your discretion. I had no idea I was in the company of such a level-headed . . . woman?"

The way he said "woman" made it a question. He was attempting to gauge her position in society. A lady looking for an adventure? A married woman searching for her paramour? Or even a ladybird?

This last shocking idea didn't shock her nearly as much as she supposed it ought to have done. After all, her presence here, unescorted and in boy's attire, was highly suggestive.

And she found that the idea of being something other than the paid companion of one of society's most venomous old ladies was unexpectedly appealing. Although she had never considered prostitution a viable alternative. Not—God save her for her impiety—because of the immorality of it as much as because she was already at the beck and call of another, acquiescing to demands for money.

"What were you going to say to them to convince them to let you pass unharassed?" Munro asked curiously when she neither denied nor confirmed his assumption.

"That I was on my way to an assignation with a person of royal blood," she answered.

She had the distinct impression she'd surprised him, though nothing in his expression changed. He only tilted his head. "And were you?"

"Not unless the young man I *was* attempting to meet suddenly discovered he owned a completely different set of parents than those he'd been led to believe were his."

"It's happened before."

She shook her head emphatically. "Not this time, more's the pity."

If only Oswald Goodwin *did* have a royal connection, he mightn't be so miserably poor, and she wouldn't have to be sneaking about meeting him in disguise.

His eyes narrowed. "I would think a woman such as yourself would be more careful about selecting her companions."

As the secrets she kept were not hers, she could no more reveal her reasons for being here than tell him her name.

"I am careful. Usually, I am quite confident of a man's situation and character before I. . . . The man I was seeking means nothing to me beyond—" She broke off, warmth seeping into her cheeks. This would never do. To have him think her an adventurous lady was one thing, but to have him think she was a prostitute was quite another. "I'm not a . . ." She searched for the proper term and decided to use the one he had. ". . . the *woman* you think. I am not"—she leaned forward earnestly—"the *woman* I appear to be."

"Really?" Humor danced in his eyes. "But your depiction is extraordinary! Why, right down to the yielding softness of your—"

His lips curved into a wolfish smile. "Well now, I confess myself utterly taken in." He leaned forward and continued confidingly, "I do hope you won't bandy about the heatedness of my response to you, will you? I should hate having to call people out over it. Quite ruins a dinner party."

"What?" she stammered.

"You are nonplussed." He stepped away. "But no more than I. I am in awe of your skill. I had heard there were clubs in the East End where gentlemen such as yourself practiced amazing transformations from one gender to another, but I never—"

"*I am not a gentleman!*"

"One would never know that, either," he said consolingly. "Perhaps you are not by birth, but in speech and manner you are the equal of any peer," he frowned, "or peeress, of my acquaint—"

"In no way whatsoever am I a man!" she declared, aghast. "I am entirely female. I am just not that *sort* of woman!"

"Oh?" He tipped his head, studying her form and face with every evidence of doubt. And with her femininity being questioned for the first time in her life, Helena could not refrain from puffing her chest out and tilting her chin at an angle that would display to advantage the long, graceful neck many, *many* men had declared flawless.

"Well?" she demanded haughtily.

His sudden smile declared his delight. "I believe you. You are female. Which is excellent, as I confess I was concerned for my powers of discrimination. Not to mention my hopes for future heirs."

She should have been insulted. Mortified. At the very least, shocked. Instead, she laughed.

And Munro, in the process of turning, checked, regarding her with a lazy smile that did not quite match the sharpening interest in his eyes.

He hadn't expected her to laugh, she realized. Just as she realized that she liked catching him off guard. She suspected it was a rare enough occurrence for him. For she had no doubt that even as she'd received any number of propositions from gentlemen, he had received more from ladies. The difference being that while she had always demurred, rumor strongly suggested that he'd often accepted.

"If I offended you back there with those boys," he said, "I am sorry. I thought it best to risk insulting you rather than your reputation."

"I wasn't insulted," she said. "I am grateful as well as indebted to you. Thank you."

The night had closed in around them as they spoke, and now the mellow warmth of an evening breeze brought with it the heady fragrance of night-blooming flowers. They were alone in the umber-steeped dusk, and he was standing too close. Or was she? She couldn't tell.

"My, but it is warm. It will be cooler by the river." She looked around and, seeing brighter lights at the far end of the path, hastened toward them.

He caught up and escorted her silently to where the South Walk intersected with the Cross Walk. Here it was brighter and more crowded, with people arriving to see the fireworks. She started into the throng, but he stopped her on its edge.

"That kiss—" he began.

"Just a kiss," she lied.

"You are most understanding." He covered her hand, his thumb sweeping lightly back and forth against the tender surface of her inner wrist, leaving a tingling trail of electricity along her flesh, a tingling heat that pooled in her core and melted her thoughts.

With a mental snap, she rallied her concentration. She had never swooned in her life. She was not going to start now. She might look as sweet and fragile as French pastry, but she wasn't. She never had been. Discovering that had disconcerted more than a few suitors. "Your kissing me was a most expedient way of extraditing me from an unfortunate situation."

She smiled, retreating behind the mantle of her much-vaunted composure while she still had the chance. He regarded her with an oblique expression. How could someone wicked be so handsome, she wondered. How could someone so handsome be anything but wicked?

"I am impressed you regard that kiss so clinically," he said in an odd tone, releasing her hand. "Now, why don't you tell me what you are *really* doing here?"

"I told you. I came to meet a young man."

"For what purpose?"

"Do you suppose that is any of your affair?"

"As your champion, I claim the right to know."

He would not leave it alone until he had an answer. "For the usual purposes, I suspect," she answered stiltedly.

"And you come here often. For the *usual* reasons?"

"Often enough."

"Liar," he said with something that sounded oddly like fondness. "You are not a habitué. I'd stake my sword on it."

"Why? Because you have already been so successful in your wagers this evening?" she asked dryly.

He laughed. "Touché. Still, this wager I would win. You don't even know the direction of the river."

"How do you know I don't?"

"Because you stated you wanted to go toward the river, and yet you are now heading directly away from it." He bent his head down nearer hers. "Now. Again. What are you doing here?"

She could not tell him. She had sworn to keep Flora's secret. There was, she had learned long ago, one way to stop a line of questioning, and that was to divert it.

"All right. If you must have an answer. I met a young man who is not welcome in the house where I . . ." she hesitated, "where I live. So, we arranged to meet here." It was close to the truth, with a few notable exceptions.

"He is married?" he asked quietly.

"Yes."

Did a shadow cross the handsome face? "And are you?"

"No!"

"Then why would you waste your time on a married man?" He sounded just the slightest bit amused, and she realized that her shocked denial had seriously undermined her chances of appearing carefree and insouciant. But she was an excellent actress. She had spent years, day in, day out, playing a role contrary to her nature. So she would don another mask and make him believe it.

Brazenly, she regarded him from beneath her lashes. "Because I am tired of being virtuous and dutiful. I am determined to have . . . an adventure."

His eyes narrowed and a tiny muscle leapt at the corner of his mouth. Did he believe her? She could not tell. She held his gaze boldly. A heartbeat. Five. Ten.

"Then what happened to your married swain?"

She shrugged. "Apparently he was more parochial than either of us anticipated."

"So," he leaned forward, and his gaze swept over her mouth with the impact of a caress, "you've not yet fulfilled your goal?" His mood had abruptly changed from playful to intense.

She drew back, trying to stifle her alarm. "As much as I care to."

As though her answer released him from some role he had no desire to play, he stepped away, taking her hand and returning it to his sleeve, once more casual. He inclined his head. "Then let me see you to the gate. It should be easy to find a carriage for hire this early in the evening."

Leave? She stepped back. She couldn't leave. Oswald might yet be waiting. "Thank you, but that won't be necessary."

"You already have a carriage?"

"No." She shook her head. "I will have to hire one. Later." She doubted she would find Oswald now, but at least she had to try.

"Then may I offer you my escort for the evening? I am deemed by some a right"—his voice hardened ever so slightly—"prime adventure."

"That won't be necessary."

He did not like being denied. "Do you have any concept of the sort of attentions a young, unescorted woman invites in a place like this?"

Of course she didn't. She hadn't ever *been* to a place like this. Not unaccompanied. "I think I had a fairly representative taste earlier this evening, did I not?" she asked, investing all her formidable poise into the query.

"No," he replied flatly. "Those were boys. There are *men* here who do not play at acting like animals, they *are* animals. So, if you must stay, allow me to be your guide for the duration of your . . . adventure." His beautifully molded lips curled on the last word. "I can guarantee you of my expertise."

Of that, she had no doubt.

"Thank you, but no." Oswald Goodwin would never approach her if he saw her in the company of another man. Besides which, her intuitions—which had always stood her in good stead—told her that it would be far more dangerous to remain with Ramsey Munro.

Because electricity seemed to arc in the very air between them. Because she couldn't look at him, his face, his chest, his throat, his mouth, without feeling unnerved and fascinated. But most of all because she wanted to stay with him. More than she had wanted anything in a very, very long time.

"Hey!" A demanding tug on her sleeve broke the tension. She looked down into the dirty, upturned face of an urchin. "Here." Without fanfare, the boy shoved a bloodred rose at her, the bloom open and blowsy atop a long, thornless stem.

"What's this?" she asked.

"Some cove give me a groat to give it you," the boy

said. "And now I done it. Ta!" With a cocky flick of his hand, the boy darted back into the crowd, leaving Helena clasping the rose.

It must be from Oswald. A sign that he was nearby, watching and waiting for her to be alone. She looked up to find Ramsey regarding her with an odd expression.

"There. He is come," she said with far more pleasure than she felt. "You needn't sacrifice your evening after all. So, once again, thank you, Mr. Munro. Good night."

She began to turn, but he stepped in front of her. "It hardly seems fair that you should know my name when I do not know yours."

She hesitated, bemused with the notion of naming herself. It must be something easy and happy and tough and courageous. Something unlike who she was and more like what she wanted to be. "You can call me Corie."

And before he could reply or detain her, she slipped past him and hurried off down the path.

Who would have thought the hesitant eagerness of a young woman's kiss could affect him so viscerally? To the point where he had forgotten, for one singular moment, everything but her? He must not be as jaded as he'd thought. He supposed he ought to remedy that, Ramsey Munro thought sardonically.

Thoughtfully, he watched Helena Nash go. And Helena Nash she was, in spite of her claim to the contrary and the London veneer that hid her Yorkish accent. He'd almost challenged her a half-dozen times in their short interval together. But if she wanted to pretend to be somebody else, well, she wouldn't be the first lady to do so, and he certainly had no right to unmask her.

His gaze followed her amongst the crowd. Dressed in knee breeches, and what with the way she filled them out, it would not be hard to follow her. He'd only have to mark the direction in which the men's heads swiveled.

He tossed a few coins to the vendor of the nearby kiosk selling cheap dominos, took one, and flung the cloak about his shoulders. He let the hood fall well over his brow, shadowing his face. Then he followed Helena into the throng. He contented himself with staying back amidst the revelers and watching. Over the years he had grown very good at keeping his distance from Helena Nash.

For nearly four years he had been faithful to his promise to lend his body and his talents to the care of the Nash sisters. His obligation to the middle sister, Kate, had ended with her marriage to Christian MacNeill, his boon childhood companion. And Charlotte was still a relative child living under the protection of a wealthy, well-connected if slightly ramshackle family. Only Helena had required any concerted attention. And while at first that attention had been perfunctory, over the years it had changed, become a personal hobby. The thought brought a grim smile to his face.

She fascinated him. So cool. So calm and quiet and yet . . . How many times had he seen the volcanic flash in her blue eyes and wondered what had given birth to that passionate heat? Or perhaps only his imagination provided the secret fire beneath her icy façade. The enigma had kept his interest alive and growing ever more intent.

Though he had warded her for years, he had rarely allowed himself close enough to hear her voice. And now he'd actually spoken with her. And kissed her. And

the fire he had so often wondered about had proved to
be real.

Too real.

He watched her as she threaded her way through the
throng, the abrupt turn of her head revealing her quick
scrutiny of the crowd. The rose in her hand bobbed as
she turned, stopped, and started again.

"Who sent you that rose, lass?" he murmured. "Who
could draw you out of that witch's tower to a dark forest
like this?"

She'd said she'd come here for an "adventure." Had
she? His gaze hardened.

Of all the people he might have expected to see on the
infamous Lovers Walk, she would have been the last.
Certainly not dressed as a boy. Definitely not alone. She
should have been safely locked in whatever garret room
Lady Tilpot kept for dependents of indeterminate social
standing, not sauntering heedlessly into a pack of drunk
youngsters hell-bent on proving their manhood.

He was glad he'd been there, having earlier completed
a transaction that had put into his pocket five hundred
pounds toward his entry fee in the International Dueling
Tournament—the means of securing a future far less
uncertain than his current one, which relied solely on
teaching overindulged peers his skills with a sword. As
he'd been leaving, he'd chanced upon the young Turks
and, seeing an opportunity to gather a few more high-
paying clients to his salle, set about piquing their interest.
Then . . . *her*.

She turned, her smooth brow furrowing, and he
melted back into the dark press of trees. The wind whispered like a ravished lover, and the babble of merry-

makers seemed overly excited. Of course his presence in such a place hadn't surprised her—he'd strove to achieve a certain notoriety in the last years—but his kiss had.

Had anything ever tasted more provocative? Had his body ever quickened so immediately, so overwhelmingly? And all for a kiss that did nothing to appease the hunger it inspired. It left him rampant and wanting.

She had felt it, too. He had known the moment the inferno burning him up from the inside had set fire to her own desire.

So why did he reject the notion that she wanted an *adventure?* After all, she was five and twenty years old. Why should he find objectionable the idea of her seeking the means of placating the same tormenting urges that raked his body? Because that was not the Helena Nash he had spent hours guarding and studying and learning with an intimacy few lovers knew.

Yet he conceded there was much he did not know. For instance, while he had expected her to be mature and composed, he had not anticipated laughter. He had not anticipated she would trade sallies with him, challenge him and tease him, that she would abandon the diffidence that women in her situation practiced, women who made their way by guarding their tongues and their thoughts.

He did not know Helena Nash nearly as well as he'd assumed he must after years of watching her, and that notion intrigued as well as unsettled him.

Ahead, Helena slowed and finally stopped, looking once more around her. She had not found whoever had sent her that rose. That rose. He shrugged off the niggling sense of unease its presence caused. The significance roses held for him, he knew all too well, was quite different from that which they inspired in most romantics' hearts.

Helena headed out the nearest gate.

He exited a dozen yards behind her and slipped between two hacks as she approached the head of the line of waiting carriages. The driver scrambled down out of his seat and assisted her into the vehicle before climbing back up top. Waiting to see if anyone joined her, Ramsey pulled off the domino and tossed it to a young street sweeper leaning on his broom who would sell it the next masquerade evening for twice what he made for one night's work. Whomever Helena had intended to meet, and for whatever reasons, had disappointed her. The man must be a great bloody fool.

The hack lurched out into the traffic as Ram watched it go. "You're a long way from home, lass," he murmured thoughtfully before turning and heading for the river bridge. "But then, aren't we all?"

Manchester, England
October 1787

The stooped custodian led Ramsey Munro down the narrow, dimly lit corridor of the Manchester Poor House, ripe with the stench of urine and sweat, to the small chamber at the far end that served as a receiving room for the indigent boys. It was here he had been brought two weeks before, after the constable had found him howling beside his mother's corpse, which was crushed beneath a crate that had plunged from a third-story warehouse block and tackle.

The warden stopped outside the door and eyed Ramsey pityingly. "Better to go with this mon what come fer ye and flee later, on the road. Away from the city. Yer too pretty by half to last long in here. I'm surprised ye've lasted this long, but then, being put in the cell fer two days out of every three for fighting don't leave much opportunity for the other lads to do mischief on ye, do it?"

Ramsey didn't bother answering. His mouth, both lips split from his latest battle, still hurt, and he felt weak and lightheaded. The worst part of being put in the cell wasn't the total isolation but being forced to subsist on the mealworm-riddled bread and water that provided the only nourishment during his incarceration. Still, the custodian's advice was good. It would only be a matter of time before a few of the larger boys joined forces to overtake him.

The custodian eyed him once again and shrugged, pulling open the door and pushing him through. He blinked in the sudden light. He'd been in the isolation cell for two days this time, and it was kept purposefully dark.

"My heavens, child, what have they done to you?" The voice was Scottish, thick with a Highland burr. The unexpected accent nearly brought tears to Ramsey's eyes. But he was nine years old, not a child, and the last time he had cried had been at his mother's side, and he could think of no reason that he would be brought to tears again. He was done, he thought fiercely, with tears.

"Nothing, sir," he managed to mumble through his swollen lips, squinting up at the tall figure dressed in a monk's robes. The man stood a little above medium height but was so thin he appeared taller. His thick hair had the sheen of pewter, and time had carved lines on either side of a wide mouth and hawk-

like nose. But his eyes were gentle and clear, and Ramsey had the distinct impression that those eyes missed little of what was worth seeing.

"I am Father Tarkin, the abbot of St. Bride's, and I have come to take you there. To take you home."

The word brought a sudden rush of longing, but Ram quelled it. "I have no home, sir. Certainly I have never been to a place called St. Bride's. You mistake me for another."

"I do not mistake you. You are Cora Munro's son."

At the sound of his mother's name, Ramsey's interest sharpened. "How do you know my mother?"

"Her family was once one of the greatest of the highland clans, and she a chieftain's great-granddaughter. And I am a Highlander second only to being a priest. Of course I knew her. Eyes like mountain lakes and pride that only a warrior's seed could produce. I came here, to England, as soon as I received her letter. I am only sorry I came too late to take you both out of here, and sorry too that once I learned of her death it took me this long to find you."

Ramsey stared at him, amazed at what he was hearing. Uncertainly he raked his hand over his scalp and was reminded again of his present straits by the short nap of hair left after the poorhouse barber had finished shaving his head.

"My mother sent for you to come for us?" he asked incredulously. He had known she was growing daily more desperate, but . . .

"She sent word that she was in difficulty and asked whether I knew of someone in this city that could give her aid. I came of my own volition. And now I would like to take you back to St. Bride's."

"Why?"

The abbot smiled for the first time, and his eyes lit. "How like a Munro to ask what is on the menu despite the fact that he is starving. Suffice to say that there is an old Jesuit dictum that says, 'Give Me the Child Until He Is Seven and I Will Show You the Man.' I know you are older than that, but I still hold out great hopes for your future. Now, will you come with me?"

"What will I do at your abbey?" Ram asked, knowing he appeared churlish but unable to bend the spine he knew he'd inherited from his father.

"Work at acquiring the knowledge and skills we will teach you. There are other boys at St. Bride's. Anywhere from a dozen to twenty at a given time, and they all work very hard. I don't suppose that has ever been required of you, being the grandson of an English marquis—even if not a legitimate one."

Ramsey felt his cheeks grow warm. The abbot's comment hit directly on target. Until his father's death in a duel defending Ramsey's mother's honor, they had lived a life of splendor. Though not legally wed in the eyes of England, in every important way his parents had been married, and when Ramsey's father had come into an immense jointure on his maternal side, he had bought a great house in Scotland and provided his family with every luxury and advantage money could buy.

Ramsey had been given fencing lessons, equestrian lessons, tutors in classics, and instruction in decorum. But with his father's death it had all ended. His mother and he had been sent from the only home he had known like servants dismissed at their master's death—with naught but a few personal possessions and nowhere to go.

"Do you think you are capable of hard physical labor as well as intellectual work?"

He held the abbot's gaze. "Aye."

The abbot smiled, apparently satisfied. "Good. Then we are agreed. You will come with me forthwith."

"On one condition."

The abbot, in the process of turning away, spun back in surprise. "You are dictating terms now?"

Ramsey could not tell if the monk was amused or angry, but there was a hint of steel in those soft, pale eyes. Ramsey gulped, nodding once, well aware of his hubris but not willing to yield. "I do not want anyone to know my . . . who my grandfather is or who my father was or my mother."

The abbot's brow furrowed and the silvery shelf of his brows dipped. "But why, my boy? You have a long and proud heritage on your mother's side and a venerable one on your father's."

"The clans are dead and gone," Ram said tightly. "As are my parents. My grandfather would not raise a hand to aid my mother when she petitioned him for help. I am nothing to him and he is nothing to me. I am Ramsey Munro, and that is all I will ever aspire to be. Promise me."

The abbot studied him a long moment before nodding slowly. "All right, Ramsey Munro. It shall be as you wish."

FOUR

FOIBLE:
the outer third of the blade;
the tip end, which is the weakest section

PHYSICAL DESIRE? Wasn't that just another name for lust?

Though Helena arrived at the Tilpot townhouse after dark, she felt relatively safe from discovery. It was Lady Tilpot's whist night, and her employer would be out well past midnight. Slowly, Helena climbed the three flights of backstairs that led to her room.

Her response to the night's events was unseemly, but not incomprehensible. Even when she had been the privileged daughter of a well-to-do gentleman, she had been uneasy about the celebrity her looks had occasioned. Since her father's death, she had had to be vigilant in guarding herself against improper advances that, as one accounted as beautiful as she was poor, had been a nigh daily occurrence before she'd found her current situation with Lady Tilpot.

It was only because Munro's kiss, his attention, his *virility* had been so unexpected that she had been so affected. And she was wise enough to realize that the entire unanticipated episode had been flavored with forbidden pleasure. Yes, her current state was understandable. What wasn't so understandable was why the memory of his kiss wasn't fading. It was over! Done!

She reached the top of the stairs eager for solitude in which to sort things through. Unfortunately, Flora, yellow curls abob and hands wringing piteously, was waiting for her at the door to her chambers. With a feeling of resignation, Helena reached past the girl and opened the door, motioning her in. 'Twas probably just as well, anyway, not to dwell on the carnal details of the evening's excursion. She already had enough here to fully occupy her attention.

"Did you see him?" Flora asked eagerly once inside.

"No. Mr. Goodwin never arrived," Helena said, frowning slightly. After he'd sent the rose, something must have occurred that prevented him from meeting her. She tossed the wilted bloom atop the washstand and pulled off the boy's cap. Her pale, flaxen hair, no longer confined, cascaded down her back.

"Oh." A world of disappointment invested the short word. "Then he was detained and will be there next week."

Helena stripped off her cravat and coat, shedding the antique outfit that had belonged to some Tilpot retainer in an earlier century, and returned it to the bottom of her chest of clothes. Then she pulled on her wool dressing robe, tied the belt tightly, and steeled herself for what needed to be said next.

"I am sorry, Flora," she said without turning around, so she would not need to witness the effect of her words, "but I can no longer act as courier between you and Mr. Goodwin."

One, one thousand, two, one thousand . . . Right on cue, she heard Flora crumple to the floor. With a sigh, she turned, regarding the young girl with as much exasperation as affection. At one time she would have thought Flora looked like a fragile little orchid lying there, her pale skirts gracefully mounding about her. But lately when Flora crumpled—a more and more frequent occurrence—Helena was put more in mind of a used handkerchief, damp and unprepossessing.

"Do get up, Flora."

"You are our only friend, and now you are abandoning us," came the muffled reply.

"I am not abandoning you," Helena answered with some heat. Tonight, she had nearly been impaled by a drunken boy. If Ramsey Munro had not made that bet—

With a dawning sense of dismay, Helena realized she owed him a hundred pounds and had made no attempt whatsoever to repay him.

"Helena?" The pretty, pale little face lifted from its wet muslin bed. "I am sorry. I am sure you would never abandon us. It is just that I am so . . . so . . . overwrought! Please, what happened?"

Flora. She would address the problem of her debt to Munro later. Right now, Flora and her problems took precedence.

"I followed Mr. Goodwin's instructions to the letter," she answered, "but he was not at the appointed meeting place, and in spite of my continued and best efforts to find him, I could not."

"Then the worst has happened! He has been *taken!*" Once more, Flora flung herself facedown on Helena's floor.

"Shhh. Your aunt may be back," Helena said, dropping heavily down on the edge of her bed.

"I don't care!" Flora wailed but, Helena noted, at half her previous volume.

"You ought to care," Helena said sternly. "You won't have a farthing from Lady Tilpot if she finds out what you've done, and it is four more years before you turn twenty-one and come into those farthings your father left in trust for you.

"So, until that time, unless Mr. Goodwin uncovers some extremely wealthy and—I am sorry to say this, Flora, but honesty compels me to do so—extremely *undiscriminating* person who fancies unburdening himself of great wealth by giving it to your young wastrel, you are obliged to live on her sufferance."

Characteristically, Flora ignored everything but the least pertinent of Helena's words. "You didn't used to think Oswald was a wastrel!"

A lapse of judgment Helena regretted daily. "I admit that at one time I thought him charming."

"He *is* charming."

"He is also a scoundrel."

The big brown eyes blinked in wounded wonder. "How can you say that, Helena?"

"Who else but a scoundrel would take advantage of a young girl and elope with her as soon as her guardian and her guardian's *extremely* culpable companion leave for a week in Brighton?"

"He brought me back before anyone realized what we'd done," Flora offered defensively. "Except you, Helena. You're ever so clever." She gazed at Helena with frank admiration. "But the rest of the world knows nothing of our elopement, and thus my reputation is intact."

"Do not ascribe noble motives to what is in actuality

very trite. The reason Mr. Goodwin returned you forthwith was because you screamed the inn roof down the first time you saw a bedbug," Helena replied. "And do not deny it, Flora. You told me as much yourself."

Flora did not try to deny it. She simply shuddered. "I discovered . . . *we* discovered that I am unsuited to a modest lifestyle."

"Are not we all?" Helena asked dryly, rising and going to the table upon which stood a ewer and a basin. "Now, sit up and wipe your face. Besides, if Mr. Goodwin is not an out-and-out scoundrel, at the very least he's an opportunist."

She splashed a little water into the basin and dabbed the edge of a facecloth into it before wringing it out and handing it to the girl.

Flora pushed herself to a sitting position, accepted the towel, and began dutifully cleaning her face. That was the thing about Flora, she was so easy to distract and so malleable—except for this unexpected backbone where Oswald Goodwin was concerned.

When Helena had first taken the post as Lady Alfreda Tilpot's companion, it had been a good ten days before she even realized that another female resided in the huge, fashionable townhouse. In the face of Lady Tilpot's overwhelming and prodigious domination, far more vibrant personalities than Flora's had wilted and faded. It was a miracle that Flora had any spine at all.

It had been precisely to bolster Flora's self-esteem that Helena had encouraged the harmless flirtation between Flora and Oswald Goodwin. He'd arrived one afternoon with a group of other eligible young bloods and rooted himself in a settee, clearly as terrified of Lady Tilpot as he was smitten with Flora. Flora had noted his poet's eyes and sweet smile, and Helena had noted Flora noting him.

Flawless antecedents, empty purse, as threatening as a lapdog, he was the perfect candidate to encourage a very young, very sheltered girl's belief in her worth—beyond the 20,000 pounds Lady Tilpot dangled shamelessly in front of a seemingly endless parade of marriageable young men.

When had the lapdog become the fox in the hen-house? Helena would never have imagined Oswald Goodwin would take advantage of a young girl. Indeed, she had been so confident in his guilelessness that she'd facilitated a few meetings between Flora and him, even allowing them a few moments of private conversation—with herself seated within a decent thirty yards, of course. He had never even touched Flora's hand!

He most certainly hadn't kissed her like Ram had—no, no, *no*, Helena told herself firmly. She was not going to think of that. *That* had been a chance moment of madness, a never-to-be-repeated excursion into a world of earthy sensuality. *That* was his world; *this* was hers. The two would never overlap again.

Unless she found she had no recourse but to hand-deliver the hundred pounds. . . .

"Why do you accuse dear Ossie of being an opportunist?" Flora's voice broke through Helena's erstwhile thoughts. She'd finished with the towel and was folding it neatly.

"Well, unless your aunt can affect an annulment, he looks to be wed to a very rich wife, doesn't he?" At the scowl darkening Flora's little face, she hurried on. "And if you manage to keep your marriage secret until after you come into your inheritance, then he has the benefits of being assured a wealthy future while being able to enjoy an irresponsible present, doesn't he?"

"That," Flora said, "is a horrid thing to say! What has come over you, Helena? This is so unlike you!" Flora exclaimed. "Where is my angel? My dear, beautiful friend? I can scarce credit such unkindness has come from one so lovely! So angelic!"

"Flora—"

"Yes," Flora insisted. "Angel! How else could you be so serene despite all the hardships life has dealt you? How could you put up with my aunt if you were not a virtual saint? And you are *so* beautiful." The girl gazed at her adoringly, and Helena sighed.

The beauty that everyone so often remarked upon had seemed to Helena to appear overnight in her sixteenth year. Then, as now, her "beauty" had never felt . . . well, *real*. Unprepared for the sudden and overstated attention, she had retreated behind her natural composure. People, she had discovered, loved aligning themselves with pretty things—too often without thought or concern for what the veneer they idolized might shelter.

Even her sister Kate seemed to consider Helena's poise an indication of a dearth of inner resources. She had certainly never asked Helena's aid or opinion after their parents' deaths but had simply assumed command of their remaining family. And Helena, unwilling to further burden her already overextended sister, had unhappily let her life be directed by her. Until Lady Tilpot. Until she had found an opportunity to put to good use years of perfecting a graceful reticence.

"I want to be just like you, Helena," Flora was saying,

her big eyes wide and earnest. "I want to be admired and respected and—"

"Flora!" Helena broke in sharply. "I am not respected. I am *fashionable*. It is not the same thing. Not at all."

Flora's brow puckered in consternation.

Helena had little hope Flora would understand. Security, family, her station in life, her celebrated beauty, all of the things that Flora had and that at one time Helena had possessed, too, had proven illusory.

Her much-vaunted beauty? After her mother's death she had grown so gaunt only pitying gazes followed her. Her status? Vanished with the entailed estate. Security? Died with her father. Her family? Scattered to the winds, Kate following the drum on the Continent with her new husband, Colonel Christian MacNeill, and Charlotte unofficially adopted into a family of scapegraces and rattlepates.

Helena had no control over the vagaries that had molded her life, but she did control how she reacted to them. An impecunious orphan could find a good deal of satisfaction in that. Still, she must try to discourage Flora from the course she had followed.

"When one has a certain degree of beauty, little else is expected of one. And even only a moderately pleasant disposition, which would normally not draw any attention at all, in a pleasing-looking person is given the status of a virtue. Which is hardly wise, is it?"

Flora regarded her blankly. Subtlety had never worked with her.

"Flora, people expect little of a pretty girl. But that does not really matter. What matters is this: When there are few expectations made of one, one begins to have few expectations of oneself. Therein lies the danger. One might settle for being less than one might otherwise be."

"But you *are* perfect!" Flora declared, and then her gaze fell and her lower lip extended in a pout. "Or you used to be."

"Hardly."

"But lately," Flora continued as if Helena had not spoken, "well, it grieves me to have to say this, but you have become positively hardhearted!"

At this Helena nearly laughed. If she had been hard-hearted, she would have flown from this house a month ago on the prospects of the portion Kate intended to give her of the huge treasure she and her husband had found in Scotland. Only two things kept Helena from going to the bank, arranging a loan—which she had been told by her brother-in-law's representative would prove no problem—buying her own house, and retiring to live in a modest but extremely comfortable style.

The first was that the last four years had taught her to be wary of anticipated windfalls. Her only current income was from Lady Tilpot, and as miserable as she was, she paid well for the privilege of tormenting her staff. The second and more important reason was that she felt responsible in part for Flora's current predicament, she felt she owed it to the girl to stay and try and rectify the situation.

So she had not investigated getting a loan. Indeed, she hadn't even told Lady Tilpot about her unforeseen windfall, because if the old despot suspected that anyone in her employ did not live in constant fear of dismissal, she threw them out. And once dismissed, Helena did not fool herself into thinking that she would ever be welcomed back as Flora's friend. She wouldn't even be allowed through the door, and the underlings that Lady Tilpot employed were not likely to risk their positions by aiding a one-time companion.

Flora, Helena thought, was as well guarded as a princess in a tower. Except for one notable lapse that had occurred a month ago, when, Helena had arrived back from a short stay in Brighton with Lady Tilpot to discover Flora in her room, much as tonight. First glowing, then crumpling, and finally confessing her marriage to Oswald.

"You know Ossie is doing everything in his power to be reunited with me!" Flora insisted.

"Oh, yes," Helena said dryly. "His efforts have been truly noteworthy—for being disastrously wrongheaded. Whatever gave Mr. Goodwin the notion that he could win a fortune at the gaming tables?"

"He has had a bit of bad luck, is all—"

"No, Flora." Helena cut off her excuses. "He has been criminally foolish!"

She ignored Flora's gasp and plowed on, striving to make Flora understand the character of the man with whom she'd eloped. "He converted everything of value he owned into cash and frittered away the profit in the lowest sorts of gaming hells. Then, not content simply to be insolvent, he willingly placed himself in the clutches of not one but two different cent-per-centers, the money which he borrowed going the same way as his other funds.

"Only a fool does not learn from his mistakes, Flora, and I see no evidence that Mr. Goodwin has learned anything from his current troubles but how to dodge dunners!"

"That is *so* unfair!" Flora intoned, her voice wobbling. "He is only trying to accumulate enough of the ready that we might live together, independently and ... and ... comfortably!"

"I will tell you what is unfair," Helena said firmly. "What is unfair is the risks he allows his friends to take in hiding him from his creditors and helping him evade moneylenders.

"My word, Flora, the man darts about from hidey-hole to attic closet like a thief! We can't ever contact him because no one knows who'll put him up for a night or lend him the money to rent a room."

Flora, seeing that Helena wasn't about to take back her harsh words regarding the light of her life, once more flung herself on the floor. "You hate him!"

Helena felt her anger slipping away. She never had been able to maintain a decent fume. She reached down and touched the girl lightly on the shoulder. "I do not hate him. I am, er, troubled by his lack of resources."

"He's *spent* his resources!"

Helena briefly closed her eyes, once more asking herself what momentary aberration of sanity had led her to agree to being party to such nonsense. But even as she questioned her sanity, she knew there really hadn't been any alternative.

She didn't trust any of Lady Tilpot's servants to keep mum about Flora and Oswald's marriage, let alone act as their messenger. They stood too much in terror of their mistress. And it was out of the question for Flora to risk her reputation and her aunt's wrath by going abroad at night. Besides which, Helena had serious doubts that Flora could navigate her way across the street without an escort, much less find her way to Vauxhall Garden.

Which left Helena. And Helena, having finally had a taste of taking action rather than simply responding to another's actions, found it a heady and powerful sensation. And addictive.

In order to evade the eyes of those looking for young Goodwin, Helena had hit upon the plan of meeting at crowded public masquerades. Happily, this season the ton had developed a positive passion for costume balls and masques. Opportunities to dress up in a domino or mask were plentiful.

This was the third time she had slipped unnoticed among a festive throng to meet with Mr. Goodwin. Those prior meetings had been uneventful. But tonight things had changed.

Helena's fingertips drifted uneasily to her mouth. Her lips still felt slightly swollen, still held the memory of his. Odd. She barely remembered feeling any fear of Figgy. All the danger she recalled came from one source, a tall, handsome Scotsman with loose black curls and the eyes of a defrocked priest.

"Whether you approve of Ossie or not, Helena, you must go back! I would not ask you if I had any alternative," Flora said with the gravity of those who believe they are speaking the truth. "Ossie must have gotten the dates turned around, or he was delayed, or he saw someone and dared not approach you. Please try again. *Please.*"

Blast the girl. Hysterics Helena could withstand, but an honest, heartfelt appeal? She had been caught in a design of her own manufacturing, and until she figured out what was to be done—and despite her most profound prayers, she had no doubt that she, and not Mr. Goodwin or Flora, would have to be the one to figure something out—there she would stay.

Right now the only other option, terrible though it be, was to throw themselves on Lady Tilpot's mercy. The fact that Helena was even willing to consider the preposterous notion that Lady Tilpot *had* any mercy was an indication of her growing desperation.

"All right, Flora."

The girl's smile appeared like the sun after a spring storm.

"But only once more." She returned Flora's brilliant smile wanly. "And you must promise to refrain from sobbing on my floors anymore. The carpet bleeds."

FIVE

MANIPULATORS:
the thumb and index finger of the sword hand

ONE WEEK LATER, Helena devoted herself to the crowd in Lady Tilpot's salon. It was primarily a young fashionable male group, and as such preferred to stand rather than try to sit in their skintight trousers. Coupled with Lady

Tilpot's interior design—one that relied heavily on displaying as many ornate family heirlooms as the salon could hold, this made it difficult to navigate through the stuffy, overheated room. Still, Helena did her best, juggling duties that included seeing that the refreshments remained plentiful, conversing with chaperones and grandfathers, and making certain that Flora showed herself to the best possible advantage. The only problem with this last being that it was impossible to act the foil to someone who was not there.

Earlier, Flora had pleaded a headache, which Helena could not help feeling grateful about. Without Flora in attendance to view—and be viewed by—the current crop of bachelors being offered on the Marriage Mart, the guests were bound to depart early. Afterward, Lady Tilpot would leave for her Thursday night whist game, affording Helena an opportunity to attempt once more to contact Oswald Goodwin at Vauxhall Garden.

"No, no, Mrs. Winebarger," Lady Alfreda Tilpot called out to a Prussian lady who had just dropped her fan. "Do not trouble yourself with dislodging The Creature."

Lady Tilpot, flat-faced, flat-chested, and round-rumped, rested her flounder-eyed glare tellingly on the little calico cat perched on Mrs. Winebarger's knee. Lady Tilpot abhorred "livestock" in the house. "Let Miss Nash retrieve your fan. She must do something for her salary. Miss Nash! Fetch Mrs. Winebarger's fan!"

Helena rose at once. She understood the underlying reason for the summons: Lady Tilpot had decided she needed to be reminded of her station. And everyone else in the room, too. She needn't have worried.

In her debut season, Helena had realized that she was being judged like a mare at Tattersall's, and had courteously but adamantly refused to partake in the sales. She wasn't any more likely to elope with one of this current flock of stable builders—or dynasty builders as the case may be—than she had been then.

Her trouble, she knew, was that while everyone else seemed content for her to be pretty, she wanted more. She wanted some man to look at her and wonder what she was thinking, what strengths of character she owned and what weaknesses. She wanted someone to take the time to know her, to discover her, to *see* her.

She excused herself and went to see to Mrs. Winebarger, curious because the Prussian lady was not one of Lady Tilpot's usual guests. For one, she was far too lovely, being small with a voluptuous figure, large blue-green eyes and autumn-colored hair. For another, she was somewhat notorious, and Lady Tilpot was as moralistic as only a secret sinner can be.

The tittle-tattle Helena had overheard amongst Lady Tilpot's cronies was that the Prussian woman had once, in order to win a bet, disguised herself as a lad to gain employment in a prince's household, a position she had held for an entire week before being discovered, thus winning, along with the bet, the sobriquet Page. Indeed, it had been Mrs. Winebarger who had been the inspiration for Helena's own costume.

"Regardless of The Tilpot's instruction," Mrs. Winebarger said softly as Helena bent to retrieve the fan, "I would have picked up my own fan had I not wanted to speak with you."

"Ma'am?"

"I have watched you. You are as out of place here as I," she said. "My husband and I were invited only because Robert is one of those favored to win the International Dueling Tournament. But then at the last minute, he was unable to accompany me, and The Tilpot found it impossible to uninvite me."

That explained much, thought Helena. Though bigoted, no one could accuse Lady Tilpot of stupidity. She had recognized that all the young men she wished to attract to Flora's hand were engrossed in the current mania for fencing. As this tournament grew near, fencing experts from any number of countries were arriving daily. Lady Tilpot was using the top celebrities to lure eligible young gentlemen to her soirees.

"I see you understand," Mrs. Winebarger said, "I allow myself to be used for her purposes because it amuses me. But you . . ." She patted the cushion invitingly. "Come, sit here beside Princess and me."

"Princess?" Helena asked, seating herself. The little charcoal, butterscotch, and white cat did not look like royalty. Her mismatched ears were tatter-edged, her pink nose scarred.

Mrs. Winebarger nodded. "But of course. She is a great princess in disguise." Gently, she fingered the raggedy ear tabs. A deep, throaty sound rumbled out of the small animal. "Happily, I see her for what she is, not what the world has made her. Now, tell me about the assembled company."

Helena began with the well-known earl listening uncomfortably to Lady Tilpot, his head bobbing in time to her red-faced tirade. "I suspect the earl is tendering his regrets for his son's—and only heir's—absence, a sore disappointment to Lady Tilpot."

"And who is the bald fellow joining them?"

A stooped man approached Lady Tilpot obliquely, his expression deferential. He had the sort of face whose age was impossible to gauge, being as smooth and unlined as the dome of his head. He had, Helena thought, rather well-composed features, with eyes that were at times old and saddened and at others bright with unexpected humor. Unfortunately, his physique was not nearly as appealing and in no manner improved by his ill-fitting clothing, his coat bunching across the shoulders, his breeches hanging too loose at the knees and stretching too tightly about a little pot belly.

"That is Reverend Tawster."

"Ah," Mrs. Winebarger said, "Lady Tilpot's pet vicar. I heard that the last one decamped."

Helena bit back a smile. "Reverend Tawster is not so bad as his predecessor. He occasionally even questions Lady Tilpot."

At Mrs. Winebarger's disbelieving glance, Helena dimpled. "Admittedly, only very occasionally." Truthfully, she rather liked Reverend Tawster. She felt a little sorry for him. He so obviously wanted to lead a good life, a goal at odds with his just as obvious enjoyment of good living.

She turned Mrs. Winebarger's attention to a cluster of gentlemen near the fireplace and in short order named an Irish earl's son, two viscounts, and a baronet.

"And that handsome man standing by himself?" Mrs. Winebarger asked.

"Lord Forrester DeMarc, *Viscount* DeMarc," Helena answered, her voice cooling. The viscount looked the very picture of a London Pink of the Ton in his buff trousers, midnight blue coat, and yellow waistcoat, clothing that accentuated his tall, athletic figure.

An occasional smile, thought Helena, would recommend him more than the superior expression he currently sported. But then she doubted anything could recommend the viscount to her. Last week DeMarc had manufactured some excuse that found them alone in Lady Tilpot's morning room. He had stared at her, smiling in a disagreeably knowing manner the whole time, yet had not said a single word.

Helena had long ago discovered that simply ignoring a gentleman often dampened his attentions—particularly as she had no money or connections that would make the effort of a dalliance worthwhile. But DeMarc did not take the hint.

There was a possessiveness in the way he watched her that she found presumptuous, especially since his consequence refused to allow him to spend more than a few moments in polite conversation with her before he moved on to more distinguished persons.

"I have heard of him."

"Have you?" Helena asked lightly before discreetly pointing at the only other young lady in the room, a bubbling composition of titian curls, green eyes, and effusive bosom. "That is Miss Jolene Milar."

"Jolly" Milar had not gained her nickname because of a cheery disposition, but because of a certain laxity in her morals. Luckily, Lady Tilpot did not know this. If she had, not even the fact that Jolly's brother was one of the ton's richest bachelors would have gotten the girl through the front door. A married woman's early peccadilloes might be overlooked if the incentive was great enough, but in an unmarried girl they were completely unacceptable. "Her brother is a Great Catch."

Mrs. Winebarger leaned forward. "Which leads back to my original question, why *are* you here? It cannot be out of affection . . . ah!" Her lovely eyes widened. "But I am mistaken! It *is* affection. But not for The Tilpot, certainly? A young man?"

Helena felt the heat rising in her face.

"Miss Nash?"

Helena swiveled to face Lord DeMarc, all too aware of her flaming cheeks. "Sir."

"You are flushed," he remarked stiffly. "I trust that the conversation"—his gaze moved accusingly to Mrs. Winebarger—"has not proved too heated?"

At his implicit censure, Mrs. Winebarger laughed, her voice tinkling like bells in the stuffy room. "Ah—Viscount DeMarc, am I correct?"

DeMarc inclined his head. "Madame."

"My husband speaks of you." DeMarc's gaze sharpened. "He says you are rumored to be formidable with a smallsword."

"I do not recall meeting the gentleman," DeMarc said with grudging interest.

Mrs. Winebarger shrugged. "He goes to many of the best salles. He watches. He speaks with the masters about who is to be counted a worthy opponent and who can be safely disregarded. Perhaps he has spoken with your master?"

"And what master would that be?"

Mrs. Winebarger cocked her head. "Why, Mr. Ramsey Munro, is it not?"

Helena's hand checked in Princess's silky fur, Ramsey's image exploding in her mind's eye, a fallen angel, a holy sinner. She could taste his kiss again, the flavor of his breath, the texture of his tongue against hers, acute and immediate, as if during the entire past week the memory had been lurking, waiting for an opportunity to ambush her senses and upend her world.

"I have studied in many salles, under many instructors," she heard DeMarc say, "but I would not count any of them my master. Certainly not Ramsey Munro, as proficient a sparring partner as he is."

Across the room, Jolly Milar's head snapped around like a fox scenting a fowl, and she started toward them.

"No? Perhaps this is just as well," Mrs. Winebarger replied. "It would be unseemly for a master to fight his pupil, and I hear Mr. Munro is determined to enter the contest himself."

"Not that Munro would know or care what was or was not seemly—he's notoriously lax in all matters of protocol. But may I ask where you heard this rumor?" DeMarc asked.

"Once again, my husband informs me," Mrs. Winebarger returned.

"How singular," DeMarc said with poorly hidden distaste, "that your husband has chosen you to be his confidante."

"Why so?" Mrs. Winebarger asked, completely unimpressed with his disapproval.

"Here in England, we protect and exclude our wives

and children from those matters in which they are not involved. Social as well as political."

"It is the same in my country. But my husband"—Mrs. Winebarger's eyes grew soft—"is a unique man. For instance, this rumor regarding Mr. Munro's purported desire to enter the tournament oversets him nearly as much as it delights him."

"Why is that, ma'am?" Jolly Milar asked, joining them.

"A true swordsman cannot help but want to test himself against the best, and Ramsey Munro is the best," Mrs. Winebarger said.

Yes, Helena thought, *of course Ramsey Munro must be the best. He wouldn't be anything less.* Elegance and deadliness unleashed in a hiss of steel, a whisper of movement, or a heated kiss.

"*One* of the best," DeMarc corrected. "But that being so, I sincerely doubt Ramsey Munro has the ready to post the entry fee. Five thousand pounds is a great deal of money to a man like Munro."

But he had handed that boy a hundred pounds . . .

"And what sort of man would that be, Lord DeMarc?" Mrs. Winebarger asked.

"A man with an undeniable and extraordinary talent with a sword. But a common man, nonetheless."

"There's *nothing* common about Ramsey Munro," Jolly Milar declared and burst into girlish giggles. "Why 'tis rumored all of London is littered with his past lovers."

Past lovers. Well, of course. She'd known. Rumors about his conquests were legion, and if lately they were not quite as widespread, perhaps he had learned discretion. How could one doubt his success with women, looking as he did, having the address he did, having the mouth and hands? Helena swallowed, smiling politely. DeMarc's aquiline nose pinched, and even Mrs. Winebarger looked sharply at the girl. "You know the gentleman?"

"He is not a gentleman," DeMarc said coldly.

Once more Helena silently agreed: Ramsey Munro was not a gentleman. She'd known that, too. The letter Munro and his companions had brought with them to her mother's house had stated that fact without compunction or apology, but simply by way of expressing their regret that whatever aid they could give her family would be neither financial nor social.

"He's the Prince of White Friars, sure enough," Jolly said with a little snort. "And his throne is at the end of his salle, and there he reigns supreme."

"How do you know this?" Mrs. Winebarger asked.

"I've been there," Jolly replied pertly.

"To the salle?" DeMarc's expression was incredulous.

"Oh, it is all the thing!" Jolly spouted enthusiastically. "We all go down and watch on Saturdays. *All* the young ladies."

By now, their group had attracted Lady Tilpot's attention. Hating to be excluded from anything that promised gossip or unpleasantness, she heaved herself to her feet and, grabbing Reverend Tawster's arm in a death grip, waddled forth with the apologetic-looking vicar in tow.

"That is indecent!" DeMarc declared as Lady Tilpot and the Reverend joined them. "Isn't it, Vicar?"

"What?" the vicar asked. "Going to a sporting exhibition?"

"The salles are schools for young gentlemen, not exhibition halls," DeMarc said. "Any woman who disports herself there can scarce be called a lady."

"Truly, the world is too lax in what it allows, but perhaps more grievous errors than visiting a salle might occupy our prayers and our outrage?" Reverend Tawster suggested mildly.

Helena smiled encouragingly at the vicar and could have sworn he closed an eye in a wink.

"Not at all," Lady Tilpot pronounced.

"Lady Tilpot, you disagree with your vicar?" Mrs. Winebarger asked.

"Completely. It is our young people who will inherit society one day, and as such we cannot hope for too much as regards their behavior. We must be constantly vigilant of any indications of vice or moral rot and be swift to excise them."

"You are correct, of course," the vicar demurred, "but I think it important to trust that our young people are proud of their heritage and thus would do nothing to diminish their noble names."

"Unless they are the not so very well bred." Lady Tilpot looked directly at Helena.

"Certainly you are not referring to Miss Nash?" Reverend Tawster declared, looking aghast. "Though I have known her but a short while, in that time she has never deported herself in any but the most exacting and nicest manner."

"Certainly not," declared Lady Tilpot coldly. "I would not tolerate anything less in my household." She regarded Helena with a pursed smile. "But," she continued sententiously, "as nice as her manners might be, blood will tell. Clearly, somewhere in Miss Nash's background lurks an Unfortunate Connection."

Helena felt her mouth stiffen. She must not rise to the provocation. She never rose to the provocation.

"That is out-and-out rubbish!" Mrs. Winebarger's amusement had apparently evaporated. She met Lady Tilpot's apoplectic glower with a cold stare. "Unless I am very much mistaken, her father was Colonel Roderick Nash."

Mrs. Winebarger turned to Helena and her gaze softened. "Was he not? A man respected in life and honored in death."

"Indeed, yes," Helena answered softly, gratefully. Yet . . . why would the Prussian lady know that? True, her father had been a military man of some renown, but not to the degree that his name would be commonly known amongst the ton. "I am surprised you know of him."

"My husband follows the wars very closely. He is a great admirer of your father and"—she glanced at DeMarc—"as my husband's confidante, I have learned a great deal about the gentleman. For instance, I know that while on diplomatic duty in France, he volunteered to trade himself for three Scottish prisoners, young men whom the French suspected were spies and who were slated for execution."

Her voice lowered, grew commiserative. "I also know that after the exchange"—her voice dropped sympathetically—"he was executed. He died a hero."

Mrs. Winebarger's words brought it all rushing back to Helena: her initial raw grief, exacerbated by Kate's anger at her father for sacrificing his life for three strangers; the shock of discovering that their family could no longer reside at the entailed estate; the stunned realization that they must leave York. And into this quagmire of desperation and grief had come the very prisoners Colonel Nash had died rescuing, vowing that they would do whatever their savior's family asked of them, no matter what that might be. What would these people say if they knew that one of those prisoners had been Ramsey Munro?

"Her father is certainly to be honored," Lady Tilpot said after a moment, and then only grudgingly. "But her sisters are another matter. The widowed one has only lately made an infamous match, wedding a common Scottish soldier. Tell them it is true, Miss Nash."

"Indeed it is," Helena acknowledged with a sense of relief. At least here she needn't feel guilty over her failure to defend her relatives. Kate and Christian did not need, nor would they want, her championship. They paid no attention to Society.

"That alone might be overlooked as a peculiarity. But the younger sister presents clear evidence that the Nash family tree is hiding Undesirable Elements."

The little hairs on the nape of her neck began prickling. Kate could, and always had, taken care of herself, but Charlotte—impulsive, passionate, independent Charlotte—would go wherever her heart and fancy led.

Soon after their parents' deaths, Helena and Kate had decided that as Charlotte would have little else to recommend her in life, she should at least have the advantages of a good education. They had done all they could to pay for her attendance at an exclusive school. But when her schooling had ended, Charlotte had flown from their care at the first opportunity, ingratiating herself with the family of a school chum, Baron Welton's only child.

Helena was honest enough to admit that at first she had welcomed abdicating the difficult task of sheltering and guiding a headstrong teenager to an established society family. Later, when it had come to their attention that there was little sheltering and no guiding whatsoever going on in that family, her attempts to extricate Charlotte from the Welton household had been met with her sister's blatant refusal to leave.

With an impish and unapologetic smile, Charlotte had informed her that she had no interest in living in poverty, that she liked her fashionable clothes and pretty room, and that she was of an age where neither Helena nor Kate could do a "bloody thing about it." And then she had winked.

Lately, Helena had heard she was developing undesirable friendships. She had tried communicating with Charlotte on the subject on numerous occasions, but always unsuccessfully. When she went to the Welton household, Charlotte was always gone. The few lines she wrote in response to Helena's alternately pleading and demanding letters had been brief, unconcerned, filled with the latest news regarding her wardrobe and the current *on dits* about her adopted family.

It had been exasperating. There were no other avenues by which to reach Charlotte. The fast crowd the Weltons ran with was hardly the type to be invited to Lady Tilpot's house. Ultimately, Helena had had to admit the indisputable fact that Charlotte neither wanted to, nor would accept, Helena's "interference" in her life, and as unhappy as it made her, Helena did not see what else she could do.

Consequently, the name of her younger sister on Lady Tilpot's pursed lips brought every protective instinct rushing forth in Helena, and with them guilt. Indeed, Helena suspected she had transferred a great deal of her guilt over Charlotte, whom she could not help no matter how she tried and who did not want her help, to Flora, whom she could and who did.

"Well, Miss Nash? Have you nothing to say for yourself?" Lady Tilpot asked.

Helena bit down hard on her inner cheeks. If she was too pert, Lady Tilpot would discharge her on the spot, and Flora would be alone. She need only bear Lady Tilpot a few weeks more. A few weeks. She could do that. "Charlotte," she finally said in a tight voice, "is quite well received."

"Yes," Lady Tilpot admitted, "but for how long?" And, having fired off this last shot, she turned with an air of finality to her vicar. "Reverend Tawster, would you be *so* kind as to give me your arm? I wish to sit."

The vicar obliged, perhaps suddenly realizing on which side his bread was buttered. And judging by his soft-looking belly, he did like butter.

"Now, then," Jolly turned back as soon as Lady Tilpot and the vicar were out of earshot, as if Lady Tilpot's views on good breeding had been a burp, a little embarrassing and best ignored, "what I was saying about Ramsey Munro was how all the young ladies visit his salle on Saturday afternoons and—"

"Miss Nash, I fear the conversation grows tedious for you," DeMarc's cold voice cut across Jolly's.

Helena regarded him with irritation. She'd wanted to hear what Jolly knew of Ramsey Munro.

"You can hardly know the people of whom Miss Jolly speaks, and I doubt your circle of acquaintances overlaps with Mrs. Winebarger's." He held out his hand. "I am sure you will like to show me Lady Tilpot's collection of etchings, eh?"

Without being inexcusably rude, there was nothing she could do but rise and take his arm. He escorted her to the other side of the room, where Lady Tilpot had arranged a portfolio of etchings for her guests' viewing.

He did not even pretend to look at them. "There. Now you have my complete attention. That ought to please you."

Helena blinked, uncertain whether or not she had heard him correctly. "Sir?"

"I am sorry you were subjected to that woman."

Once more Helena regarded him, startled. Was he going to champion Charlotte against Lady Tilpot? Perhaps she had misjudged—

"The Prussians are universally acknowledged to be coarse, and that Milar creature." He shuddered delicately.

No. He would not be championing her.

She struggled to find a rejoinder, but it was impossible. She could hardly dispute him by saying the conversation was not low, and she could scarcely agree. So she said nothing. And she *hated* saying nothing. Just as she had hated being unable to defend Charlotte to Lady Tilpot. But she would do what was necessary, at least for now, in order to find a happy ending for the star-crossed lovers.

"You bear your state with laudable patience, Miss Nash," he murmured fondly.

Apparently, the role of silent sufferer was one DeMarc found admirable. The man probably liked his dogs cringing, too. Helena lowered her eyes so he would not see her ire. "Sir."

"You little minx. Look at me. No one is watching us. You've been discreet." Her head snapped up. He smiled. "But not too discreet. I have noted your interest. Others have, too. I see how you look at me. I see your smile."

Amazement turned to dismay.

"My only question now is, what to do about it?"

No. Oh, no. She couldn't afford to hurt his feelings. A man like Forrester DeMarc would take any rejection poorly. But she could not encourage him, either, and not only because she had no desire whatsoever to do so. If Lady Tilpot suspected Helena of using her soirees for Flora to attract men for herself, she would dismiss Helena at once.

She couldn't leave Flora. Not now. Not yet. She racked her brain looking for some suitable response.

"Too kind," she finally murmured.

"Miss Nash!" Lady Tilpot's peremptory call unfurled across the room like a lash, and for once Helena felt only gratitude for that petulant, demanding bark. "Stop monopolizing Lord DeMarc and come here."

Without a backward glance, Helena obeyed.

SIX

PREPARATION:
a nonthreatening action intended to create
the opening for the initial phase
of an attack

THE AFTERNOON SHADOWS had lengthened into long mauve streaks when Helena placed the shillings in the Vauxhall Garden attendant's hand. This time she did not keep her eyes lowered behind her black silk mask. Last week's experience, rather than discouraging her, had given her confidence. The excitement of the other attendees was contagious, their faces smiling and their laughter spicing the air.

A ragamuffin girl standing just inside the gate pressed a violet nosegay into Helena's hand and then, tilting her tough little face up, inspected her thoroughly before saying, "I don't know rightly if yer a man or a woman, but either way that'll be tuppence."

"Give me the flowers for a penny, and I will reveal my secrets," Helena said, teasing the child.

Without preamble, the girl snorted. "I ain't *that* interested. Besides which, me ma told me as how if anyone ever says anytin' about revealin' anytin' to me, I was to scream bloody murder. So, will it be tuppence then, or I'll start screaming?"

Helena laughed and tossed her a groat before tucking

the flowers under the lip of her soft hat and moving on, amused and fascinated that this little scrap of a girl would own such self-assurance and aplomb. She could not remember ever having been so summarily dismissed.

It was the mask, she realized. No one could see her countenance or hair. Always before, her looks had attracted conspicuous attention. It was novel for her to move anonymously through a crowd. Here, dressed thus, she could say whatever she wished and never pay the penalty for a chance indiscretion or pointed observation, for laughing too loudly or saying something inappropriate. That was the danger of masks, Helena realized, no doubt of it: the euphoria of freedom. And of such freedom she'd had scant experience.

Before this past month, she had never gone anywhere like Vauxhall Garden. In fact, she had never been anywhere at all without the escort of at least a maid or footman. This was heady stuff, indeed. She might—

"I could do anything I wanted to you. Right now. You're mine," a hoarse voice whispered close to her ear.

Helena spun about, but the crowd was thick, and the owner of the voice might have been any of a dozen people surrounding her: the fat man in the Tudor robes, the woman in kimono and plaster mask, the sailor or American Indian princess. She forced herself to calm down. The words probably hadn't even been meant for her. The feeling of being followed that had dogged her all week had stimulated her imagination. She was simply reacting to her sudden freedom with the ingrained conviction that nothing came without a price.

Her pleasure dimmed by the distasteful episode, she made her way to the centerpiece of the gardens, called the Grove, and from there to Lovers Walk. With any luck, Oswald would be there tonight. She fervently hoped so. Flora's constant tears were mildewing her pillow shams.

"My dear, my exquisite, my kind and *generous* Miss Nash!" The harlequin raised Helena's hands to his lips and pressed a fervent kiss upon her knuckles. Helena gazed sardonically at the tinkling bells decorating the foolscap bent over her hands; Oswald Goodwin could not have found a more fitting disguise. At least this time Flora's husband had been waiting for her at the shadowy end of Lovers Walk.

"Thank you so much for coming," Oswald continued. "I cannot apologize enough for my failure to meet with you last week—"

Helena pulled her hands free of his and wordlessly withdrew Flora's note from inside her velvet jacket. She handed it to him, glad to be rid of the thing; it was so drenched in perfume that carrying it had given her a headache.

His face alighting with joy, Oswald took the note, held it to his nose, and inhaled, his eyes slitting in a delirium of bliss. Grudgingly Helena felt her ire fading to simple exasperation when she saw the unfeigned pleasure with which he broke the seal. Whatever was to become of Flora and him? She did not doubt his love was real—but how deep was it? Would it survive years of separation? Poverty? Hardship? Social banishment?

He read for a few seconds and looked up, holding the paper to his heart. "She is well!" he breathed rapturously.

Helena refrained from pointing out that if Flora had

been ailing, Helena would hardly be here delivering love notes.

He read a little more and once again clutched the paper to his breast. "She misses me!"

"So she has informed me," Helena answered dryly. "Many times."

His large hazel eyes filled with tears. "I miss her, too."

"Yes, yes," Helena said impatiently. "It will be grand when you can be together again. And speaking of this, at the risk of sounding meddlesome, what exactly are you doing by way of hastening that happy day's arrival?"

She could barely believe it was herself speaking to him this way. She was always most circumspect, never sarcastic. But, drat all, it felt good—no, it felt *wonderful*—to give vent to her frustration over the lovers' inability to do something for themselves. If they insisted on involving her, then they would have to put up with the consequences.

It must be the mask again.

"You could never overstep yourself, Miss Nash!" Oswald declared, once more grabbing her hand and raising it to his lips. "Our angel! You, who facilitated our joyous union—"

"I did not!" Helena snatched her hand back, aghast. "I facilitated a meeting—not a *union!*"

"Whatever term you prefer." Oswald waved her protest away. "We are together now, and it is all because of you."

She wanted to be reminded of this about as much as she wanted to be reminded that Mrs. Winebarger's cat had had fleas. She glared at him from behind the black silk mask.

"And as such," he said, "you can *never* be too presumptuous. Never! We are in your hands. Utterly and confidently."

And *that* was just what Helena feared and did not want and refused to allow. She might be partially to blame, but she was not entirely at fault. Oswald and Flora would have to make *some* attempt to remedy their current plight.

"Most affecting," she said with determined brightness. "Now that we have established my culpability for your marriage and further determined that nothing I do can possibly free me from the obligations implicit in such a charge, tell me, Mr. Goodwin, what are *your* plans to become one, in fact as well as spirit, with your bride?"

Oswald Goodwin, not the brightest luminary in anyone's sky, blinked in a puzzled manner. "Ah . . . I have a plan."

"So far, so good."

He looked around. "A failure-proof plan."

"Better yet." Helena smiled encouragingly.

His restless gaze settled on her and grew thoughtful. "You know, Miss Nash, I am loath to say so, but I doubt anyone could possibly mistake you for a lad, even dressed as you are. You're too deuced curvy. In fact, I might suggest that you eschew masculine attire in the future as being too conspicuous."

At this patent attempt to turn the conversation, Helena released a sigh. "I expect you are correct. Believe me, I have no plans to wear it again. Now, what is *your* plan?"

"Well," he rubbed his hands together, "I have come into possession of a bit of information that, if acted upon in a timely fashion, will enable me to magnify a small sum of money—as yet to be secured—into considerable wealth."

Helena stared at him. "I pray you undeceive me, but I could have sworn you just announced that, having been provided with a *tip*, you plan to bet money—money you do not have—upon something whose outcome is so uncertain others are willing to wager even larger amounts on the exact opposite result," Helena translated. "Tell me this is not so."

He shuffled, and his foolscap bells tinkled. "I can't."

"How *could* you, Mr. Goodwin?"

"Could I what?" Oswald blinked innocently.

"Gamble!" Helena said in a furious whisper. "In case you have neglected to notice, you have already lost everything you own!"

Oswald's pleasant face turned crimson. "This is different, Miss Nash," he said miserably, earnestly. "This is an Absolute Certainty."

She threw up her hands. "Oh, Mr. Goodwin—"

"Please, Miss Nash," Oswald broke in. "In just a few weeks' time, I swear I shall be as rich as a nabob, with plenty of the ready and then some to spare. Enough to buy off the moneylenders and still furnish Florie with all the fripperies and whatnots her dear little heart desires!"

"Because of a wager."

"Not a wager. An investment. An investment in a very sound commodity that will enable Florie and me to live like Midas for the rest of our days, and I swear on my honor," he stated sententiously, "that afterward I shall never gamble again."

"Hm."

"Really."

"Is there nothing I can do to dissuade you from digging yourself deeper into the hole into which you have purposefully flung yourself and into which you are now attempting to drag Flora, too?"

He winced, but met her eyes bravely enough. "No. Sorry."

"Ach!" She crossed her arms tightly over her chest and turned on her heels so she wouldn't have to look at his stubborn, lovesick, genial face.

"Miss Nash?"

"And when," she asked tightly, "is this great plan to come to fruition?"

"Within the month," he chirped at once. "By then, I shall have collected my monies, paid those sums I owe various people," he hesitated sheepishly, "and still have plenty remaining to take Flora from her aunt's house and set her up in her own home. *Our* own home."

She turned back. He was beaming, and she realized that nothing she could say would dissuade him. "And if you lose this bet?"

"I won't."

"But, say, the world stops spinning and the heavens fall and you *do* lose? What then?"

"Then?" His face fell into such abject misery that for an instant Helena felt every bit a blackguard. He blew out a lengthy breath. "Then I shall have no recourse but to present myself to Lady Tilpot and ask her aid."

"And in response she will do everything in her power to see that your marriage is annulled," she said with ruthless candor.

"That is a chance I will have to take." Tears sprang to Oswald's eyes. "I can't ask Flora to live alone under

Lady Tilpot's tyranny until she comes into her inheritance. If this does not work, I shall throw myself on her mercy . . ."

And end up in debtors' prison, Helena thought morosely. At least until Flora could bail him out four years hence. *If* her affection for the young miscreant lasted that long. Which wasn't very likely, given that Flora's commitment to her conjugal vows hadn't even stood the test of a few bedbugs.

No, Helena was not confident about the couple's future. Not at all. But, she reminded herself, there was little she could do about it. God willing, maybe this latest havey-cavey plan of Oswald's would actually bear fruit. Miracles did happen, and they say that God watches out for children and fools, and as far as Helena was concerned, Flora and Oswald qualified on both counts.

"Have I convinced you of my sincerity?" Oswald asked.

"Oh, yes," Helena said because there was nothing else to say. "I believe you are utterly sincere."

"And you will support my decision? Because Flora holds your opinion in the highest regard, and she will feel so much better if I can write and tell her I have your full blessing."

"Full blessing" is hardly how Helena would have phrased it, but she supposed that anything that might help the couple out of their current predicament was worth commending.

"I suppose—"

"Oh!"

"What is it?" Helena asked, swinging around. Midway down the path from where they stood, a pair of men in friars' robes had stopped, their heads close together. Even from this distance and in the gloom of the poorly lit lane, their interest in Oswald was apparent.

"I . . . have to go!" Oswald declared, edging backwards. The men on the path stilled like hounds on point. "I will send word through the *London Post* where next we are to meet."

"Next we meet? *Next* we meet! There will *be* no—"

"Look in the advertisements for one from 'Harlequin,' " he cut in. "And remember, no boy's clothing! A dress. A *pink* dress!" he shouted, and bolted.

The men raced after him, passing Helena on a dead run. Within a minute she was alone on the path, the sound of receding footsteps beating away into the darkness.

"Wretched dunners," Helena muttered, because as she hadn't secured the all-important love letter from Oswald to Flora, she would be obliged to find Oswald next week or risk having her furnishings ruined by Flora's torrents of tears. And where, pray tell, was she to find a pink fancy dress?

Perhaps, she mused as she started down the dim path, she could forge a love letter from Oswald that would satisfy Flora. What would one write in a love letter? *Dearest one, I long to see you again.*

Frowning, she paused beside a rail separating the path from a Greek folly. That wouldn't do. Far too tame. She tried again.

My darling, last night I dreamt I gazed into your eyes and. . . .

No, no, no. She had to put herself in a lover's place, try to imagine what she would write—

My Sin, My Transgression, My Pleasure,

How ardently I yearn to see you. How desperately I fear I will never do so again. I dream of you and wake to find myself alone but for the memory of your brilliant eyes and wicked smile, inspiring wanton feelings within me that I cannot imagine owning. But I am unrepentant. I long for your touch, your kiss—

"Hello, *Corie.*"

SEVEN

〈◇◇〉

CONVERSATION:
the back-and-forth play of the blades in a fencing match

"NOT A VERY LOYAL SWAIN you have there."

Helena swung around, backing into the rail. Ramsey Munro strolled toward her out of the gloaming, a conjuration of that magical time betwixt day and night. He was dressed again in the dark, conservative style she realized was typical for him, the gold rose pin at his throat his only embellishment. His eyes were soft and brilliant, his smile wry. A frisson of fear awoke in Helena's blood like an opiate, piercing and disturbingly pleasurable.

"That wasn't the much ballyhooed married man, was it?"

"Yes," she said a little breathlessly. She must remember

to keep her voice disguised. Her normal accents might prod the memory of a man like Ramsey Munro. There were not all that many Yorkshire women in London.

He shook his head sadly. "Not a terribly impressive specimen. Despite all that ardent hand-kissing."

"You think not?" she asked, trying to find her equilibrium. He was so devastatingly elegant and wicked-looking.

"No, indeed. He lacks address." He stopped only when he was almost upon her, coming far too close, unacceptably close. She could *feel* him, a tingling that disturbed the air between them, a magnetism that drew her.

"Perhaps his address is not important to me."

"I hadn't considered that."

"Perhaps I only require that he be slavishly devoted," she suggested archly, warming to this unfamiliar but fascinating role.

He smiled. "Ah. I see. You desire a sycophant."

"No, no," she said glibly, her confidence growing as the conversation continued. "That implies falseness. I desire to be worshipped in a most sincere fashion."

"Well," he said, "you'll certainly find sincerity amongst the young. It is one of the few qualities that, owning in abundance, they insist on distributing in excess."

"Spoken from the vantage of one in his dotage, no doubt?"

His eyes glittered in the dusk of approaching twilight. "Darlin' lass, there is more than one way to count age. Experience being but one of them, and in that I proclaim myself positively venerable.

"That being so," he continued, falling back a step and leaning casually with one hand on the rail, "tell me, how is it a fresh-faced youth like yon boy has managed to secure the affections of not one but two ladies? To marry one girl and then seduce another all by . . . what? Twenty? Twenty-one? I confess, I am all wonder."

She did not want his curiosity about Oswald piqued to any degree. And that meant she would need to deflect it. A task, she acknowledged, with which she would have no trouble proceeding.

"First," she said smoothly, "you assume *he* was the seducer."

Aye. That had startled him.

"And second," she continued, infusing her voice with the same liquid velvet he'd employed, "not everyone finds experience as appealing as, say, artless energy." She smiled, and his smile flashed in answer.

Merciful heavens, this was intoxicating! She felt drunk on their wordplay, as if they were fencing, parrying, nicking and retreating.

"Miss," he said in a low, vibrant voice, "I could scarce live with myself if I were to leave you doubting my vigor. In the name of all the underappreciated experienced men in the world, how then might I convince you to test me?"

"If you were to view what I would propose as a test, sir," she said sweetly, "then I fear you have already failed."

He grinned. "Bold words, but then bold words are easily spoken from behind the safety of a mask."

Everything about him bespoke his unassailable sophistication. Yet she'd glimpsed a bit of the nature of the man who owned that perfect alignment of flesh and bone. She had some knowledge of the masks that beauty makes. "You speak from experience."

"How so?" He lifted his hand, inviting an explanation.

"You are the one hiding. I am, as you see, without a mask."

"Are you?" she asked.

He burst out laughing. "How delightfully unanticipated you are, lass. I swear, if your wrist and footwork could keep pace with that facile mind, you would make one hell of a fencer."

"Perhaps I'll come by your salle some day for a lesson," she suggested, preening a little. "Teach the lads a thing or two about verbal fencing."

His eyes flashed. "I can promise you, should you appear in my salle dressed in your current attire, the play would be much more physical than verbal."

She'd forgotten she wore boy's clothing: breeches and linen shirt, white silk cravat and velvet jacket, a soft, antique hat covering her hair. He smiled, one side of his beautifully shaped mouth beginning a slow, carnal climb a second before the other side followed. It was a ravishing, lopsided smile, and her heart beat faster even as the heat rose in her throat. "Surely your students are not such ruffians," she protested.

"It wasn't my students I was speaking about." He pushed off of the railing and stepped in front of her, blocking her way past him.

Now, the heat exploded fully in her cheeks. She sidled back and he let her go, and she had the lowering idea that he was laughing at her. She did not want Ramsey Munro laughing at her.

"As diverting as the conversation has been, I had best be going, but first . . ." She reached up to unbutton the top of her ruby-colored velvet jacket and had the pleasure of seeing his dark brows flicker up in surprise. Touché! "But first I owe you a hundred pounds."

"Pardon me?"

Though she hadn't expected to see him again, she had prepared for the eventuality. Turning aside, she loosed the ties at the throat of her linen blouse. She could feel his gaze as she reached beneath the soft material and plucked a thin sheath of folded notes from her cleavage. She turned back, holding it out in front of her.

"You don't really expect me to take your money?" he asked, more in amusement than offense.

"Yes. Why would you not?" she returned.

"Why not?" He regarded her with an unfathomable expression. "Well, because despite any number of strenuous and fair objections, I still like to maintain the illusion, if only to myself, that I am a gentleman."

"Pshaw. You cheerfully forfeited your money in order to protect my identity. I am therefore in your debt. Let me repay what you lost." She pushed the currency against the hard wall of his chest. He didn't even glance down.

"Honesty compels me to say that I don't recall being all that cheerful about the situation. I think you underestimated the danger you were in, lass."

The soft caress of the Scottish-flavored endearment swept through her, stirring her senses. "Perhaps you are right."

Once more, a black brow climbed in query.

"After all," she answered, "I have remained here with you. And seeing as to your reputation, Mr. Munro, that hardly seems advisable, does it? Tell me"—she tilted her head—"should I be afraid?"

He closed what little distance remained between them, looming above her. Once more she backed up, but this time he followed her retreat until the rail pressed against her hip. He bent down, his beautiful Lucifer's face so close she could smell the faint tang of brandy on his breath. "Now *that*," he murmured, "is a question I've been asking myself."

Her breath caught, and her fist, still pressing bank notes against his chest, dropped. Suddenly, the deepening twilight surrounding them felt warmer and more intimate, and his dark beauty seemed dangerous. Perhaps even lethal—

"No."

"No?" she echoed faintly, fear and pleasure swirling within her in an unholy mixture.

"No, you have no reason to be afraid," he said. He frowned, backed away. "After all, you know something of me, while I know nothing about you. Clearly, you have the advantage."

He was right, and she wanted it to stay that way. She did not want him to know who she was—Helena Nash: mute, pretty mannequin, companion to society's most malicious matron. She didn't want him to know, because *he* would never have stood for such treatment.

But she had.

"That," she said, "remains to be seen."

"You are most perceptive, darlin'."

"And foolish?" she softly wondered aloud.

But he'd heard her. A wicked smile curved his perfect lips. "In your own words, my dear, that remains to be seen."

She could not remember ever feeling so richly, vibrantly *here*, as if her whole being was concentrated in this moment. She was acutely aware of every aspect of her surroundings: the warm air blowing ripe and moist from the Thames, the gravel beneath her slippers' thin leather soles, the whir and rustle of the trees' leaves above her, and the soft murmur of distant voices.

"Please take the money. A woman has a code of honor, too." She held out the paper bank notes.

He studied her face intently for a long moment and then reached out. Before she could react, he'd clasped her upper arms lightly and turned her around, facing her toward the brightly lit end of the path. "I think it is time for you to go home."

She didn't want to go. She would have to go back to Lady Tilpot's, to being a silent and decorative doormat. "I think I will stay a bit longer."

"No. I do not think that is a good idea."

"Are you warning or threatening me?" she asked, meeting his eyes.

Munro laughed. "Oh, my darlin' lass, if I was a threat to you, I would hardly need to apprise you of that fact. You would already know it."

Of course he was right. He could simply take from her what he wanted, and she had no doubt that he could do so without any effort at all. Everything about him was tempered and strong, elegant but deadly. Like his rapier, Ramsey Munro was a handsome means of destruction. Yet there was no denying his attraction. He was entirely unique in her acquaintanceship, a razor's edge separating the suave gentleman and the lawless Scot. Which was he really?

"You know what I think?" His fallen-angel mouth

curled in a sweet smile. Dusk caressed the angles and planes of his face with warm shadows. Moonlight gleamed in the blue-black softness of his curls and glowed in the deep patina of the gold rose pinned at his neck. "I think you *are* a lady. A lady who has never walked these paths, or those like them, before. An intelligent lady, a little too mature for recklessness, a little too young for caution."

It wasn't at all what she'd expected. It was so much worse. He'd read the very heart of her. How could he have known?

"And I find I cannot leave you to your own devices, at the mercy of whatever or whomever else might find you."

She waited.

"So," he continued lightly, "I have a suggestion that might satisfy both you and this unexpected impulse toward chivalry in myself." His voice was summer-night warm. "I will take your hundred pounds if you let me be your escort for this night."

She stared at him, fascinated and tempted. His hand rose, as if he were about to touch her cheek, but then he let it drop. He let his voice caress her instead.

"Come, lass," he said. "Let me show you things you have never seen. Take you places you have never gone. The gardens are but the gateway to a world you cannot imagine."

No words, no promises could have been more seductive. Nearly four years of quiet endurance stretched behind her, untold hours of crushing boredom, of being obliged to hear the same dreary conversations, the same dull topics approved for virgin ears. She wanted more. She wanted the exhilaration that came of watching a man, *this* man, react to her words rather than her face.

She wanted to see the world through another's eyes. To begin to live, when for so many years it had seemed to her she had simply slumbered.

As if on cue, laughter mingled with music flushed from far down the lane, the siren call of unchecked merriment. She would like to be part of that gaiety, to be caught up in the noise and crush of heated bodies, swept into a current of jubilant humanity.

"Yes," she whispered before realizing she spoke.

His eyes on her face, Ramsey Munro wrapped his long fingers around the hand still holding the paper currency and lifted it to his mouth, pressing a kiss against her knuckles. Heat speared through her, weakening her knees as he returned her trembling hand to her side, the money gone. She looked into his eyes and knew. He understood exactly her reaction to him: It was the same as any other woman's.

Well, he might recognize her reaction, but he was doomed for disappointment if he thought she would succumb to it. *She* could not be one of his past lovers "littering London." But oh! How very much she wanted *him* to be hers.

"Before we begin, I need to make one thing perfectly clear, Mr. Munro."

He inclined his head inquiringly.

"You are not to touch me, handle my person, kiss my hand, or in any way importune me."

He conspired to look shocked. "But I would never importune you."

"You know what I mean."

"I do?" He grinned with unabashed wickedness.

"Yes."

"Very well, then." He placed one hand over his heart. "I swear I will not set hands on you unless you desire I do so. Even to help you into a carriage. But"—his eyes danced—"do you think you might see your way clear to taking my arm when we walk? For the sake of my vanity?"

She eyed him suspiciously.

"I would hate for it to be bandied about that Ram Munro trotted all night at the heels of a lovely young woman who could not even stand to touch his decently clad arm. It would be so very lowering."

"All right," she agreed. "But how do you know I am a *lovely* young lady? I may well be a harpy beneath this mask."

His gaze took in her body in a long, slow visual drink, his eyes turning lambent with sexually charged awareness.

"Well, darlin'," he said, his soft Scottish burr becoming more pronounced as his voice deepened, "your throat is as long and pale as a swan's, and your lips, I know for a fact, are soft as silk velvet, and even behind your mask, the color of your eyes is enough to set the morning sky weeping with envy.

"And if that describes the aspect of a harpy," he continued, taking her hand, "then I pray God you were sent to plague me."

From behind the hedge, Forrester DeMarc forced himself to watch. He did not move, even when Ramsey Munro kissed the backs of Helena Nash's fingers as he took the folded bills from her and tucked them in his waistcoat. He stayed motionless, though his skin felt scorched and his breathing whistled from the contracted corridors of his chest.

Helena. His Helena. His blonde angel, as delicate as a fairy princess, giving money to that creature, that panderer of flesh. His stomach roiled, and he fell back a step, closing his eyes to blot out the sight of them. But he could not blot out her image, her lips soft and full beneath the black silk mask, parted slightly, the flash of widening eyes, the shiver of excitement telegraphed across the space separating them.

And Munro! Like a wolf, he watched her. His *hunger,* his insatiable want, a palpable thing. It made DeMarc ill just thinking about Helena being the object of such lust. Well, he wasn't going to tolerate it.

She was his.

Two months ago he'd walked into Lady Tilpot's, bored and disinterested. He'd noted first her great beauty, as any man must: smooth, milky complexion; perfect patrician features; the polished flaxen hair; quiet blue eyes framed by honey-colored lashes. But the world was filled with great beauties, arrogant creatures sure of their power over the pitiful fools who flung themselves at their feet. Creatures like Sarah Sweet.

But that had been years ago, he reminded himself, and he'd been young and idealistic. He was no longer so naïve.

No, it had been Helena's mouth that had alerted him that here was something different, something unique. It was pliant, soft, and quiet, hinting at a sweet helplessness that Sarah had never owned. At the same time, others commented on what had at once been blindingly apparent to him: Helena Nash was smitten with him.

She had not merely smiled at him. She had smiled *because* of him. He knew with absolute conviction that she, too, recognized the deep unity between them. From that moment on she had been his.

He'd needed only to crook his little finger to have her. But what to do? What to make of her? Because while she was far below him socially, she was not so far below him that he couldn't take her as his mistress, as he had Sarah Sweet, without repercussions. So he had waited while he decided what to do about her.

And then this . . . *betrayal*.

He closed his eyes, the taste of bile coating his mouth.

He'd gone back to the Tilpot townhouse earlier this evening in search of a snuffbox he'd mislaid, only to find Reverend Tawster still trying to escape from Lady Tilpot. Together, he and the toady little vicar had left the townhouse. For some time afterward, the vicar had kept him on the front steps, enthusiastically extolling Helena Nash's attributes—as if DeMarc did not already know them. But suddenly Tawster had frowned, peering past him.

"That isn't . . . ? " Reverend Tawster had shaken his head. "I am imagining things."

"What is it, Vicar?" DeMarc had asked, turning to see what had captured the parson's attention. He saw a slender boy in a cloak moving out of the alleyway behind the Tilpot townhouse. There was something familiar about the way he moved. "Who is that?"

"I don't know, I thought I saw her face—"

"*Her?*"

The vicar had smiled apologetically. "That's just it. Of course, it is not a woman. Why would a woman be dressed as a lad? Especially—"

"Especially what?"

The vicar's gaze darted away from DeMarc's. "I really must be going. I am already late for evening offices. I trust we will meet again soon. Goodbye!" And with that, he scurried away, his hands twining worriedly in their kidskin gloves.

DeMarc spared him little thought; he'd been consumed by a need to know whom the vicar had thought he'd recognized in that boyish form. So he had gone after the slight figure, instructing his carriage to follow the hansom cab the woman had hired.

And there, in Vauxhall Garden, the bright globe lights had revealed what the vicar had seen: Helena Nash.

DeMarc's fury compounded his sense of betrayal. That she would seek such low entertainments! Be dressed so shockingly—no, so scandalously! But far worse, that she could forget for an instant *her duty to him* was unconscionable! *Insufferable.*

So he had followed her, trailing far behind, and when she hurried down the notorious Lovers Walk, he followed her there, too, gall rising in his throat when she met a young man. Then she'd sent him away, and he'd thought she would leave.

She hadn't.

He came. His sparring partner. His instructor. His . . . what had that foolish Prussian woman had the audacity to proclaim him? His master. Ramsey Munro.

He came, and she had blossomed in his presence like some wickedly ripe flower, and Munro . . . ? He fair shimmered with carnal appetite.

DeMarc opened his eyes. They were gone.

But he knew where to find her. Just as he knew what to do to remind her to whom she belonged.

EIGHT

<>

INSISTENCE:
forcing an attack through a parry

RAMSEY MUNRO LED HELENA along Lovers Walk until it intersected with another path called the Druid's Walk, he informed her politely, because of the many coyly posed and cunningly illuminated statues amongst the greenery. From there, they entered the broad, brightly lit Grand Walk.

Here the clandestine atmosphere gave way to a festive one. A monkey leapt from his trainer's shoulder to steal the feathers from ladies' hair and return them with a bow as he held out a small tin cup for a coin. Jugglers wove through the multitudes, and cartmen selling cakes and savories rolled along the avenues while boys laboring under great canisters of arrack punch strapped to their backs hawked mugfuls for half a bob.

Helena drank it all in, the color, the noise, the scents

of garlic and perfume, wood smoke and bakery goods underscored by the briny stench rising from the Thames. People of all sorts and sizes, some richly costumed and others covered by cheap dominos, sauntered by, laughing and joking, listening to the various musicians, watching the mummery shows, and pausing to inspect the elaborate dioramas.

Helena could not help but notice that as many women covertly inspected Ramsey Munro as they did the exhibits. But it was not only the ladies who were drawn to him. Several times gentlemen clapped him on the back with exaggerated bonhomie. His discomfort with such familiarity was obvious, but he greeted their blusters politely. Oddly, his tolerance for their brazenness did not extend to her. He stepped in front of her at their approach, obliquely shielding her from their curious glances.

"A student?" Helena asked after the last such encounter.

"An applicant."

"You are highly regarded."

"I am currently en vogue," he said, regarding her lazily, yet she could not help but feel that razor-sharp attentiveness lurking behind his detachment. "I fill a special niche in society. I live at the sufferance and behest of my betters. Which is, I suppose"—his mouth tilted up at one side—"a good deal better than not living at all."

"You teach fencing," she said. "That is hardly scraping and bowing."

"Not all bowing is a matter of bending at the waist," he said. He held out his arm, and she placed her hand upon his hard, muscled forearm, keeping pace with him as he moved. "I am regarded as something more than their servant, something less than their tailor."

"Hardly," she disagreed. "Those gentlemen would never greet their tailor so enthusiastically."

"You think not?" he asked in a bored voice. "Perhaps you are right. I have a skill they pay me handsomely to teach. Since it is not a skill that makes a person in any way more useful or even more ornamental than say, a tailor's craft, Society, following the vagaries for which it is noted, deems it more romantic than those more practical services. And thus my own poor self more worthy of their interest.

" 'Who is he?' they ask themselves. 'Where did he learn to gut a man in two slight moves? How terribly savage! And how can I learn to do it, too?' "

Put thus, it did indeed seem absurd. But his words gave rise to a hundred questions. Where had Ramsey Munro been these past four years? Where had he been before that? Before the French prison? What had he been five years ago? Ten? She frowned. *Who was Ramsey Munro?*

"Men are at heart bloodthirsty beasts," he was saying, drawing her along as easily as if they were strolling through Hyde Park after Sunday services, "fascinated by violence and those who are able to harness it to their purpose. Tell me, do you not find it quixotic that I am invited into their drawing rooms when the tutor or governess who has custody of their offsprings' character isn't allowed through the door?"

He stopped before a blooming topiary. "Oh, not *every* drawing room door." He flashed a smile. "Some people maintain standards."

"You sound as if you despise the skills you teach."

"No. Not a bit of it," he corrected her with unwilling gravity. "But then, I was taught swordplay as a discipline, not a sport."

"A discipline?"

"Yes. The mind translated to physical expression, precision and instinct honed by long years of practice before being married to imagination. I never even held a sword until I had mastered the elemental footwork. It took me a year to do so, and I was an adept student.

"Given my druthers, I would teach it the same way. Hone my students' skills like my masters honed their blades. But I haven't the time. I haven't—" He broke off, essaying a brief, shattering smile before turning his bright gaze away from her, concealing once more the core of him.

"Bedamned!" he drawled. "As improbable as it is, I swear I begin to bore even myself! I commend you, miss, on your apparent ability to perambulate while asleep. Because I cannot for the life of me conceive how you could have remained awake during that self-aggrandizing little sermon."

"On the contrary, I found it fascinating."

"Did you?" he asked, looking amused and cool and invulnerable. "Lud, my dear, you must contrive to get out more often. Shall we continue on?"

He set out to charm her, droll and wry and a little bit wicked in his observations. He led her from amusement to amusement, purchasing ribbons and silk flowers to pin to her sleeves, plying her with the delicious arrack punch and tiny iced cakes, and stopping once beneath a giant beech tree to listen to a string quartet play one of

Handel's sonatas. In short, he did exactly as he had promised. He showed her a new world and made her feel irresistible.

Luckily, she had been admired before. Luckily, she would not read anything into that. Luckily, her head could not be turned by the intensity of his regard. She knew better. She would not become smitten with him. Ramsey Munro was adept at making a lady feel attractive and interesting. Wasn't that a rake's stock-in-trade?

Their path eventually led them toward the crescents of dinner boxes lining either side of The Grove, where a party of masked revelers had begun a riotous country reel. Helena had paused, her foot tapping to the beat of the snare drum, when she felt a slight chill creep up her spine. She looked about, unable to shake the unpleasant feeling that sinister eyes watched her, but she saw no one. She glanced at Ramsey.

"See that lady over there?" he asked, nodding at a buxom American Indian princess twirling arm in arm with a young sailor.

"Yes?"

"She is a famous marchioness as well as a newly made grandmother. Her reputation is impeccable, and her social hauteur alarming by any standards. Yet here she is, enjoying herself immensely all because she knows she can be as anonymous as"—his gaze slipped down and touched her face—"as you."

Helena regarded the breathless woman collapsing, laughing, into the arms of her sailor. "Who is the sailor?"

"A sailor." He grinned at her skeptical look. "Truly. He is a junior lieutenant in His Majesty's Navy. I spoke with him earlier. His ship arrived from Egypt last week."

"But if she is so great a lady, is she wise to risk being here?"

"Wise?" he asked. "Perhaps not. But she may well feel the risk worth the reward. She will go home tonight happy and tomorrow will perhaps be a bit brighter for remembering what it was to be young and carefree. And dance a reel."

She looked up at him and his smile was almost winsome, hiding nothing. "And the young lieutenant," he continued, "will someday tell his children how once upon a time, for a few bright moments, he held a marchioness in his arms and made her laugh. No," he mused softly, "perhaps she is not wise. But some things cannot be gainsaid, no matter how unwise."

His gaze drifted over her masked visage. "Are you always wise?"

She wanted to tell him no, that she was not always wise, that she wanted—oh, very much!—to be *un*wise. But he knew nothing about her other than that she was a lady, and the only inference she could make from his interest was that she presented him a challenge. She shook her head sadly, regretful not that he was amusing himself by attempting to seduce her, but that she was wise enough to realize it.

"Yes, I am always wise."

"I was afraid you were going to say that." He turned away from her for a few seconds, ostensibly to watch the dancers, and when he turned back to her, his charming smile had returned in full force, and nothing clouded the extraordinary blue of his eyes.

"Where next, little tourist?" he asked. "There is a hermit lurking somewhere nearby who will tell you your future for a penny. Or I believe Mrs. Bland is scheduled to sing some of her famed ballads in the Rotunda, and the fireworks are scheduled to begin at ten o'clock."

"Oh, I won't be able to stay that long," she declared.

He frowned. "Why not? It's only another quarter of an hour."

A quarter of an hour?! Dear Lord, how had it grown so late so swiftly? Flora would be beside herself waiting for news of Oswald. She had forgotten Flora. She had forgotten everything.

"I have to go." She wheeled about. He caught her arm. "No."

"I do," she insisted, guilt filling her. "I have to. Someone waits for me—"

His hand tightened. "Who? A man?" he asked. "Another *adventure*?"

"No!"

"You promised me this night. You made a bargain." He was angry. It flared in his eyes and in the set of his mouth, even though his expression remained cool and his tone offhand. "And I accepted your bargain. Because of your insistence that a woman has a sense of honor."

Oh! He didn't fight fair! "I will keep my promise if you insist, but I would not like to do so when it will cause another pain. She will be most anxious for my return."

"*She?*" he repeated. "You expect me to relinquish what I want simply to appease some 'she'?" His lips curled. "Clearly our evening together has not brought you any insight into my character."

But it had.

"Be reasonable, Mr. Munro," she said. "You don't want me."

"Don't I?" he asked with icy politeness.

"You want what you bargained for, and now you feel you are being cheated."

"Is that what I am feeling?"

She ignored that, dared not read anything into it. "Yes. I ask again that you release me from our bargain. Please."

He studied her behind half-closed lids a long moment before finally uttering in a hard, careless voice, "As you will."

"Thank you."

Wordlessly, he escorted her beneath the arched passageway that led to the entrance and exit gates. The cobblestones magnified the sound of his boot heels beneath the vaulted ceiling, the light from the lanterns diffuse. From here she could see Kensington Lane, where the hacks and carriages stood in line awaiting their fares. He stopped. "You will have no trouble finding a conveyance," he said.

The realization washed over her that her adventure was ending. She hesitated, feeling abruptly forlorn. She turned, looking up into his face. "Goodbye, Mr. Munro."

His expression was enigmatic. "Goodbye."

She held out her hand, determined that he would be able to recall her as a well-mannered distraction if not the unassailable femme fatale she'd wanted him to think her. He looked down at her hand with a bemused expression.

She cleared her throat. "You are *supposed* to take my hand and bow."

"Ah!" he said pleasantly. "Thank you for the instruction. One quite forgets what is required of one."

"Balderdash."

He took her hand, snapped his heels together, and

bowed low over her fingertips, brushing his lips across her gloved knuckles. Then he straightened, but neglected to relinquish her hand.

She strove for the right tone: sophisticated, a trifle put out, a bit amused. "Very good, Mr. Munro," she commended him. "Now you are to let go of my hand."

"Yes," he answered, his eyes fast on her face. "Yes, of course. But if I hadn't promised you—"

He broke off.

"Promised me what?" she asked curiously, breathlessly.

"That I would not touch you without your express consent, I would be kissing you right now."

"You would?" she swallowed. She couldn't be that brazen. . . . No, tonight she could be anything she wanted to be. "You could always . . . ask."

He gave her his wicked, wonderful, lopsided smile, a deep dimple scoring his lean cheek. His fingers tightened fractionally around her hand. "Ah, but lass," his burr was there in full force, deep and vibrant, "I have two great failings. The first being that I never ask permission."

Her face fell.

"And the second being that I'm a bloody . . . great . . . liar."

He jerked her against him with a single yank, wrapping his arm about her waist and lifting her until her face was even with his. His hand cupped the back of her head as his mouth covered hers.

It was a hard, punishing kiss, in no way demonstrating his former languid expertise. His heat poured into her, through her. His mouth moved fiercely, possessively on hers, his crushing embrace not giving her any room to struggle.

And she abandoned herself to it. To him.

With a sound of frustration, she pulled her arms free, lashing them about his neck and clinging to him, bewildered by the need he incited, the need she felt roiling through him, setting her afire.

"*Jesu!*" He muttered thickly against her mouth and, still holding her above the ground, moved back into the deeper shadows of the archway, back behind the column of the far arch, back until her shoulders felt the brick wall behind her.

He pinned her there, his hips tight against her, forcing her to comprehend the message sent by the hard, masculine presence pressed against her belly and recognize its answer in the heated sensation pooling between her thighs. Wanton. Wicked. Irresistible. Reason clamored for caution, for restraint, shouting at her to retreat. To struggle.

She didn't. She couldn't.

And Reason, finding no place to take purchase, ceded ground to Instinct, and Instinct flourished. She closed her eyes and answered his fierce kisses with her own. With a will of their own, her hands delved beneath his jacket and smoothed over the warm linen shirt covering him. They flowed up his hard flanks around to his back and up along the shallow channel of his spine to the heavy planes of his shoulders.

He shuddered. He trembled beneath her touch.

A deep growl issued from his throat as he lifted his hands to her face, bracketing her cheeks between his palms, tipping her head back as he dragged a searing kiss up her chin, along her jaw to beneath her ear.

"Kiss me," he whispered thickly. "Kiss me as if you want me. Make me believe it."

As if? As *if*? She *did* want him. Desire ripened within her like a rare orchid patiently waiting for years for just the right dark, heated, moonless night to bloom. He was that dark night.

She speared her fingers through the thick black locks and pulled his head down to meet her mouth. She kissed him eagerly, impatiently, and when his tongue pushed between her lips, she opened her mouth and met it with her own.

She had wanted this forever, from the moment she'd seen him in Lovers Walk. From the moment he'd set her afire with his kiss, she'd hungered for him. She'd lain in her bed at night, and in those fever-kindled moments between dream and wakefulness, this is what her imagination had been filled with. This. *Him*.

She was only dimly aware of him untangling the ties at her throat, of his fingers brushing aside the linen blouse. He stroked the soft swells of her breasts where they pushed above the tight banding. His head dipped and Lord! She gasped at the sweet drag of his mouth, the raw scrape of his incipient beard across her tender virgin flesh. She gasped, aye, but at the same time arched into the tantalizing sensation and—

He froze.

His already hard form tensed even more and his head snapped up and jerked around, like a hound scenting something evil. He eased back, his clasp loosening until her feet touched the ground. She grabbed helplessly at his biceps, praying he would not abandon her now, because her legs would not hold her upright.

"Mr. Munro?"

"We are being watched."

The blood drained from her face. For an instant his gaze touched hers, and the grim set of his mouth disappeared into a savage line. He looked from side to side, from the empty archway leading into the street to the one leading into the gardens. Through either portal she could see people strolling past, heedless of them. But while the shadows might conceal them from a casual passerby, they would not conceal them from a secret spectator.

She did not doubt what he said for an instant. Hadn't she too felt the touch of a malevolent gaze earlier this evening?

She shivered, and Ramsey wrapped her closer against him, shielding her with his body as his gaze searched the area. She glanced down and saw that her breasts were exposed above their bindings, soft and milky in the umber drift of darkness. And with that, reality rushed in, dissolving the heated spell. She stood in the arms of a man who did not know her name, in the shadows of a public pleasure garden, the tops of her breasts reddened by the beard of a stranger, accepting from him the sort of kisses she suspected few wives enjoyed.

Enjoyed.

She closed her eyes at that treacherous turn of phrase. Aye. But it didn't make it any less vulgar. Her body burned at how far she'd been willing to abdicate her pride for pleasure's sake. How much further would she have followed her body's siren call? Thank God she did not need to know.

She pushed against him. "I have to go. I have to."

His head swung back to her, his eyes fixing on her face. They glittered in the half-light. With an oath, he stepped back and reached between them. She shrank against the wall, but he only closed her blouse, retying the stays with ruthless efficiency before taking her elbow and turning her from the archway. Swiftly he escorted her out onto the street.

"You don't need to—"

His look cut off her words. He led her to a cab, motioning for the driver to stay atop his seat.

"I don't expect you'll give me your address to tell the driver," he said.

She shook her head. "No."

"Of course not. You can tell him en route." His expression was closed and impartial. He'd wanted her; he'd lost her. But he was a gentleman. He accepted his loss without rancor. If only she could.

He wrenched open the door and pulled out the block of steps from inside. She ducked inside, and he closed the door behind her. From outside she heard him shout for the driver to head back to the city, and at once the carriage lumbered from the curb.

That was it then. That was all there would be.

She could not help herself. She grasped the edge of the window and pushed her head out, craning her neck to look back. He stood at the curb, exactly where she'd left him. And then the carriage turned and he was lost to her sight.

Unhappily, she sat back on the cracked leather upholstery and only then did she see it lying beneath the window on the other side of the carriage. A single red rose.

NINE

FLORENTINE:
a fencing style where a secondary full blade is used offhand

RAMSEY HEADED BACK INTO THE GARDENS, intent on finding whoever had been spying on them. He still felt the touch of that evil gaze. The idea that it had also touched Helena, creeping over her like filth, filled him with cold fury. So he searched. For half an hour he searched before finally conceding that whoever had been watching them had vanished.

Uneasy and with nothing more keeping him at Vauxhall, he struck out for White Friars.

He could still feel her body, supple and yielding against his, her mouth beneath his. Desire thrummed through him as keenly as if he still held her pinned against the wall. Who would have thought that Ramsey Munro's acclaimed sangfroid would be shattered by a masked slip of a female in boy's clothing, no matter how well she filled them out?

But they had not watched her like he had. They hadn't spent years learning the still language of her composure: the way her pupils dilated with ire, the gentling of her mouth when she was amused, the downward glance that hid the mental ripostes she dared not utter. They had not grown ever more fascinated by the seeming enigma of her while forcing themselves to stand within arm's reach of her at the opening of a new exhibit or in a crowded street fair, knowing she must not turn those clear, cool, blue eyes upon him. Must not know that he watched her, guarded her.

He picked up his pace. His salle was miles away, but the night, as he was all too grievously aware, was young, and his need for physical activity—*any* physical activity—acute. As he moved toward the wharves, the district in which he traveled grew shabbier. At first the changes were subtle, but they became more pronounced as he went. The houses grew smaller, the shops meaner, the public houses more decrepit and numerous, the sounds spilling from them more raucous.

Ramsey paid his surroundings scant heed even though he knew he was being observed, his pace calculated, the worth of his clothing tallied. Evil intent followed Munro the way a cat trailed a fishmonger's cart. He could taste the threat in the atmosphere the way other men tasted the rain on an incoming wind. He'd not survived unscathed for two years in prison through sheer luck.

Yet it took only a stabbing glance from him to quell any unseemly interest emanating from the denizens of the fetid streets. Because just as he could sense potential danger, those who lived in places such as these could tell the difference between prey and predator, and Ramsey Munro was definitely a predator.

Last week's chance encounter with Helena had been a matter of grace or punishment, prize or penalty, depending on one's mood. But tonight?

He had told himself he was going to Vauxhall Garden as a likely place to get information about the identity of the man who had nearly gotten Kit MacNeill killed earlier this year. But the truth was that he'd come hoping to see Helena Nash again and see if he could satisfy himself as to the mystery she presented.

Who was she?

Perhaps she was what she declared herself to be, an adventure-seeking newcomer to the world of pleasure. Until now she had lived a grimly proper life. If she wanted something to relieve the drudgery of her daily life, he was certainly in no position to take exception to that.

Then why the bloody hell had he wanted to? Even as he'd bruised her mouth and fumbled at her breasts like a randy boy with his first maid, why had he wanted to caution her against him and every man like him?

He did not know himself, his motives, his impulses. He'd thought he understood himself with an unsparing clarity. That he might not displeased him greatly. He tensed, sensing another close by, and then relaxed.

"Have you found anything out?" he asked.

"Gar! I never goin' ta get used to you doin' like that," Bill, a raggedy, rubber-faced man complained, slouching out of a darkened doorway to fall into pace at Ram's side. "Ain't natural. How'd ya know'd it were me?"

"You breathe like a bellows."

"Coal dust," he said proudly.

"What news have you for me?"

"I been along the wharves and got me mates doin' like-wise, and no one seen no one wid any rose-shaped scar burned into their hides. Not this six months past. Nor have any of the whores along the docks or even the grander whores toward town.

" 'Course, memories be short when they're drowned in gin, and most of the lads down here get on land and don't stop drinking till they ship out ag'in. But still, a tav-ern owner or some wench would remember a brand like the one you described, let alone some Frenchie. Sailors right hate the Frenchies, they do."

Ram's eyes narrowed as he mentally tallied the efforts he'd made to ascertain who had threatened Kit MacNeill and his bride and left a circlet of dried yellow roses tied about a dead rat's throat six months earlier. It had to be someone from St. Bride's. No one else knew of the yellow roses that grew in the remote abbey, no one else knew their special importance to the men who'd once been or-phans there, or the oath of fidelity they'd made to each other, which that rose had come to symbolize.

There had been four of them, raised to believe in an-cient oaths of fidelity, holiness, and honor: Douglas, their leader, passionate and dedicated; Kit, the ruffian, strong and imposing; Dand, clever and irreverent; and him. When the abbot had requested volunteers to go to France as spies, they had all come forward. They had all gone. They had all been captured. They had all been marked by the experience, and in a most tangible way.

His fingers fell to his right pectoral muscle. Even with

the linen shirt between his fingers and his flesh, he could feel the raised edges of the brand. He could still smell the stench of his own flesh scorching.

Then, after months so dark they seemed now like nightmares, they had been betrayed by one of their own. The betrayer had to be either Dand Ross or Toussaint, the exiled French priest who'd helped devise the original plot. Neither seemed possible, but there could be no other explanation. No one else knew the things that the prison warden had gleefully disclosed.

And, having gotten his information, the warden had set about guillotining them. One by one. Douglas had been first. Dand was to go second. But then, on the eve of his execution, their releases had been secured by an Englishman, Colonel Roderick Nash, their freedom purchased with his life.

Freedom had not, however, freed them. Suspicion haunted them, corroded their brotherhood. Accusations were made, but as there was no proof, no one acted. They were hindered by their ignorance as much as by their one-time brotherhood.

After the survivors had returned to England and made their vow of aid to the colonel's family, Ram had left Kit and Dand behind. Then, about six months ago, Father Tarkin had written to Ram from St. Bride's of Kit's forthcoming marriage.

Ram had stared at that short note a long time. He'd thought of a hundred reasons not to go, a dozen not to care. But in the end, he'd gone. He'd ridden from London to northern Scotland, having decided that he would ask Kit one last time if it had been he who'd betrayed them. He hadn't anticipated Kit would ask him the same question. But he had. Just as Kit had accepted, without question or doubt, Ram's denial, Ram had accepted Kit's. It was enough. It was a benefice in a world rare shy of charity.

After, Kit had told him everything that had transpired during his journey across northern Scotland with Kate Nash Blackburn. Ram had suggested that while Kit was off leading His Majesty's men in battle, he might revisit the painful question of who had betrayed them. Because it never really had been closed. Kit had agreed.

He'd felt the past's cold touch a dozen times these past few months. For himself, he did not care if Dand, with his quick wits and fast fists, or Toussaint, with his swordsman's skills, found him. Let either come. But Kit's bride, Helena's sister, had also been visited by their unknown adversary, making it clear that no one close to them or to the late Colonel Nash was safe from whatever evil that French prison had spawned. Charlotte, cocooned by the Weltons' enormous wealth and status, he deemed safe enough, but Helena, at the mercy of an old tyrant and sent scurrying across London on the veriest of whims, was far more vulnerable.

He would not allow anything to hurt her.

"Ye heard anythin' from yer foreign mates?" Bill's query broke the thread of his dark thoughts.

Over the years, Ram's fame as a swordsman had grown to the point where he'd developed an international correspondence amongst the cadre of men who considered themselves experts. He had used these sources to try and locate their as yet unnamed adversary.

"Not yet," Ram continued. "But if it's Dand he'll be

wearing a rose brand, and if it's Toussaint . . . Well, how hard can it be to find one French priest?"

St. Bride's Abbey,
the Scottish Highlands 1792

"Good!" The new priest, Brother Toussaint, purportedly at one time an officer in the old French regime, said approvingly as Ram countered his feint.

Behind them, Ram could feel the eyes of the spectators: Douglas Stewart, analytical and concentrated; Kit, studying with the fierce determination with which he overcame every obstacle; and Dand, loudly suggesting that a good kick in the groin would end the matter most decisively—and he didn't much care whose groin was kicked.

The only other boy the French exiled priest would agree to teach, John Perton Glass, sat apart from the rest. The years, and the hard work the abbot insisted all the boys do, had pared the fat from John but done nothing else in the way of improving his personality. Surprisingly, he showed some actual talent with a sword.

"Only a Frenchman could teach you the principal parries so well," Toussaint said now.

"When I was a boy," Ramsey answered, panting a little with exertion.

"You are still a boy."

Ram smothered his irritation. At fourteen, he had long since ceased to consider himself a boy. Toussaint knew this just as he knew mentioning it now, while they were engaged in a bout, would distract him.

"Tell me. I insist on knowing. How came you by these skills? A poor orphan such as yourself." This last was delivered with great irony, and Ram felt a stab of irritation. He did not want to be reminded of his past. He didn't need it. He had these brothers.

Ram glanced sideways to see their reaction. They, too, looked decidedly uncomfortable. By unspoken agreement, they had left the years before St. Bride's behind them, like a discarded carapace, empty and meaningless. Except, well, some things were simply self-evident.

Clearly, Kit had led a rough life before his arrival, and Douglas, who had been here the longest, was the most dedicated—always envisioning the noble deeds that they would someday do. Only Dand remained a complete puzzle. At times he seemed to come from a background nearly as elite as Ram's and at others he seemed as wary and rough as Kit.

"Come. Tell me."

"I read a treatise on it."

"Ha!" The Frenchman laughed. "What orphan here has your sangfroid? Your education? You came here, or so the other brothers tell me, already knowing Latin and Greek. What Highland orphan knows Latin at the age of nine?"

"A pious one?" Dand suggested innocently from the sidelines.

Two could play such a game. "What of your talent, Brother Touissant?" Ram asked mildly, the sweat pouring down his face, stinging his eyes. "For one who has eschewed being an instrument of war, you seem oddly well tuned."

Toussaint's smile was pleasant, but his eyes narrowed thoughtfully. "You are very neat at turning aside all sorts of feints, my young swordsman," he said quietly. "Be careful, *though. In pressing an attack, you may ultimately leave your-self vulnerable."*

And with a sudden flourish, he slipped the tip of his blade around Ram's, the impetus jerking the sword from his hand.

"Like so."

TEN

ATTACK IN PREPARATION:
an offensive action taken while one's opponent is still setting up his attack

RAMSEY EMERGED from the alleyway onto a street where an earlier rain had swollen the gutter to overflowing, leaving pools of filthy water. The street was choked with traffic where a dray had tipped over, spilling its contents. A driver stood atop the overturned vehicle, shouting and swinging his whip at the swarms of ragged children who darted in to pluck at the soggy baled contents.

Ram leapt across the reeking channel onto the sidewalk and headed up the avenue. Two blocks further on, he mounted a set of steep marble stairs leading to the front door of his salle. The townhouse, erected a generation earlier by a merchant with too many pretensions to build modestly and too much pride to build in a more fashionable neighborhood, rose three stories high. Soot stained its classic façade, and the pediments were chipped and broken, but it still managed to exude a certain dignity.

Ramsey unlocked the door and his assistant, Gaspard, jumped to his feet from the chair he'd been dozing in and hurried to help rid him of his coat. Ram accepted the ministrations with a distracted word of thanks.

"Is the decanter full, Gaspard?" he asked.

"Yes." The man's single eye—the other being covered with a black patch—narrowed disapprovingly. Ram did not take exception. They had become acquainted in Le-Mons dungeon, where they had both been held. Ram legitimately for his intentions if not his acts, and Gaspard simply because he had taught his former monarch's nephew a few dueling moves one summer long ago.

After he'd been freed, and after he and his one-time brothers had disbanded, Ram had wended his way to London, where he had found his former cellmate in a dingy salle, sharpening swords. Ram had offered him a position. They had been together ever since.

"Any correspondence from Scotland or the Continent?"

"A communiqué from your land agent in Scotland." Two years ago Ramsey had set about discreetly, through secondary agents, acquiring the lands his mother's family had once owned, with an eye to rebuilding the estate forfeited after the Battle of Culloden. It would be years before he could afford all of it. Unless he won the International Dueling Tournament.

"And four young men appeared at the salle early this evening applying for instruction."

"Do you recall their names?"

"One was a Lord Figburt, I believe."

Ah, the boys from Vauxhall. Grand. Now he had four new lads to play nursemaid to, a message from Scotland to answer, notes from paid agents to go through, letters from associates and would-be opponents to answer, and still attend to the preparations necessary—physical, mental and financial—to mount a worthy challenge in the tournament. Plus Helena Nash.

It was going to be a long week.

"Thank you, Gaspard. You needn't bother staying up. I shall see to my own needs."

"Very good, sir. But there is one more thing." His remaining eye shifted away.

"What is it, Gaspard?" Ram asked.

"The marquis of Cottrell is in the drawing room."

A very long week indeed.

Ramsey entered a room banked in night, the only light a beacon from a lamp set on the sideboard. At once, he saw the silver-haired old man standing beside a display of smallswords. He'd taken one out, a bright piece of Toledo steel, and was balancing it delicately across his fingertips. Upon hearing Ram's entrance, he returned the blade to its display case.

"I heard you have put your early training to commercial use," the marquis said without turning, "and am given to understand that this is your salle."

"Poor," Ramsey answered calmly, "but mine own."

The old man picked up another sword. A rapier from Solingen, Germany. "You have collected some fine weapons."

"I have retained the more significant of my childhood lessons. An appreciation of a good blade is one of them."

"Ha!" The old man gave a short bark of laughter and turned. Old age had not yet completely robbed him of his sublime good looks, though advancing years draped the fine features in crepey flesh, and cataracts filmed the cold, implacable eyes. How he must hate that.

He was slower, too, the inner resolve no longer translating quite so quickly into graceful action. His joints were sticky, his hands slightly curled even though they held nothing. And nothing was what Ram felt looking at him.

"Your father was taught by the great Angelo, you know," the marquis said.

Ram pulled a heavy armchair around and collapsed into it, sprawling with studied indolence. "I seem to recall some such thing, yes."

The marquis regarded the younger man closely, trying to gauge what manner of man he dealt with. But Ramsey Munro gave nothing away. He had hoped to surprise a reaction from him by coming to him at night, unannounced and unanticipated, but a stiff spine inhabited that good-looking temple of flesh and blood. Stiff or hard. Harder even than himself? the marquis wondered.

"Your father was the best natural swordsman I have ever seen," he remarked.

"Apparently," Ram returned dryly, "you never saw the man who killed him."

The marquis's lips twitched. "You are being deliberately vulgar."

"Am I?" Ram reached out and swept up the decanter

of claret residing on the table beside him, spilling an inch of liquor into a glass and lifting it to his mouth. "And here I thought I was being remarkably restrained," he said over the rim. "But I am sure you did not come here in so clandestine a manner at so clandestine an hour to comment on my parent's fencing skills or lack thereof. Especially since I have refused to meet you in any venue or under any circumstances these last three years. Yet here you are. Which leads me to wonder, to what do I owe this . . . honor?"

At the calculated pause, the marquis smiled for the first time. "Begad, you are a cool one."

"It's a cold world, sir."

The marquis's smile faded. He stared at Ram, willing him to break the silence. But Ram only took a sip of the claret, replaced the goblet on the table, and stretched out his long legs, crossing them at the ankles. Then, settling his hands negligently on his flat belly, he regarded the marquis with a faintly interested air, as one might a child, with dutiful—and bored—politeness.

It was a tack designed to belittle and enrage, and it worked.

The door swung open, breaking the silence, and the one-eyed butler who'd shown him to the drawing room lumbered in under the weight of a heavy silver platter crowded with such accoutrements as might grace the sideboard of any fashionable young buck. Crystal dishes heaped with foie gras and toast, sugared grapes, and sugarplums crowded the platter, while a Sèvres teapot rose gracefully above the heaped bounty. Apparently the sources that had informed him that Ramsey eked out his living in as frugal a manner as possible had lied.

"Ah, Gaspard," Ram said laconically. "Raided the neighbor's larder, I see? The marquis's consequence will be gratified. That will be all."

So the butler had worried over the impression his master made. Thank God, someone had sense enough to know when appearances mattered and when they did not.

The butler cast his single eye worriedly at him before assaying a quick bow and noiselessly retreating, closing the door behind him.

"Pray, sir, have at it," Ram said. "I would hate to think Gaspard had embarked on a career of crime only to have the fruits of his labor ignored." He waved his hand at the small feast.

"No. Thank you," the marquis replied. "You are very like him in manner," he said. "Your father. Proud. Un-yielding. Resentful."

"Kind of you to tell me," Ram replied calmly. "It's a comfort to know at whose door to lay my character flaws. Not to mention quite inspiring. For we can only improve on baser clay, eh, sir?"

"And caustic," the marquis shot back. "His tongue was caustic, too."

At this, Ram's smooth brow furrowed in distress. "Can we not say 'witty'? Sounds better, don't you think?"

With an effort, the marquis quelled the anger leaking through his cool façade. He took a deep breath and then, thinking better of his earlier refusal, poured himself a glass of claret. He had spent nearly four years coming to this point. At first simple logic had kept him from coming here. He'd been certain that Ramsey would eventually answer his summons. He was, after all, the marquis of Cottrell. Then, later, pride had kept him from coming.

He was, after all, the marquis of Cottrell. And finally, the very thing that had held him away, drove him here. He was, after all, the marquis of Cottrell.

The last of the Cottrells.

Quickly he tossed back the wine. He looked down at Ram, the glossy tumble of black curls, the pale skin and beautiful blue eyes.

"You look like him, too. By God, you do!" he muttered.

"Had the look of a catamite, did he?" Ramsey asked in a bored voice.

The marquis could not stifle his gasp of outrage. "How dare you?"

"But, sir, I only repeat the last words I had from you," Ram replied innocently. "Let me think . . ."

He tilted his head back against the seat cushion and closed his eyes as if trying to recall something.

"Ah, yes. I am sure of it. Pray, sir, think back," he encouraged in bright, biting tones. "My mother and I came to your house in Mayfair. Your servant told us to wait in the back hall. Like tradesmen. I seem to recall a tweenie polishing the brass door plate.

"You finally appeared, and my mother asked, 'What is to become of my son?' She was crying. I recall that *quite* clearly because I had never seen her shed tears before." He paused and looked across at the marquis. "And you answered, 'The brothels in all likelihood—he has the look of a catamite.' "

Ramsey lifted his shoulders in an elegantly apologetic shrug that in no way apologized. "Thus, when you remarked on my similarity to my father, well, I naturally assumed that he too had the look of a—"

"Enough!" The word exploded from the marquis's mouth.

The facile smile died on Ram's lean countenance, leaving behind a fiercely scornful expression. "Yes," he said softly, "Precisely what I am thinking."

"He was my son! I was in pain! I spoke wanting only that someone else would feel such pain as I."

Ram's eyes slit. "Now, *this* is a surprise. I thought you had denied my father. 'My son has been dead for over a decade,' I believe you were reported to have said when informed of his death."

"Do not throw my words back at me!" Palsy shook the marquis's hand, and blood rose in patches beneath his skin, mottling his flesh. "I blamed your mother for his death," he went on without a hint of remorse. "I still do. If he had done his duty and married within his class, he would still be alive."

"My mother was the daughter of an earl. Last time I checked, they outranked marquises," Ram replied, finally stung out of his insouciance.

"Her father had been stripped of his title and his lands. She was a Scot and a papist!" the marquis returned angrily. "She refused to convert regardless of my wishes or how it would affect your father or yourself. She was no better than the regent's bawd, Mrs. Fitzhugh, and as she was not yet twenty when they 'wed,' your parents' union was not even legal!"

"It must have been most vexing when your son refused to deny his marriage to my mother," Ram replied flatly.

With an obvious effort, the marquis brought his fury under control. He would not win the young man by alienating him. All hope of his line continuing, the noble name and title being handed down through future generations, was lost. Unless he could convince Ramsey Munro to accede to his wishes. For that purpose, he could control his ire.

"It doesn't matter what he denied," the marquis said. "The state doesn't recognize his marriage. Or you."

"I shall contrive to live with my disappointment."

"You don't have to."

Ram glanced up from the grape he'd been assiduously peeling. He even smiled. Blast his insouciance.

"Your mother left you nothing," the marquis said flatly.

"The exact same sum the butcher of Culloden, your friend the duke of Cumberland, left her family."

"Cumberland was no friend of mine. Nor do I care about some Scottish family's loss. If they had wanted to keep their lands, they should have supported the crown."

"Forgive me for boring you."

The marquis ignored him. "But most of all, I do not care because it is in the past. The past is dead. Like my son. Like your mother."

"You mean sons, don't you?" Ram asked softly.

A quake ran through the marquis at this sudden stab to his heart, and Ramsey smiled, noting his shiver. It was not a pleasant smile. Damn. Of course he would know. Everything that had been reported to him about Ramsey Munro suggested he would.

"I believe you sired three males after my father," Ram said. "One died in infancy, and another died some years later in an accident at Eton. The last was killed five years ago. All dead without heirs. Without, or so I am told, even siring a few handy bastards."

He would *not* be provoked. "I would declare you my legal heir."

"Would you now?" Ram emitted a snort of amusement and, clamping his hands on the ends of the chair arms, heaved himself to his feet. He glanced at the clock on the mantle above the fireplace. It was old, the marquis noted, and exquisitely made. No other decorations stood beside it. As a boy, Ram had a life lavish with luxuries and indulgences. Did he miss them? How could he not?

His father's wealth had been provided not by the marquis but by a vast entailment coming to him through his maternal line. Wealthy, ostracized, unheeding, and bold, Ram's father had denied his wife and son nothing money could buy: servants and carriages, tutors and instructors, sumptuous furnishings, exotic food, and fine clothing. Ram had lived like a young prince.

For nine short years.

Until his father had died in a duel defending *that woman's* honor.

Then . . . oh yes, then Ram's privileged life had changed. Now the once-entitled boy sat as a cool, dark stranger before him in a nearly empty room in a cheap part of London. Drinking stolen wine. How could he fail to want what the marquis offered? The marquis set his glass of claret on the table.

Ram yawned. "You must forgive me," he said. "I find I am suddenly exceedingly tired. Gaspard will show you out."

"Did you not hear me?" the marquis asked incredulously. "I have offered to have you legally recognized. As I have offered last year and the year before and the year before that. I can make you the next marquis of Cottrell!"

"You cannot do that," Ram said lightly. "You cannot simply make a bastard a marquis. Only the crown has that power."

Ah. So, that was why he failed to be impressed. Ramsey did not yet grasp the extent of the marquis's power. Nor did his grandson know about the plan the marquis had implemented years ago. "And those who have the crown's ear," he said.

"As do you?"

"Yes! *Now* do you understand the great gift that I am offering you?"

"Indeed, I quite understand, sir," Ram answered. "And as I wrote you last year and the year before that and the year before that, I am not interested. I am surprised you could imagine I would be."

The marquis gaped at him. "I do not believe you. You are playing a game. Trying to make me beg. Trying to make me say I am sorry. That I regret my treatment of your father and his—your mother. I won't do it. I won't!" He slammed his fist down on the table and the glass tipped over, spilling claret on the bare floorboards.

Ram looked at the pooling ruby liquid without emotion. "On the contrary, sir. I would expect nothing less from you than what you have already demonstrated."

"You think you are being noble," the marquis said angrily. "But you are being stupid. An obstinate, ridiculous *boy*. You aren't going to make your mother live again by denying me."

"No," Ram agreed politely.

The marquis's mouth flattened, and he swung away to collect himself, thwarted and infuriated. Ram's refusal to meet his provocations was unexpected and therefore unplanned for. Fury and hatred had been emotions he had been prepared to deal with. He had not anticipated an imperturbable young man capable of more disdain than Lucifer.

He tried another tack.

"Accept my offer," the marquis said quietly, forcing himself to the same degree of chill politesse his grandson evinced. "You cannot want to live like this, an outcast, a beggar eating the scraps from your betters' tables, knowing all the while that they are not your betters."

Ram smiled. "They are extremely tasty scraps, sir."

The marquis ignored his flippancy, his gaze fixed on Ram's face, looking for any sign, the slightest fissure in his composure. "How you must hate it, as heir to your mother's pride as well as your father's."

"Hate what?"

"Society's pity at the same time as their patronage. It must taste like ashes in your mouth."

Nothing.

"Do they greet you when they chance upon you in the streets? Do they invite you into their clubs? Yes? But only to give exhibitions of your prowess. Like a circus bear."

Not a flicker.

"Do their wives and daughters speak to you?" Was that a slight tightening about the corners of his mouth? Had his words found a sore place? There was but one way to tell: Press harder. "But what a foolish question! Of course they do. Look at you!

"Yes," the marquis mused thoughtfully. "I am certain they speak to you . . . after dark. Or in the back stairwell of their mansions, while their husbands lay in sodden slumber at their gaming tables." A mistake there. The tension in Ram's smooth countenance disappeared. The marquis hurried to recoup the lost ground.

"No," he said. "No. There would be no husband waiting for *your* lady, would there? You would not tolerate someone else's dregs.

"Who then? A widow? Or perhaps an adventurous young lady? Does she allow you liberties in the hushed seclusion of her carriage or in the leafy bowers of the pleasure gardens? But then . . . does she refuse to acknowledge you the next morning during her ride in the park?"

There! A flash of some deeply rooted emotion in the pacific coldness of that brilliant gaze.

"Indeed," he said softly, "I am quite certain the ladies do more than just *speak* to you."

"I will have Gaspard show you out."

"You have too much pride to be kept, like a secret pet, by some lady. You are no male whore."

"You don't know anything about me," Ram said. But tightly.

"On the contrary. I know a good deal about you. I have had you investigated: your finances, your associates. I know you better than you assume. For instance," he said, "I know you have your father's inability to accept substitutes or compromises. I know you have his charm.

"I doubt any woman could stand proof against him when he wanted something badly enough. I doubt many have managed to stand proof against you. Indeed, your reputation is widespread."

Ram scoffed. "You can't have it both ways. One minute my Cottrell looks doom me to a future as some sort of cicisbeo, the next I am so fatally attractive to members of the opposite sex that I have but to put forth a suggestion, and they race to ruin themselves at my behest."

"I have not made myself clear," the marquis answered in a silky voice. "They do *not* stand proof against you, at least not for a few hours. But I suspect they recover their senses quickly enough once they emerge from your bed. Ladies such as you would wed, bed, and beget your heirs upon, ladies of *quality*, are quite careful about that sort of thing, recalling how much the cost of love is once passion has been spent."

"The sort of ladies *I* would wed?" Ram echoed incredulously. "You know nothing, *nothing* about what I want. I assure you, sir, should I someday be overcome with the need to propagate, there are plenty of virtuous—"

"Virtuous shopkeepers' daughters?" The marquis laughed, shaking his head. He had him. He could see the dull color bronzing the pale, fine skin, the slight flare of his nostrils. The fool was in love. With a lady.

And she would not have him.

"No, Ramsey Munro. You were born to splendor and privilege, like a young caliph, a connoisseur, trained from the cradle to appreciate only the best, the finest, the most exquisite. Look around. You have precious little, and yet what you do own is exemplary.

"How many nameless paupers own a Japanese blade from the seventeenth century? And how many nameless bastards wear gold roses in their cravats? Yet you do."

There. He could see how close to the bone he'd cut. "Think about my offer."

"I don't have to. I don't want anything that belongs to you. I don't want your name, your money, or your title."

"But whoever has you so enthralled, *she* might. If you

take my offer she might actually accept the use of your name for a lifetime, rather than the use of your body for a few hours." The marquis rose with the aid of his ivory walking cane. He moved in a cramped, arthritic manner to where Ram stood.

"Oh, yes," he said. "I can see there is a woman. I read the signs. I've seen them before. With your father.

"And like him, you must have her, and you will never accept her on any terms less honorable than those you impose. But she, whoever she is, won't have you. Not openly. Indeed. You ought to know that by now. Was there not one particular young lady a few years ago?"

"Get out." Ram's hands curled into fists by his side.

The marquis smiled complacently. "What gentlewoman would give up everything—honor, family, society—for *you* as you are now? At least with your father, there was ample inducement to fly in the face of convention and society. Your father was heir to a title and wealthy beyond reason. You are a bastard, and a poor one at that."

"I said get out!"

"Tell me one thing. This young gentlewoman . . . do you think she's even told you her real name? Or is she too discreet—or too embarrassed—to bother telling you any name at all?"

The marquis's glance flickered to the trembling fists at Ram's side. A shiver raced through him at the sight, a sensation long unfamiliar and now unaccustomed. He hesitated. For all his covert study of Ramsey Munro, he did not know how far he could be pushed. He did not know what had been done to him in that French prison or what he had become in there.

Still, he must do what he had come to do. He would not leave without doing everything in his power to secure a legitimate line for his name. "You are so like him, Ramsey. You will kill yourself with wanting. But you needn't," he whispered urgently. "You can have anything you desire."

"I do not desire anything from you. Except your absence from my house."

The marquis opened his mouth to speak but snapped it shut. Let his words work in his absence. He swung around and laboriously lumbered out into the cold, narrow, and poorly lit hall.

"You will," he muttered as he passed the one-eyed butler holding open the door. "You will."

Gaspard closed the door behind the handsome old man.

"Gaspard!"

At once the Frenchman hurried into the drawing room to see what Ram required. His master stood in the precise center of the room, his legs wide, as though he stood on the deck of a sea-battered ship rather than on dry land in London's White Friars. His shoulders were bunched against an unseen gale, and his head was lowered. At Gaspard's entrance he glanced up, his face ravaged and his lips curled back over clenched teeth. Like Lucifer himself upon being told of his eminent expulsion from heaven, Gaspard thought, mindful of the sacrilege but incapable of expelling the thought.

"*Oui?*" he asked, faintly.

"Whiskey, Gaspard," Ram demanded in a husky voice. "Two bottles. No, three. And keep the light out when the blasted dawn breaks."

ELEVEN

～∞∞～

FLANCONADE:
Italian. A thrust to the side of the body exposed just under the elbow

THE EVENING OF THE 12TH, 55 Beard Street, Cheapside. A revel in masque. Three shillings, Harlequin.

"Miss Nash."

Helena, having just found the advertisement Oswald Goodwin had promised to place in the *London Post*, jumped at the unexpected sound of Lady Tilpot's voice. It was half an hour before the guests were scheduled to appear, and Lady Tilpot generally preferred to make an entrance after their arrival.

"Calm yourself, Miss Nash," Lady Tilpot commanded, waddling in. Helena held back a start of surprise. Lady Tilpot had eschewed her normal funerary colors for white lace. A great deal of white lace, which fell from her plump, narrow shoulders in a more or less uninterrupted line to a broad circumference at her feet. She looked like a sugarloaf. "You are becoming deuced agitated of late."

She lifted her beringed hand and waggled her fingers. At once the footman scurried forward to hold her chair as she settled her bulk into it. She waved him away. "You may go await my guests, John."

In Lady Tilpot's household, as in many of the great

households, all footmen went by the ubiquitous name "John" regardless of their given name. The footman withdrew, and Lady Tilpot returned her attention to Helena.

"Pardon me, Lady Tilpot," Helena said, surreptitiously tucking the newspaper between the cushion and the arm of the chair in which she sat. "I was engrossed in reading and, soft-footed as you are, you caught me unawares."

The appeal to Lady Tilpot's vanity worked. Her teeth appeared in what passed as a smile. "I suppose that is understandable. Still, you must try not to be so skittish."

"Yes, ma'am." The charge was not unwarranted. There had been a time—not but a few weeks ago—when she would not have had to try. But now restlessness hounded her waking moments, and passionate encounters with a Celtic prince, a dark overlord, and a warrior angel filled her nights. Knowing she was not likely to see Ram again, she hastened into sleep to find in dreams what she could not seek in her waking hours.

Yet it was not solely Ramsey Munro that accounted for her nerves. Her recent feelings of being followed had grown. Even something as innocuous as a trip to the circulating library had her jumping at shadows and looking over her shoulder.

And then there were the roses. Seven, one for each day since she'd been to Vauxhall. She found them in chance locations and odd places: waiting at the milliner to pick up Lady Tilpot's new hat, or coming back from the greengrocer's, or on the shelf at the circulating library.

At first she had found the roses rather charming, but not anymore. They were not like the perfect specimen she'd been given at Vauxhall two weeks ago. Now they were overripe or desiccated, some had the outer petals ripped off, and today's had been so thick with thorns hidden beneath the rampant leaves that it had drawn blood when she'd picked it up.

"Did you hear me, Miss Nash?" Lady Tilpot demanded.

Startled, Helena looked up. "Ma'am?"

Lady Tilpot scowled. She disliked having Helena's attention focused on anything or anyone other than herself. "Do try to remember in whose employ you are. It is important that my household run perfectly today because *today* the duke of Glastonberry's nephew is coming to call, and he is *only fifth in line for the title. That* is why I have arrived early, to greet the young man."

"Should not Flora be greeting him?" Helena asked.

Lady Tilpot rolled her eyes. "Flora? *Flora?* No. Oh, she will make an appearance eventually, but you are naïve if you think it is Flora that the young man has come to see. It is not. 'Tis Flora's family. 'Tis . . ." She paused, and her double chin hiked an inch higher in the air. "*I.*

"*Family*, Miss Nash, is far more important than the personal attributes of a prospective spouse. What is the prospective bride's breeding? The character of her relatives? These things are far more significant than a chance arrangement of features or"—her eyes fell on Helena's blonde tresses—"an unusual shade of hair color."

"Yes, ma'am," Helena murmured.

"I know what you are thinking." Lady Tilpot leaned forward. "You are thinking of your own family and how they reflect so poorly upon you, and comparing them to Flora's obvious advantages."

A month ago, even a few weeks ago, Helena would have kept her gaze lowered in the face of this wretched piece of nonsense and remained mute. But while she could bite back the retort welling in her throat—she must for Flora's sake—she could not avert her eyes. Not today. Maybe not ever again. She met Lady Tilpot's challenging stare coolly and without wavering. Her regard, so unlike her usual demeanor, clearly confounded her employer. Lady Tilpot frowned, fidgeted, and smoothed the thick cascades of lace across her lap.

"True, you will likely remain a spinster," she finally intoned. "But not to worry, my dear. You have a place with me, and I foresee no reason you should be dismissed from your current situation, all matters remaining the same."

"I am not worried," Helena said flatly. She had spent little time planning her future. For years she had never allowed herself the luxury of looking forward to it with anticipation.

She had thought that she aided Flora out of a sense of duty and obligation, but now she wondered if she had not been looking for an excuse to begin living again, to become the woman she had wanted to be. Someone who would be loved as Mrs. Winebarger was loved, as an equal. Someone capable and vital and . . . unafraid.

"Well, have you nothing to say in the face of such charity?" Lady Tilpot demanded irritably.

"Your words inspire me, ma'am," Helena said.

"Humph." Lady Tilpot sniffed. "Flora is lucky that I know my duty. I will not wed her to anyone but a gentleman of the first degree. But one who also has the fortune and character to match her own!"

Lady Tilpot studied Helena. "But you, Miss Nash,

haven't Flora's wealth, her name, or me to look out for either of them. Far better for you to stay with me, whom you are so similar to in temperament and character."

Had Helena not had the habit of equanimity so firmly ingrained, her mouth would have dropped open.

"Do you think I had not noticed that, despite the great differences in our relative positions in Society, there are certain similarities between you and me? I hope I am not so bigoted I cannot appreciate a likeness when I see it, and I see that you, like me, are sweet-faced, angelically natured, but undemonstrative, avoiding the emotional muddiness that soils the common life.

"Clearly you are as repulsed by the notion of intimacy as I. I applaud you on your youthful wisdom." She paused and looked Helena up and down. "*Relatively* youthful wisdom."

Helena ducked her head to hide her mounting horror. Is *this* how Society thought of her? Remote? Undesirous of human touch or concourse, and happily so?

She stared at her lap, barely heeding Lady Tilpot's continued chatter. Would she be well on her way to becoming the person Lady Tilpot described if Flora's elopement hadn't roused her to action? Or had it been Ramsey Munro who had awakened her?

The thought of Ram brought with it an urgent wave of longing mixed with panic. Would she ever know such sweet excitement with another man? Could anyone else ignite her senses to such a degree?

"Aunt Alfreda?" The door opened, and Flora, dressed in a confection of pale pink muslin and satin bows, and looking like a bonbon at a sweet shop, hesitated in the doorway. An intellectual Flora might not be, but she possessed a sort of feline intuition. Whatever telepathic whiskers the little puss owned were shivering now. Her eyes widened anxiously. "Is everything quite all right? Should I go away and come back later at a more fitting time?"

Lady Tilpot sputtered with exasperation. "Our guests are due to arrive in a few minutes. Just when do you suggest that better time might be, Flora? After they'd *left*?

"Now stop behaving like an idiot, come in and seat yourself. There. Just so. Fluff your hair, child. Flat hair is the bane of your family, I am afraid. Now, tuck your shoes beneath your hem. Pinch her cheeks, Miss Nash. She is entirely too white—"

Both Flora and Helena were spared this last as the footman—a darker John than the one that had earlier attended them—appeared in the doorway and announced the first guests.

"Clearly he is smitten with you," Reverend Tawster said, glancing at DeMarc while assiduously licking the sugar from his fingertips. The vicar had declared himself inordinately fond of sugarplums, and now, filled with the warm feelings induced by excess, had apparently decided to try his hand at matchmaking.

Helena considered DeMarc, standing with spine-breaking exactitude near the door, his chin high, the light gleaming in his thick blond hair as he regarded the rest of the company with ill-concealed condescension. Though she considered him the most likely candidate to have sent her the roses, she couldn't imagine any possible way he could be responsible for their appearance in such odd places in this house. She must have an admirer amongst the staff. As for the rose in the carriage—? An earlier fare must have left it. And Oswald had clearly sent the first. She was becoming imaginative. That is what happened when you went about pretending to be someone you were not.

She quit her study of DeMarc. Twice in the last week they had met, and he had done no more than incline his head. Lord DeMarc, she decided, had finally recalled the great social gulf separating them.

"I think you are mistaken. He is here for Flora."

"I suppose you are correct," the vicar agreed, popping another sugarplum in his mouth. "But aren't all the men here for that same reason? Excluding myself, of course. But then," he sighed, "I am hardly the stuff of a young girl's dreams."

"You are here as Lady Tilpot's spiritual advisor," Helena assured him. "A far more heroic role."

"You are, as ever, diplomatic, Miss Nash." He frowned a little, studying her with great intensity. "But . . ."

"What is it, Mr. Tawster?"

He shook his head. "I fear I was about to be quite forward."

"Pray do not feel that way," she said. "I consider you a friend."

"Do you?" His smooth face reflected his unconcealed delight. "How charming of you!" The delight faded, replaced by concern. "It is just that . . . are those bruises beneath your eyes? Oh, do not misunderstand me. You are, as always, surpassingly lovely. But is something troubling you?"

"Troubling me?" Helena repeated, surprised by the vicar's insight. "No. That is, nothing that you need concern yourself over."

"Oh? Oh!" His expression collapsed into misery. "I *have* been too forward! Pray forgive me!"

"No, no! You haven't. Really."

"Then let me ask you something. You see, I have grown fond of you. In a most brotherly sort of way," he hastened to add. "But I am *not* your brother.

"I worry that you are alone in the world, and that if something *was* troubling you, you would have no one to whom you might turn. I hate to speak ill of my benefactress"—his voice lowered miserably—"but I do not see her in the role of your champion.

"And while I would be pleased and flattered to be your spiritual advisor, as far as achieving any secular results, I am not well equipped." His smile was self-deprecating. "I can hardly fight a duel for you.

"Pray ease my mind on this account if you can. *Is* there someone you could rely on for practical assistance, should it be necessary?" He regarded her worriedly, his light brows knit.

Was there? She hadn't ever asked herself such a question. "I have my sister Kate," she replied slowly. "And my brother-in-law is a most capable man."

"But they are on the Continent, are they not?"

"Yes."

"Is there no one else? An uncle? Cousin? A family friend?"

Ramsey Munro. If she was ever in true distress, she thought, she could go to him. Because he would do everything in his power to aid her—he'd sworn an oath to do just that—and "everything" in Ramsey Munro's power would be a great deal, indeed. The realization washed through her, calming and easing.

She smiled at the vicar. "Pray, do not concern yourself, Vicar, I am not without resources," she said.

The little vicar regarded her dubiously. "I hope so, Miss Nash. It is a terrible thing to be alone in the world. A terrible thing. And if ever you feel in need of a confidante, or advisor, regardless of what appearances suggest, I am very good in that role. I beg you remember that, Miss Nash."

"Thank you, sir. I will," Helena promised.

TWELVE

❦

FLICK:
a cut-like action that lands
with the point

"HERE YOU BE, MISS." The carriage stopped, and Helena clasped the cloak tighter at her throat and adjusted the gold-lacquered papier-mâché mask that concealed her face. Tentatively she emerged from the carriage and paid the driver before looking around a neighborhood unlike any into which she had ever ventured.

On either side of a narrow street filled with people, buildings were jammed seamlessly together, disappearing twenty feet overhead into a brackish Thames fog. Gaslights floated like spirit lamps in the drifting morass above cobbled streets shimmering with oily condensation. Lights flared up from doors standing open at the bottom of short flights of stairs, portals to subterranean worlds below street level.

Taverns, she concluded, from the groups of people going up and down from those brightly lit holes, men in rough jackets and women in multicolored gowns and shawls. She looked about for a street number but could find no indication of the address Oswald had given. To her eye, nothing resembled an assembly hall or even a more modest private club. All the houses looked the same, disreputable and secretive.

Finally she spied a trio of women in fancy dress climbing a short flight of stairs to a nondescript door. Two wore masks like Helena, and the last was bare-faced and nearly bare-bosomed, trailing feathers and raucous laughter. Hurriedly Helena followed them.

"You are certain he is here?" the one in back asked her companions.

"Indeed, yes. I have it from Jonathan that he is obligated to appear. He is being *paid* to perform a demonstration. Deliciously vulgar, isn't it?"

"*I* would pay for a demonstration," the woman with the low décolletage announced.

At the top of the stairs the door suddenly opened on a barrel-chested man with blistered cheeks and a bulbous nose. He eyed them without interest and held out his hand. With an air of long practice, the women gave him some coins and filed in. Helena followed suit.

Inside, a throng of costumed merrymakers waited

while the liveried servants scurried back and forth to take their wraps and coats and cloaks. Excitement filled their voices as they chattered and primped before a giant mirror.

Turning, Helena felt her cloak being swept from her shoulders and at once felt her fellow masqueraders' interest. She regarded her reflection with unease. Though thirty years out of style, the French robe à l'anglaise, a ball gown she had found in the wardrobes in Lady Tilpot's attic, still looked wicked and sumptuous. Yards of deep rose-colored velvet covered the wide skirts, creating a small train in the back. The tightly fitted sleeves tied above the elbows were embellished with deep lengths of Brussels lace. In front, the velvet overrobe cinched in at the tiny waist before flaring open to expose a gold-embroidered stomacher and two tiers of gilt-trimmed flounces.

Slowly Helena's gaze rose to the extremely daring square décolletage. She could not imagine Lady Tilpot ever having worn such a gown. She could scarce believe she was appearing in public in it herself. If it weren't for the anonymity promised by her gold-painted mask, she wouldn't have.

The servant, mute as a mime, motioned the revelers to follow him. They fell in behind him, whispering and giggling like children as he led them down a long, dimly lit corridor that stank of old lamp oil, expensive perfume, and overripe bodies. At the end of the passage, he flung open a door.

Light and noise poured over her, filling her ears and eyes. Horns bleated and violins shrieked above the laughter and gabble of hundreds of voices. Candelabras and chandeliers reflected a thousand candles, throwing back the sheen and shimmer of satin and silk in every conceivable color and vibrancy, gowns and headdresses and gloves and fans and masks, bedizened with feathers and fur, gems and paste, hammered silver and gold wires. Animals and characters from books and mythology, history, and drama, populated the huge ballroom.

Before Helena could get her bearings, she'd been swept into a stream of moving bodies. She craned her neck to stare up at the minstrels' gallery, where more crowds hung over the rails, shrieking and babbling, fans gesticulating madly to move the air over the press of hot bodies, glasses tinkling as champagne poured from the bottles circulated by a troop of footmen.

Overwhelmed, she fought free of the churning mass of people and edged back toward the wall, trying to catch her breath, her heart pounding as she looked for Oswald. There were so many people. So much movement. So much noise and color.

At one end of the room, a dais had been erected, and it was from here that the squawks and shrieks of misused instruments came, their masters being otherwise occupied with the women sitting on their laps. One man, dressed as a satyr, ran amuck through the crowd, tooting on a horn. A butterfly, broken wing askew, pounded at the keys of a pianoforte.

Helena stared, horrified and fascinated. She couldn't believe she was here at this . . . bacchanal! It was completely beyond anything in her experience, a Vauxhall gone mad! She must leave. She must go. She must find Oswald and tell him these assignations were ended.

She looked around for a harlequin, but the lurch and

bump of the crowd kept shifting her further down the length of the ballroom, the press of bodies so close she could scarcely breathe. Then, as swiftly as she'd been sucked into the stream of humanity, she was spit out again into a small, deserted area beneath the minstrels' gallery. Gratefully she sank into a chair standing forlorn and empty against the wall. The noise thrummed against her ears, and her skin felt moist with the breath of hundreds of gyrating bodies.

"More! More! More!" A chant had started in an area in front of her, along with cheers and hoots.

"More? The devil take you all, you would eat a man alive to satisfy your appetites, wouldn't you?"

Helena froze. She would know that voice anywhere. Ramsey.

He laughed, and the sound was both amused and filled with rage. "All right, then. Who next?"

She rose to her feet, but the press was too thick to see through.

"Both of them? At once?" Again, that terrible, discordant laugh. "Well, why not? Why the hell not?"

She tried to push her way through, but no one would step aside. Thwarted, strangely apprehensive, she finally scrambled atop her chair to see what held the others transfixed.

Ramsey stood in the center of a tight circle of spectators, having shed both coat and waistcoat. His white shirt was damp, clinging to his torso, and though he still wore a cravat about his neck, the ever-present gold rose winking from the rumpled folds, it looked like a noose waiting to be tightened. He'd rolled up his shirtsleeves, and his forearms flexed as he swiped a flashing rapier through the air, missing by scant inches the faces and forms of those standing nearest. They hissed and scrambled back out of the blade's path, and he grinned savagely, and though his gaze was fixed on the tip Helena *knew* that he had gauged to a hair's breadth how close that shining tip came to slicing open flesh.

She stared, amazed at the change a single week had wrought in Ramsey. His skin, ever pale, looked bleached in stark contrast to the damp, tumbled black hair clinging to his neck and brow. And he seemed somehow lighter, too, as if the hours had set about paring every bit of softness from him and leaving nothing to pad the flesh separating skin from muscle and bone. Only his eyes held color, a deep blast-furnace blue, as though the devil himself inhabited Ram's tensile form, staring out of those beautiful eyes while burning him up from the inside. And like the very devil he smiled, his handsome mouth provoking and mocking and wretched. Unimaginably wretched. She'd always suspected the devil would wrench pity as well as horror from the human heart.

"Well, come, I haven't all night," Ram gestured to a man in a powdered wig. Muttering and grumbling, the gentleman shrugged out of a blue silk coat, while beside him another man in the black velvet of a Spanish grandee shifted his weight experimentally back and forth on his toes, jabbing at the air with a rapier.

"Hadn't you best don one of those new wire helmets, Munro?" someone called out.

Munro, in the midst of executing a feint that sliced the tip off a plume adorning a lady's turban, snagged the woman's arm and dragged her giggling to his side, and in a stage whisper asked, "Does he consider my opponents' talents so slight that he fears they will forget the rules of engagement and sever me from my mortal coil?"

The woman shook her head, eyes wide.

Ramsey smiled into her face. "I should be so lucky."

"But there are two of them, Munro. And you are . . . you are . . ."

"Foxed? Jug-bitten? Properly shot in the neck?" Ramsey asked, his expression beatific and dangerous and desperate. "So I am. And so saying, 'tis my challengers who ought to be wearing those damned baskets, not I. Because otherwise I might kill one of them, and, well, I can ill afford to kill my clients. However would I pay my tailor?

"So find them a pair of those curst mesh baskets!" he demanded, leaning heavily on his sword's point, his eyelids falling half shut.

He was, Helena realized, not only drunk, but exceedingly drunk. Dear God, he could not really intend to fight?

"Damn you to hell, Munro," sniffed the grandee, swatting away the wire contraption one of the servants offered him. "Can't act the gentleman and leave me the part of craven. *En garde!*"

Having dispensed with any question about helmets, the man lunged forward. With a collective gasp, the encircling crowd fell back, the ladies tittering wildly.

And Ramsey laughed. He laughed even as his sword arm flew out, the buttoned foil driving as unerringly straight and true as Gabriel's burning sword, engaging the grandee's. Ramsey flowed backward and sideways, graceless as Lucifer plummeting to earth on burnt wings, he blocked and parried, lunged and retreated, elegance and precision so ingrained he flew even when he staggered.

Helena's breath closed in her throat as suddenly the fight was joined by the other man, who, having finally dispensed with his coat, attacked. It was incredible. Unfair. Too much. Ram would be hurt.

But Ramsey only backed into a corner, using the surrounding spectators as a shield. The man in shirtsleeves growled in frustration and plunged forward. Ramsey shifted, turning his torso sideways. The man's point flew past him. Grabbing his guard, Ram leaned back, forcing the man into a prolonged lunge as Ram's own rapier's tip pressed firmly into his challenger's shirt, right above his heart.

"One gone," Ramsey said lightly and swept his foot nonchalantly beneath his opponent's heels, sending him crashing to the ground. The crowd howled with delight.

And now the grandee pressed forward again.

"What the hell was that, Munro?" the grandee panted, his face reddening.

"Scottish play," Ramsey answered. By contrast, he did not seem in the least winded. "Crude. But effective."

"Thought . . . you were a disciple of . . . Angelo's?" The grandee pressed a high attack, forcing Ram to lift his sword and expose his side.

"I favor whatever wins," Ram returned. Steel clanged as the man drove suddenly downward. Ram parried and went on, "Sir John Hope presents some interesting conjectures. 'Rules,' he calls them." He might have been discussing a book in the reading room of a gentlemen's club.

"Tell me," panted the grandee.

" 'Whatever you do, let it always be done . . . calmly.' " His arm swept down to counter a sudden feint.

" 'And without Passion.' " He followed through by taking the grandee's blade and sliding his tip along and around it on a hiss of steel.

" 'And Precipitation. But still with Vigor—' " He attacked, his body following the line of his blade in. The grandee gasped and tried to parry, yielding ground— but not enough. The kiss of steel on steel filled the air, " '—and all Briskness imaginable.' "

It was as though Ramsey's blade had teeth, holding the grandee's high and then slinging it low, his riposte quick and clean. And then, so quickly Helena could not see how it had happened, the buttoned point of Ramsey's blade rested at the base of the grandee's throat. The crowd burst into applause.

"Magnificent, isn't he?"

With a start, Helena looked down. Oswald Goodwin stood beside her, his foolscap bells tinkling softly as he lifted up on his curled-toed shoes, trying to see better.

"You're likely never to see better swordsmanship than that, Miss Nash," he exclaimed with fervent hero-worship. "Why look! He's going to go at it again!"

Anxiously Helena watched. Ram wove slightly where he stood, his eyes drifting without purpose or focus over the circle of animated, masked faces. His smile faltered, and he waved his hand impatiently.

"Who next? Come! One amongst you must be an adequate foe!" he exhorted them. When no one answered his challenge, he swung away from them contemptuously. At her side, she heard Oswald murmur, "I have to see better. I *must!*"

She barely noted his leaving. All she could see was Ramsey, encircled by an ever-tightening group of people in masks and costumes, their voices high, their eyes glittering feverishly, their shrill laughter like the howls of a dog pack. All except for one figure.

Across the circle stood a man dressed in the black, stylized mask of some fantastical bird of prey, a short beak jutting above his lips and shadowing the shape of his jaw. Unlike the other spectators, he stood motionless, his attention not on Ramsey Munro but on *her*. She could feel his cold scrutiny.

"What of it?" Ram shouted again, and then, as if he too had caught the scent of something hostile in the currents that moved through the room, he swung about and caught sight of the dark bird of prey. "How about you, sir?" he demanded. "You have the look of a man who's at least held a sword."

The man shivered visibly but then only shook his head slowly in negation. "No?" Ram studied him a second longer, his head cocking to the side. "I know you—"

"I'll have a go!"

The voice of a young man broke over the noise. Ramsey turned as a young rajah strutted into the circle, paste jewels adorning his turban, rings on his hands, pearls at his ears. Ramsey threw up his hands in mock defeat. "Good Lord, Figburt, if your plan is to blind your opponent, you have succeeded beyond your wildest imaginings."

It was the boy from Vauxhall.

"Now, dab the milk from your lip and get you gone from here before I have your mother pounding down my door demanding to know what I have done with her whelp."

The crowd roared with laughter.

"Not I, sir," the boy said staunchly. "Not until I have tested my sword against yours."

"Oh, for God's sake, Figburt. What do you think you need to prove?"

"That you can't disarm me."

"Ah," Ram said. "A bit of revenge?"

"Aye."

"Far be it from me to caution against vengeful endeavors. But wait a second, lad. If we are to be reenacting that memorable night . . ." His unfocused gaze roamed about the ring of faces, falling on a young woman, her garish yellow hair tumbling down her mostly naked bosom. He snagged her wrist, yanked her forth, and dipped her over his forearm.

Helena felt the blood leave her face in a rush.

"For luck."

His mouth descended on the girl's. At once she flung an arm around his neck, pulling his head, while the other hand settled high on Ram's thigh, moving upward. The crowd hooted and whistled, and some clapped.

Helena felt as if she'd been struck. As if *he* had struck her. She reached out, seeking a bolster that wasn't there. The girl's touch moved even higher, seeking a more intimate purchase. Helena squeezed her eyes shut, faint and mortified, and opened them to look straight into Ramsey Munro's eyes, stark and damned and riveted upon her. The girl still writhed suggestively against him, his body still stood bowed over hers, but his eyes belonged to Helena.

She didn't want him.

He'd already belonged to too many.

She stumbled off the chair and pushed her way back through the throng, reeling along the perimeter. In front of her, a door stood ajar. Without thought she dashed through it and into a back alley erratically lit by smoking lanterns and adrift in mist. A light rain had begun, soaking the shadows and making the cobblestones slick beneath her feet. A couple locked tightly together blocked the passage leading to the main thoroughfare, sounds of animal urgency coming from them.

My God. Helena wheeled in the opposite direction, hurrying past stacks of crates and boarded doorways, piles of refuse and heaps of broken bottles. Above her, the blind, dark eyes of windows stared down with inimical indifference. A rat squeaked, and she doubled her pace as the thick, warm drizzle grew heavier.

Her hair fell from its elaborate coiffure, and the flour whitening it ran in rivulets down her bare shoulders into a river between her breasts. The velvet skirts grew sodden. She paid none of it any heed. A litany of self-castigation had begun in her mind.

Fool! Fool, to flirt with this life, *his* life. *Fool*, to think one could come near a burning angel and not be singed. *Fool*, to wish she had been the one in his arms . . .

The passage turned, and she found herself in a small yard occupied by a broken handcart, the only other egress a narrow black slit in the corner. She stopped as a sudden feeling of danger fell over her.

She was not alone. Someone else was with her. Someone who meant her ill.

She backed up, blinking in the fine rain as she looked for the source of the menace, but the alley from which she'd come was hidden in rain and fog. Was the danger lurking behind her or waiting in that black slit ahead? She strained, listening, but all she could hear was the sibilant hiss of rain.

"I can save you."

She froze. The plaintive whisper reverberated in the tiny yard, making it impossible to tell from where it had come. She bent down and yanked free one of the cart's broken wheel spokes, lifting it high and brandishing it like a cudgel. "Go away."

"What do you think you are doing?" the voice whispered angrily. "Look at you. Your hair like a whore's, your bosom exposed. Disgusting! You shouldn't be here."

"No," she agreed, her voice quavering, "I shouldn't. It was a mistake. I'll go now."

"Are you patronizing me?" The voice was cold. *But was it closer?* She turned slowly, inching toward the wall, the spoke high in her hand.

"No."

"You best not. You best remember who you belong to."

Who she *belonged* to? She trembled, confused and terrified. *"Who are you?"*

"Do you *dare* play games with me?" A dark figure suddenly materialized out of the gloom, coming rapidly toward her, anger vibrating from him. It was the bird of prey. "Think, my dear. Who else? You know. And if you don't, I'll teach you!" He swooped toward her, the back of his hand raised to deliver a blow.

She stumbled backward over the cart and fell, catching herself at the last minute against the wall, her shoulders banging painfully against the damp brick. She jabbed out with the wheel spoke. At the sight, the man stopped and laughed.

"Pitiful," he snickered, leaning toward her. "Unfortunately, my dear, you are no Ramsey Munro."

"No," said a voice. "But I am."

THIRTEEN

〈∞〉

CORPS-A-CORPS:
French. Literally "body-to-body";
physical contact between two fencers during a bout,
illegal if performed intentionally

THE MAN KNOCKED AWAY the spoke Helena held and grabbed her arm, yanking her to her feet and shoving her at Ram. Ram caught her as the birdman fled, escaping into the black maw in the corner. Ram's arms wrapped tightly around her, holding her fiercely.

"Are you all right?"

She nodded. He started to set her aside, to go after the man. She clung to him. "Please. Don't leave me. He's gone."

A muscle leapt in his lean jaw, but he did not let her go.

"What are you doing back here? In case, you hadn't noted, this is hardly Lovers Walk."

She froze at the implication of his words, an implication she had intuited when their eyes had locked across the ballroom: He'd recognized her as the brazen young woman in breeches whom he'd kissed at Vauxhall. She stiffened.

"Don't worry," he said, his lips curling slightly. "Your precious anonymity is safe, *Corie*. I am no closer to knowing who you are now than I was at Vauxhall. But I am not deaf, darlin'. Your married beau shouted for you to don a pink dress for your next tryst. And thus when I saw a woman in a pink gown standing beside the same fool I'd seen at Vauxhall, I inferred your identity. But not your name. Your *real* name."

There was only one reason Ram could imagine why she was so eager to remain nameless: Because whatever she had done or wished to do was best done in secret, under the cover of masks and darkness. Things she would be ashamed to admit to or lovers she did not want to acknowledge. And even more bitter than the knowledge that what she wanted she wanted for only short, intense, and stolen moments, was the knowledge that she didn't want it from him. She wanted it from this *harlequin*.

He fought the jealousy surging white hot within him. He had no right to judge her. No right and no reason. For a week he had been haunted by the marquis's suggestion, sought to wash away with innumerable bottles of wine the images his grandsire had painted in his mind of a woman seeking a covert lover, someone a little disreputable, a little dangerous, someone she would never acknowledge in the light of day. He'd been here before. But that that woman was Helena Nash!

Abruptly, Ram released her, turning partially away. The rain fell in earnest now, and his soaked shirt molded transparently to the corded and cut musculature of his chest, adhering to his ribs and the tight corrugation of his belly.

He was magnificent. A selkie. A watery demon. Dark hair covered his chest and whorled around flat nipples. A raised imprint of what looked like a stylized rose was stamped into the flesh of his right pectoral. It was strangely, perversely sensual.

"Where *is* your harlequin?" he asked roughly. "Surely it is his part to be saving you from unwanted advances? Or," he looked down at her, his expression coldly interested, "*were* they unwanted? Am I *de trop*? If so, I do most sincerely beg your pardon."

Crystalline blue eyes stared at him through the cutout eyes of her mask. He could see the minute his words took hold, the minute she realized how gravely he'd offended her. Now she would slap his face and leave. And he would be free to go.

But she didn't slap his face. Her chin rose, her eyes catching the tiny bit of light left in the dark yard. "You are not suggesting that I *wanted* that man to accost me?"

He shrugged with elaborate indifference. "Why not? It would be a prime adventure."

"I came this way by chance. I had no idea anyone was following me."

"I see. You thought to leave the party alone, and here you had not one but two men following you, the crow and mine own poor self. You are exceedingly popular."

"Why were *you* following me?"

Because I saw your body stiffen as you watched that poor trollop try and incite a bit of interest from me. Because I saw how it offended you, and thus it offended me. So I followed you before I understood I was doing so. Because that is what I do where you are concerned now. All my caution and discretion have been burnt to ashes by desire, and scattered to the winds, leaving only impulse and reaction. The very things a swordsman disdains if he wants to live.

"Because the way by which you left led to a place I knew was unsafe for a woman alone." It was some of the truth.

"Then, once more, I owe you my thanks and ask that you guide me to where I might hire a hack."

"I don't want your gratitude, at least not for such slim service."

Her head snapped up at that, and he smiled at her, idly tipping his shoulder against the wall and blocking her exit. He was a cad, an unspeakable roué. He didn't care. He allowed his gaze to drift over her suggestively. Let her think he was drunk and dangerous. Hell, he *was* drunk, had been drunk, more or less, since the marquis's visit. Because, damn the old man, he'd awakened demons Ram would rather have left sleeping.

And as for being dangerous . . . He didn't have to pretend there, either. Because she'd fled without her cloak and, drenched in the tepid London rain, her skin shimmered with pearl-like incandescence, her hair coiling in dark, wet strands down snowy white shoulders and over the pale bosom exposed by the low neckline.

She looked like something carved from milk ice, something that could not possibly withstand the heated furnace of a man's passion. If only he knew that wasn't true. If only he didn't know that her warm ruby lips were a far more telling barometer of her ardor than the cool, ice-blue eyes, the pale hair, the long white limbs. But he did.

He reached out and ran his fingertip along the damp edge of her gilt-painted mask. He had no pride. He had nothing left but desire: to hold her, to kiss her, to make love to her. He wouldn't think anymore. Not about why she was here, why he was here, what tomorrow would bring and what yesterday had left behind.

"That's twice now your fool has left you to your own devices," he said. "Or, rather, that you have fled from him. Can it be that you are still so untried that you think the chase is the best part of the game?"

She didn't reply. She just stood under his light, feathering caress, the rain beading on her shoulders and trickling down her bosom. He curled his finger low against her bared breast, catching one swollen drop just before it disappeared into the dark crevasse between her breasts. She shivered as he lifted his fingertip to his lips and sipped the drop off.

"It doesn't even compare," he whispered enticingly. "True, there are some poor sots who never reach the blissful, fiery end. They seek, they pursue, they struggle and strive. Their hearts race, their lungs labor."

His gaze traveled down her flushed body. "But they do not find the satisfaction such sweet labor strives to achieve. In the end, they are left frustrated, impelled by a goal that exists beyond their reach, but not, alas, beyond their ability to imagine. Come, lass. Your harlequin is but a boy. Such an experience as you want requires a man."

Her masked face rose. "A man with vast experience in achieving that fiery finish?"

He disliked the note hidden in the breathless query. He had no answer for it. Sexual concourse he'd had too many times, and too many times the moments after the little death had been empty.

He ignored the hollow memories, intent on only one thing—Helena. "That is what you are here for, is it not?"

He heard her breath catch and hold. Could see her fascination and her fear. Not a sound disturbed the moment. The fog rolled about them like a warm blanket, obscuring everything it touched, softening hard edges and obliterating ugly lines.

"Let me guide you, my wee tourist," he coaxed softly. "Let *me* be your adventure." His mouth hovered inches above the sweet, curved juncture of her neck and shoulder. She smelled of dried lavender and wet powder and rain. "Tell me yes. Give me leave."

She trembled under his light, buffeting breath. His lips brushed her shoulder. Only then did her breath escape, rushing out in a sigh of dismay and acceptance and . . . excitement. She could not deny the excitement.

"Why me?" she whispered. "There are other women far better—"

"There *is* no other woman," he murmured against the creamy column of her neck. "There is no one but you."

She wanted desperately to believe him. His voice was so grave, low and unsteady. But the image of that blowsy beauty with her hand between Ram's legs flashed across her mind's eye, like acid spilled on a painting, destroying his assertion, destroying her ability to believe him.

She pushed him away. "I can't—"

He clasped her shoulders and spun her around, pulling her back hard against his chest, facing her forward, away from him. His mouth fell on her neck, and, as if echoing the abrupt shift in mood, the misting rain grew heavier, harder.

She should struggle. Free herself. But an answering hunger roused within her like a starving animal intent on feeding. She reached up and back over her shoulders, her fingers raking through his thick, wet curls and her head falling against his broad shoulder. Behind the beautiful mask, her eyes drifted shut.

He dragged his mouth up her neck, beneath her jaw, the soft skin beneath the lobe of her ear and then down, to her delicate collarbone. He trailed the tip of his tongue against the elegant bone, taking more of her weight as her knees weakened under the sensual onslaught.

She tried to turn in his embrace, but his forearm lashed around her waist, holding her in place, locked against him.

"Don't struggle," he muttered thickly. "Just feel." She did.

He could sense the tension seeping out of her, the incremental surrender to pleasure. To him. The rain drove down in spears now, stinging and warm, as drenching as the desire that flooded his thoughts, his plans, his conscience, and his reason, drowning them all.

He spread one hand wide against the hard panel of her stomacher, and finding a stiff board where tender flesh should be, he yanked open the lacings and pulled the busk out, dropping it to the ground. Beneath it, she wore only a fine batiste chemise, the shadowy inference of the nipples beneath.

He pulled her tighter, fanning his hand across her upper chest and brushing down. A little sound of pleasure purred from her throat, and his hand dipped beneath the sheer material, cupping one firm, plump breast.

She would stop him now. Surely now she would end this.

He dipped deeper, lifting her breast free of the loosened material. She did not resist. Her arms linked back around his neck, her throat arching, tendering its delicate length to his use. He used it well. He kissed her, nipping her skin, feeling her pulse jumping against his lips, his tongue. Against the very center of his palm, her nipple beaded into a taut little pearl.

God help him, never had he been so quickly, so wholly, aroused. Desperately he sought to tame the desire, to throw up barricades, to appeal to absent conscience and reason. He failed.

He needed. He would have.

He spun her around, bowing her back over his forearm, her exposed bosom pale and wet and irresistible. With a shiver, he gently squeezed the soft breast, lifting the enticing nub to his mouth and taking it deep inside. Beneath the thin veil of rain, her skin flushed, plush and warm, like honey and flowers and whiskey—potent, mind-wrecking whiskey. He suckled, and her breath jumped and started in her lungs, little gasps, sighs, and moans from behind the mask. And as he suckled, gilt paint washed off the mask, running in sparkling rivulets down her throat and shoulders, down her breasts, staining the rose-colored velvet and gossamer lace wedded to her skin.

He fed on her pleasure, feasted on her arousal, licking

and sucking and tasting her, and still he needed more. He swung her up, carrying her to the wall, setting her on her feet, and bracing his arms on either side of her head, shielding her from the driving rain.

"Kiss me. Take off your mask and let me have your lips, your mouth, your tongue."

Her head snapped up, and he cursed at the sight of the pretty disguise, its presence a cold knife gutting him.

Does she wear a mask? What name has she given you? Or has she even given you a name? A week of steady drinking hadn't obliterated the marquis's words.

"Take it off. Take off that curst mask!" Longing and pain filled his voice, ripping away his habitual insouciance and hauteur. With a growl, he raised his hand to snatch the thing from her countenance, but her hand intercepted his, catching his wrist with a strength born of desperation.

"No! No," she panted. "Please!"

"Why?" he demanded. "Does anonymity spice the sin so well? Or are you so important a personage that, if revealed, your identity could topple the great thrones of Europe?" he sneered.

"Who are you, then, madame, a princess? A grand duchess? A great heiress?" he asked, daring her to lie, to reveal herself as the adventuress she had already declared herself to be and that he, fool that he was, would not believe. Well, he would believe now. He would *make* himself believe.

His scorn lashed at her and yet, even with her bodice undone and her breasts bare, even in the rain, dripping cheap gold paint and half-clad in sodden velvet, she'd only bow her head, and the nape of her neck filled him with inexplicable tenderness and a sickening compulsion to beg her forgiveness.

"Well?" he shouted, hating that she'd stripped him of the one thing he'd always owned: his much-vaunted, hard-won self-possession.

"No," she whispered gravely. "You have it wrong. I am no one."

No one. No words could have more completely destroyed him.

"You're no one, boy," the tired old woman at the workhouse had said. *"The bastard of a Scottish bit. Penny a dozen these days. Ha'penny. Do no good to put on airs here, boy. You're* no one. *Best remember that."*

He tried to hold on to his rage, but each tremulous breath she drew eroded it. "Why must you wear a mask?"

"Because . . ." She hesitated, pulling the chemise up to cover her bosom. "I could not stand for you to be disappointed."

"Disappointed?" Surely she was mocking him now. There were few women in London who could challenge her beauty. Yet she sounded sincere. He would stake his life she spoke the truth, but how could she fail to know what all London celebrated?

And then another explanation offered itself. She did not know he knew her name. In her mind, if she took off her mask, she would reveal herself as the daughter of the man who had saved his life. A man who had been a respected, honored military hero. Of course she would not want him to know that Captain Roderick Nash's daughter was slumming in White Friars.

So perhaps, she meant to tell him the truth, after all, truth wrapped up in a lie. Perhaps she feared he *would* be disappointed, but not for the reasons he would expect. Better that he thought she hid some physical deformity or imperfection than that she dishonored her father's memory.

He turned his hand, breaking her hold, and lowered it to his sides. "How then am I to kiss your mouth?"

Helena hesitated, her gaze scouring his face, looking for the trap, a falsehood, some sign that he was not to be trusted. She could not find any. He stood in the rain like a statue, his soaked shirt welded to his broad chest, the long arms beneath cabled with muscle. His chest rose and fell as though he was winded, but his eyes were calm.

Go! she told herself, *flee while he is in this amenable mood*. But . . . his voice was so raw.

"Close your eyes," she said softly.

His shoulders dropped. "You needn't worry. I won't stop you from going this time."

"You told me once that I should beware of two things regarding you, and one of them was that you were a great liar."

His brows dipped low. "I will not lie this time."

"Then if you will let me go, it is no great thing to you whether I leave while your eyes are open or closed, is it?" she asked, amazed by this fearless, foolish Helena Nash who'd supplanted the reasonable, cautious woman she knew. "Close your eyes."

He shut his eyes, and she laid her hand over them and she stretched up on her tiptoes, steadying herself with a hand against his broad chest. His heart beat thickly against her palm.

She brought her lips near to his ear. "If you will give

me a promise that you will keep, then give me this one. *Do not open your eyes.*"

She pulled her mask off, letting it drop and hang from its laces around her throat. Then she kissed him, gently melding her lips to his.

For one breathless moment, he accepted her kiss. Emboldened by his seeming tractability, she combed her free hand through the silky wet tumble of demon black hair, pulling his mouth more firmly against hers. She arched against him, kissed him with all the passion she'd kept so long buried. She kissed him as if she could not stop, as if she meant to drown in his embrace.

No woman had ever kissed him like this before. He had no words to describe such exquisite, such honest and unreserved desire. He tipped her head back, her hand still covering his eyes, and found her mouth already open, waiting for his tongue, dependent on him to show her what to do, how to find pleasure's apex.

It undid him.

Such carnal innocence. Such blistering virtue. He pressed her against the wall, pushing his thigh between hers, reaching down and pulling up the layers of rich cloth until he felt the satiny warmth of tender flesh.

A sound hummed deep in her throat. She wanted. He wanted. Nothing stopped them. His hands slid up the backs of long, slender legs and found the soft swell of her buttocks. Lust surged through him like a spear, bringing him to the point of pain. He filled his hands with soft female flesh and lifted her, pushing against the layers of damp velvet and taffeta and lace. He forced himself to hold there, like that, her hand blindfolding his upper face, their mouths locked in passionate combat, his cock pressed against the juncture of her thighs. So she could understand what would happen next. What was inevitable.

She made a sound between a purr and a moan. Her hand dropped from his eyes and her arms locked around his neck, her face against his shoulders. Her breath rushed against his ear, panting with desire. And she moved, she rocked against his erection.

He let her. He let her use his body, find the hardness that eased the painful pulse of arousal, all the while trying desperately to quell his own demon, the demon that wanted to take her here. His body ached. Desire raked him. He tipped his head back, his jaw tightened with the restraint he practiced as her hips rubbed against him, her movements erratic and unpracticed. And he knew, virgin or not, she'd little or no experience with what went next.

A virgin? Yes. Or near enough made no difference. Clumsy enough in her desperate pursuit of the ancient rhythms that if she was not a virgin he cursed the man who'd initiated her into womanhood. And with that came a sly, mocking whisper that trickled through his heated mind: He was no better. Because there was only so much of this he could stand before he spilled his seed or tossed up her skirts and entered her.

In the rain. Against a wall. In a bleak back alley.

No. No, no, no. He would not think that. He would block out everything but the feel of her rocking with awkward, soul-shattering little jerks against him. He would hear nothing but her breathless gasps and sighs, rising from where she'd buried her face against his throat. He would give himself to her use, and then he would have her.

Why not? Why not give them both what they so desperately wanted?

Somewhere down the alley, a window shrieked open and a voice called out, "Me bed is empty, gents. Anyone fancy a bit of sport? Three bob fer anythin' you wants!"

He had his answer.

With a savage sound of self-denial, Ram pulled away from her. She made a soft sound of dismay, her arms tightening imploringly around his neck. He could only stand so much.

"No," he rasped, his chest heaving with the effort he exerted. "No. Not here. Not like this. Put your mask back on!"

"But . . ."

"Put on your mask if you would not be seen!" he ground out, lowering her to her feet and averting his face as he felt her trembling hands find the dangling mask and raise it to her face. He looked down at the mask; her eyes caught a tiny bit of light behind the peepholes, and they were wide and awash in tears.

His anger battled with pity and yearning. "If you want a lover, God knows, ma'am, I'm your man. You know my name. You know where to find me. You have only to come to me. Any time, day or night. In any guise and in any fashion. I'll beg if you like. But I won't do this here. Not like this."

She wouldn't come to him. He knew it even as he forced the words from his lips. Given time, given distance, she would come to her senses.

His harsh words penetrated her haze. He wanted her, she was certain. No degree of inexperience could blind her to that. He'd wanted her as much as she had wanted him.

She supposed she should be grateful, but she wasn't: She was resentful, edgy, insulted in spite of the fact that she knew he acted in her best interest. "Why?"

"Why?" he asked and turned his head back round to look down into her masked face. "Because what I want from you cannot be given in a back alley tryst. Because if we stay here any longer I will take you against that wall, and there will be nothing about it worthy of either of us. I want more. What do you want?"

Your arms around me. Your lips covering mine. Your body pressed hard and impatient against mine. She stared mutely up at him until, with a curse, he grabbed her by the wrist and pulled her into the center of the little yard. The rain had eased, in the way of London rains, and the ground shimmered with rainbow-filled pools.

"One of us is going to be honorable. One of us is going to be a fool. I fear, my dear, I am destined for both roles. Now, let us go before I forget my intentions and only seek to fulfill yours."

FOURTEEN

FROISSEMENT:
an attack that displaces the opponent's blade
by a strong grazing action

HELENA SAT IN THE CARRIAGE, staring unseeing at the street outside. Her mask, now washed clean of most of its gilt paint, lay unnoticed in her lap. She felt amazingly calm, except for the shivering. Ram had handed her into the carriage without saying a word. Nor had he lifted his hand in farewell.

She didn't know herself. Despite her heated responses, she did not think herself wanton. Not until Ram Munro. And that, she suspected, was a problem.

Because even now, looking down at her damp gown, trickles of gold drying on her shoulders and bosom, even knowing she looked every bit a disreputable doxy and, even more, had acted like one, she did not regret this night. Except that the promises that had begun with Ram's kisses and been compounded against a brick wall had not been kept.

Abruptly, despair washed over her. Where was he? Was that trollop who'd so brazenly handled him touching him now? Was she lying with him, beneath him?

As her sister Kate's closest friend, Helena had been the recipient of all of her confidences. There was little about the intimate relations between man and woman that she did not know. Even if until this night most of it had been only an academic understanding.

She knew she had left Ram in a state of acute physical distress, a state in which men were most likely to do whatever was necessary to ease themselves. And should that tart make herself available to him, well, there was no reason to suppose that he would not avail himself of her offer—despite his rough declaration that there was no other woman but Helena.

She wanted to believe him, and she'd half convinced herself that he'd meant it. He had sounded so genuine, so angry. As though he didn't want her to be the only woman, but could not deny it. But, her stubbornly pragmatic mind insisted, if *that* was true, than that meant he had become infatuated with a costume, a mask, a role she had played only a handful of times. How could he declare her "the only woman" when he did not *know* her? When he had never even seen her face?

Ram Munro did not strike her as the sort of man to be beguiled by a chimera. Yet she hated the only alternative, that he was a hard-hearted seducer of women, saying whatever was necessary to have what he wanted.

She rubbed her temples, trying to think clearly. Either way, she should stay away from Ram Munro. She must not even entertain the possibility of accepting his outrageous offer to become his paramour. It would destroy her.

But to go to him as his lover. . . . To feast on the sensations he alone called forth. *Would* he beg for her favors if she asked? Of would she end up begging for his?

"Ma'am? We be at the address you give me." With a start, Helena realized that the carriage was standing motionless beside the curb. From the tone of the driver's voice, it had stopped some time ago.

"Oh. Of course." She opened the door to find the driver waiting outside. Quickly she descended and reached into her pocket for his fare, but he held up his hand.

"Gent already paid me, mum. Plenty well, too. Said I was to see you safe to whatever door you wanted. So which one is it?"

"That won't be necessary," Helena said. "I'll be fine."

The driver regarded her dubiously but climbed back aboard his rig. Then, doffing his hat, he clucked at his horse and drove off. She looked around. She stood at the head of the familiar tree-covered carriage lane that separated the back gardens of the great houses in Hanover Square, where Lady Tilpot lived, from the less elaborate but still exceedingly desirable ones on Adam's Row.

She had only to go a hundred yards along the lane before slipping through the gate leading into the Tilpot House kitchen garden and from there into the home itself. By prior arrangement, Cook, the only one of Lady Tilpot's staff whose position was sacrosanct, had left the door unlocked. But looking down the long, silent alley, she remembered what she had forgotten all evening: the man in the bird mask, his hand raised to strike her, his voice throbbing, "I'll teach you!"

But that was miles away. She was safe here.

She started down the leafy corridor, following the muddy track. It was early yet, and many of the carriages were still out conveying their owners to halls and private dinners, musicals and lectures. Resolutely she started forward.

She had gone halfway when she heard the distinct sound of footsteps behind her. She peered over her shoulder, but the light spilling from a vacant stable door concealed whoever stood in the darkness on the other side. She turned back, moving quicker now. The footsteps behind matched her pace. She grabbed up her heavy, wide skirts and ran.

He caught her before she had gone a dozen yards.

His hand clamped down on her forearm, and he snatched her and threw her to the ground, as easily as a falcon dispatches a dove in flight. The taffeta petticoats cushioned the impact of her fall but could not stop the air from being driven from her lungs or her hair from tumbling free of its pins. She whipped around to face her attacker, shoving the heavy, wet tresses from her face.

Forrester DeMarc stood over her, his body rigid, his lips thinned to a bloodless line. "Why did you make me do that?"

She stared up at him, as amazed by his question as she was frightened by it. His gaze fell on her bosom, and with a hot flood of embarrassment she lifted her skirts and covered herself from his gaze.

"Who saw you like that?" he demanded, pacing in front of her. "I'll kill them. I'll cut their eyes out. No one sees you like that but me."

"*You?*" The paralysis freezing her voice cracked. "What do you mean? I don't belong to you."

"Bedamned, you do! You pursued me. Now you're mine."

"What?" He was mad. He stopped in front of her, staring down at her with venom-filled eyes, and she scooted backward. "It was you," she whispered. "In the alley. And you sending the roses."

"Don't play games with me, Helena."

"I'm not."

"That's all you've been doing lately. Playing games. You flirted with me, fawned on me, set snares to inveigle me. You did everything in your power to make me notice you. Do not try to tell me otherwise."

"But I did not! I treated you with no more consideration than any of Lady Tilpot's guests."

Before she could duck out of his reach, he grabbed her arm, hauling her to her feet with frightening strength. She tried to squirm away, but his grip tightened painfully.

"You are lying," he said between clenched teeth. "Why are you lying? Are you trying to make me jealous?"

"No!" she denied.

He shook her like a terrier does a rat, his fingers digging deep into her skin. "Do not lie to me!"

"I'm not! I don't know what you are talking about. I haven't set any snares for you. I do not want your attentions. You are mistaken. Please, my lord! You are hurting me!"

"Do not want my attentions? Didn't set snares? Ha!" His laughter held a note of hysteria. "Your machinations are obvious to everyone, my dear. Not two days ago, someone remarked on how obvious you were."

"Who would have said such a thing? It is absurd."

"I don't know what game you are playing, Helena. But I will not have it. You are mine, and you will learn to remember that."

She stared at him in horror. He truly believed it, she realized. He really was mad.

"Let me go, my lord. I will be better," she whispered, trying desperately to sound contrite. "Please. Lady Tilpot is due back at any moment, and she might go to my room and discover I am gone. And then," she said carefully, "I would have to tell her what happened."

He tilted his head. "Are you threatening me?"

"No," she denied hastily. "But I should hate to have to explain the bruises on my arm."

His expression reflected only mild contempt. "Tell anyone you like that I made them." He leaned closer. "I'll deny it. Do you really think anyone will believe you? Me, a viscount, or you . . . a *nothing?*"

He was right. Without a witness, it was his word against hers. "Please. Leave me alone."

"Leave you alone? Oh, no. That is the one thing I will not do, my dear. I will most assuredly not *leave you alone*. Whenever you walk out Lady Tilpot's door, I shall be watching you. Wherever you go, whatever you do, my eyes will be upon you. Whoever you talk to, I will know about it. And"—his teeth clicked together—"until I decide what to do about you, you are to be on your best behavior."

She swallowed, hypnotized by the arrogance and cruelty in his voice. He might have been disciplining a dog.

"Do you understand?"

She nodded, but it was not enough; his fingers squeezed until she winced. "You have a voice. Use it. Do you understand?"

"Yes!" she squeaked. "Yes. I understand."

"Good." Abruptly, as if he had just realized the thing

he held was soiled, he released her arm and wiped his fingertips on his sleeve. "Go then. Run. Run into that house, and do not dare to come out unless it is for a decent purpose, with decent people."

She nodded frantically. Anything to get away from him.

His eyes narrowed on her. "Mark me, Helena. I will know if you do otherwise. I will be watching you. There is nowhere you can go that I will not follow. Nowhere you can be where I cannot gain entrance. Do you understand?"

"Yes," she whispered.

"Go!" he shouted.

She needed no encouragement. She picked up her skirts and bolted, running heedless of any noise she made, arms stretched out as she banged through the garden gate and scrambled sobbing up the path and through the kitchen door. She slammed it shut behind her, driving the bolt home, and dashed through the empty rooms and up the staircase, flying to the safety of her room.

She burst into her room, pushed the door closed and twisted the key in the lock. With a terrible sense of foreboding, she realized that it did not make her feel any safer. She doubted it ever would. With a muted sob, she turned.

Her bed was covered with roses.

FIFTEEN

INTERCEPTION:
a counterattack that intercepts and checks an indirect attack

"WHERE HAS SHE BEEN?" Ramsey Munro asked Bill Sorry five days later.

"Nowhere." Bill took a long draught of the beer from the mug the pretty tavern girl had set before him. She had set a great deal more before Ram Munro, but the blighter didn't appear to notice the bounty put on display for him. Poor sot.

"She must go out sometimes," Ram insisted. He didn't dare go to Hanover Square himself lest Helena see him and realize he knew her identity. So he had sent Bill Sorry to watch over her in the guise of a workman repairing the square's iron fence. Except, according to Bill, there was little to watch. She'd kept close to the house, venturing out only rarely and always in Lady Tilpot's company.

"She must go out sometimes," Ram insisted.

"Well," Bill scratched his head, "she come outside yesterday and waited with Lady Tilpot and the niece until the carriage come round and picked them up. But she went back inside soon as they left."

"How did she look?"

"Beautiful, of course." Bill wiped his mouth with his sleeve. "Ain't ever seen a woman to match her looks. Her hair's like . . . like"—he looked down at his mug—"it's the color of clear ale."

"Sauterne," Ram corrected absently.

"If you say so," Bill agreed. "Pretty, whatever you call it. But she looked scared, too, and . . ."

Ram reached over and seized Bill's wrist. There was surprising strength in those long, elegant fingers. "And *what?*"

Bill shrugged uncomfortably. "Alone. She looked . . . alone. I don't know why, but that's what I thought when I seen her, and then I thought how terrible that was." He shook his head, as if to clear away such impractical non-sense. "Stupid that, eh?"

"No," Ram said, releasing his grip. "No. It is terrible."

"Damnation!" Dand Ross dropped the rose vine he'd been tying up to a wicket archway and sucked angrily on his bleeding fingers. "If a knight really did give these bleedin' yellow roses to St. Bride's for taking care of his family during the plague, then I'm thinking he might not have been all that happy to see them alive and well on his return from the Crusades 'cause these things is as bloody like to kill someone as please them. These aren't thorns, they're bloody daggers!"

Douglas Stewart wiped the sweat from his eyes and stood up from where he'd been fitting shale into a new stone wall divid-ing the rose garden. "You know, yesterday you took a half-dozen stripes across the back of your thighs without a whimper, and here today you are bleating like a goat kid over a few scratches."

"That was because yesterday I did something to deserve those stripes," Dand explained with heavy patience. "And I have done nothing to deserve being stabbed by these bleedin'

roses except spend the last five years tending them with a mother's care."

"Your mother must have been a rare piece of work, then," Ram drawled carelessly as he heaved a heavy stone into the trough he'd dug earlier, "if you are emulating her tender care."

Kit MacNeill, muscles bunching with his exertions, emerged through the doorway with a barrow piled high with more stones just in time to hear this last. "Dand didn't have a mother. He was spawned with the rest of the demon whelps in hell. At least that's what John Glass tells the younger boys."

"May be true!" Dand, ever impious, grinned. "But I heard John tell them the same thing about you."

"Blast John, anyway," Douglas, by far the most thoughtful of their quartet, frowned. "He has those lads thinking we've some sort of secret cabal going on in here."

"Well, don't we?" Ram asked. The others paused in their labors and regarded him interestedly.

"What do you mean?" Kit, the most forthright, asked.

"Dand said it himself. We've been working in this garden, reclaiming it, or so Brother Fidelis says, for Mother Church for five years. But doesn't it strike you as odd that none of the other lads ever works in here? That we're the only ones?"

Douglas nodded. "I have thought about that. A great deal."

"And Brother Toussaint," Ram continued. "Why would the abbot want him to teach us swordplay and other martial techniques? I know some of the others have instruction, too, but not to the extent that we do. Not nearly." He rolled his shoulder at the painful memory of the long hours spent practicing the various drills the ex-soldier monk gave them.

"But why?" Dand demanded.

"Because we're being groomed for something," Douglas answered gravely. "Something important. Something which re-

lies on us working together, as one, something which relies on our . . . our brotherhood."

It made sense. It felt like the truth. Ram looked around. The others thought so, too. Kit was looking stern—but then, Kit always looked stern—and Dand was nodding with uncharacteristic seriousness.

"Well," Kit finally said, "if that's what the abbot wants, I have no complaints. You are brothers to me, and I'd give my life for any one of you."

Only Kit—big, rough and taciturn—could have said something so quixotic without rousing Dand into making a flippant reply. Or himself, Ram supposed honestly.

"I would, too," Douglas proclaimed.

"And I," Dand muttered. He looked at Ram and his eyes, momentarily sober, lightened. "What of it, Ram? Are you not feeling the urge to declare your life forfeit for mine?"

"Christos!" Ram declared with an extravagant sigh, unwilling to let the others see how much they meant to him, this family he'd found after he'd lost all else. He supposed the others must feel the same. No. He knew they did. "I suppose if I had to die for someone it might as well be one of you. But only so you would be obliged to spend the rest of your miserable lives singing my praises. Yes, indeed. I rather like the thought of that. It would irk you so. Particularly Dand."

"I think," Douglas said slowly, "I think we ought to swear allegiance to one another."

Leave it to Douglas to make a ritual of something that needed no formalization. But Dand, grinning wickedly, held up his bleeding hand, nodding. "And trade blood on it?" he suggested with feigned innocence. "I'm ready."

"Aye!" Douglas declared enthusiastically. "The blood of the rose."

And without waiting for the others to agree, he seized hold of the thorn-covered vine Dand had been tying, piercing his palm in a half-dozen places and wincing with the pain of it. "Damn, that hurts. Now, the rest of you! And then we swear loyalty to one another!"

And amazingly, they did.

At the sharp sound of the snap, Helena jumped.

"I am sorry, Miss Nash!" The footman who'd been opening the napkin before placing it on Helena's lap apologized, his expression more surprised than contrite.

"That's all right, Simon," Helena said. She knew her behavior had given rise to speculation amongst the staff. She was anxious, jumping at shadows. She had to stop. *This* had to stop.

She glanced across the luncheon table to find Flora's reproachful gaze on her. Guiltily, she began a minute scrutiny of her hard-boiled egg, though she knew Flora would not assail her in front of the servants. She had avoided Flora since the misadventure in White Friars five days ago. No. That was whitewashing. She had not only avoided Flora, she had abandoned her.

When Flora had crept to her room late at night and knocked on her door, Helena had ignored it. When a tearful Flora had caught at her sleeve in the hallway yesterday, pleading for a few minutes of her time, Helena had demurred, promising a "later" she had no intention of keeping. She was a coward. A rank, pitiful coward.

She had even fleetingly considered fleeing from here, leaving Flora to her fate. It was not only affection and obligation that kept her from doing so. She had nowhere to go. Nowhere she would feel safe, that is. The thought of borrowing money against her expected settlement from Kate was no longer even a possibility. She could not even imagine living alone with only a few newly hired staff. What if *he* someday decided that something she had done warranted punishment? At least here there were always people about, a small army of servants as well as a formidable employer.

She glanced again at Flora, picking listlessly at her kipper. Not even the jonquil brightness of her fetching gown could conceal her melancholy. Helena felt a wrench of guilt. She would talk to the girl soon, but right now all her concentration centered on Lord DeMarc.

The few times she'd ventured out of the house alone, DeMarc had been there, waiting, watching. He never approached her. He never even ventured close, but he was always there: across the park where she stopped for chocolate, in the Rotunda of the circulating library, lounging in his coach at the side of the street when she walked to the milliner's shop.

The only times she had been free of him were those times she had been accompanied by Lady Tilpot. Then he vanished, either apparently satisfied that she would do nothing of which he disapproved, or unwilling to have his surveillance known.

"Miss Nash!"

At the sound of Lady Tilpot's voice, Helena's hand flew to her throat, startled.

"If I didn't know better," Lady Tilpot said, waddling ponderously in on the arm of a footman, "I would think you had been gambling."

"No, ma'am."

"Gambling *to a bad end.*" The old lady waited for the

footman to haul out the massive chair at the head of the table and then settled down like a discontented pullet. "The way you start and fidget and shy. All the earmarks of someone who has wagered monies they do not own and now are ill prepared to pay."

"Not I, ma'am," Helena said.

"You, of all people, should eschew gambling," Lady Tilpot said, ignoring Helena's denial as she ignored everything she did not want to hear. That she rather enjoyed the idea of Helena sneaking out to lose what few pennies she had at the gaming tables, lost to an addiction she could not control, was unpleasantly obvious. "You have neither the disposition nor the know-how nor the cunning nor the . . . the . . ."

"Money?" Helena suggested.

"Well, of course, that," Lady Tilpot said with a roll of her eyes. "But I was *going* to add that you do not have the understanding necessary to be a successful gambler."

"I am sure you are correct, ma'am," Helena answered.

"Of course I am correct. Now *I*," she patted her hair, "I am well armed with necessary weapons to battle Dame Chance on the green baize field."

At this improbable and highly poetic flight of fancy, Helena looked up. She knew Lady Tilpot enjoyed her weekly game of whist with her fellow misanthropes, but she thought it merely an excuse to trade venom. "Is that so, ma'am?"

"Indeed, yes. Why, just two evenings ago I won three hundred and forty-four pounds and ten shillings."

"My felicitations, ma'am," Helena said.

"It is a pittance of what I could win."

"I have heard that in some of the great houses, fortunes trade hands between ladies," Helena said carefully.

"And have you also heard the scandal that attends them?" Lady Tilpot asked sarcastically. "Oh, certain people are accepted in Society because their husbands are powerful. But a woman alone in the world, without some male to stand behind, a woman such as I, must be careful."

"How provoking for you," Helena murmured.

With a sharp rap, Lady Tilpot lopped the top off her hard-boiled egg. "Two things are sacrosanct in life, Miss Nash, both of which, once lost, are irreplaceable: standards and reputation. Have I not said this often to you, Flora?"

Flora, lost in her own musing, came to with a little start, and nodded vigorously. "Indeed, yes, Auntie."

"But," Lady Tilpot waved her knife instructively in Helena's direction, "there is a point in life when one might reasonably expect that a sterling reputation might absorb some small tittle-tattle, and I am nearing that age. Yes, yes! I see your shocked expression, and I understand your amazement, but it is true. I am approaching my middle years—

"Here now! Drink some water! Good heavens, Miss Nash, what are you thinking to gobble your food so fast?"

Gratefully, Helena raised her glass to her lips. At sixty-six years of age, Lady Tilpot had been looking at the retreating backside of middle age for some time.

Helena cleared her throat. "Ma'am, I would be very grateful if you could spare me a few moments at your convenience."

"It is convenient now," Lady Tilpot mumbled around a mouthful of food. "What is it you want? More money? And for what, I should like to know?

"Living like a daughter of the house in one of the finest homes in London? Listening in on the conversations of London's greatest intellectuals? Running a few simple errands? Reading a few pages for anothers' weary eyes? Warming a glass of milk on an occasional night to ease an overly agile mind? Once in a while being asked to find a flower amongst the market stands that does not clash with one's benefactress's gown? Acting as an occasional courier between her and unpleasant tradespeople? Looking for a lost—"

"I was not going to ask for money," Helena broke in.

"Oh?"

"I was going to ask you for your advice."

At this, Lady Tilpot's eyes grew round with amazement and then narrowed with satisfaction. " 'Twas only a matter of time." She set down her knife and fork, picked up her napkin, dabbed delicately at her lips, and said, "Well, then. What is it?"

"It's . . . it's a most private matter." Helena darted a quick look at Flora, who had, if possible, paled a shade. Could the poor chit be imagining that Helena was about to disclose her secret? "Concerning only myself."

Flora relaxed.

"Pshaw. Flora is the soul of discretion, and the footmen do not hear anything. Do you, Johns?" The footmen stared mutely ahead.

"I would prefer privacy, ma'am."

"Nonsense. You'll hurt Flora's feelings. What is it? I insist."

Helena took a deep breath. "It is Lord DeMarc, ma'am."

Lady Tilpot's brows snapped together in consternation. "DeMarc? Forrester DeMarc? Can't believe he's tryin' to get to Flora through you! Don't tell me it is so!"

"Not precisely, ma'am," Helena said, searching for the right words. "I am sorry—"

"Good!" Lady Tilpot exclaimed "Because I won't believe it. Man has far too much a notion of where the line is kept to be sneakin' about, using a paid companion to insinuate himself with my niece.

"Why, good heavens, Miss Nash! Lord Forrester DeMarc is one of the most formidable egg peelers in the ton! Top lofty, a bit too high in the instep, if truth be told, and worth a plum."

"Yes, ma'am. But it is not Flora in whom he is interested."

It seemed to Helena that everything in the room came to a dead halt. Not a soul breathed. Not Flora, not the footmen, not Lady Tilpot, certainly not Helena herself. Lady Tilpot simply stared at her, dribbling a little egg.

Finally her mouth started working, but the word she whispered was so faint, Helena did not catch it the first time. She leaned forward. "Ma'am?"

"Me?"

Dear Lord. Helena swallowed, marshalling her courage. "No, ma'am. I believe Lord DeMarc is . . . that is he . . . It is me, ma'am."

"What?" Lady Tilpot fell back in her chair

"He has intimated an interest in me."

"But how wonderful!" Flora said, clapping her hands

in delight. "How marvelous! And you are so well suited! Both so proper and handsome!"

Flora reached across the table for Helena's hand, clasping it and squeezing lightly. "No wonder you have been so distracted. Well, Helena, I understand now. Indeed, I do!"

"Flora," Helena turned to the beaming girl. "You have it wrong—"

"Indeed, yes!" Lady Tilpot snapped. "As do you!" She shook her head, but there was no anger in her expression, only exasperation. "I do not have to know what transpired between you and Lord DeMarc to know that it was, on his part, innocent of any *objective*."

She fixed a baleful glare on Helena. "Pray, do not think that you shall enlist my aid in forcing the poor man into making an offer for a woman he could never consider his equal.

"Now"—she held up her hand, stopping Helena's protest—"you are lucky, Miss Nash. Not only that you have been with me for three years, but that I am an excellent judge of character. I do not think that you purposefully connive at Lord DeMarc's downfall. You are not a conniving sort of woman. I would not have you as my companion if you were.

"But you are mistaken. Oh, do not look like that, Miss Nash. I do not fault you overly much. You are a spinster, after all, and what spinster, however sensible she might think herself, is ever really that sensible when she looks about at all the young women she knows who are married with families and children and consequence, and she has none of these things?

"It is not unusual for someone in your station to embellish a smile, a kind word in passing, a little courtesy, into the sort of attention she must once have imagined she would receive from a beau, a suitor . . . a husband. But you really must not be deceived by these daydreams."

"I was not deceived," Helena said firmly. "He watches me. He is following me!" She knew her voice had grown shrill, but she could not help it. The sleepless nights, the anxiety, and DeMarc's persistent pursuit had made her frantic.

The worst part of it was that standing up for herself did not provoke the rage that was Lady Tilpot's usual response to any sign of backbone amongst her staff or family, but only a pitying shake of her head. "No, my dear, he is not. And yes, my dear, you are deceived, and you will see this soon enough. These things pass. Believe me, they pass.

"Now, the guests will be arriving in a few hours, and Lord DeMarc will be amongst them. I trust you will not make a cake of yourself." Her face turned cold. "And you will *not* embarrass the viscount."

She turned to her niece. "Flora, you *would* wear the jonquil dimity. Miss Nash will find the ribbons for your hair. You best go now. *Now.*"

They went.

"I am not interested in Lord DeMarc. He is repugnant to me."

Flora sank down onto the cream-colored satin slipper chair in her rose-colored room. The bedchamber was adorned in a style as decorative and delicate as its inhabitant, cluttered with furniture in gilt and satin, dressed with silk draperies, festooned with ribbons, flowers, and bows in delicate watercolors. Living in it would be like residing in a milliner's workbasket. "Then you must tell him, without offending him."

"That is the problem, Flora. He is unbalanced. Do you recall what your aunt said about my building a fantasy around the viscount's innocent attentions?"

"Yes. It was a terrible thing to say. I am so sorry—"

Helena shook her head impatiently. "It doesn't matter what she thinks of me. What matters is that she is right—but about DeMarc. He thinks that I am—I don't know! He thinks that in some way I belong to him, and he will do everything in his power to see that I don't escape him."

Flora stared at her, her eyes wide in her heart-shaped face. "But that is terrible. Someone must stop him!"

"Who?" Helena said, sinking down next to Flora. Always before she had been the strong one, the confidante and comforter. That their roles were reversed struck Helena as odd, and would have amused her in any other circumstances. "Anyone I tell will likely have the same response as your aunt. DeMarc is a peer. I am a paid companion."

Flora did her the favor of not objecting. "You will have to stay away from him until his infatuation fades."

Remain trapped by his obsession in this house? For how long? A few days? Weeks? Months? Until DeMarc decided otherwise? Helena's lips tightened.

In her entire life, Helena had never allowed herself to be ruled by her fears. As a young girl she had wanted what she assumed every girl wanted: a home, a family, a part of a community in which she would prove an asset. But the young men who came to call had seemed unable to see beyond "the chance symmetrical arrangement of features" Lady Tilpot had so aptly described.

They had no notion of how to speak to her or what to say. They were only good at admiring those things over which she had no control and for which she could take no credit. They made her feel empty and afraid: afraid of the future, afraid she might in truth be no more than a decorative addition to some lord's home, but most of all afraid that she would eventually marry one of them just to have the whole hollow courting ritual done with.

But she hadn't given in to those fears. She had not, no matter how much she knew it disappointed her parents, accepted any of the offers that had been made.

But she was afraid now. She hated being afraid. And more, she *resented* being afraid. DeMarc had done what death and personal catastrophe had failed to do. She started to bury her face in her hands but made herself stop.

"I don't know what I am going to do," she said, touching Flora's hand. "But thank you. And I am sorry, Flora. I fear I underestimated you. I have been so consumed by DeMarc and this . . . this situation that I didn't feel I could bear your disappointment when I told you that I did not deliver your note to Mr. Goodwin."

Because I ran away rather than watch Ram Munro kissing another woman, and later, because I was in an alley with Ram Munro, learning why a woman could risk everything for a man. Because I was not thinking of you, Flora.

She flushed guiltily. "I am sorry, Flora. I have been unconscionably selfish."

"No, no," Flora said hastily. But her eyes glistened suspiciously. "You have things other than Ossie and me to concern you. I understand."

Flora took a deep, shaky breath. "But I must contact Ossie. I cannot wait. I must speak to him in the next week or two." She swallowed bravely. "I suppose I shall go myself. If you will just tell me—"

"Flora!" Helena interjected harshly. She had thought the girl was finally maturing. "You cannot be thinking of risking your reputation—and, more importantly, your aunt's wrath—by seeking out Oswald Goodwin in those places where he currently lingers. That's ridiculous. You can wait until another means can be found to contact him."

She disliked having to say the next. "Really, Flora. It is time to grow up."

"I *am* grown-up, Helena. That is why I have to see Oswald," Flora answered as a tear slipped down her dewy cheek. "I am going to have a baby."

Flora was pregnant. With every hour Helena's situation grew more formidable. She had to do something. She could not let Flora brave the streets. So, she must. And that meant braving DeMarc's madness.

"May I sit next to you, Miss Nash?"

Helena, lost deep in her own thoughts, looked up to find Page Winebarger standing before her, the little cat Princess tucked into the crook of her arm. "Pardon me, ma'am. I was not attending."

"It is quite all right. You are distracted. And I am imposing on your reverie."

"Not at all," she said. While she was accompanied,

DeMarc would remain at bay. All afternoon DeMarc had been extremely careful to demonstrate his indifference. By neither glance nor remark had he singled her out for his attention.

Lady Tilpot had certainly noticed. She was triumphant. Twice she had cornered Helena to whisper, "He barely knows you are alive, my dear!" and "I fear I must lend you my dictionary, Miss Nash, for you have clearly mistaken the meaning of 'oblivious' for 'infatuation.' "

But Helena was not deceived. The manner in which DeMarc always managed to be within a certain distance of her chilled her. She shivered now, and she could have sworn he smiled even though his gaze seemed firmly planted elsewhere.

She hated him suddenly with a vitriol that shook her, hated the prison his obsession had built around her, hated her fear of him and her inability to escape that fear. What right had he to intimidate and terrorize her? She had done nothing to deserve his vile fixation!

"Miss Nash?" Mrs. Winebarger said softly. "Are you quite all right? You look rather fierce."

With a start, Helena realized the Prussian lady was regarding her solicitously. "Thank you, I am fine. I see your husband once more has had to decline Lady Tilpot's invitation."

Mrs. Winebarger idly stroked a purr from her calico companion. "The tournament consumes his thoughts as well as his hours. I think," she leaned in confidingly, "that for the first time in a very long while, he feels he has a real rival. Perhaps two."

"Mr. Munro?"

Mrs. Winebarger nodded. "And Lord DeMarc. The

viscount seems determined to mount a formidable challenge. Why, in preparation the viscount has been getting in thrice-weekly matches at Mr. Munro's salle."

So that is where he disappeared to when Helena went with Lady Tilpot on her rounds.

"Does he?"

"Indeed. My husband says he will be there tomorrow afternoon." She looked sanguine. "It is important to know one's opponent's habits. And DeMarc is a very serious opponent."

"Mrs. Winebarger," Helena said slowly, an idea taking hold. "I have a great favor to ask you."

"But of course, what is it, my dear?" Mrs. Winebarger asked, looking not in the least offended.

"I would like you to ask Lady Tilpot if I might escort you on some errands tomorrow afternoon. I am usually obliged to accompany her, but if you asked her, she might well agree."

"And what errand will we be running, Miss Nash?" Mrs. Winebarger asked, a twinkle of interest in her eye.

"We will be going to Mr. Munro's salle, L'École de la Fleur."

Mrs. Winebarger broke into a wide smile. "But of course, my dear," she said kindly. "It is about time you indulge your feminine curiosity."

SIXTEEN

FEINT:
attacking into one line with the intention
of switching to another or pulling out
before the attack is complete

"THANK YOU AGAIN, Mrs. Winebarger," Helena said the next day as the Prussian lady's carriage deposited them outside Ramsey Munro's salle.

"Think nothing of it, my dear. It was worth asking if only to hear the preposterous excuses The Tilpot came up with for why it was impossible for her to lend your company to me." She dimpled mischievously as she shifted the sleeping Princess from her lap to a cushion beside her. "But I had only to hold out for her the carrot that Robert might escort me to her soiree next week, and suddenly the impossible became not only possible but it was her sincere pleasure to accommodate me. And not just for the afternoon, but any time I like."

The carriage rocked to a stop, and Helena's courage faltered.

"Is it true that ladies with a risqué reputation frequent Mr. Munro's salle?" she asked as Mrs. Winebarger's tiger went ahead to ascertain the particulars of the situation.

Mrs. Winebarger peered out at the street. "That is the *on dit.*"

"He has his choice of any of them, I suspect," Helena murmured.

Mrs. Winebarger looked around. "Having a choice and availing oneself of it is not the same thing, Miss Nash. Mr. Munro is an extremely handsome man and a marvelous swordsman. His grandfather was just as handsome and just as good a swordsman."

"His grandfather?"

"The marquis of Cottrell." Mrs. Winebarger glanced at her curiously. "You did know he was born on the wrong side of the blanket?"

"I never gave it any thought," Helena replied honestly.

"Didn't you? How unconventional. You'll probably see the old man today. He has taken to attending the practices. Although, according to my husband, he and Mr. Munro apparently don't speak."

"Your husband is most au courant."

"Yes. The world of true dueling enthusiasts is a very small one. Ah! My tiger has found the attendant. Shall we?"

They descended from the carriage and climbed a short flight of steps to where a trim, middle-aged gentleman wearing an eye patch bowed disinterestedly.

"We have come to watch the practice," Mrs. Winebarger announced.

"Yes, ma'am," the attendant said in a voice that suggested he'd heard the same countless times. "This way, ladies."

He preceded them into a wide, unfurnished foyer, where a cluster of a half-dozen females donned shawls and hats, apparently getting ready to leave. At once, Helena identified Jolly Milar, her brown curls bobbing excitedly as she whispered to a young lady in an extremely a la mode mint-green gown, her short ruffle of ginger-colored hair tilted—dear God.

"Charlotte?"

Helena's youngest sister turned, eyes the color of green agates, bright with amusement. But that was Charlotte, perpetually amused. Perpetually unconcerned. Perpetually on the brink of disaster. And then she was across the room, flinging her arms around Helena's neck, as unaware of the proprieties as she was unconcerned with them.

"Charlotte, what are you doing here?" Helena asked in a low voice.

"Helena!" Charlotte cried. "But this is wonderful! I swear, Helena, I hold out hope for you yet."

Remembering herself, Helena ushered her winsome little sister over to Mrs. Winebarger and introduced her. Mrs. Winebarger, displaying her usual sensitivity, murmured a greeting and excused herself to give her tiger some last-minute instructions.

Gratefully, Helena swung on her youngest sibling. "Charlotte, again, what are you doing here?" Her troubled gaze passed over her sister's companions. In addition to Jolly, she recognized Charlotte's boon companion, Margaret "Magpie" Welton, but she did not know any of the other young ladies. They were a gay, bright-eyed, and vibrant lot. *Very* vibrant.

"Why, I came to watch some fine athletes disport themselves. But as we have been here for nearly two hours, we are most sharp set and decided to go find some refreshment. Hopefully, with some of those same ath-letes following us, n'est-ce pas?" Charlotte winked and then laughed at Helena's expression.

"More to the point, sister mine, what are *you* doing here?" she asked, tucking her arm through Helena's. "Tell me, darling, have you come to see the Prince of White Friars? Or has one of his pupils caught your fancy?"

"No one has captured my fancy," Helena lied.

"Oh, fie on you, Helena!" Charlotte said impatiently, the short cap of loose curls glinting as she tossed her head. "One would think you had no fancy to capture. True, you were never what one would call corky, and al-ways kept the line, but I never would have called you straightlaced. And you had bottom, my dear, true pluck.

"It's that Tilpot creature who has done this to you. You simply must escape her clutches before you become the Ice Maiden Society thinks you are."

"What?" Helena exclaimed.

" 'Pon rep!" Charlotte exclaimed. "I cannot believe you are actually unaware of the sobriquet with which you've been dubbed. But then, you aren't really ever *in* Society, are you? Not real Society. That old cat and her cronies hardly qualify."

She pursed her lips, but her eyes danced. "Yes, dear sister, 'tis true! You are known as the Ice Maiden. Helena the Unassailable."

"Good Lord."

"Don't poker up like that. I would *love* to be thought unattainable." She sighed before darting an impish look at Helena. "Until I desired to be attained, that is. Regrettably, I doubt I could lend the necessary verisimilitude to such a pose."

"Charlotte!" Helena exclaimed again uncomfortably. That had ever been Charlotte's style and Helena's bête noire: Charlotte's unrepentant candor. Some thought it a delightful, if reckless, child's prank, but Helena suspected that defiance made Charlotte say the things others only thought.

"This must be your sister," one of Charlotte's companions, an extravagantly tricked out young woman, enthused.

"Yes. My sister, the most beautiful woman in London," Charlotte said with unfeigned pride. And that was the other hallmark of Charlotte's unfortunate, wondrous, disastrous personality: her unhesitating and unconditional affection coupled with her absolute refusal to be overruled in anything she wanted.

Then, with the same ruinous honesty, Charlotte continued, "Just think what she'd be if dressed well."

The young woman laughed. "Well, you weren't exaggerating. She is stunning." She tugged on her glove, apparently not expecting to be introduced. Helena could only conclude that the fashionable-looking beauty, whoever she was, knew she was not someone Helena would approve of Charlotte knowing.

"Come along, Lottie," Margaret Welton called breathlessly. "Jenny thinks the Comte Sancerre is drinking coffee on Bond Street because you said you would be there this afternoon! And if we don't go now—oh! Hallo, Miss Nash! Fancy seeing you here!"

"Miss Welton," Helena inclined her head. There was

now no possibility of her appearance here going unnoticed, and less of it going unremarked. Magpie Welton was as gregarious as her nickname suggested, and as discreet as a town crier.

Charlotte understood. She bit her lip to suppress an amused smile. "That is the trouble with spotless reputations, Helena," she whispered. "Any mark shows."

Charlotte looked around, her color high, her smile brilliant, and called, "I am coming, darlings!" before turning back to Helena and bussing her affectionately on the cheek. "There, my dear. For luck. And I have *always* thought he was gorgeous!"

Before Helena could respond to this outrageous comment, Charlotte had danced back to her companions. Like butterflies, they flitted down the corridor and milled about the doorway until it opened and out they flew.

"Ahem." The one-eyed attendant drew Helena's attention. "There are several other ladies presently watching the practice, and as there are such a lot of you, I must beg that you respect the participants' need for concentration and remain mute. Now, if you would follow me?"

Helena and Mrs. Winebarger fell into step behind him, Helena taking the opportunity to whisper urgently to her benefactress, "Ma'am, if I might beg one last favor?"

"You may," Mrs. Winebarger returned.

"After the exhibition, I would like to find my own way back to Lady Tilpot's."

Mrs. Winebarger's brows flickered into a concerned frown. "An extraordinary request, Miss Nash. I am not sure I approve. Certainly The Tilpot would not."

"Please."

"Very well," she capitulated. "You are hardly a green girl, and I can hardly have claimed not to have done some rather interesting things in my own life. But be careful."

"Thank you!" Helena breathed as the attendant pushed open a sturdy set of doors at the end of the hallway and stood aside.

They entered a ballroom stripped bare of every ornamentation and superfluous bit of furniture to create a great open expanse, the light flooding in from the uncurtained second-story windows above. The only reminder of the room's past function was the gigantic crystal chandelier sparkling overhead. A dozen straight lines had been painted on the bare wood floorboards, and along these, several men dressed only in tight-fitting trousers, shirts, and waistcoats lunged and retreated, thrusting swords against invisible opponents.

Along the far end of the ballroom clustered a group of ladies and gentlemen. As Helena approached with Mrs. Winebarger, she saw what held their rapt attention: the viscount DeMarc locked in battle with Ramsey Munro. A referee stood anxiously by, waiting for the first strike.

This was not the Ram Munro who'd shuffled with fallen-angel grace as he'd countered and parried the moves of his hapless opponents at the debauch in Cheapside. This Ram Munro moved with a dancer's artistry and control, his body poised and tensile, back straight, shoulders angled, long legs supple as he crouched.

But DeMarc appeared equally adept. Moreover, as combatants they were quite evenly matched, both being tall and lean with long reaches and powerful legs. Their bodies moved back and forth as if locked on some straight, invisible track, the space between them remaining as exact and fixed as in some elaborate dance set to the staccato chatter of swords.

Some movements, too subtle for Helena's novice eyes to see, drew murmurs of approval; others garnered slight inhalations of concern. At the far end of the cluster of spectators, an elderly gentleman stood with a discontented expression on a countenance so handsome he could only be related to Ram.

"Inside!" he shouted in annoyance. "Inside!"

Ram gave no indication that he heard. "I see you have been practicing your diagonal parry, DeMarc," he said in a conversational voice.

"Kind of you to notice," DeMarc answered, but without Ram's sangfroid. "Am I mistaken, or are your beats more concentrated of late? The tempo seems accelerated."

Ram shrugged. "A duel is much like a seduction, Viscount. Each lady—as each opponent—succumbs at her own rate, neither too quickly nor too slowly for the man who understands the virtue of patience. And the rewards."

The viscount lunged, the point of his blade dipping low. But Ram countered, intercepting the blade and returning the line of action higher. Thwarted, the expression on the viscount's face tightened like a closed fist. "You know, Munro, you really are an exceptional swordsman."

"Too kind," Ram murmured.

"But you are *not a* gentleman."

Ram flashed a smile at his aggrieved opponent. "Do tell."

"A gentleman does not talk about seduction in front of ladies."

"What ladies? Are there ladies here?" Ram sounded amazed, but his eyes did not stray from DeMarc. Delighted laughter spilled from those same ladies. "Viscount, I begin to perceive why it is you have rarely beaten me—"

Some slight movement, some tiny opening must have presented itself, for Ram abruptly stopped speaking and the swords' conversation took over. An insulting hiss, a rebuke, and a disparaging sneer. Then, as quickly as the chatter had begun, it stopped. The duelists fell back a pace from one another, the odd, contemplative air returning to the match.

"And why is that, Munro?" DeMarc asked, but his breathing was a bit heavier now, and a light sheen covered his forehead.

"If you have noticed there are ladies in this room, you are simply not focusing enough on the match. Now I, on the other hand, could not say if ladies surround me or dancing bears."

More laughter. Beside Helena, Mrs. Winebarger fought back a smile.

It was all nonsense, of course, meant to make DeMarc look ridiculous. For if Munro was as riveted on the match as he claimed DeMarc ought to be, he would hardly be contemplating things as absurd as dancing bears or making provocative comments about DeMarc's lack of focus. No. Ram Munro knew to a degree where every person in the room stood.

Except for her and Mrs. Winebarger. He had not

looked up since they had entered, and they were half hidden by the other spectators.

"That being the case," Ram went on, "how can I be held accountable for ungentlemanly comments I make in front of ladies I do not note?"

"Well you know there are ladies present, Munro. As you are most *well known* to several of their number. I would say further on the matter, but then I am in truth that which you only pretend to be."

A lazy smile turned Ram's lips. "Too brown, Viscount. I have never pretended to be a prig."

DeMarc's jaw clenched. He attacked, pressing forward, his footwork assured and deft. With a grin, Ramsey parried, deflecting the blade just before it hit his padded chest.

"So predictable, DeMarc." His tone had lost its superficial politesse. "You have excellent skills, a very good instinctive reading of your opponent, but you allow your emotions to set your strategy."

His sword cut over DeMarc's testing blade, passing through his guard, and flirted within inches of the viscount's shoulder, only to be enjoined and parried, "In a duel there is only room for two people. Nothing else must matter."

"*Pris de fer!*" shouted the elderly gentleman, annoyed and disgusted. Once more, Ram affected not to notice.

He engaged DeMarc's sword, was parried, and immediately engaged again. Their blades held, each man exerting equal force pushing against the other's sword. The muscles in Ram's forearm corded. "Not your wife, your brother, your father, or your child."

In an effort to regain the control that was slipping

from him, DeMarc turned to present a smaller target. Helena could visualize DeMarc's plan: He need only push Ram's sword, and by extension his arm, sideways across his chest, and, for a short, vital instant, an area beneath Ram's outstretched arm would be exposed. DeMarc would then disengage his sword and strike through to the vulnerable target.

Others saw it, too. Around her little gasps burst from a number of ladies' lips just as Ram abruptly released the countering force. DeMarc's sword, without the expected resistance, drove too quickly and too far, leaving his own chest unprotected.

It was brilliant. "Bravo!" she called out spontaneously.

Ram's eyes, which had been locked on the action, darted up at the sound of her voice, and in that telling instant he lost sight of his target. DeMarc, trying to drag his sword back in time to parry the strike he must have known was coming, instead drove forward, his tip plunging into the padding above Ram's heart.

"Point! Halt!" the referee shouted.

The duelists stepped back from one another, DeMarc openly triumphant, Ram openly distracted. His gaze flickered across the crowd. He couldn't have recognized her voice. She had always been careful to keep her voice low and disguised. But in the alley in Cheapside . . . had she remembered then?

"So, Munro, what was that you were saying about my never having beaten you?"

Graciously, Ram inclined his head. "Well done, Viscount."

"Bah!" A sound of disgust drew the duelists' attention, and Helena looked around to see the marquis disappear out the door. When she looked back it was to find De-Marc staring at her, his face tight and his body rigid. Ram was quitting the floor, pausing beside the one-eyed attendant to exchange a few words before exiting the salle.

"Does anyone wish to challenge Viscount DeMarc?" the attendant called out. At once, two young men appeared on the edge of the cleared space, vying for the right to take on the man who'd bested Ramsey Munro. There was no way DeMarc could demur without looking as though he feared his win had been a fluke.

Helena merged with the crowd. She waited a moment or two while the duelists took their marks and then slipped into the corridor where the attendant had taken up a position by the door.

"Sir. Would you please take this to Mr. Munro at once?" she said, handing him a folded note requesting an immediate audience.

The one-eyed man looked at her dubiously and took the proffered letter, bidding her to wait. She paced along the bare corridor impatiently. What would she do if he said no? He couldn't. She reached into her reticule and pressed the tiny yellow silk rose she'd cut from one of Flora's gowns. The attendant reappeared.

"Ma'am. If you would follow me?" He led her to a room at the top of a flight of stairs and ushered her in to what was to all appearances a sort of masculine sitting room, though woefully lacking in amenities.

A pair of high-backed chairs upholstered in fading blue damask faced each other in front of the fireplace, while a lovely old walnut desk sat in the pool of light coming through a bank of narrow, undraped windows. A bookcase stood on one side of a door on the far wall, and a simple glass case displayed a trio of ornately wrought swords on the other side. And that was all. No carpet, no drapery, no pictures on the wall.

"Mr. Munro will join you directly." Without waiting for a reply, he left, shutting the door behind him. The sudden vacuum caused the door on the far wall to pop open a few inches, and with some embarrassment Helena realized that it led to Ram Munro's private chambers and that she was looking obliquely into a mirror hung above a washstand. But then Ramsey's reflection appeared in the mirror, and she forgot all matters of circumspection.

She jerked back a step, fearful that he might see her. But when nothing happened, she leaned forward, craning her neck to see if . . . yes. Oh, *yes*.

He stood in front of the mirror, naked to the waist, his dark head of curls glistening with the water he must have just splashed over his face and neck. Moisture beaded on the fine mat of dark hair covering his chest and trickled down the sharpcut vales and contours of a finely toned, muscular torso. She swallowed as he straightened further, and she saw again the rose shape emblazoned high on the sloping plane of his pectoral muscle. It looked to her like a scar, pearlized and angry.

Then, as she stood transfixed, breathing rapidly between parted lips, his head fell forward and he gripped the edges of the washstand, the muscles of his forearms and biceps bulging as if he were trying to bury his fingers in the hard marble surface.

With a sudden jerk, his head snapped up, and he met his own gaze in the mirror. For a long moment he studied his reflection. She could not say what he saw there, in the privacy of the moment his face shed its usual sardonic mien and he looked . . . young. Both apprehensive and expectant. And . . . awed. Yes. Awed.

It must have been his defeat in the fight that made him look so. She could find no other explanation. Yet he did not look unhappy. Not at all.

Then, with an unreadable quirk of his lips he pushed away from the washstand, snatching up a towel from some unseen rack, and roughly began drying himself off as he disappeared from view.

She pulled back, her pulse racing. This was a mistake. A terrible mistake. How could she be with him and not long to be in his arms, feeling those clever, wicked lips on her? He would know. He would realize she was "Corie," the woman who'd responded so passionately to—

A door clicked behind her. She spun around, her hand moving to her throat to catch at the heartbeat stuttering there. He stood motionless in clean, white shirtsleeves and dark, pressed trousers, his damp, dark hair curling over a fresh collar, his shirt cuffs rolled up over lean, muscular forearms.

His gaze was grave. No spark of carnal interest. No leap of stunned recognition. Of course not. A dozen ladies might have been in his arms since that night.

"Helena," he said with a quiet, bemused sort of gravity. Was there welcome in those syllables? No. Impossible. He was simply testing his memory, asking which sister she might be. That was all. She struggled to remember her reasons for being here—and found them.

"Mr. Munro." Thank God, at least she needn't feign an accent anymore, but could speak naturally in her native Yorkish tones. "It is kind of you to remember me, particularly as our one meeting was so brief and years ago, and even kinder for you to agree to see me in such a remarkable manner."

She could have sworn his chin jerked up a fraction, as if he'd taken a blow. He stood quite still. Long enough for her to note the luxury of black lashes, the marble sheen of a newly shaved jaw, the way the light refracted the blue of his irises. Then he was coming across the room, his manner exquisite, his smile formal with just the right degree of familiarity.

"Of course I remember you, Miss Nash," he said. "Pray, to what do I owe this pleasure?"

Taking a small breath, she stretched out her hand. Automatically, he reached out with his own. She dropped the yellow silk bud in his upturned palm.

"I want you to teach me swordplay."

SEVENTEEN

BIND:
an action in which the opponent's blade
is forced in a diagonally opposite line

RAM DIDN'T LAUGH OUT LOUD, a reaction Helena had half expected. His hand closed about the small silk rose as he motioned for her to have a seat. While she settled herself in one of the chairs, he rang for a servant, and after giving the one-eyed man directions, returned.

"Gaspard will bring us tea." He seated himself opposite her, his long legs stretched out nonchalantly, his gaze hooded. "How fares your family, Miss Nash?"

She stared at him, startled. "Sir?"

"Your family. Your sisters. I heard of your mother's death, of course, and beg you accept my belated condolences. Miss Charlotte, I believe, still resides with the Weltons?" Seeing her wide-eyed stare, he nodded. "As I thought. And, of course, I know of Mrs. Blackburn's marriage to my old companion Kit."

"You do?"

He smiled. "Of course. I was at the wedding."

"You were? I didn't see you."

"I was attempting to be circumspect." He cocked his head, smiling a little. "I saw you. You were very severe. Very concerned and trying terribly hard to accept your sister's choice of groom."

He was right. She had been worried. But she would have wagered much that no one would have been able to read that in her face or manner. Except . . . he had.

"Why were you trying to be circumspect?" she asked, amazed at her boldness.

His smile was unexpectedly charming. "I wasn't sure I would be welcome."

"Why is that?"

"A long and tedious story, Miss Nash. Suffice it to say Kit MacNeill and I had certain suspicions regarding each other that precluded me from standing up for him at his wedding."

"*Had?*"

"We have since learned to trust each other again. It's far too tiring to maintain a decent suspicion without proof." She didn't believe him. He was playing a role, hiding behind a mask of sophisticated ennui.

Her eyes narrowed. "Why have you gone to the trouble of keeping apprised of my family's situation?"

He shrugged apologetically. "I made an oath. I am afraid I take that sort of thing ridiculously seriously," he drawled, his blue eyes waiting and watchful. "But there it is. The last remnants of an education too steeped in mythology, I suspect. All those heroes with their pledges and labors and duties and decades-long quests."

"I see." He'd quite disconcerted her. Had he been keeping abreast of her own situation, too?

As if he read her mind, his smile grew vulpine. "And how is Lady Tilpot?"

"Fine," Helena said a little breathlessly. He *had* been watching her. How far had his obligation extended? How much did he know?

"I am delighted to hear it. Now then, Miss Nash, perhaps you can tell me more about this desire of yours to learn swordplay."

She pulled herself back to her present situation. "There is nothing to explain. As you said, you swore an oath to answer my needs as best as possible."

"I did," he replied in equally sedate tones.

"Well, I need to learn to protect myself." She was proud of her self-containment. She met his gaze straightforwardly, using the old trick of looking through a man's eyes rather than into them. No lowering of her lashes, no demure glance to break eye contact, no suggestion that the paid companion was in any manner being coy.

Except it was impossible to look through Ramsey Munro's blue gaze.

"My dear Miss Nash. If you are in need of protection, I can provide that far more easily than I can teach you to wield a sword. Now, tell me, whom requires sticking?"

She flushed. "I do not require you to 'stick' anyone, sir. I would prefer greatly that no one is stuck at all. But, if the need to protect myself arises, I would like to be able to do so myself."

"I see." He stood up. "I think you had best go home, Miss Nash."

She stared at him, her lips falling apart. "But you promised."

"I am quite aware. But I promised to meet your needs, not your whims, and all that you have told me is that you have a whim to learn swordplay should some happenstance arise that puts you in danger. To which there is a very simple answer. Stay out of dangerous places."

"But I . . . I can't," she blurted out.

The handsome cast of his features hardened, his voluptuary's mouth tightened. *"Can't?* Why? Are you impelled to visit places other young ladies fear to go?" His tone held the rasp of derision. "I can hardly think so, ma'am. So, if you do frequent dangerous places, I can only conclude that you choose to put yourself in peril for whim's sake.

"Do not look so cheated, Miss Nash. If you still feel the same way, oh, say a month hence, return to me. By then the tournament will have ended, and I will have the time to indulge you." As she continued staring dumbfounded up at him, he turned his hand over and dropped the little rose into her lap. "Keep this until then."

"How dare you?" Slowly, she climbed to her feet, her

eyes locked with his, her voice shaking, the silk rose falling unseen to the floor. "How *dare* you patronize me?"

Nothing about her was composed or cool now. She burned with indignation. "Despite your information about me and my sisters' circumstances, you know nothing about us, Mr. Munro. Nothing about *me*.

"You do not know what circumstances have led me to your salle or what has led me to closet myself alone in this room with you at the risk of my reputation."

"No," he said flatly. "You are correct. Why don't you tell me?"

He wouldn't help her unless she explained, and she could not explain everything. She had sworn to protect Flora and Oswald's identity, and until she was released from that vow, she could only allude to the situation.

"Be seated, Miss Nash."

Reluctantly she retook the seat as a rap on the door heralded the arrival of Gaspard, carrying a tea service. He set the service out on the desk —there being no table—as Helena considered what she might say to win Ram's aid. When he had left, she began without preamble, "I am being followed."

Ram cocked his head. "I am sure you have many followers, Miss Nash."

"No," she said impatiently. "I am being followed, dogged, my steps hounded."

"Most unpleasant," he said sympathetically. "But the obsessions young men form for their inamoratas are fleeting. You have only to remove yourself from public view for a while and, fickle as men are, when you return to Society I have little doubt you will find your admirer's fancy has fixed on a more available—or at least visible—lady."

"I cannot remove myself from the public," she said tersely.

"Oh." He sounded no more than faintly intrigued. But his fingertips drummed on the end of the chair's arm. "Why is that?"

She took a sip of the tea she'd been offered. "I am looking for someone."

"Someone in particular?"

"Yes. A gentleman."

"Can you not find this gentleman a week hence? A month? Is it so necessary you have him now?"

"*Have him?*" The expression snagged her attention, but only briefly. She was too frustrated to bother over his word choice. If Oswald's creditors got hold of him, he might not be here in a month. She had heard grim stories of how some of the cent-per-centers dealt with those who reneged on their loans. "He very well may disappear forever."

"And this would be unendurable?" he asked coolly.

At the thought of Flora enduring the scandal of her pregnancy alone, Helena's teacup rattled in its saucer. Quickly, she set it down. "Yes," she said quietly.

"Then, ma'am, tell me who hounds you, and I will stop him."

"Stop him how? Stop him from what? Being on a public street? Lounging in a public coffeehouse? Accepting an invitation to an acquaintance's house? Viewing an art exhibit at a gallery?"

"Ma'am?" Ram insisted.

"Lord Forrester DeMarc."

His brows shot up in surprise. "Viscount DeMarc? The man I just fought?"

"Yes."

His amazement was unfeigned. "I can scarce countenance it. He is far too proud to dangle after a woman in such an obvious manner as you describe. He is far too proud." His gaze narrowed. "You are certain?"

She should have known he wouldn't believe her. DeMarc *studied* with him. "He is not obvious. He is most subtle. And yes, I am certain."

"If what you say is true, then I will escort you when you go in search of your young man."

Ramsey see her in her costume? Realize her identity? Know her to be the woman who'd all but begged him to take her in a dark alley? Her cheeks burned at the idea. He saw the bright flush on her cheeks, and something withdrew in his expression, a subtle shift, a door closing.

He thought she didn't want a witness to her tryst, she realized. Of course. What else was he to think? Still, it hurt that he thought so little of her. Which was stupid. He didn't know her.

"No," she said, lifting her chin. "You cannot. That is the problem. The gentleman I am seeking will not come to me if he sees another man in my vicinity. So you see it is imperative I keep DeMarc from following me, just as it is imperative that I go alone."

"Dear God, woman," he said with a trace of anger, "no man is worth imperiling yourself. If you really fear DeMarc so much, you would be a fool to risk yourself for an assignation."

"I do not know *what* I fear!" Helena exclaimed, exasperated. Would DeMarc hurt her? She did not know. She only knew that she was afraid, afraid to walk alone down a busy street in broad daylight because he would be walking fifty feet behind; afraid to look out a window because he would be there, standing at a street curb or reading a newspaper on a bench; afraid to turn a corner because he might be waiting for her.

"DeMarc believes that I have purposefully beguiled him," she continued, her hand rising in an unconscious, imploring bid for understanding. "I think he is unbalanced. He *wants* me to know that he follows me, spies on me, watches my every move."

"And you have not purposefully beguiled him? Teased him into this state?"

The cool question shocked her more than anything else he could have said.

"No," she whispered. "No. I am not . . ." But then honesty jolted her with sensually explicit memories, and she could not continue her mechanical denial. Her cheeks grew chafed with hot humiliation. That is exactly the woman she'd been a week ago.

She struggled on, tongue-tied with misery. "He has even gained access to my bedchamber. He spread them on my coverlet as a sort of warning that there is no place sacrosanct. No place where I am invulnerable."

"Spread what across your coverlet? Left what?"

"Roses," she said dully. "All those roses."

"Roses?"

Something in Ram's voice caused Helena to look up from the crumpled kerchief she'd twisted into a ball in her lap. "Yes. I find them everywhere. Like the one that—" She stopped herself before she mentioned the boy at Vauxhall who had pressed a rose into her hand on the night they'd met. Anxiety was making her careless.

Ram's brow furrowed. "But DeMarc is extremely allergic to all manner of flowers. We held a bout in a garden once, and DeMarc attended. He reacted most violently, ultimately having to withdraw from the match."

"You choose not to believe me." Helena shook her head. "I do not care. What I care about is whether you intend to honor your pledge to serve me at my request. I am making that request now."

Ram stood up and she followed suit, determined not to let him cow her with his skepticism. He had no reason to trust her. He did not know her. Perhaps she *was* overestimating her danger, but she did not want to search for Oswald when she was afraid to leave the house. Added to which, she needed to slip out from under the viscount's constant observation or else, even if she did find Oswald, he would only run away upon seeing DeMarc. And then, if DeMarc confronted her later . . . when she was alone . . . She drew a shaky breath.

"You make little sense, Miss Nash. You refuse to let me accompany you, and yet you insist you are in danger."

"I *fear* I am in danger. I am not so dull-witted nor so certain of my situation that I don't realize that what I perceive to be a danger may be in fact no more than an annoyance. You doubt DeMarc's . . . *interest* yourself. But I dislike fearing anything, Mr. Munro. It is not a pleasant way to live. Perhaps you have never been afraid?"

It was an unworthy taunt—particularly knowing his history and that he'd endured nearly two years in a dungeon—but from the slight tensing of his shoulders she saw that it had hit its mark.

"I have come to you seeking the means to rid myself of my fear, precisely because I myself am uncertain of whether DeMarc poses a real or an imagined danger," she said with as much dignity as she could find.

"I would *think* you would be appreciative of my refusal to give in to hysteria and insist you guard my every step for as long as I desire. I would *think* you would see this as a relatively simple and expedient way to repay a debt of some standing, one *you* maintained you owed, not one I insisted upon."

She looked him straight in the eye. "All I want, Mr. Munro, is some knowledge of how to protect myself so that I might have the confidence necessary to go about freely. Surely you can understand that?"

He considered her for a long moment. "A well-thought-out argument, Miss Nash," he finally said. "Are you always so lucid?"

An image of his arms holding her against a damp brick wall as she pulled his head down to meet her rising lips bloomed in her mind's eye. "No." Her gaze dropped. "I fear I am not."

He smiled, but his gaze was still assessing. "All right, Miss Nash. I will teach you. Come to me on those days DeMarc prepares for the tournament, and Gaspard will bring you up here by the servants' staircase."

He bent down suddenly and swept something up from the floor. Then he straightened and reached out, securing her hand. His touch electrified her. His fingers were lean and long, as gracefully wrought as one of his beautiful, deadly swords, and just as strong. He prised her hand open and placed the little silk rose in the center of her palm, then very carefully, with almost ritual gentleness, folded her fingers back atop it. "We shall count your lessons a percentage of my debt. Keep this until it is paid in full."

"Thank you," she said, aware that fear marched alongside her gratitude. Gratitude that he'd agreed, fear that he would find her out.

Fool. From the vantage of his window, Ramsey watched Helena wait while the driver withdrew the stair block from within the carriage. When he'd received the note he'd thought—God help him—he'd thought she'd come in reply to his hushed, irreverent plea to become his lover. For those few, eviscerating moments his heart had hammered in amazement and gratitude.

Then he'd heard her light York-accented voice, so unlike the husky, cool whispers in which she'd spoken before, and he'd known: She'd come to him as a stranger.

He should have known better.

As he watched her from above, she looked up over her shoulder as if she had felt his gaze, but the darkness of the room concealed him. Even on this dank midafternoon, her blonde hair glistened like new-pulled taffy, and her skin shimmered like mist-cloaked alabaster. He had forgotten how beautiful she was. But then, it wasn't her beauty that had attracted him. Beauty was not always a boon.

But she *was* beautiful, like a gorgeous statue wrought in the finest marble, smooth and cool and quiescent, unaffected by the gawking crowds, aloof, immutable, her isolation a mystery and a challenge.

Except he knew it to be a lie. He knew her refined, unassailable façade masked a passionate nature. He almost wished he didn't. Almost. He raked a hand through his hair as she disappeared into the carriage and drove away.

Whatever else he believed after their conversation, he no longer believed Helena Nash searched for a lover gone missing. Not only because a woman like Helena Nash did not take lovers, but because there had been nothing about her in the least ardent or eager as she spoke of the man she wanted to find.

There had been desperation, yes. Even anger, but not affection. And most certainly not passion. He knew the taste, the cadence, the sound of her passion. Its memory had damned him to too many sleepless nights.

So who was she looking for, and why? Unconsciously his hand lifted to the gold rose pinning his cravat. From her manner, he would almost think that she owed moneylenders, except that he had never heard of anyone having to search for a moneylender whom they wished to repay. Then *who?*

And what was this of *roses?*

Ram stood at the doorway to St. Bride's walled garden. His neck was blistered from the sun, and his fingers were cracked and embedded with dirt. His thighs ached from bending down all day, and his shirt clung to his back, sweat-stained.

But the soft late-afternoon air whispered balm-like across his face, and the perfect clarity of the mountain sunlight etched each rose vibrantly against the deep green banks of foliage that carried them. A few thrushes trilled from deep in their thorny bowers, and the trickle of water bubbling from the well answered their music with its own. Objectively, Ram did not think anything in the world could match this place for beauty.

"Do you love them or hate them?" a voice asked seriously.

Ram looked around. Surprisingly it was Brother Martin, the abbey's crabbed and crabby herbalist who stood beside him, his thoughtful gaze fixed on the blazing and brilliant-hued beds of roses he so often, and so publicly, denigrated as nature's useless fribbles. Brother Martin also very publicly had no use for St. Bride's orphans, unless he could make use of them to weed his own extensive herb garden, so that he stood here now, speaking to Ram for the first time as a man, if not an equal, gave Ram pause and made him consider his answer.

"A little of both, I suppose," he finally said.

Brother Martin nodded. "That's the way of things out there in the world. Hate and love, longing and aversion, two sides of the same coin, and why that should be is a mystery, and beauty for beauty's sake one of God's greatest conundrums."

"How is that?"

Brother Martin glanced at him sideways. "Well, young Munro, is beauty without merit a waste . . . or a gift?"

"Why do you dislike the rose garden so much?" Ram asked suddenly.

"I don't," Brother Martin said, frowning as he turned away, their momentary equality apparently ending, "I like it too well."

"Mr. Munro?" Gaspard stood in the doorway.

With a start, Ram turned from the window. "Ah, Gaspard. Good. I need you to send a note." He could not follow Helena himself. There was something between them. She could feel his gaze, his presence, too easily. But he could send someone else. Someone who would be watching the viscount DeMarc as well. And closely. That left out Bill Sorry.

"Yes, sir. At once." Gaspard came into the room, holding out a sealed envelope. "This came for you a short while ago. I thought it best not to interrupt you and the young lady."

"You aren't implying anything improper went on in this room, are you, Gaspard?" Ram asked in the casual tones that those who knew him well found it best not to ignore.

"No, sir," Gaspard said, repressing a flicker of surprise. "Not in the least. I did not presume a need for discretion as much as prudence. The young lady looked most resolved."

At this Ram smiled. "Aye. She is that. But you are mistaken, Gaspard. A need for discretion in regards to her is most important. Not a word of her visit or any subsequent visits are ever to leave here. Do we understand one another, Gaspard?"

"Absolutely."

"No scandal will ever touch her in any manner," he said, his voice losing all semblance of its customary nonchalance. "Her name will never be misused, whether by the lowest knave or the highest prince."

Gaspard's remaining eye blinked, but he managed to stifle his amazement. He had never heard Ram talk in such a manner, more as though he was making an oath than stating an intention. "No, sir."

"Good." Ram smiled suddenly, as if fully aware that he'd disconcerted the Frenchman. He relaxed, taking the note Gaspard still held out, albeit with none-too-steady fingers, and tapping the envelope thoughtfully against his jaw. "I have never lost my concentration like that. Never. It quite oversets me."

At once Gaspard realized Ram was referring to his bout with DeMarc. "It was the woman," Gaspard said sympathetically.

"You are not comforting me, Gaspard."

"It is not meant to be a comfort, sir. It is meant to be a warning." And suddenly the older man grinned. "How do you think I lost this eye?"

Ram smiled back, knowing full well that the loss of Gaspard's eye had nothing to do with a woman, and tore open the envelope, withdrawing a thin sheet of paper scrawled over in a hand he did not recognize. As he read, the smile died on his lips.

"What is it?" Gaspard asked. Ram's gaze was riveted, fixed on some inner thought, and it seemed not to be a pleasant one.

"Arnoux," Ram answered. "This letter is from Arnoux."

"The guard from LeMons dungeon?" Gaspard asked incredulously.

"Yes," said Ram. Dissipated, cynical, and bored, Phillipe Arnoux had been no better and no worse than the rest of the guards who had had the "care" of the prisoners in the dungeons; he was only younger. A member of the minor aristocracy who had had the foresight to back the rebellion, he had moved from one regiment to another, finally ending up with an attachment to the prison.

When he beat a man it had been a desultory business,

meaning no more to him than whipping a surly cur from his path. The only time he had exhibited any real fervor had been during the sword fights the guards had arranged between some prisoners and themselves. Duels arranged, they claimed, to sharpen the skills of their men. Duels in which the victor must always be the guard.

Oh, the prisoners—undernourished, vermin ridden, and weakened by captivity—were allowed to defend themselves. But it had been made abundantly clear that if a prisoner caused any lasting injury to a guard, he would pay with a finger. Or a hand.

Or an eye.

Ram had been a special favorite, being not just good, but exceptionally good. He had gotten better. For while it was most assuredly not a very fair way of orchestrating a duel, those unfair duels where he fought to keep from being maimed at the same time as he held back from causing any lasting harm, had honed his skills far better than all the lessons his father arranged for him, even better than those lessons the monk Toussaint had taught him at St. Bride's.

Arnoux had been the best of those who'd challenged Ram.

"What does he want? What does he say?"

The corner of Ram's mouth lifted in its old, cynical curve. "He is arriving in London under special diplomatic protection as part of the retinue of a French contestant."

"What? He wishes to lift a toast to old times?" Gaspard said bitterly.

"No. He wants to tell me who betrayed us to the French."

Gaspard's eye widened.

"And he wants a lot of money for the information."

EIGHTEEN

❧

BALESTRA:
Italian. A forward leap,
typically followed by an attack

"INDEED, MR. TAWSTER, I have it from my friend's own lips that Ramsey Munro challenged a roomful of gentlemen to a duel to the first blood."

Helena, studying Mr. Turner's latest painting in the Royal Academy show at Somerset House, swung about looking for the speaker. Ramsey? Dueling? *Was he hurt?*

At once she saw Lord Figburt, sitting on a marble bench between the vicar and Lady Tilpot. Only concentrated effort kept Helena from demanding the essentials. She strained to hear more.

"Yes. I have heard the same scandal broth myself. Won them all, didn't he?" the vicar asked in awed tones. "Blessed Virgin, but he must be extraordinary!"

Helena's shoulders relaxed, and she shut her eyes as relief poured through her. Ram was not hurt. It had been two days since she had gone to his salle, and during those two days there had scarce been a moment when she had not thought of him.

He had been keeping apprised of her and her sisters' situations for years, obliquely, without interference or communication. He had been all the while preparing to honor his oath to her family. Such commitment to a vow, such honorable intentness, touched her deeply, struck an answering chord.

"More's the pity," Lady Tilpot sniffed. "The fellow is infamous. Some woman's name is bandied about, and he has the audacity to challenge his betters! Probably just some Cheapside trollop."

She exchanged superior looks with her friend Mrs. Barnes, who'd joined their excursion. As with most of this Wednesday afternoon crowd, they were far more interested in inspecting each other than the paintings. But it was "the" place to be seen, and therefore Flora must be here. Helena looked around for the girl.

Flora was heading toward what the wits had christened the Exhibition Stare Case, due to certain nasty young men's predilection for gathering round the base of the spiral staircase when a young lady mounted it to see what could be seen from beneath. At the last minute Flora veered off, something bright and pretty having caught her magpie eye, and Helena returned her attention to the speakers.

"Still, that does seem rather excessive," Mrs. Barnes was saying in knowing tones. "Even for a baseborn blackguard."

The blood rose in Helena's cheeks. It had been her name being bandied about. She was certain of it. She had returned to her rooms after seeing Munro two days ago to find an unsigned letter awaiting her. And with it a desiccated rose. "There are consequences for acting the wanton," it had read.

It had to have been DeMarc. He had seen her at Ram's salle, and his views on the women who went there were clear. Thankfully, the viscount, whether he'd not been invited or had chosen not to attend, was not with them this afternoon. Now she wondered if his absence was a matter of cravenness. She had no doubt that his revenge had been in sowing the germ of a dreadful rumor, knowing full well that if any blemish attached itself to her name, Lady Tilpot would send her packing.

But she doubted DeMarc was afraid of looking her in the eye after such a despicable act. He was more likely to come to gloat. Something else must have kept him away.

She had tried to do her best to act on Flora's behalf. Each day she scoured the newspapers looking for some message from Oswald. There had been none. And each day that Flora's pregnancy progressed, the girl's apprehension for her erstwhile husband grew. She was making herself sick with worry. For the sake of the child she carried, Flora needed to hear from Oswald.

"No, not a common woman," Lady Tilpot agreed thoughtfully. "It must have been a lady. How delicious. Who was the lady who prompted the challenges, do you suppose?" She placed her chubby finger alongside her nose, her little raisin eyes glittering. "Come, Lord Figburt, do tell us."

"But ma'am"—the boy's face had gone red—"I can scarce say as I do not know. Mr. Munro *won* the challenges, as you know, every single one, and as such, those whom he fought would scarce be worthy of the name of gentleman if they revealed the identity of the lady Munro went to such lengths to protect."

Lady Tilpot's little chins quivered with irritation. "Bosh! Someone must know. And I shall find out."

"Please, ma'am," Lord Figburt said unhappily. "I did not mean to incite your interest, I only mentioned the matter because it was by all accounts a magnificent, nay, an unparalleled exhibit of swordplay. Munro is superb!"

Helena listened in amazement. Could this be the same boy who had drunkenly accosted her in Vauxhall Garden? Earlier today, when he had been introduced to Helena, he'd met her gaze with respectful admiration, but not a whit of recognition. He'd matured in a few short weeks, his bearing straighter, his expression courteous. Ram's doing. He obviously idolized and therefore sought to emulate his master.

"Hm." Lady Tilpot did not bother hiding her irritation. "Well, young man, I am of the opinion that it is unwise for members of the lower classes to fancy themselves maestros and so forth. Leads to that Jacobin nonsense that has destroyed France."

"France is hardly destroyed." The women looked at Mrs. Winebarger, who, having finished her contemplation of the latest portrait of Prince George, had returned to her companions. She had not come with them but had exclaimed at the happy chance that had led to her meeting them there. Lady Tilpot and Mrs. Barnes could do nothing but agree. For her part, Helena was delighted. She liked the lady.

Her current comment was met by a stony and lengthy

silence that was only broken when Mrs. Barnes, puffing aside a feather, intoned, "You are Prussian, are you not, Mrs. Winebarger?"

"Yes."

"Ah, then. That explains it."

Mrs. Winebarger's cheeks pinked, and young Lord Figburt plowed into the even stonier silence. "He won't be in the lower classes any longer."

"Excuse me?" the vicar said, looking confused.

"Ramsey Munro. He is going to be a marquis."

"Ha." Mrs. Barnes revealed the edge of a set of extraordinarily yellow little teeth. "Ha. Ha. Most amusing, Lord Figburt."

"I didn't mean it to be amusing, Mrs. Barnes. I am quite serious," the boy said earnestly. "Ramsey Munro is being made heir to the marquis of Cottrell."

"Cottrell?" The vicar's eyes widened. "Why, yes. There is a resemblance, isn't there?"

"Of course there is, Vicar," Lady Tilpot said instructively. "As soon as the young man appeared in town, it was clear who his parents were. Or, at least, who *one* of them was.

"Cottrell's son was a ne'er-do-well. Left town under quite questionable circumstances and went to live in Scotland. That being the case, Lord knows how many Cottrell eyes one might find north of Edinburgh. I am sure the countryside is awash in them.

"He died in Scotland, too. In some tavern brawl over a woman, I believe. So it would seem that the seed has not fallen far from the tree." Her lips puckered with amusement.

"But—" Lord Figburt began, his young face ruddy with his determination to defend his paragon.

"But nothing, young man; the marquisate falls under the directive of primogeniture," Mrs. Barnes declared and received a nod of approval from Lady Tilpot. "A bastard cannot inherit. Ramsey Munro is a bastard, and that is the end of it."

"I dislike to disagree, ma'am—"

"Then don't."

"I must. You see, the present marquis has lately discovered that Mr. Munro's parents were indeed legally wed and in the Church of England. So Mr. Munro is not"—he colored, swallowed, and glanced at Mrs. Winebarger—"er, merry-begot."

"What?"

Every head in the Great Room turned to see what had occasioned such a noise. Lady Tilpot scowled and then, seeing Helena's profile turned in her direction, called out curtly, "Go find Flora, Miss Nash! The girl will get a crink in her neck what with staring up at all these pictures so long. Crinks ain't charming."

In a daze, Helena rose. Her head swam as she moved automatically through the crowd. *Ramsey Munro was going to be the marquis of Cottrell.*

Ramsey Munro, swordsmaster and probable rake, had lived much as she lived, in a world of impoverished gentlefolk, untitled gentry, and the bastard children of their peers, existing on the fringes of Society, not a part of it, yet not apart from it. Ramsey Munro, bastard grandson of a marquis, was someone an impoverished gentlewoman might know. Ramsey Munro, the heir to the marquisate of Cottrell, was far above her touch.

Well, she thought, a little light-headed, a bit numb, just as well. She had Flora to think about and Oswald to find.

And tomorrow was her first fencing lesson.

NINETEEN

ENGAGEMENT:
when sword blades are in contact
with each other

RAMSEY MUNRO, eyeing his students in the salle, heard the clock chime the hour with a mixture of anticipation and dread, and that amused him. Ten minutes. All the years he had lived, the things he'd done, and the things that had been done to him, and here the imminent arrival of this young woman had him confounded and anxious and aroused. Ten minutes and Helena would be whisked discreetly to his private chambers on the upper floor while Viscount DeMarc made his cuts in the salle. That she did not come for the reason one would hope when a young lady was whisked discreetly to one's private chambers only made the situation more piquant.

"Make some attempt, Lord Figburt, to keep your feet from slapping the floor," he called out as he walked down the line of students.

The door opened behind him, and he heard Gaspard greet DeMarc. He ignored the viscount's entrance, knowing that to do so gave grist to the gossip mill that had him refusing the viscount's subsequent challenges out of fear of losing. In truth, he simply did not quite trust himself to cross swords with a man who purportedly hounded Helena. Which, he supposed, was again amusing.

He was far too old to succumb to callow possessiveness. He should have been able to meet the viscount's usual stiff superiority with an ironic lift of his brow. But he couldn't. He looked at the viscount and wanted to grab him by his perfect white cravat and drag him into the kitchen and demand to know if he was bothering Helena. But Ram resisted.

DeMarc infatuated with Helena was one thing—more than one man had fallen under her cool, enigmatic spell, himself being a prime example—but *obsessed* with her? He would have said DeMarc was incapable of being obsessed with anything other than his own consequence. And yet he knew better than to dismiss DeMarc out of hand. There was something not right about him.

He forced himself to nod a greeting. DeMarc was not the first man he despised to whom he had taught swordplay. In LeMons dungeon he had taught a smuggler named Callum Lamont some of his skills.

"Why are you teaching me?" the filthy young man had demanded as he dropped the stick he'd been using as a sword and backed away from the delicately swirling tip of Ram's own makeshift wooden rapier. "You and your friends there ain't exactly chummy with the rest of us here."

"You saved my friend's life."

"And you always repay your debts?" the man sneered.

Lamont had enough ability and a native cunning that he might actually be a threat someday. To someone. But that would mean he would have to be freed. And no one left LeMons dungeon. Not alive. At least teaching him served to pass the long, tedious hours of imprisonment. Hours broken only by torture and interrogation. And the man had kept Kit from being knifed in the back. For whatever reasons.

"That's right, ain't it?" Lamont demanded. *"You four think you're just better than the lot of us. You think you can still afford things like honor and nobility. And what's it gotten you? An appointment with the guillotine. Bah! What's it worth to you now, I wants to know? Why bother?"*

"Call it a habit," Ram answered unconcernedly.

"It's pride," the man enjoined. *His gaze fixed on Ram's weapon.*

Ram considered. "All right. Now, do you intend to use your arm as a sword, because I can promise it makes a poor substitute for steel. Or even wood."

Aye. Lamont had had the right of that at least. He had pride. Too much. Ram started back down the line toward the viscount. "Viscount, welcome."

"Mr. Munro," the viscount returned, his manner decidedly cold since he had seen Helena in the salle.

Clearly he had disapproved. Had DeMarc been the originator of the rumors attached to Helena's name? But the notion of the poker-faced, stiff-rumped viscount whispering into some tale-monger's ear was, again, incongruous.

"Would you care to scrimmage?" the viscount asked loudly enough for everyone in the vicinity to hear the challenge. Subtlety was not the viscount's strong suit. Another point against his using roses and whispers to frighten Helena.

"Nothing would afford me greater pleasure," Ram replied. "But, alas, I cannot. My grandfather's solicitor insists on a confabulation."

What better way to distract DeMarc than with the teeth-grinding matter of Ram's nascent gentility? The diversion worked. The viscount's skin stretched tight across his forehead.

"A mixed blessing, your newfound respectability. I foresee you spending a lifetime floundering desperately," DeMarc's upper lip curled back over his front teeth, "through the paperwork, that is."

"Oh, I understood you quite clearly, Viscount." For a few seconds Ram considered staying and giving the viscount the lesson he'd requested. And a few others besides. After all, how long could it take?

Then, with an inner sigh, he realized that the only characteristic DeMarc owned in greater quantity than his snobbery was his skill with a sword. He was taking this tournament seriously, too. Each day he grew more adept, more capable. Teaching him a lesson might, in fact, take too long.

And Helena waited.

"Perhaps later," Ram said. The viscount shrugged and went in search of another opponent as Ram watched.

Roses. Even supposing DeMarc could suppress his physical reaction to them, why choose a flower he could barely tolerate to terrorize Helena? Either the viscount knew of the association between Ram and the Nash family and the significance of roses in their shared history, or someone else had suggested the device to him, or it was a coincidence.

Ram disliked coincidences.

But how to approach DeMarc to ask him these things? And when was the right time for such an interview? He didn't want to tip his hand too early, before his own agents had collected what information they could.

So far, Bill had learned that, yes, DeMarc did spend a great deal of time in the vicinity of Miss Helena Nash. But, as Bill had scrupulously pointed out, that also meant that the viscount spent a good deal of time in the vicinity of Flora Tilpot, a pretty young heiress with a most considerable fortune.

As far as roses . . . no one had ever seen the viscount with a rose. But that did not mean the viscount did not have someone else acting for him. Except there was no evidence of that, either.

Perhaps they came from some other source? Some other besotted idiot? A footman Helena had ignored? A merchant? Even a florist? He could easily understand any man coming under the spell of her quiet-unquiet eyes, being charmed by the way she bit her bottom lip to keep from laughing, being beguiled by the ironic arch of her honey-colored brows. But few had seen those aspects of her except for him.

She had created for public viewing a face at once dignified, serene, and unresponsive. He stood in the rare company, he thought with a flash of hunger, of those few men who had seen Miss Helena Nash without her mask on. Any mask.

He glanced at the clock. It was quarter past the hour. He left the salle and took the servants' stairs up to the second level, pushing soundlessly through the swinging green baize door at the top and moving rapidly down the carpeted corridor to the corner room, where he'd arranged for Gaspard to take her.

"—do you think he will win?" he heard Helena ask.

"It depends on his competition, n'est-ce pas?" Gaspard answered.

The reprobate. Gaspard was to have come to Ram at once upon Helena's arrival, not sit here basking in the lady's beauty. That was Ram's place.

He settled his shoulder against the wall, shamelessly eavesdropping. She was here. In his house. In his room. The sense of pleasure this brought confounded him. Another source of amusement. He should abscond with the wench, he supposed idly, haul her off to Gretna Green and thereby assure the rest of his days were filled with delicious self-irony.

He smiled ruefully. Probably best to abscond with a woman *before* one taught her to fence . . .

"Then Mr. Munro *will* be entering the competition?"

"I do not know. Last week . . ." Gaspard's French accents fell away invitingly, "he was planning to enter in hopes of taking the winner's portion of the gate. But now his need is not so pressing."

"The gate," Helena repeated uncomprehendingly.

"*Oui*, Miss. The gate, the sum total amount of admissions paid by the spectators. The winners at the various levels are not only awarded a purse made up of the entry fees charged the combatants, but they also receive a percent of the gate. The higher the level at which they win, the greater their percentage. The winner of the entire competition stands to make a great deal of money. And then," his voice lowered suggestively, "there are also the private wagers."

"Mr. Munro would fight for money?" The shock Ram heard in her voice brought reality crashing back in on him. Whatever circumstances might have made her a paid companion, she was a lady, and not just any lady, but the most respectable of ladies. His grandsire might make him a marquis, but would he ever be gentleman enough for her? His hand rose briefly to touch the mark seared into his pectoral. How many "gentlemen" had been branded in a French dungeon?

"Filthy lucre, ma'amselle?" Gaspard sounded defensive.

"Pardon, monsieur. What a buffleheaded prig I must sound," she apologized, and he was struck by her tone. No mumbled girlish embarrassment, only a woman's candor. "It is just that from the reverence with which Mr. Munro spoke of his art, I thought he would only enter a competition to test himself."

"Ram Munro has been tested more times than any mortal man should be, miss," Gaspard declared loyally. "He does not need to pit himself against others to know his own abilities."

A long pause. "You mean in France, don't you? What happened—"

No. "Gaspard?"

Ram entered the room without any apparent haste. *No, my love. Even you cannot go there.* "Ah. Here you are."

His factotum swung around guiltily. "Sir?"

"There's a certain young jackanapes belowstairs who requires a lesson. Milord Figburt has decided to challenge anyone who carries a pointy stick. I would like your stick to be very pointy, indeed." As he spoke, his gaze fell hungrily on Helena.

She had dressed for their lesson in a simple ecru-colored gown printed over with charcoal gray florets, the bodice covered by the light material of a close-fitting bottle-green spencer. She had laid a chipped straw hat on the table beside the smallswords Gaspard had provided, uncovering a gleaming and neatly coiffed head of hair.

"Lord Figburt, you say, sir? Impertinent pup! It will be a delight. Miss Nash? A pleasure." Gaspard bowed to Helena and hastened from the room.

For a moment Helena eyed Ram warily, a combatant sizing up her opponent. Ram could appreciate the examination. He held his arms out to his sides and turned in a slow circle. "I hope you approve your choice, Miss Nash," he said, "because it is a bit late to be checking teeth."

Her expression gave nothing away. No amusement. No embarrassment. My, but she had trained her countenance well. He preferred the Helena of Vauxhall Garden with her laughing, passionate mouth and husky voice. This mask was much more difficult to penetrate. "You mistake my interest in you, Mr. Munro," she said.

"Damn. I was afraid of that," he said regretfully, and was rewarded by the slightest quirk of her lips. "But tell me, what were you speculating on, then?"

"I was wondering that, as the newly discovered heir of the marquis of Cottrell, you are still teaching in your salle."

One brow rose. Now *this* was an interesting development. Undisguised inquisitiveness? From the distant, self-contained Miss Nash? "Miss Nash, Society is ripe with stories of your beauty, your serenity, your good nature. I do not, however, recall any stories that glorify your frankness. Is this perhaps a newfound virtue?"

Ah! *There*. Finally. He'd teased a smile from her. "I am not sure anyone would count it a virtue, Mr. Munro."

"I would." At her blush, he smiled. "As to your kind interest in my late rise to the exalted position known as 'heir,' I have discovered that the situation's primary occupation is anticipating the death of one's progenitor." She was definitely biting her bottom lip to keep from smiling.

"But," he intoned resignedly, "I am leery of promises of impending death—death, in my experience, having the nasty habit of either sneaking in uninvited or refusing to make a timely appearance altogether. That being the case, I have decided to hedge my bets and keep alive my current means of providing for myself."

Her lashes slipped down to cover her gaze, but not before he saw the appreciative gleam in them. "You are extremely impious," she said.

"Aren't I, though?" he murmured, enjoying the way the light from the window limned the curve of her cheek. "Do you think my impiety puts me in danger of losing my immortal soul?"

"No," she said, her smile not so much shy as unused. "Simple impiety, I would presume, falls well down the list of what threatens your soul."

"Oh, Miss Nash. I fear what I will create in you," he said, shaking his head.

She looked taken aback. "Sir?"

"You already fence better than most of my students." *And you are far too appealing, transforming before my eyes into a woman as formidable of mind as she is of form.* He picked up one of the two smallswords Gaspard had left on the table. "Shall we begin?"

"Of course." At once, she was all business. Her eyes had darkened, and he realized that for a few minutes she had forgotten the need that had sent her here.

She unbuttoned the spencer and shrugged out of it, placing it on the table. Beneath, her dress was modest, the neck modest, the sleeves short little puffs. She *might* be able to move in that.

"I am ready." Uneasiness had crept into her voice. *Damn.* "What do I do?"

Smile again. Want me. "Take a stance as if you were confronting an attacker."

She nodded, squaring her shoulders dutifully and pokering up as tall as her five and a half feet allowed. Very courageous-looking. Very stiff. She had to relax.

"No, Miss Nash. We are not facing a firing squad; we are trying to present the smallest possible target."

She nodded again, very seriously, and crouched low, looking up at him expectantly. She looked like an enchanting little blonde hedgehog. But she was still painfully rigid and heartbreakingly earnest. "No, Miss Nash. We are not preparing to roll down a hill; we are preparing to defend ourselves."

With a sound of frustration, she drew upright. "Fine. Then how should *we* be standing, Mr. Munro?"

"Hips square, thighs lightly flexed, back subtly arched, shoulders turned slightly. Relaxed, supple, pliant."

She contorted into an impossible alignment, somehow managing to do everything he had bid her and still be all wrong. "Like this?"

"No." He tried very hard not to smile. He did not succeed.

Her light eyes narrowed on his smile, but she straightened, her lips pressed tight. He didn't suppose anyone had laughed at Helena Nash in a good long while. At least she'd forgotten her former anxiety. "Demonstrate."

He took the position. She came closer, examining his stance minutely as she walked in a slow circle around him, her gaze traveling unhurriedly over his body, measuring his arms, assessing his torso, moving with slow deliberation down his thighs and along his arms. With each passing tick of the clock, the touch of her gaze grew to feel more like a caress. Though when she stopped behind him he could not see her, he smelled the light floral scent of her perfume and heard the soft sound of her breathing. The bloody cut of his trousers suddenly seemed painfully tight.

"Do you think you have it yet?"

"Not yet." She came back within his field of vision, her head tilting one way and then another as she considered him. A strand of pale hair fell loose of its pins, unraveling in silky slow motion down her cheek to dangle flirtatiously on her shoulder. It gleamed like mill floss. The tip of her tongue peeped out as she concentrated, touching the very center of her bowed upper lip. Her tongue had tasted of oranges, been warm and eager . . .

"*Surely* you have studied the pose long enough?" he asked in a stilted voice.

"Not yet." She cleared her throat— No. She stifled a laugh.

The minx was *laughing*, getting a little of her own back for his teasing. Two could play at this game.

He abandoned his pose, and then slowly, giving her a chance to erase her telling grin, turned around and faced her. "Do you think you can replicate my stance now?" he asked equitably.

"Oh, I think so." Confidently, she struck the same pose he'd held. Honesty forced him to admit that she did a more than fair approximation of it. But he was in no mood to extend mercy.

"Pitiful," he said.

Her head snapped around in comical disbelief. "What?"

"I have seen carriage posts more supple."

Her skin pinked, but she gamely attempted to arch her back more fully, and in doing so badly overcompensated.

"Ah! I see," he said sagely. "You are planning a career as a contortionist and are demonstrating your skills for me. Brava. Now, shall we try fencing?"

She scowled. "Don't mock me. *Show me.*"

Just the invitation he'd been waiting for. He moved in behind her looping his arm around her waist and pulling her tightly against his chest. At once she stiffened. He ignored the tensing of her body, molding her soft curves to the hard line of his torso, spreading one hand flat over her belly, her bum nestled intimately against his groin, her shoulder blades pressed like wings into his chest.

He bowed over her and slid his free hand languorously down her bare arm to clasp her slender wrist. He pulled her arm up, bending it gently so that her elbow fit snugly into the crook of his arm. Then he wrapped her hand around the hilt of the smallsword. He enveloped her with his body, fitting himself over her lithe, well-curved form.

Her heart jumped into a patter. He could feel its anxious rhythm like rain strikes against his breast, light and urgent. Her belly muscles tensed beneath his broad palm.

He lowered his lips and whispered, "Relax, Miss Nash. Swordplay is just another dance: a dance of death."

A shiver rippled through her. He could feel the light aura of heat rising from her skin. "It's a dance mercurial and elegant, stylized and spontaneous," he murmured. "The wary salute, the irresistible invitation, the passionate encounter, the breathless disengagement.

"Easy, Miss Nash. You're trembling. Lie back against me."

"I can't."

Such honesty. 'Twas much more provocative than false bravado.

"Why is that?" he whispered, brushing the silken hair at the nape of her neck.

"You have me articulated so far forward, sir, that if I relax I'll fall over."

His head jerked up as though she'd doused him with ice water. Which she had. Verbal ice water.

"I'll catch you," he said, trying to recapture the warm, intimate tone he'd been using.

"Is that supposed to be comforting?" she asked. "Because I am decidedly *not* feeling reassured. And I do not believe you mean me to be, do you? Tell me, Mr. Munro, by saying you will catch me if I fall, do you desire that I feel grateful, secure, or threatened?"

Well, damn, she had him there. He straightened a little, giving her question serious consideration. "I'm not sure," he admitted.

"Ah." She nodded, craning her neck around to look him in the eye. "I understand. You are at variance with yourself."

"I am?" Lord, but she was fascinating. Even more fascinating than beautiful. Which was saying a good deal.

She twisted around even more so that she could speak to him eye to eye, and thus he found he was actually holding her suspended now, one arm around her waist, the other still supporting the arm he held out above them. They must look like some bizarre statue, he thought dazedly, Man and Woman caught in some eternal struggle to see which one would poke a hole in the ceiling.

He looked down into her eyes. Their expression was sympathetic.

"Yes," she said. "You see, masculine conceit requires that as you are holding me intimately, I must feel some maidenly trepidation, a fluttering within, a frisson of fear coupled with heady expectation. I suspect it would be even more necessary for your masculine pride that I feel thus if you were carrying me. Or catching me."

"You have a point," he conceded, lowering their arms and wresting the sword from her hand. She relinquished it without complaint, and with her newly freed hand clutched at his bicep. She needn't have worried, he wasn't going to drop her. This was far too interesting. Besides, he had her balanced effortlessly now, as if they usually conversed this way.

No, this is not what he had planned. Yet there was no denying it had its own tantalizing charm. He'd never discussed seduction with a woman before. At least not a woman he wanted to seduce.

She nodded again, even more sympathetically. "On

the other hand, as a gentleman you *despise* the idea that you might cause me alarm when it is your duty, indeed, *your sworn pledge* to safeguard, protect, and even serve me."

He studied the lovely, guileless face raised so earnestly to his. She had a chipped front tooth, he realized for the first time. A tiny thing, but as piquant in that perfect oval as mint in sweet tea.

" 'Tis a quandary for you," she said soberly. "But while you may not have always followed your nobler instincts, knowing that I value my virtue, I believe you will stop before . . ." She trailed off, took a small breath, and went on. "I know you would like to lead me astray, but please don't."

"Lead you astray? How charmingly you put it."

Her gaze fell. "I don't know how else to put it."

"And you are quite sure that that is what I meant to do?"

"Yes." Well, she'd been right, of course. He must grant her that. "It is what you do. You are quite notorious, you know."

And then he noticed that his seductiveness didn't appear to be all that, well . . . seductive. She looked uncomfortable, a bit repelled. And he knew why. That last bit had revealed a great deal about what she thought of him and what she thought him to be.

"And you think I have taken the seducer's part many times before."

She didn't need to answer. It was there in her eyes.

"Too many times," he said, and was proud of how bored he sounded, how unaffected.

"How could you not when you are offered what other

men must actively seek? I saw how that woman at the—"
she broke off, and he realized she'd been about to say
something about his kissing that woman at the courte-
san's ball, but that would reveal she'd been there.

She didn't know that the woman had been nothing
more than a pathetic and unsuccessful attempt to purge
her from his thoughts. And he couldn't tell her. Because
then she would know he'd discovered her secret, and for
whatever reason it had become, almost without volition
and certainly without reason, imperative to him that she
tell him herself.

He wanted her. He wanted her trust even more. He
wanted, he realized in some horror, for her to have faith
in him. Dear God! He must indeed be going mad. And
because he wanted her admission, he must present himself in the most disreputable of lights. It was enough to
make even the most cruel gods laugh.

"The woman at the . . . ? " he prodded, angry now because he could not refute her and angrier still that even
if he could refute the trollop at the ball, he could not refute the others. Those others whom he'd bedded that
first year after he'd been made to understand how little
he had.

Because she was quite right. He hadn't refused that
which had been so generously offered. The fact that he
had not accepted nearly as often as she presumed af-
forded him scant satisfaction. The fact that he had availed
himself of those offers and stopped availing himself of
them long *before* her held no meaning to anyone but himself.

"In the salle," she muttered, her gaze shifting away
from his, "I saw how a number of them watched you."

She gave him no latitude; neither would he give her any. "You said *'that* woman.'"

She flushed. "There was one in particular."

"Hm," he said, looking at her lying there in his arms, her heart not a hand's breadth from his, her breasts moving in gentle agitation, her eyes luminous with her lies. "You must point her out to me when you leave. Seeing as how your virtue must remain unassailable." Damn, he'd been unable to keep the edge of bitterness from that.

"But though I am . . ." He could scarce choke the word out. He had never considered himself such, but if she had branded him with the title, he would wear it. ". . . a rake, I am not a cad."

"I know you are not," she said quietly, making his heart pound with the restraint he must impose on arms that wanted to snatch her roughly closer. "I am untried, but I am not naïve."

No. It would have been better for them both if she had been. If she'd been a seventeen-year-old virgin, fresh from the protection of her father's country manor, never having dealt with men who wanted anything other than a dance or honorable wedlock, a girl who had never been pursued or propositioned by men who desired her solely for her beauty, a girl who'd never had to learn to keep her thoughts hidden. *That* girl would not know about what men like him had done.

But then, that girl wouldn't be this woman.

"So I see," he said.

She released a little breath, relieved. "So," she said with a return to her former guilelessness, "I do appreciate the quandary you find yourself in, and I appreciate the fact that you have chosen to subordinate your baser impulses to your native decency."

Then she batted her eyelashes.

There was no other word for it. In a performance notable for its understatedness, it was a glaring misstep.

She had *handled* him!

From the very moment he'd wrapped his arm around her, she had adroitly led him to this, to stepping away and leaving her virtue and dignity intact.

"Very good," he said with terse admiration. "Excellent. If you had dispensed with the last bit, you would have finished me to a turn."

Her eyes widened.

"But, those lashes . . ." He shook his head. "A disappointment, I don't mind telling you. Such a tired old chestnut. Really. 'Twas beneath you."

" 'Tisn't a chestnut," she said, making no effort even to pretend not to know what he was talking about. "It is a standard. A tried-and-true method."

More of her willful tresses had uncoiled from her coiffure, falling in long ribbons that bobbed and swayed with each insignificant movement. His gaze swept over her delicate collarbone, the first modest hint of cleavage above the discreet neckline coloring with a slight flush, spreading like rosy dawn over a snowy landscape.

"You have had much success with the technique?" he asked. If she saw the glint in his Satan-bright eyes, she did not heed it.

"Hm?" She stared up at him. Her lips had parted slightly and looked invitingly soft and accessible. What was she playing now?

"Oh, no," he said firmly. "We are beyond pretense.

Have you managed to dissuade many overfamiliar swains in a similar manner to the one with which you just so expertly managed me?"

"Hm?" She blinked. "Oh. A few. Though not many have gotten far enough along in their—" She flushed. "Well, *you* know."

"I suppose I am flattered?"

She smiled, damn her, as if that was *exactly* what he should feel.

"And what do they do," he went on smoothly, "after you have them tongue-tied and wretched as hell but altogether uncertain how they went from holding a woman who had enflamed their senses to one who much more resembled their spinster governesses?"

"Generally, they release me," she suggested artlessly.

The minx stood in need of a lesson. Exasperation at her machinations, irritation at how easily he had been manipulated, and fury at her assumptions about his profligate sexual history mixed together in a potent brew.

"Far be it from me to disappoint."

He dropped her.

It was not a very long fall, as she was already lying supine in his arm, a mere foot or two above the floor, and he didn't release her entirely, so her fall was broken. But still, it caught her by surprise.

With a soundless "oh!" she landed in a swirl of muslin and unadorned petticoats, exposing pretty, slender calves clad in silk stockings tied with pale green satin ribbons. What little of her coiffure had remained intact tumbled over her face.

He regarded her expectantly, hands on hips, preparing himself for indignation or anger or even, though he profoundly hoped she would bypass this last, mortification. She looked up, pushing back a curtain of gleaming blonde hair, her beautiful, composed face no longer composed and self-possessed but bright with . . . *laughter.* "Touché!"

No scowls, no temper, no reproach.

And with that—a simple, gaily tossed out "touché!"—Ramsey Munro, poor sot that he knew himself to be, realized he was in love with Helena Nash.

TWENTY

〈∞〉

DISENGAGE:
a small movement of the blade under the opponent's blade with the intent to escape

RAM STOOD LOOKING DOWN at her with the oddest expression on his face. When Helena was a girl, there had been an episode when the sugarplums that their father had liked left on the sideboard to ease any midday hunger pangs had started mysteriously disappearing. So one day he had enlisted Helena to stand guard with him in the butler's pantry, which led off the dining room. After an hour's wait, who should saunter into the dining room but their lapdog, Milo.

Milo had taken a casual look around, leapt blithely atop the table, and begun gobbling down sweets. Whereupon her father, armed with a slingshot, had promptly pelted the little bugger in the arse with some dry peas. Milo had shot straight up in the air and spun around, looking exactly like Ram did now, somewhere between panic and astonishment, with a dollop of horror thrown in for good measure.

What was the man thinking?

She hadn't meant to be so forward. She hadn't meant to ask him about his inheritance. She hadn't meant to let him see her irritation when she'd been unable to strike the requested pose. She most *certainly* hadn't meant to mention his conquests. But from the moment he touched her, she knew that the attraction she had hoped desperately had been a result of moonlight, masks, and madness, was just as potent in a bright, empty room when he thought she was a beautiful cipher rather than a hedonistic romp. And that is when she realized that he could have from her anything he wanted with only the smallest of efforts. And what could the future marquis of Cottrell want from a paid companion he had just become reacquainted with except what he had had, by own admission, from countless other ladies?

Self-preservation leapt into play. She must not be seduced by him. It meant too much to her. She could not be simply an afternoon interlude to him.

"Are you all right?" he asked gruffly, and she came to with a jolt, realizing she'd stopped laughing and was staring up at him. "Because you stopped laughing all of a sudden, and now you look deuced strange. Is something hurt, after all?"

"No, no," she mumbled, smoothing her skirts down over her legs. He reached down, and she put her hands in his, allowing him to lift her to her feet. She began feeling a bit uncomfortable at his continued unreadable expression.

"I suppose I shouldn't have dropped you like that." He looked a little angry, grudging, and those were expressions alien to Ramsey Munro's devilishly clever, handsome face.

"I suppose there was some provocation," she admitted. "Shall we call a truce?"

"A truce. Yes."

She tilted her head. He really was behaving most strangely. "And can we continue the lesson?"

"Yes. Of course." He shifted his shoulders as if his shirt was binding. Which, given the way the white material stretched across his broad shoulders, may well have been the case. But he hadn't seemed physically uncomfortable earlier. Then he squared them, much like he was facing the same firing squad he'd accused her of confronting earlier.

"First, the grip." He picked up the smallsword that had fallen to the floor and brought it to her, holding his hand out and showing her how to hold the hilt.

"This," he pointed to the flexible tip of the smallsword, "is the foible. It is the weakest part of the blade, but also the most flexible."

"This," he tapped the bottom of the blade, near the hilt, "is the forte, the strongest part of the blade."

"I see."

"Your goal is not to duel," he told her, now fully a teacher, impersonal and informative. "Your goal is to protect yourself. The concepts of point of line and right of way are immaterial."

"We shall focus on footwork, the parry—" At her questioning look he explained, "The parry is the blocking of an opponent's blow. The feint is attacking in one direction with the intention of switching to another. And finally you shall learn to lunge, to pierce another man's body with a sword."

He watched her closely, gauging her reaction. "You do understand that, when all is said and done, that *is* what dueling is about, that is *why* one learns to fence? So one can stick the tip of a piece of steel into another living being and take his life?"

She felt the blood drain from her face but nodded gamely. With a sudden grimace he threw up his hand.

"This is ridiculous! You don't want to hurt anyone. Look at you! You're a lady, not some vicious bit of Haymarket wares. Why on earth would you need to know this?"

"I told you. Lord DeMarc—"

"Lord DeMarc is a pompous prig who probably reacted poorly when you showed no interest in him. He may even have expressed himself in a manner that seemed menacing, but as to being an actual threat—" He shook his head. "You were frightened. You still are. You have probably never dealt with a man with such conceit, who reacted so strongly to being rebuffed. But believe me, Miss Nash, though it might be rare amongst gentlemen, it is not rare amongst men.

"You have had an unfortunate experience. But you do not need to arm yourself in order to—"

"To what?" she interrupted him. She stood very straight. "To be free to go where I desire when I desire to go there?"

"Yes."

"You are wrong," she said in a low voice. "You think because a man wears his cravat in a certain way or pays his gambling debts or drinks without getting drunk, or because he rides well or *fences* well, that he abides by all of a gentleman's codes of conduct. And for the most part, you would be right. Men are mostly what they appear to be. A scoundrel is a scoundrel, a gentleman is a gentleman. But not all of them are.

"You do not know Lord Forrester DeMarc, Mr. Munro. You have never seen his expression when he looks at me, heard the frantic tenor of his voice when he speaks to me. I have. But because I challenge what you think you know of him, you suspect my judgment rather than his character."

He returned her gaze with a shadowed one, neither embarrassed nor convinced. She could hardly blame him. In his situation, she might well have felt the same. She still scarce believed it herself.

"Perhaps all that is needed is for me to confront DeMarc?" he finally said. "Suggest that his interest is unappreciated and unreciprocated—"

"No!"

"But why?" he asked.

"Because DeMarc would go to Lady Tilpot at once. If she thought I had caused any of her guests embarrassment, she would dismiss me from her service."

"And would that be so onerous? I am sure your sister and her new husband would welcome you in their home."

"I am certain they would, too," she answered tightly. "But as you know, they are on the Continent, and I would not like to have to travel to join them."

"Nor would I like that," he murmured, frowning.

"And I can't very well ask the Weltons if I can share Charlotte's room!" Her shoulders suddenly drooped, weighed down by his suspicions and her uncertainty. "Believe me, Mr. Munro. I have given my situation a great deal of thought. I believe I am doing the best that I can." She smiled wanly. "So please, shall we start with the parry?"

TWENTY-ONE

DISARM:
forcing your opponent to release his grip on his weapon

"MERCIFUL HEAVENS!" Jolly Milar, her eyes fixed on Lady Tilpot's ballroom door, started frantically fanning herself. Helena, sent by her employer to keep the scapegrace from sneaking off with one of the young bucks attending the gala ball, turned as a hush fell over Lady Tilpot's three hundred guests.

Standing in the corridor outside the wide-flung double doors, calmly handing his walking stick and hat to the wide-eyed footman, was the marquis of Cottrell, Ignatio Farr. And beside him, looking around with elegant detachment, stood Ramsey Munro.

He carried himself with that aura of superiority and

casual easiness that so many men emulated and so few managed to achieve. Dressed all in midnight blue, the only ornament on his person was the gold rose pin securing his cravat.

Helena's breath caught. What was *he* doing here? Lady Tilpot would never have invited him to her home, regardless of his newly acquired status.

"Poor Tilpot." Helena looked around to find Mrs. Winebarger smiling knowingly. "One could almost feel sorry for her. Look at her, trying frantically to think what to do with this unlikely and unwanted pair! Where to seat them at dinner? *Should* she seat them at all?" Mrs. Winebarger laughed lightly. "What a pickle."

Helena followed her gaze. Lady Tilpot sat frozen in her chair, her lips a little slack, her eyes darting nervously, gauging the reactions of her nearest companions. Standing behind her, Reverend Tawster looked nearly as taken aback as his benefactress, but where Lady Tilpot wore an expression of confusion, he wore one of rapt amazement.

On one side of Lady Tilpot, Mrs. Barnes sat with pursed lips and an expression of speculative delight. She was center stage at what might well prove the juiciest *on dit* of a rather lackluster season. On Lady Tilpot's other side, Flora, a vision in diamante spangled lace, looked around, sensing the sudden shift in the atmosphere but having no idea what had caused it.

"Alas for The Tilpot," Mrs. Winebarger continued in a low voice, "she is between the proverbial rock and hard place. Her friends expect her to cut the audacious Mr. Munro directly, but she is not so stupid as that. His grandfather, the marquis, is a powerful man. A very powerful man, you know."

Helena didn't. Not for the first time, it occurred to her that the Prussian lady was extremely knowledgeable for a relative newcomer to these shores. Then she forgot all about Mrs. Winebarger as Ramsey's unhurried perusal of the room moved to her. He checked and inclined his head, the movement rife with amused irony. And with that she knew: Ram's appearance here was his concession that she might have a better understanding of DeMarc than he did. He had come to see for himself her situation.

It might seem a small thing, yet she did not know another man who would have given her opinion such weight. And was it a small thing? Certainly if the evidence of the murmured conversations erupting behind quivering fans all over the room was any indication, it might prove more than he'd bargained for. He had exposed himself to embarrassment and possible humiliation.

For her sake.

Her heart jumped in her chest. Emotions crowded her thoughts, vying for expression. But she knew that was absurd, she was absurd, mistaking gratitude for . . . She refused to countenance such nonsense, and so she tamped down her unruly heart and turned to look for DeMarc, whom she had been avoiding all afternoon.

She saw him at once, his blond head trained like a hound toward the door, his figure tense as he stared at Ramsey. Then, following Ramsey's gaze, his own dark gaze turned toward her. The animosity she saw there took her aback.

With a little thrill, she looked at Ramsey. He *must* have seen DeMarc's livid face, his curled lips and black gaze.

But Ramsey wasn't looking at her anymore. He'd bent his head toward his grandfather, listening to whatever the old man was saying as they entered the room, and now made his unhurried progress through the crowd. Startled heads turned, chests puffed out indignantly, and plump, overdressed matrons scattered before him as he moved through their midst very like a sleek young tomcat through a dovecote, heedless of the clucking, unconcerned by the ripples of hysteria he caused.

It was grandly amusing.

"Look! He's going to pay his respects to Lady Tilpot!" Jolly breathed. As they watched, Lady Tilpot leaned over to Flora and hissed something in her ear. The girl popped up at once, bobbed a quick curtsey, and darted away.

"Oh, dear. This does not bode well for Mr. Munro's social ambitions. The Tilpot will not have him know Miss Tilpot," Mrs. Winebarger said with a sigh. Helena watched a little crowd gather behind Lady Tilpot like a flock of sheep at the pasture gate, each jockeying to be close enough to hear the upcoming exchange, yet not so close as to appear indiscreet.

"I think it will be all right. The man has extraordinary élan!" Reverend Tawster whispered excitedly from beside her. She hadn't heard him approach. She regarded him now in surprise, and with newfound respect. Though clearly interested, the vicar had ceded his front-row seat to those with more prurient interests.

"Up to the nines on all counts!" Jolly agreed enthusiastically, her fan fluttering above her bosom.

"Smart lad," Mrs. Winebarger murmured as Ram waited unconcernedly while his grandfather crossed with stately deliberation to Lady Tilpot's side. He did not make a leg. He canted forward sharply at the waist, raised her plump hand to within a few inches of his lips, and stared directly into her rounded eyes as he murmured something.

Every fan in the vicinity ceased moving as their owners strained to hear what he said. They were thwarted. Whatever he murmured caused Lady Tilpot to squirm and then, with a sniff, make an imperious motion for Ramsey to draw near.

With a look of mild and utterly unconvincing surprise, Ramsey stepped forward and executed a perfect bow, one that quite shone down his grandsire's. "Lady Tilpot," he said clearly. "A pleasure, ma'am."

"Welcome to my home, Mr. Munro," Lady Tilpot said loudly, and then, shooting a nervous glance at the marquis, added even more loudly, "My niece is presently occupied, but she will return shortly. I must make her known to you."

A little thrill of conversation rippled through the masses at this. Ramsey replied politely that he would be honored, and with that Lady Tilpot ceased to look as though she expected him to rip off his clothes and run amuck through her ballroom. He bowed again and joined his waiting grandsire. The crowd shifted and dispersed.

"And thus Ramsey Munro enters Society," the vicar said in an odd tone.

"You look disappointed, Reverend," Mrs. Winebarger said.

"Perhaps I am, a little," the vicar admitted. "There is

something so romantic about a rogue aristocrat, don't you think? Still, I am sure this is all for the best." And with a small, self-deprecating smile, he excused himself.

The rest of the evening passed more or less uneventfully. Helena had not expected Ramsey, as the heir to a marquisate, to be introduced to her in such a large throng, nor was he. There were plenty of others vying for that honor who stood well above her, innumerable young ladies and fashionable misses with mothers dutifully pushing their progeny forward, daughters of knights and those bearing old, illustrious surnames. Now that Lady Tilpot had stamped Ram with approval, going so far as to publicly introduce him to her only niece, universally acknowledged to be one of the ton's most well-guarded heiresses, that portion of society that lived to care for their reputations and appearances, followed suit.

And Helena was jealous. For the first time in years she wished that she had a beautiful gown. Something exquisite, gossamer-light and shimmery, something that flowed down her body like the Grecian-styled, high-waisted gowns the other young ladies wore.

Not that there was anything wrong with her dress. It was in keeping with her station, fashioned from coral-colored batiste that tied beneath her breasts with a silk bow, short puffed sleeves, and a modest lace-trimmed neckline. Her hair, coiled atop her head, claimed no ornaments.

While she received many admiring glances, no one asked her to dance. Least of all Ramsey. But then, neither did he dance with any other lady, seemingly content to lounge with the young bucks and older military men at the far side of the room, making himself as pleasant a guest as one could want. He treated the giggling and tittering young women who sauntered by him to respectful nods and admiring looks, he listened attentively to the gout-riddled old general who stomped over and bellowed in his ear, and he performed a pretty bit of nonsense with an ancient baroness's handkerchief, which the coy old cat had flung at his feet.

Indeed, with each passing hour Lady Tilpot's demeanor grew more and more triumphant, until by ten o'clock Ramsey Munro's presence in her home had been magically transformed from potential disaster into Lady Tilpot's personal social coup of the season.

"Yes, yes," she was saying to her cronies as she accepted the cup of punch she had sent Helena to fetch, "of course I knew Mr. Munro was coming. Aren't his grandfather and I old friends?"

Not that Helena had ever heard.

Lady Tilpot must have caught a glimpse of Helena's thoughts in her sardonic expression. She disliked being caught out. "Helena," she snapped, "Flora is sitting with the marquis by the door leading to the garden. She is a sweet, innocent, but essentially silly girl who will be boring the dear marquis to tears."

Ah, such warm commendation. No wonder Flora had eloped at the first opportunity.

"Do go over and relieve him of her company."

"Of course."

"Now, as I was saying, Ramsey shall be attending next week's soiree, of course, and then . . ."

True to Lady Tilpot's words, Helena found Flora seated in one of the small settees placed about the perimeter of the room for the relief of the dancers. Her gown shimmered under the lights of thousands of candles, reflecting back the gems adorning the little bodice. She looked like a piece of woven glass, glittering and brilliant.

The marquis sat in his own chair next to hers. He looked far from bored. He looked steely-eyed, grim, and, yes, a touch disconcerted, but definitely not bored. She hurried over, trying to imagine what Flora—sweet, unassuming Flora—could have said to provoke him.

"But of course you are! You are attempting a rapprochement with your grandson," Flora was saying softly, tears shimmering in her eyes. "I find it frightfully noble!"

Oh, Flora! Helena enjoined the girl silently. She knew better than to make grossly personal comments like this! But pregnancy had addled her senses. She'd always been sentimental. Now she'd become bold *and* maudlin, a horrifying combination.

"Flora, dear," Helena said easily, coming up to her side. "You look flushed, and the gardens are only a few feet away. Wouldn't you like a nice bit of cool night air?"

"No, thank you, Helena," Flora said with only the quickest glance at her, then her limpid gaze reattached itself to the marquis. She looked like she might reach over any minute and pat his hand.

Please, Flora, don't pat him.

The old man's gaze flickered over Flora, and for a second Helena was convinced he was about to give Flora the blistering set-down she unfortunately deserved. Helena delved into her pocket for a handkerchief, preparing to stem the anticipated tidal wave of tears. But then, amazingly, the marquis relaxed.

"Young people today," he said. "Have you no sense of decorum? No capacity for self-containment?"

"I think Mr. Munro excessively self-contained," Flora said, looking across the room at the marquis's polished grandson.

The marquis followed the direction of her gaze. "Yes. He is. Which I find most praiseworthy." His telling gaze rested on Flora. But Flora didn't catch his meaning.

"How sweet!" she said, delighted.

"Sweet." The marquis sounded as if he might choke on the word.

"Yes!" Flora clasped her hands together in front of her chin. "To find each other after such a long, arduous search!" She sniffed, her eyes awash in tears, and Helena knew she was not thinking of Ramsey and the marquis's separation but hers and Oswald's.

"It is so . . . won-wonderful!" With a supreme effort she blinked back her tears. "And having found him, to then realize that you find much of value and worthiness in him! You must be very gratified."

"It really doesn't matter whether I am or not. Any feelings I have for Ramsey are entirely moot."

"Why is that?" Helena blurted out before she could stop herself.

The marquis, who had been ignoring her as a lady to whom he'd not been introduced, now turned that inimical gaze on her. "And you are?"

"Oh!" Flora said, aghast. "I hadn't realized . . . That is . . . This is Miss Helena Nash, Marquis. Helena, Ignatio Farr, the marquis of Cottrell."

"Milord." Helena bobbed a curtsey.

The marquis's gaze settled on her with awakening interest. "Ah. The beautiful companion. And my grandson's charge. Pray sit, girl."

How did he know that? Helena wondered as she took a seat beside Flora.

He spoke as if she had voiced her thoughts. "Do you think for an instant I would allow the marquisate to fall into the hands of a stranger, Miss Nash? I am not a romantic. Not by inclination, not by desire. I have had every aspect of Ramsey's life thoroughly investigated. I doubt there is much I do not know about Ramsey Munro"—his lids fell over his light eyes—"or those who are important to him."

Heat climbed into Helena's cheeks, and she was uncomfortably aware of Flora regarding her with a very interested expression. Oh, no. She did not think she could bear to be questioned about Ramsey by Flora, who would make the most absurd leaps of logic.

The marquis turned back to Flora. "As to finding Ramsey, Miss Tilpot, I had never lost him. Oh, I might have displaced him for a year here and there, but for the most part, I have known where he has been most all of his life."

"But . . . then why did you go so long without acknowledging him?" Flora looked confused. The romantic gleam had dried in her eye, and she seemed to be coming to the slow realization that she was facing a man without a single ort of sentiment in his veins. Such a creature was as alien to Flora as a hobgoblin.

"I have nonplussed your young friend, Miss Nash. But not you," the marquis said consideringly. "Hm."

"As for your question, miss," he returned his gaze to Flora. "You deserve no answer for such impertinence, but

I choose to indulge your curiosity, anyway." He glanced sideways toward Helena, and she had the uncanny notion he was speaking to her, not Flora.

"You assume that I did not acknowledge Ramsey, when it was quite the reverse. Ever since his return from France, I have sought some means by which to convince him to let me make public those documents that prove he is my legitimate heir. It is Ramsey who has refused me."

Why? Helena wondered, but then, hard on that thought came another. *And why had he agreed now?*

"Marquis." Helena, lost in thought, hadn't heard Ram's approach. Now she looked up to find him standing over her, his hands clasped lightly behind his back. He did not look at her. Instead, he regarded the marquis mildly. "You are monopolizing two young ladies when the room is awash with unhappy young men who are too afraid to approach."

The marquis gave Ram a flat look of disbelief. "No need for the company manners, Ramsey. It is not necessary to charm me. We know each other too well to be deceived."

"Perhaps it is not you I am trying to charm, sir." Ram smiled.

"Or deceive?" The marquis smiled.

Dear Lord, Helena thought in exasperation, being with these two was like flinging oneself in the midst of a fencing bout, all sharp words and verbal feints, little cuts and bloodletting flicks. "Flora, dear. You really are flushed, and the air is growing ever so much more heated. Would you care to take that walk *now?*"

Flora, who'd been regarding Ram and the marquis in bewilderment, cruelty always having a way of passing straight over her head, rose. At once, the marquis stood up.

"Gentlemen," Helena said sweetly, and, nodding to them, linked her arm through Flora's and led her through the door into the garden.

"A stop hit," Ram murmured behind her.

"Indeed. Impressive," she heard the marquis agree.

TWENTY-TWO

SIMPLE:
an attack or riposte that involves
no feints or blade play

THE GARDEN WAS QUIET except for a servant collecting punch glasses and a pair of smooth-faced old matriarchs inspecting the herbaceous border at the far end of the yard. Paper lanterns bobbed gently overhead, strung along the paths that meandered among the perfectly manicured beds. Flora turned eagerly to Helena as soon as they stepped onto the grass walk. "Have you had a note from Ossie?"

"Ossie? No." Helena shook her head. "I am sorry, Flora."

Flora's lovely little face crumpled. "Oh. I thought when you insisted that I join you out here, you had news."

"No, I just wanted to get you out of the vicinity of those gentlemen."

"Oh, you needn't have worried, Helena. I was handling the old marquis splendidly well, and as for the notorious Ramsey Munro"—she gave a little shiver—"I am glad to have made his acquaintance."

Helena regarded her curiously. "You are? And why is that, pray tell?"

"Well, he is reputed to be one of the most dashing men in London, not to mention the most handsome. So, it is really a rather good thing to have met him because it tested my love for Ossie."

"It did?" In her frankness, Flora reminded her so much of Charlotte, or rather the young lady Charlotte would have been had she had the same advantages Flora benefited from. But had Flora benefited? Yes, Flora was sweet, charming, completely devoted, and numbingly naïve. And as such, completely unfit for any sort of life other than the one she currently led. Charlotte, Helena thought for the first time, well, Charlotte would not merely endure, she would triumph.

"Yes," Flora prattled on earnestly. "Because now I can say with utter conviction that having met the most dashing, handsome, notorious gentleman in London, I felt not one flutter of attraction."

"Come, Flora, that's doing it a bit brown," Helena said.

"All right," Flora conceded, "but only in the most academic fashion. Like viewing a handsome picture, say, one of Mr. Turner's more tumultuous seascapes. Yes, it's all very exciting and dark, but one wouldn't want to be in the painting, would one?" she asked seriously.

"No."

Flora nodded sagely. "Mr. Munro—" She paused, "Is there a courtesy title attached to the marquisate, do you imagine?"

"I don't have any idea. Pray continue, Flora."

"Oh. Mr. Munro is simply too dangerous, too deuced awake on every suit, for a girl to ever feel comfortable with him."

Yes. He is canny and knowing and dangerous, which is precisely why a girl would feel comfortable with him. At least, why she did.

At the far end of the garden, Helena heard a sudden heavy rustling in the shrubbery. She looked up curiously but saw only the same two elderly ladies, now pitched into a heated debate about aphids. She turned back to Flora. "Mr. Goodwin will be transported to know he has no rival in Ramsey Munro."

At the mention of her beloved's name, the animation fled Flora's face. "I would that I could tell him myself," she said wistfully. "Oh, Helena, what am I to do? Soon it shall become apparent that I am breeding, and then Aunt Alfreda will send me off to some terrible place like . . . like . . . like Ipswich!" Her voice lowered dramatically. "I shall die in Ipswich."

"No, you won't die in Ipswich. Besides, Mr. Goodwin is probably figuring out some terribly clever way to amass a fortune and reunite with you, even as we speak."

Flora eyed her as if suspecting irony, which, of course, she had every right to do as Helena was, in fact, being ironic, but she didn't want Flora to know that. So she smiled. More rustles and snapping and popping came from further up the hedge, as though something was making a slow and painful progress through the dense underbrush. Had Mrs. Winebarger's cat, Princess, escaped her mistress for a bit of a hunt?

"Truly, Flora," Helena continued in a distracted voice. It sounded too big to be a cat and was definitely coming closer. Surely not DeMarc? She had seen him not five minutes ago, speaking to the vicar. "I am certain Mr. Goodwin desires to see you as much as you do him, but finds it impossible. You simply must have patience, my dear. Take care of yourself and your unborn child. Be brave for his sake."

She could have made no better appeal. Resolutely Flora lifted her quivering little chin. "I will be brave. And now, I suppose I best go back in to Aunt Alfreda," she said. "She doubtless has a line of 'eminently eligible young men' to whom she has promised my dances. Are you coming?"

"No, dear. You hurry along." Flora, biddable as ever, headed for the door until, as an afterthought, Helena called out to her. "Flora?"

"Yes?"

"I have to know. What with all the young men being thrown in your way and your beauty and sweetness and, well—excuse me for being vulgar, but—wealth, however have you kept them from asking Lady Tilpot for your hand?"

Flora, blushing while Helena listed her qualities, dimpled with a trace of shy pertness. "Oh, that's easy," she said. "If ever a gentleman gets a little too warm in his attentions, I simply tell him that I could not possibly consider living in a household that did not include Aunt Alfreda."

"I see," Helena said admiringly and Flora, seeing her aunt waving at her through the doors, hurried away.

Perhaps Flora, too, would triumph—

Beside Helena, a shrub emitted a low groan of despair. "Florrrra!"

Dear God, Helena knew that moan! It was Ossie. The bush started to shake and leaves began dropping in a shower as the boy struggled to break free and follow his beloved.

"No!" Helena hissed, jumping up. Her gaze darted to the two old ladies who'd paused in their debate to see what was going on. "Mrs. Winebarger's cat," she explained loudly, "seems to have gotten caught."

They sniffed and went back to their conversation.

"Stay where you are, Mr. Goodwin," Helena implored. "If those ladies see a man come out of the shrubbery, they will scream down the rafters, and either you will be pursued as a thief or, worse, my follower! Then Lady Tilpot will dismiss me!"

"Ohhhhhh."

"There now, puss-puss," Helena crooned loudly, covering Oswald's voice, then hissed in a fierce whisper, *"Do be quiet!"*

"But to be so close," whispered the quaking shrub. "And for her not to know. She looks well. No, she looks beautiful," he whispered. "Perhaps she is better off without me."

"Doubtless, yes. But your child might think differently."

"She looks like an angel of—" The shrub went still. "Child?"

"Yes, you— Yes. Flora is breeding."

"Ah!"

"Careful! Don't you *dare* fall out of that bush."

"But . . . how?"

"Clearly, you have a better idea of that than I. But I would suggest the usual method," Helena said, amazed at herself. "Now tell me quickly: How goes this plan you had contrived when we last met?"

"Well. Yes, very well," the bush said distractedly.

"And have you enough funds to claim your bride?"

"Soon. Very soon."

"When?"

"Two weeks, give or take a day."

"Can you not—"

"Miss Nash." At the sound of Ramsey's voice, Helena whirled around.

"Mr. Munro!" she exclaimed. She couldn't let him near the bush. He would know at once someone was hiding there. "Pray, wait right where you are," she called out. "I . . . I . . . my, ah . . . my dress has caught in the shrubs whilst I was trying to extricate Mrs. Winebarger's cat, and I would not like you to see me until I have facilitated a repair."

The two old ladies at the end of the path had turned at the sound of Ramsey's voice and stood regarding him with deeply offended expressions. Ram returned their look. He dared not risk Helena's reputation by coming to her when she had expressly asked him not to do so. "Very well. Do you require any assistance?"

"No, no," she called gaily. " 'Twill be but a moment."

She turned back to the bush. "When can we meet?

Where? I have much more to tell you. A letter from Flora to give you—"

"Florrraaa," the bush sighed.

"Enough! Where? Vauxhall?"

"No! My creditors know about that place. They haunt it," the bush muttered disconsolately. "I will think of something, but until then . . ."

The bush shook, and a hand suddenly emerged, clutching at her ankle. Helena jumped, stifling a cry. "For heaven's sake, Mr. Goodwin—"

"A note," the bush whispered as the hand released her and set a small folded piece of paper by her foot. "For my Flora. Please see she gets it."

"Fine. Now go away." Then, with a sigh for the loss of her one decent ball gown, she dropped down and rent a bit of lace on her hem as she swept the note up. Then she stood up, backing away as though she had just disentangled herself.

"There," she called, joining Ramsey near the doorway. "Free!"

"Are you all right?" His brows were lowered, hiding his eyes in shadow. He looked so handsome in his dark coat and trousers, his snowy white cravat a foil for his black curls. The moon, flirting with a cloud, suddenly appeared, glazing his lean features with a blue-white sheen.

"Yes. Now, what do you want? Is it something about the fencing lessons? Can you not meet with me this week?" she asked quietly.

"What?" he said. "Oh. No. No, the time is fine. I just . . . I saw Miss Flora leave the garden, and you did not follow, and DeMarc is nowhere to be seen, so I . . ."

She stared at him, her heart doing strange flip-flops. He looked, she realized, anxious. *On my behalf.*

"Then you noticed something in his manner," she said, ignoring the giddy lurch of her heart. "Something in the way he looked at me?"

"That would be impossible, as he did not look at you at all."

"Oh," she said, disappointed. It would be such a relief to have someone else witness what she had seen, the demon that lurked behind the sober, straitlaced viscount's handsome features.

"Which makes me decidedly uncomfortable," he replied.

Her gaze snapped up to meet his.

"Shall we walk?"

She hesitated, feeling all too clearly the critical gazes on them. "I would prefer to sit down, if you don't mind. There."

She pointed to a pair of wrought iron chairs sitting directly in front of the doors leading into the ballroom. Seated there they would be in full view of anyone who chose to glance outside. While not precisely chaperoned, she could hardly then be accused of clandestine engagements.

He smiled knowingly. "Must you always be so careful?"

"Always."

"Very well then." He waited for her to take her seat and then followed suit, stretching one long arm along the back of his chair, his fingers dangling carelessly a few inches from her bare shoulder. His fingers were strong, she recalled, and smooth. Warm and—

This was ridiculous. Earlier today she had been frightened of DeMarc and ready to jump at shadows. Now
Ramsey Munro had only to stroll into a crowded ballroom and her world felt safe, secure—no, more, it felt
opulent, rife with promise, delicious with potential.

"You were saying something about how DeMarc's not
looking at me made you uncomfortable," she said.

"You know you are an extraordinarily beautiful
woman," he stated matter-of-factly. "One has only to
look around the room to see the covert glances aimed at
you, the way men follow your progress across the floor.
Yet DeMarc did not look at you once. More, he made
every effort to turn away from where he must have
known you were so that his gaze, even in passing, would
not cross over you. Why?"

"I don't know."

"I think it is because he knows he cannot keep from
betraying whatever it is he feels for you when he looks at
you."

"I see." It sounded so strange. So unhealthy. She shivered.

He saw it and reacted immediately, moving closer and
stretching out his hand as if he would gather her to him
but then, abruptly, recalled himself. Or rather, he recalled the fascinated audience standing at the far end of
the garden. "I won't let him hurt you."

"I won't let him hurt me, either," she said firmly.
"Thank you for telling me this, Mr. Munro. Thank you
for believing me enough to give credence to my fears. I
shall be doubly on my guard."

His face tightened with frustration. "You do not have

to be. I can be on guard for you. It is what I pledged to do. Let me do it."

She regarded him with softening eyes. He sounded so angry, and he was trying so hard to control his temper, and Ram Munro, she reckoned, never lost his temper. "If I could, I would. But . . ."

"But what?" he demanded. "Trust me."

She shook her head. If he came with her, Oswald would not meet her. Besides, Flora's secret was not hers to tell. It was a simple matter of pledges and personal integrity. She must turn him toward another subject.

He looked away from her, his jaw tightening, his eyes flinty in the moonlight, his profile that of some handsome, thwarted prince.

"May I ask you a question?" she finally said.

"Yes," he said irritably. "Of course."

"Not every question deserves an answer," she rejoined softly. "I have no right to ask you anything, and you have every right to expect me to respect your privacy."

His anger left him in a flood. She sounded so contrite. He looked back at her, his expression softening. He loved her. He wanted her approval, her smiles, her understanding. And if in discovering who and what he was, she discovered who and what he was not, so be it.

"My dear young woman," his voice sounded odd, "I am yours to command. Whatever you desire, simply give me the task. Whatever you would know, ask."

"My! I hadn't realized you took your pledge to my family quite so seriously." She tried a light laugh, only it wasn't light. It was breathless.

Oh, this has nothing to do with my pledge, he thought, holding her gaze. Her eyes flickered as if she'd read his mind. His mouth curved in a slight smile. "What is it you want to know?"

"Why has the marquis waited so long to produce those marriage documents?"

"Because they didn't exist before five years ago," he answered without hesitation. "I would not allow them to be put before the public as truth until"—he paused thoughtfully—"five days ago."

If the world got wind of his grandfather's forgeries, there would be a scandal of unprecedented size, and not only would Ram be a nameless bastard again, but his salle would be destroyed. He risked much in telling her this. But he had never been in love before. If revealing his secrets could entice her into trusting him with hers, it would be well worth it. He disliked whatever it was she felt she needed to do that sent her abroad, masked and now armed with a sword, into the night.

Her eyes remained calm. She'd suspected. "But why now?"

"The reason has its roots buried in the past," he answered. "Do you recall the other men who came with me to your townhouse and pledged to aid your family?"

She nodded.

"Colonel MacNeill, of course, and another, Andrew Ross. Did you ever know *why* we were in that French dungeon?"

"A little," she said. "Kate revealed to me some of what her husband told her. You had been sent to France to set up a network of informants, the center being the place

Napoleon would least expect it—at his wife's home, at Malmaison."

"Yes," Ram said, fingering the gold rose pin nestled in his white cravat. "Josephine adores roses; she is obsessed with them. As the wife of the rising power in France, kings and queens, deposed princes, and would-be potentates send her gifts of rose plants, all the most exotic varieties. But none have ever been as exotic as a rose that grew in a small Scottish abbey, a gift from a crusader to the abbot who'd cared for his family during the Black Death."

"The yellow rose," she said.

"Aye." His faint Scottish burr deepened. "The yellow rose. We brought her that rose, and offered her our expertise as rose hunters to scour France and Europe for new varieties for her gardens. With her written endorsement, we could have gone anywhere unchallenged."

His gaze, drifting through a sea of memories, sharpened. "It was a good plan," he said. "But someone betrayed us before we could even begin to implement it. We were caught and sent to LeMons castle's dungeons."

Her gaze remained fixed on his face, the light blue color of her eyes deeper in the moonlight, her blonde hair bleached nearly white.

"Suffice it to say, the French failed to treat us with the respect a Scotsman might expect from their former allies." He smiled wryly, but then his smile faded. "They executed one of us, the noblest of us, the heart of us, Douglas Stewart."

His thoughts flashed back to Doug, his brown hair caked with filth, his light eyes fierce, the hectic color high in his lean cheeks as the guards dragged him up the narrow stairs to the guillotine. "Stay true, lads!" he'd shouted before the thick door slammed shut.

"But *who* would betray you?" she asked, her brows knit.

"I don't know," he replied. "It had to be one of three: Kit MacNeill, Andrew Ross, or Toussaint, the exiled French priest and ex-soldier who'd planned the enterprise. I always suspected Toussaint was more than he let on."

His mouth twisted humorously. "I can't think it was Kit, and for whatever reasons Kit now seems willing to accept that it was not me. Before he left for the Continent, I promised him I would find out once and for all who betrayed us.

"A few days ago I received a letter from a man who was a guard at LeMons. I had sent out some inquiries, offering a reward for any information that could lead me to our Judas. This man answered. He claims he knows who betrayed us.

"He is arriving as part of the retinue of a French duelist who's been given special permission to enter the country for the tournament. I have arranged to meet him the day the tournament ends, when he will reveal to me the name of the man I seek."

"*But* only for a great deal of money," she said, her eyes narrowing. "And the marquis has a great deal of money."

"Brava."

He regarded her with sober amusement. "The sum Arnoux demanded far exceeds anything I can produce."

He had sat through one long night pondering what to do as the past had crept in and taken occupancy of his mind. He'd thought about his lovely, imprudent mother, his fierce, devil-may-care father, and the bonny life he'd led in the Highlands. Then he'd thought about those few short, terrifying weeks after his mother's death, and how Father Tarkin had found him and brought him to St. Bride's Abbey, where three boys had absorbed him into their brotherhood as effortlessly as if he'd always been one of them, as if they were in fact brothers he had simply not known existed. And, finally, his thoughts led to a French dungeon where he and those same brothers had been betrayed, one of them killed, and the survivors irreparably damaged.

Twice he'd lost a family. His parents' death, senseless as it had been, at least had been unpremeditated. But the second time— With malice and purpose, someone had conspired to destroy them. And that same person wanted to destroy them again. Why?

Now, discovery stood within his reach. He had needed only to ask himself how much he wanted to know. More than he wanted to make an old man suffer for the slights he'd dealt his parents?

Definitely.

"I am the only living blood relation the marquis has, and that, Miss Nash, galls him. Still, his pride is huge, and he grows old, and he wants, desperately, for his line to continue."

Something dark flickered in her eyes. What was it?

"So I sent him a letter stating that I would allow myself to be found as his rightful, legitimate heir if he would at once settle upon me the sum of forty thousand pounds. The marquis met me at his barrister's office the same day."

"It must have been terribly hard for you."

He regarded her with amusement. "Must it? Why do you say that?"

"Because you didn't want the marquisate," she said with soft conviction. "It comprises obligations and compromises you had no wish for or plans to make."

His amusement turned to sharp interest. "A bastard such as myself being offered wealth and power beyond his comprehension? How could I not want it?"

"Because you wanted something else," she mused, regarding him seriously. "You wanted . . . to teach swordplay as you believe it was meant to be taught. You wanted something for yourself. *Of* yourself."

"Did I? How could you know that?" Her insight took his breath away. She was right. He had wanted the salle he'd dreamt of owning, to teach his craft not as a hobby for bored sons of wealthy peers, but as a discipline, as an art.

"Because I heard how you spoke, the timbre of your voice."

He didn't deny her perception, but neither could he affirm it. What good would it do now? The life he'd dreamt about was no longer within his reach. A marquis did not teach. There would be other obligations and duties to fill his time, other petitions for talents and acumen he did not even know whether he owned, let alone whether he could put to good use. But he would try. As he had told Callum Lamont, paying one's debts was a habit he could not break. And now he owed not only his grandfather but all those on whom the marquisate depended for their livelihood.

"And what of you, Miss Nash? What do you want?"

"To be known. To be valued. To *have* value." He realized she'd spoken without thought, from the heart, by the way her skin grew dusky in the moonlight and by the way she averted her face, as if embarrassed by her words.

I know you. I value you.

He turned his face toward the doorway leading into the ballroom. Society beauties, speculative matrons, and, bedamned! even a few respectable ladies had spent the evening casting interested glances and coy smiles at him. And the only woman he wanted to give him those come-hither glances and inviting smiles considered him a womanizer and now knew him to be a fraud.

Beside them the two older women had finally grown weary of their innocent and public conversation and were re-entering the ballroom. He smiled, amused.

"You will be celebrated," Helena said quietly. "You *are* being celebrated."

"Yes. Strange, is it not?" he asked carelessly.

He did not look back at her. The desire to touch her, to pull her into his arms and force a response from her was nearly overwhelming. All night he had played the good heir role, speaking and bowing and scraping to people he didn't give a damn for, just to see her, just to ease his own anxiety over the danger she might be in. Helena Nash was the only one he cared about and the only one who seemed not particularly impressed. *How could he impress her?*

Oh, he understood well that she responded to him physically. His sexual appetite was healthy, as was hers. But the magnetism between them frightened her, his attraction for her scared her. He must be careful, go slow. Be patient. Even if it killed him.

He looked around at her in profile. Her expression

had resumed its serene beauty, but there was a tension in the fingers curled on her lap.

"We should leave," she said, standing up with sudden deliberation. "If we are seen together much longer I will be supposed shockingly ambitious."

No. He rose to his feet, following her to the door. No. She reached the entry and paused, and he took advantage, slipping to her side and reaching out, taking her arm and pulling her roughly to him, into the shadows.

"No," he said as she stared up at him. "They will think I am overly base."

"But you're not. You are to be the marquis of Cottrell."

He gazed down at her, feeling green and foolish and raw. And so damnably exposed. "And you are to be my grave little instructress in the niceties of social behavior? I see. Tell me, then, what does a newly found heir to a great title do when he finds himself alone in a garden with a woman he most ardently wants to kiss?"

He heard her swallow, saw the deep pools of her pupils swallowing the blue discs of her irises as she stared up at him.

"He releases her and walks away." She didn't sound confident, though, and that gave him hope.

"Well," he said with a tender smile, "I am new to this role and thus bound to make mistakes."

He pulled her into his arms and kissed her with a thoroughness that left her breathless. And only then did he release her.

But it was she who walked—no, ran, away.

Hidden in the shadows of the old musician's gallery, Viscount DeMarc tilted his head against the wall and closed his eyes. But he could still see them, Munro dark and elegant as Lord Sin as he bowed above her, moonlight and gold spun into ethereal beauty so bright it hurt his eyes to see her. Helena! My Helena!

He kissed her. He kissed her as if he would drink her into his very body, and she yielded, for one long moment she flowed into his arms and then, abruptly, Munro released her and stepped back.

They didn't speak. They didn't even touch. They didn't have to touch. They were touching so many other ways, his darkness seeping like a stain into her bright, pale beauty, and she opening to it, embracing it, absorbing his hard, dark soul. No. No, no, no. It was an abomination. A desecration of their union.

She belonged to *him*, damn her.

Did Munro think he was just going to give her to him? Did she think she could just leave him?

No.

Ram Munro loved Helena Nash.

The other man who'd been watching sighed, feeling a little wistful, a little sentimental. The poor fool actually loved her.

It would never work, of course. She did not trust him, and Ram Munro, well, he was as damaged goods as a man can be who'd crawled out of hell. Ram just didn't know it. But *he* knew it. Aye.

In a very real way, he was doing Ram a favor in getting him killed. He wouldn't have to suffer watching his beloved's admiration turn to hate, realize that he was doomed to fail her, that he could never be what she needed. Never be what he'd promised to be, never fulfill the sacred oaths he'd taken, promises to old regimes and new . . .

The man frowned. He was getting confused. His head was swimming with memories and images, and it was hard sometimes to sort out which ones were real and which ones born during long hours of mental torment.

With a hiss of despair, he yanked off his glove and dug in his pocket for the thin penknife he always carried to help him focus. To help him concentrate. It was a trick he'd learned long ago in France. With a sigh of relief he jabbed the needle-sharp tip into the fleshy pad at the base of his thumb. At once, his thoughts cleared. Another little twist and lucidity returned, and with it sweet reason.

Ram was trying to remake himself. A man couldn't remake himself. Wasn't that what the Church taught? A man must die before he could be reborn again? Like he'd been reborn. Unfortunately he'd been reborn into a world still populated by those who'd known him as another. He couldn't allow that. He didn't want to spend the rest of his new life looking over his shoulder.

So they must die. All of them.

It wasn't as if this was easy for him. He looked at Ram Munro and he was filled with admiration, an almost paternal sense of pride. He'd done that. He'd been responsible in part for that proud bearing, that lethal skill with a sword, that hard, determined heart.

Was it any wonder he couldn't bring himself to kill them? But he couldn't. Not himself. He'd taken vows, too, after all.

And he wasn't a traitor.

TWENTY-THREE

<><>

VOLTA:
a turning or rotation
of the fencer's body

"Good. Now, follow the line."

Fired to greater efforts by Ram's infrequent praise, Helena straightened her arm, her blade subtly angling downward. It was her seventh lesson at the salle over the last two weeks, and each time her pleasure in them grew. She liked the physicality of the sport, and under Ram's formal tutelage had come to appreciate it as a game not only of balletlike artistry and precision but of cunning.

After that devastating kiss in the garden, she'd been hesitant to venture here again. But now she was glad she had. He had greeted her without any hint that his kiss had been anything more than a momentary aberration, and she had come to assume that it had been more an angry thumbing his nose at the situation in which he found himself than an impulse engendered by her irresistibility. Slowly, she had relaxed. And so had Ram.

He had made no further attempt to seduce her. Yes, he laid his hands on her, and often at that, but his touch was impersonal. Worrisomely, she could not claim the same indifference in her response. But every time he wrapped his fingers around her wrist to position her blade, or clasped her shoulder to turn her body, or tilted her chin with his thumb, no matter how inconsequential or fleeting his touch, her body reacted as though she was being caressed by her lover. Luckily, he didn't seem to notice.

Added to her pleasure was the unexpected boon of Lord DeMarc's disappearance. For over a week now, she had not seen him at Lady Tilpot's soirees, nor had she caught any glimpse of him lurking about waiting for her to appear. She was relieved, if not yet confident, that he had finally come to his senses. He'd sounded anything but sane that night he'd caught her in the mews behind Lady Tilpot's townhouse.

Still, as a reprieve it was a welcome one. But Helena realized that even if DeMarc should never appear in her life again, she would be loath to give up these hours spent with Ram. They were stimulating, amusing, and wholly satisfying.

Only after the lessons had ended would he discard his instructional manner. Then he insisted she stay for tea and charmed her thoroughly as they were being served by his grim, one-eyed factotum. He amused her with stories about growing up in the Highlands and made her pensive as he told her about being orphaned and brought to St. Bride's.

And he asked her questions. Questions about her sisters, about her life with Lady Tilpot. He led her into expressing her opinions on the latest brouhaha in Parliament, the Irish question, and the latest fashions. He challenged her on whom she admired and what she did not. And always, he listened as she spoke, as if what she said really mattered to him. She liked their growing friendship, a strange term for one's relationship with a handsome rake, but she could not think to call it anything else.

But he did not look at her with that lazy sexual awareness she knew signaled a man's interest, and he did not make any attempt to touch her. Indeed, he seemed to have lost all interest in her as a woman. She should have been glad. She should—

"No! Where have you gone, Miss Nash? Because clearly you are not here."

Her blade had dipped during those last uncomfortable thoughts. She blushed, and with an impatient sound he slapped away her blade, grabbed her wrist, and pulled her arm straighter.

"This is no way to teach swordsmanship," he muttered. "No footwork, no foundation, simply slashing and jabbing and poking. I am appalled that I agreed to do this. You have brought me to a new low, Miss Nash, are you pleased?"

"I'm sorry."

"In fact," he said, suddenly fierce, "this could well get you killed."

"But . . ."

"A little knowledge is a dangerous thing, Miss Nash. An attacker will come fast, and he will not be abiding by any rules."

Of course he was right. She had known all along that her goal was unachievable. But knowing even a little had given her some measure of confidence. At least she had not simply been waiting to become a victim.

"I know," she answered in exasperation. "But I have to do something. I can't just . . . I have to *do* something!"

He looked at her with an unreadable expression.

"*Passata sotto*," he finally said. "It might be construed as a sort of secret *botte*, except there is no such thing." He went on, his tone vexed. "The only advantage a vulnerable person has when being attacked is that he *is* vulnerable. His attacker will not expect him to fight. The *passata sotto is* ungainly, difficult to recover from, and easy to parry, but only if one expects it. Let me demonstrate. Lunge at me, straight at me."

He held his blade in a casual line, the tip low. She hesitated. Oh, she knew Ram could parry anything she presented, and her blade tip was well buttoned, but she did not like the idea of purposely lunging at him in his current defenseless stance.

"*Do it.*"

She did it. She lunged forward as he'd taught her, but Ram, rather than forcing her blade aside, lunged even deeper, at the same time canting sideways and dropping, his free hand flat on the floor, so that his back extended leg, torso, and sword arm formed one long, contiguous line, the end of which, the tip, lay against her ribcage. It could have been embedded in her lungs just as easily.

She looked at the tip dinting her gown. "But that's marvelous! I had no idea you could do something like that."

"It tends to be the last point in a bout," Ram said dryly, rising and dusting his hand off on his pant leg. "One either wins with it or loses."

"Will you use it in the tournament this weekend?"

"I have decided to withdraw from the tournament," he said. "There are other preparations I have to make. Time is essential, and my lack of means is no longer so pressing a concern."

"Preparations to meet the guard from the French prison?" she asked soberly. She could not dismiss a little disappointment. She would have dearly loved to see Ram duel.

"Yes," he said uncomfortably. "Now, take off your dress."

She blinked.

"You can't execute a *passata sotto* in a dress, Miss Nash. I shall have Gaspard find something. Sometimes the younger patrons leave items, and Gaspard cleans them."

He looked very grim. Far from the gentleman who'd nuzzled her neck and told her to relax into his arms. He yanked on the bell pull and then paced to the window and stood looking out at the street below, his hands clasped tightly behind his back.

That something had angered him was obvious, but as she had no idea of what it could be, she, too waited. It was not long before Gaspard appeared and, hearing his master's rather odd command, left without batting his eye in search of the requested garment.

"Do you have any idea the extent to which I would go to fulfill my pledge to your family?" Ram finally asked without turning.

"As far as teaching me a *passata sotto?*" she asked, attempting to cajole him from his present mood. Ram Munro did not have "moods"; his sardonic demeanor was as integral to his character as his Lucifer good looks and skill with a sword.

He turned around. He would not be cajoled. "Can you not at least find it in you to confide in me? Have I ever done anything that demonstrated to you that I am not to be trusted?"

"No!" she said, and then, slowly, "The day after I came to your salle the first time, do you recall it?"

He nodded, his gaze watchful.

"Was that the same day you fought duels with eight consecutive men in order to defend a lady's name?"

She'd caught him off guard. No one was supposed to have known about that.

He stiffened. "How sad that honor means so little amongst the better classes these days," he said calmly. "I see I shall have to revisit the gentlemen in question and—"

"No," she interrupted. "That won't be necessary. No one knows the lady's name. Only that a now-famous duel was fought. A man, supposedly so drunk he never even heard the original slight, was roused enough to witness it."

"I see."

She looked him straight in the eye. "Was that lady me, Mr. Munro?

He held his hand palm up, a gesture begging her indulgence. "I went to some effort, Miss Nash, to protect a lady's name. I can hardly reveal to you what I was willing to cut eight men to keep secret."

Her gaze was calm, assessing. "I respect you for that, Mr. Munro. But the same code of honor that prohibits you from revealing the lady's name or the gentlemen involved, keeps me from revealing a situation involving persons to whom I swore my aid and my silence."

"Touché," he murmured. "But—"

A knock interrupted whatever he'd been about to say,

and Gaspard entered, a pair of small trousers and a shirt draped over his arm. Wordlessly he set them on the table.

"I shall wait without," Ram said. "Call me when you have dressed."

It didn't take Helena long to shed her dress and don the trousers, having had plenty of practice with male attire these last two months. She left the white shirt open at the throat, pushing the sleeves up her forearms and stuffing the tails beneath her waistband. Then she picked up her sword and lunged.

Ah! This was ever so much better. She grinned.

"Mr. Munro!" she called.

He entered the room and crossed his arms over his chest, his gaze sweeping up and down her length, from the slippers to her delighted expression. "Feeling quite the thing, are you?" he asked dryly.

"I feel liberated, Mr. Munro. I should have been wearing young men's clothing from the first. I feel certain I will be much more competent with the freedom of movement these garments allow me."

"Really? Then you intend to go about in public from now on dressed in men's clothing?"

She flushed. "No, no, of course not." He had come too close to her secret, and she suddenly wondered if seeing her in these clothes would put him in mind of another young lady in men's clothing. She glanced at him. He was watching her with hooded eyes, dark and still angry, but without any dawning recognition.

"Shall we?" she asked.

Over the next two hours he made her practice the single offensive ploy over and over and over again. He made her lunge so deeply and so many times that her thigh muscles screamed in protest. Again and again, he had her lunge and tip sideways, catching her weight by slamming her hand into the floorboards until her palm was bruised. Time after time, he barked at her to thrust her sword up, stretching out as she did so, so that her ribs burned and her arm shook with her effort to hold the miserable few pounds of steel over her head.

And then he made her do it again.

She would not be dissuaded. She would not be discouraged.

But finally, as he picked up his sword and started to speak, she had had enough. Before he had finished a word, she'd dropped, the motion so ingrained now that her body fell into alignment, surging out and up, striking his shirt. With immense satisfaction, she heard material rip. She'd scored a point on Ramsey Munro! With a sound of glee she leapt to her feet, her face flushed with victory, her eyes brilliant with success.

Ramsey looked down. She must have caught a seam with the tip guard, and the result had rent it all the way up his side and into the sleeve. The fabric flapped loose, exposing part of the muscular chest beneath.

He looked up. "I rather liked this shirt."

"I hit you!" she said excitedly. "I caught you off guard!"

"You did," he admitted.

"So, you see? You needn't worry about me, Mr. Munro," she said, success making her giddy. "Having mastered this truly marvelous ploy, I shall be safe and—"

She didn't even see him move. One minute she was happily babbling about her new skills, and the next he'd caught her up in his arms, his lips curled back in a snarl.

His arms were hurtfully tight, and he was propelling her, stumbling, backward, and she was twisting desperately in his arms, frightened.

"Ah!" Her back hit the wall, the breath leaving her lungs in a gasp.

"You are not safe!" he said in a low, furious voice. "De-Marc has gone to ground. No one has seen him in over a week, and you do not know where he is.

"I'm a fool to have given you the tools, illusionary as they are, to make you think you are in any way prepared to defend yourself with a sword. But you, you are a far bigger fool if you think this little trick has rendered you sacrosanct."

"Let me go," she said, her own anger rising to meet his unfair accusations, his patent scorn. How dare he handle her like this? How dare he hurt her? And which hurt more, his steely grip or his biting contempt?

She pushed at him, trying to break free. "Don't you dare—"

He shoved her back, spreading her arms wide, holding her wrists tight against the wall and pinning her body with his. "If someone comes after you, they won't play by rules. They won't wait for you to essay a few practice swipes before you begin."

"So what would you have me do?" she demanded furiously. "Ask you to follow after me for the rest of my life?"

"Yes." He looked down into her face, his blue eyes blazing. "Yes." He pulled her out a few inches and thumped her back into the wall again, as if to drive some sense into her. "Yes." Once more he pulled her out and she winced, waiting for the coming impact.

He cursed, low, hard, and vehement, and then his

angry mouth was on hers. She tried to twist away and then, and then it was too late, the fire that lay banked burst into flame, and she moaned, arching into his hard body, her mouth seeking his.

With a curse, he tore his mouth from hers, snatching himself away from where she stood, shoulders to the wall, her breast rising and falling rapidly in agitation beneath the thin linen. Small and defenseless, hurt and angry.

He'd done that.

"Marry me."

Her eyes widened. "What?"

"Marry me. Let me protect you. Let me—"

She laughed, the sound broken and high-pitched. " 'Do you have any idea the extent I would go to fulfill my pledge to your family?' " she echoed back his words. "Well, yes. I guess I do. Now."

"That's not what I meant." He half turned from her, raking the black hair back from his face with both hands.

"Isn't it?" she demanded, quivering. "What *do* you mean, then? That on the basis of two weeks you have grown to love me with such ardent and honest devotion that you could not imagine life without me? Or is it that you feel that you have now so completely compromised me that your new status as a gentleman insists you act honorably?" She threw out the words bitterly. "Well, I commend you, milord. You are the first in a long line to feel so compelled."

He could not answer. He could not tell her of the years he'd spent watching over her, of his initial attraction to her valiant composure, of his growing desire for her, of his appreciation of her courage and intelligence and wit. Or finally, the knowledge that, wherever he went, however long he lived, he would never know her like again, he would never feel love like this again.

She would never believe him if he told her he loved her. So he sought some other means to win her.

"Marry me because it is sensible, Helena." He looked up as if seeking inspiration. "Marry me because I will be a marquis and you would make a fine marchioness. Marry me because I will never bore you. Marry me because our children would be surpassingly gorgeous. Marry me so that you can become the finest female swordswoman in the world. Marry me because I want you. Just marry me, Helena. I *most* ardently beseech you."

She stared at him until he realized that her lovely blue eyes were awash in tears. He hadn't meant to make her cry. He reached out and with the back of his index finger traced the curve of her cheek.

"I swear I will spend my life endeavoring to make sure you do not regret it."

"Ramsey, I cannot—"

"Please. Do not refuse me yet," he said soberly. "Promise me that you will at least consider it. Think on it a few days at least."

Her gaze fell. "It will not change anything."

"Please."

She moved back, harassed by desire and sorrow and guilt. "I will think," she murmured, and fled.

TWENTY-FOUR

⬳

PHRASE:
a set of related actions and reactions
in a fencing bout

SHE LOVED RAMSEY. The knowledge pierced her with an impact no steel could have ever rivaled.

She loved his wit and his hauteur, his irony and his nobility. Everything about him she admired. Every moment with him, either as "Corie" or as "Miss Nash," had been the most vital, gratifying moments of her life.

But, of course, she could not marry him.

Why had she told him she would consider his offer when she already knew any union between them would reap nothing but heartache? He had only newly been made heir to a great fortune. He did not even realize yet the matrimonial prospects open to him. But Helena, who had lived her life on the fringes of Society, knew very well the opportunities that awaited him. He could align himself with a great house, with power both political and monetary.

No. She would be doing them both a disservice if she told him yes. Aye, *she* could be making a brilliant match, but how long before she ceased to amuse him? Before he wanted the company of a more conventional, and less possessive, woman? Then he would take a mistress. She did not think she could stand that.

Despite all the ladies and gentlemen she knew who lived under just such circumstances, she knew she could never listen to the carriage drive away knowing he was going to another woman and then smile at him over coffee the next morning.

No. She'd kill him.

No, that was not clarity of thought. That was emotion. She took a deep breath. Yes, Ramsey Munro wanted her. But he wanted "Corie," too. And the woman at the bacchanal. And how many others before and since?

He'd only made the offer because she was a virtuous if impecunious gentlewoman, and he had made an oath to do anything in his power to protect her. He had said nothing of affection, let alone love. Oh, he wanted her. That was a factor, too. Because he could not honorably proposition a gentlewoman except through an offer of marriage. Had he not asked "Corie," a woman he clearly considered an adventuress, to be his lover?

And she wanted that. She wanted to be Ram Munro's lover.

But there was only one way she would allow herself that, one way she could spend months, perhaps even years, with him. A way that, when his attention waned and he no longer wanted her, she would not be condemned to a lifetime of witnessing his polite indifference, the gradual death of his desire.

She could become his mistress.

He was standing bare-chested in the stinking dungeon, the acrid scent of his own burning flesh filling his nostrils, a rushing sound filling his ears. His own blood, he supposed dazedly. Though he could barely stand, somehow he conspired to re-

main upright, his vision dimming with the welcome coming of oblivion.

"Pretty, don't you think, monsieur?" the warden of the prison stepped back to admire the handiwork they had made of him, pointing at his chest. "Almost as pretty as you. Perhaps next week we should brand your cheek—but there's the problem. We have tried it before, and always the brand goes straight through to the jaw. Then it is not so pretty. The ladies run in horror rather than swoon with appreciation."

"Wouldn't want to frighten the ladies," he managed to gasp.

He hadn't screamed. Or had he? It didn't seem to make any difference now. Who was there to impress? But he hadn't told them about the farmer who'd aided them or the ship's captain who'd transported him or the young lieutenant at Malmaison who'd been their contact. That . . . now that was impressive.

"That is what I like about you, Munro. Your sophistication. Your refinement. It is such a pleasure to meet someone of your stamp here. The rest of these scum . . . Bah! But you!"

"My God, Gardien, are you propositioning me?" Ram asked, twisting his lips into the old, disparaging smile. The thousands of nerve endings exposed and then seared by the white-hot brand screeched, bringing tears to his eyes. He would start sobbing soon. He would hate for the warden to see him sob.

"Because, as flattered as I am, I must decline the honor. You see, there's this chap below who's been plying me with gruel, and I would hate to be thought to be taking the better—"

The blow caught him upside the head. His last coherent thought was one of gratitude.

• • •

Ram bolted upright in his bed, gasping for breath. The memory had taken him by the throat, as it always did, coming when he was most weak, most susceptible—in his dreams. He braced his arms at his sides, gulping in great lungfuls of air. And that is when he noticed it was pitch black, the only light a sliver of illumination coming from under the door leading to the hallway. Someone had closed the heavy velvet drapes covering the windows. Someone who was still here. Someone who stood very near—

He lashed out, catching hold of a slight form and tumbling it to the bed. He felt an instant of surprise as he straddled the figure beneath him, pinning her under him. *Her. Helena.*

Dressed, he realized, in breeches. Velvet by the feel of them. And her hair. Even in the darkness it would show pale, like a faerie nimbus. She must, he realized in a fog of confusion, be dressed in her boy's garments.

"You said if I came you would welcome me as your lover." Her voice was hoarse, stripped of her native accents. "You said nothing about being a wrestling partner."

His lover? He sank back, slowly releasing her arms, striving to find the right tone, the right words, while he sorted his jumbled thoughts. "But my dear, that is exactly what a lover is."

He felt her swallow. He felt a great deal, warmth seeping through her velvet coat, the hipbones jutting against his inner thighs, the slightness of her form . . . And, abruptly remembering that he wore nothing but a nightshirt, realized that she must feel a great deal, too.

He eased off of her. She didn't move. She lay motionless on her back, a barely visible form against the sheets. He could hear her breathing, rapid and shallow. Afraid? Reconsidering the entire lover construct?

Then he felt her fingers fumble across his chest and move up to his throat. Deftly, she pulled the loose opening down across his chest and then, like a blind man learning a sculpture, her fingers traveled with mind-searing gentleness over the brand.

"I watched you while you were sleeping."

He could scarce countenance it. He slept lightly. He always had. His life had often depended on it, but some portion of his brain must have recognized her and let him sleep on, feeling safe. Ha. If this was safety, he ought to have preferred peril. For there was nothing harmless in her devastating touch. It exposed him, revealed him, made him aware of how starving he was.

"I saw this. It's a rose, isn't it?" she murmured, her fingertips playing lightly over his flesh, his life.

"Yes."

"You were . . ."

"Branded. In a prison."

"Why?"

"The warden claimed it was to encourage me to remember. Ultimately, he was right. The rose does help me remember. But not the things he asked for."

Her touch was mesmerizing, her voice a warm current he wanted to drown in. "What then?"

"It reminds me to stay out of dungeons."

She hadn't expected that. He heard a sharp intake of breath and then a surprised laugh. She linked her hands around his neck. "That is a pity. A rose, so exotic and lush, should remind you of other pleasures."

"Are you tempting me?"

"I certainly hope so."

What was she playing at? He was tired of games. His dreams had chased him from the memory of death to heart-pounding wakefulness, and his body celebrated, heavy with desire, growing harder with each moment. He was impatient, frustrated, and the self-control he so carefully maintained did not hold nearly as well here, in the dark, with her body under his.

"And how am I to respond?" he asked coolly, though his hands of their own accord, slipped beneath her shoulders, lifting her a little.

"As a man," she answered breathlessly.

"Oh, I can assure you, on that count you will not be disappointed." He smiled into the darkness. She would be glad not to see it. "No, what I meant is what mien would you have me adopt? Whom shall I be in this dark room?"

"I don't understand," she said with a trace of confusion.

"Do you prefer the polished swordsman, the sophisticated rake, the disreputable habitué of low places? Shall I be tender or careless? Rough? Interested only in my own pleasure? Shall I fill your ears with compliments? Or oaths?"

She pulled back. He could feel her inner recoil as well. "I don't understand you. I came here at your bidding. You said if I ever wanted a lover I should come to you. Now you mock me."

"And here I thought *you* were mocking *me*." He found the fastening of her coat and nimbly opened it, lifting her arms and pulling her out of the restrictive garment. Idly he unwrapped the cravat she wore and let it slide to the floor, returning to open her shirt. She did not resist. With a slow, inexorable tug he drew it over her head and fingered the fabric beneath. Thin as gossamer, warm and subtly scented. A chemise.

"How . . . how so?" Her words struggled out. Her hands gripped his shoulders more tightly now, as if she needed an anchor. He ignored the implicit trepidation in those clenched fingers. He ignored the impulse to lift her from his bed and set her on her feet and send her on her way.

"Well," he said, plucking at the bows at the top of the chemise until he'd pulled it undone and the fabric fell open. He spread it wide and felt the instant the night air raised the flesh on her chamois-soft skin. "You are the one who comes to me in the darkness, still clad in your boy's clothes. Still in disguise."

He lowered his head until his lips touched the very base of her throat and opened his mouth over the fragile skin. Her pulse fluttered rapidly under his tongue.

"Since you are playing a role, I thought you would like me to play one, too." He traced a line with the tip of his tongue along the delicate collar bone. "I have, as I outlined, a certain proficiency with many."

She trembled. He released her and her hands fell away. Sitting back, in one movement he dragged his nightshirt over his head and tossed it aside.

He looked down at her shadowy figure and, seeing just enough to find her arms, clasped her wrist and set her hand on the middle of his chest. At once, realizing he was naked, her hand clenched into a fist. "Well"—his voice was thick—"what do you want of me? What guise am I to assume?"

Her hard little fist slowly relaxed against him, the tension in her body releasing in a sort of final capitulation. "Love me."

The words, no more than a breath, cautious and uncertain in the dark, warm room, speared through him, as decimating as any blade, as transforming as any brand.

He descended upon her like an incubus, dark and hungry, hovering over her, braced on his arms. He bent his head and kissed her, buffeting her temples and her eyes with little kisses, her smooth brow and the angle of her jaw, the bridge of her nose and the curve of her cheek, with warm, burnishing caresses. Her hand opened like a flower against the dark crisp hairs covering his chest and spread flat, absorbing his heat, the rhythm of his pulse, riding the heavy rise and fall of his chest.

"Love me," she repeated.

With a groan he sank down, settling his body over hers. Soft breasts yielded as his hands flowed down her shoulders and followed the narrowing column of her ribs to the small waist and the sweet, feminine flare of hips. The velvet pantaloons got in his way. He worked the front placket open and skimmed his palms down her hips, peeling the pantaloons off, pulling first one leg up and then the other until he'd freed her of her boy's clothing.

His head swam with the feel of her beneath his hands. He rolled sideways, pulling her with him, his palm beginning a return journey up the velvety skin of her outer thigh, pushing up beneath the thin chemise and finding

her breast, plump and hard-tipped. With devastating deliberation he molded it to his palm, kneaded it, played
with her, while like a thief with his ear to a tumbler lock,
he listened, attuning himself to the slightest variation in
her breathing, each little hitch, each gasp, until he heard
the second he'd unlocked her defenses and she surren-
dered to pleasure with a quavering sigh.

Then he lowered his mouth and suckled.

She squirmed restlessly, not knowing what she
wanted, how to ask, what to give in return. Virgins,
thought Ram, with a brief flicker of humor, and then with
a little cry she arched into the pleasure he gave her, her
hands tangling in his hair, holding him tight. His heart
thundered in response, his thoughts thickened with the
scent of her, the feel of her, the taste of her.

Somehow he managed to summon some semblance of
restraint, the need to go slow imperative, more urgent
than the need to bury the rod that swelled between his
legs. He released her swollen nipple, trailing a long,
moist kiss down the nether curve of her breast, to the
shallow basin of her belly, pausing at her navel to swipe
the little knot with his tongue and send a shiver racing
through her. Stroking her arms and sides and thighs, he
moved lower.

"Please," she whispered, her voice raw and vulnerable.
"Please, Ram." Her fingers dug into his shoulders as if
she might be ripped to shreds by the force of the sensations that assailed her and sought some anchor in the
storm that moved over her, in her, through her.

His hands abruptly dipped beneath her, cupping the
round, womanly buttocks and lifting as he shifted his
shoulders, forcing her thighs apart.

"Ram?"

"Trust me. Let me make what will come easier," he whispered, blowing his words softly across a thatch of silky curls.

"That's wicked!" she breathed, scandalized, trying to squeeze her thighs together. Failing.

"Yes," he said and settled his mouth over her. She bucked, and he held her tighter, holding her down as he languidly traced the soft feminine fold along the narrow opening to the small bud at its top.

"This is sinful— *Ah!*"

He flicked his tongue against the little kernel. She shuddered. He sipped it delicately into his mouth. She reacted instantly, twisting away from and then bowing against his mouth. He lifted her closer, dragging his tongue more firmly against her this time, setting up a rhythm.

"No . . . oh, please." Her words were muffled, her body damp. "You can't . . . no, please. Make it . . . What is?"

He tongued her more quickly now, feeling the tension building in her, in the long thighs that bunched with muscles, the fingers digging frantically into his shoulders. Desire tore him, raked him across coals far hotter than any the LeMons dungeon had ever offered.

Blood roared in his ears. His muscles clenched in his belly. Not yet. Not yet. She must know there was pleasure at the end. Not just pain.

He closed his eyes and mated her with his tongue.

"Oh . . . oh! . . . No. Yes!" Her body quaked. Tension hummed through her like a blow on steel. She arched up, suspended for one long moment. She didn't breathe. And then a sob. Another. And then she was sinking back, the tension ebbing from her limbs, her body melting into the mattress.

And she laughed.

Helena laughed because she feared she might cry. Oh, Lord! No wonder! All the things Kate had told her. Oh, she understood now.

"Generally young ladies do not respond to my love-making with laughter." Ram's silky voice slipped like warm brandy over her thoughts, heating them again almost at once. Was that to be her fate now? A few words from Ram and her skin heated, her breasts grew heavy and sensitive, and her mouth ached for his?

She lifted her arms and found him braced over her, the hard, dense musculature, the lean flanks, broad shoulders, and narrow hips. He went very still, breathless in anticipation. Of what? Her touch?

Her hands slipped from the broad shoulders down his chest, combing through the soft curls, testing the idea. He shuddered but remained motionless, suspended above her while she traced the rose brand with her fingertips. She wanted to kiss him, and in this dark, magical sphere she could do whatever she wanted.

She wrapped her arms around his neck and pulled herself up, kissing his lean, still face, the roughness of his morning beard tingling against her sensitized lips. She kissed his chin, she kissed his throat. She moved lower, brushing soft buffeting kisses along his breastbone and over the angry, raised welts of the rose brand.

"I am accounted, by almost all who know me, a most temperate man." His voice did not sound temperate. It sounded harsh. The honeyed brandy tones had gone raw and smoky. "But you are challenging that notion, my love."

"Am I?" she murmured, nipping now. His skin was so deliciously warm, veiling the strength of sinew and tendon so gorgeously. A light dampness covered it. Proof of the self-restraint he'd claimed.

"I wanted to make this easy for you. Gentle."

"What?" she asked, trying to pull him down on top of her, suddenly overcome with the need to burrow into him, to meld her body to his, to be absorbed by all that beautiful, potent masculinity.

"This," he said and swooped down. She met his lips with an open mouth, her tongue seeking his. Wet, passionate, they traded kisses with drunken abandon, his body pressing down on hers, his shaft a thick, hard presence throbbing against the inside of her thigh.

He reached between them, spreading the folds he'd drenched with her climax, finding again that acute, nerve-rich little piece of flesh and brushing it with his thumb. Her hips canted upward, wanting more, clinging to him as he tormented her with rough, shaking hands, pulling her legs apart, setting his knees between them. He replaced his finger with something blunt and hard.

"More. Ram," she begged raggedly. "*Please.*"

He thrust into her. Her eyes flew open, the spiraling buildup of sensation fleeing before this sharp intrusion. She shrank away from the thick presence pushing into her, stretching her. He caught her hips in shaking hands.

"No!" he grated out. "Be still!"

She bit down on her lip, forcing herself to remain motionless. She could hear his breathing, harsh and uneven. His head dropped, his forehead coming to rest against her shoulder. She waited, tense and a little frightened. She knew it hurt most women, but she'd thought, because of what had gone before, she'd assumed—

He kissed her throat. He angled his head against hers and kissed the skin beneath her ear, a gentle brush of lips. She flinched. His clasp gradually eased, though that part of him still buried deep within her body gentled not at all, but stayed hard and thick.

"I am sorry," he said and kissed her lips with exquisite care, with thought-blurring tenderness. "I have never done this with a virgin. I am . . . I am not . . ." he trailed off, his voice raw. "I would have done this better if I but knew how."

She loved him.

She reached up and cupped his cheek with her hand. He turned his face into her hand, kissing her palm, kissing her wrist. Desire fluttered within her. She shifted, the feeling of him inside her no longer so painful, and the movement pulled a chord of pleasure from her. "This is making love?" she asked.

He moved, slowly withdrawing his shaft. She did not want him to, and that surprised her. She followed his retreat.

"No," he said. "Like this."

He eased himself back inside, the drag on her feminine fold bringing a jolt of reawakened hunger. He started a deliberate return, and this time she met it, lifting her hips to accommodate him, as want began to take hold of her.

"Dear God," he muttered thickly and began thrusting, his hips taking on a slow, possessive cadence that caught the most sensitive part of her feminine flesh against the ridge of his erection. She wanted more. She wanted to feel him hilted all the way within her, his body flush with hers. She spread her legs wider, angled her hips, answered the increasing pace of his thrusts. He growled low in his throat and he grasped her legs behind the knees and notched them over his hips, making his possession deeper, each thrust demanding more.

Her body welcomed it. Welcomed his rough ride, his sweat-slicked torso moving against hers. And when he caught her hands and braided her fingers with his, stretching her arms high over her head and holding her pinned there, she recognized the thundering pulse that spiraled in ever tightening circles. She felt him in her, on her, strong, virile, a riptide of sensation . . . pleasure spearing through her . . . a harsh cry of masculine release and . . . there . . . there . . . ah! *there!*

She collapsed, spent and exhausted as he eased off of her. Her thoughts formed, dissolved, and swirled. Her body felt alien, lax, indolent. Hedonistic, she supposed. Saturated with so much pleasure she could hold no more. She could like being a hedonist. She reached for Ram, wanting to explore again all the planes and contours that made him. But he'd sat up.

"I'll get some warm water and a towel." His voice was tender, concerned.

That would be delight— No! "No!" she scrambled upright, gathering the sheets around her body as if he could see her. "No." If he brought water, he would bring light. He would see her. She was not ready. Not yet. She wanted to stay a hedonist, exist outside the world for just a little longer. With him.

The room was silent. Outside, beneath the window, a

dray cart lumbered by, the harness bells tinkling in the still of early dawn.

The mattress creaked as Ram stood up.

"Why 'no,' Helena?" he asked coolly, "Are you still resolved not to marry me?"

TWENTY-FIVE

RETREAT:
step back; opposite of advance

AT THE SOUND of her name, Helena bolted upright. "How long have you known?"

The drapes suddenly swished open, light spilling into the room. She snatched the sheets to her breasts, blinking. He turned around, his hand still on the pull, magnificently, entirely, naked. He didn't even notice. He stood as haughtily and indifferently as he had in Lady Tilpot's ballroom. His arms were long and smoothly muscled, his powerful legs covered with the same dark hair that grew in a thick tee across his chest and down his belly. Her gaze traveled lower. His erection lay quiescent now among a thick brush of black hair. Heat exploded in her cheeks, and she looked away. "Answer me."

"I've always known. I knew the minute I saw you in Lovers Walk who you were."

He'd known? He'd kissed her like that in Vauxhall,

nearly taken her against an alley wall, then met her as Helena Nash, pretending to seduce her, pretending not to know already exactly how ardent a response he could draw from her. He'd let her come to him, forfeiting her dignity, all the while knowing she . . .

"You bastard."

Backlit by the tall window, it was impossible to read his expression. "Well, yes." So silky, that voice. So dry. "But I thought we'd already covered that point."

"You've been toying with me! Just like you toy with those men to whom you teach swordplay."

"No. I haven't."

"Yes," she insisted, mortified and furious. She climbed off the bed, snatching up her pantaloons and yanking them on. He didn't move.

"Am I supposed to say I'm sorry?" he asked. "Because, if you desire I should do so, I will, but pray recall, Miss Nash, that you are the one who began this masquerade. I simply went along with it."

She grabbed the white shirt from where it had been thrown across a nearby chair and flung it over her head. "You should have told me. You could have stopped the masquerade at any time!"

"And what?" The silkiness had gone, anger hummed in his voice, "ruined your *adventure?* I wouldn't think of disappointing a lady."

"Bastard!"

"Again? Really, if you are to haunt low places, I will have to teach you some new words. 'Bastard' is so pitifully pedestrian."

She choked back an angry response, feeling the burn of tears rise in her eyes. No. She would not cry.

She spied her cravat on the floor and snapped it up, looping it around her neck before shoving her bare feet into her slippers.

"Helena—" She rounded to find him coming toward her. The light fell full on his face now. No more shadows. He looked hard, angry, his eyes brilliant. "Helena, wait."

"Why? So you can laugh some more?"

"I'm not laughing."

She flung back her head and her hair lashed back. "Oh, how wonderfully amusing it must have been for you. The dignified, unassailable Miss Nash twining herself about you like a cat in heat. Oh!" She covered her face.

He grabbed her hand, spinning her around to face him. "What? Are you so much above my touch that the thought of wanting me brings blazes of humiliation to your cheeks?" he demanded between clenched teeth.

She had never seen such emotion on his countenance. His eyes burned, the muscles in his jaw leapt, his lips curled in a snarl. "And if we are to discuss the wheres and whens of disclosure, Miss Nash, when were you going to tell me who you were? Or did you intend simply to keep coming to my bed in the darkness until you tired of your bastard lover?"

"No!"

"When, then?" he demanded, his hand tightening painfully about her wrist. "When were you going to reveal your name to me, 'Corie'?"

She stared up at him, furious, unable to answer. She didn't know. She hadn't thought that far ahead. That had been the problem with this, with her reaction to him from the beginning. She hadn't thought. She had simply . . . wanted. Because she loved him.

She was such a bloody, bloody fool. He mustn't know. All she could salvage of this night were a few shreds of pride. She lifted her chin, heedless of the tears spilling down her face.

His brows snapped together in sudden anguish. "Don't."

"Let me go."

"No. This is wrong." He shook his head. "We are talking at cross purposes. Marry me."

"That won't be necessary. I assure you, I am not breeding." Her courses were imminent, a day away at most.

"This has nothing to do with necessity," he said, anger flashing anew in his eyes. "You must know that I—"

"Mr. Munro!" A series of violent knocks sounded on the bedroom door. "Mr. Munro! Please!" Gaspard called frantically.

"Not now, Gaspard!" Ramsey thundered, his eyes locked with Helena's.

"But, sir! You said if ever the lady came I was to tell you no matter what," Gaspard called through the door. "She is here! And she is most upset. She insists on seeing you!"

Pain, terrible and swift as thought, shattered through Helena. Her eyes widened in shocked betrayal.

"No." He stared at her. "No." He shook his head violently, reaching out for her, but she scrambled back out of his reach, groping for the door.

"Helena, you misunderstand." His voice was tense but his gaze hopeless. It was condemnation enough.

"Oh, no," she said, her lips wet with her own tears. "I understand. Pray beg my pardon of the lady, and tell her I didn't realize I was impinging on her time."

She jerked the door open and ran.

• • •

Ramsey cursed savagely, pulling on the robe Gaspard tossed to him and striding into the hall after Helena. She'd disappeared. Bloody hell and damnation! He raked his hair back. He'd had her, his Helena, in his arms, in his bed, and he'd driven her out. Because of his pride, his fucking pride!

She was right. He should have told her right from the beginning he knew her identity, but he hadn't. At first, because he had given unwilling countenance to her spurious claim of wanting an adventure and later, later because he had wanted her to come to him. He'd wanted her to prove her, hell, what? That she loved him by an act of faith?

And why should she when she'd never received the same from him? God, how wrong headed could he be, and now . . . now he'd lost her.

A vacuum opened in his heart, leaving only a gaping open wound that threatened to swallow him whole and pitch him into a blacker place than any LeMons dungeon had held. He squeezed his eyes shut, gritting his teeth. Merciful God, what had he done?

"Ramsey!" With a savage growl, he swung around at the sound of the female voice.

Page Winebarger's hand flew to her chest and she backed away from the ferocity on his face.

"She's gone, Ram. Helena! I spent all night looking for her, driving around the town before coming because I knew you would . . ."

He shut his eyes tight for a brief second, and she saw his nostrils flare as he took a deep breath. He was striving for control, she realized. Ram Munro, the most perfectly composed man she knew.

She held out her hands in pity and entreaty. "I am so sorry. I lost her, and DeMarc is nowhere to be found, and oh, Ram! I fear the worst! Forgive me! I swear I have done my best in the favor you asked of me! Please, dress at once. We must find her."

"She's safe, Page."

"No," Page shook her head. "She's missing—"

"She just left me."

Numbed, Helena climbed the servants' stairs to her third-floor room. Of course, there would be another woman. Just as, of course, he'd known Helena's own identity. A man like that? He probably knew a woman by her individual scent. Probably memorized individual curves, the sound of a specific woman's cries, the way she kissed . . .

The tears began again, and she pressed her fist against her lips. She must not cry. Not anymore. She must strive for composure. Wasn't that who she was, composed, dignified, unassailable Miss Nash? If she could just return to who she'd been, she would be safe again. Tranquil. Numb.

There'd been clues all along. He'd not wanted to teach her swordplay, but of all the objections he'd made, he'd never mentioned the most obvious: that a woman does not carry a sword. *Unless she's not dressed as a woman.* And when she'd appeared at his salle and he'd said "Helena," he'd been calling her name, not recalling her face from a long past meeting.

Oh, God. Why hadn't she told him? Why hadn't she revealed who she was to him from the first? But she knew the answer. Because it had been too exciting, too fascinating, his world of no rules and no consequences. Except there were consequences. She'd fallen in love.

Stand in queue, Helena, she told herself. Wait your turn.

Damn these tears, anyway.

She'd always thought of herself as better than everyone else, she realized now. A little superior in her mind if not in her status. A bit finer in her self-containment. A little above it all.

She bit her lips. She just wanted to be back in his arms again, and that scared her. She needed her pride. It was the one thing no one had ever been able to take: her pride. But what good was it now?

Should she return to him and say, "Yes, I will marry you," and for the next decades try not to hear the whispers about his latest conquest while her heart broke over and over again?

Yes. No!

Should she be his mistress instead? A piece of property to be replaced when a brighter, fresher face caught his eye? Oh, he would do it well. Ram Munro would do everything well. He'd see her set up in a house with a tidy little sum in the bank but . . . she would see him with his latest love. In the park. At the opera. Driving in St. James.

Was future heartache worth a year with him? Four years? Ten?

No. Yes!

With burned and vacant eyes, she stopped before her door. A clock chimed the fifth hour from somewhere deep in the house. She untwined the cravat from her throat, and something pricked her thumb. Listlessly she looked down at her hands. Ram's gold rose pin sparkled on its bed of white silk. In her haste to leave she must have picked up his cravat rather than the one she'd worn.

She touched the little carved rose with trembling fingers, trying in her mind to invest the smooth metal with his body's warmth. Tortured, branded, set to rot in a dungeon, and he'd emerged able to smile at years of horror she could not even imagine.

"Stay out of dungeons," he said he'd learned from the experience. How many men would have come through with their spirit intact? And yet . . . and yet he wore a rose outside as well as beneath his clothing. How complicated he was. How complicated things were. She didn't know herself. She pushed open the door—

"Helena!"

She jumped back at the unexpected sound of Flora's voice coming from inside her room, and then tentatively moved forward. A large mound of blankets and coverlets shifted on her bed. "Flora?"

Flora's big brown eyes peeped over the edge of a heavy wool blanket. "What are you doing here?" the girl asked anxiously. No, not anxiously, angrily.

"I sleep here." She was not about to start explaining to Flora her whereabouts. "What are you doing here?"

"I left you a note. I slipped it under your door just after ten o'clock last night."

"What note?" Helena asked, bewildered. She was in no state of mind to deal with Flora's pregnancy-related idiosyncrasies.

"I asked you to trade rooms with me at midnight, and when I came up here and you were gone, well, I naturally assumed that you . . ." She trailed off, her wide eyes narrowing. "If you haven't been in my room, where *have* you been? And dressed like that?"

"I . . . I have been looking for Mr. Goodwin, of course."

"All night?"

"Yes." Helena nodded, feeling stupid and callow.

"Oh, my dear!" The coverlet slipped lower, and Flora sat up, holding her arms out. "My darling friend. But you needn't have! If only you had read the note. For, indeed, Mr. Goodwin is here!"

With a flourish worthy of the best magician, Flora whipped off the coverlet, revealing a red-faced but beaming Oswald Goodwin. Thankfully, wearing a nightshirt.

Helena stared at him, open-mouthed. "What is Mr. Godwin doing in my bed?" she asked, and then, "No. Do not answer. Get him out of my bed, please. At once."

"Of course, Miss Nash," Oswald said and slipped to the far side of the bed, where he pushed his arms into what Helena tentatively identified as one of Flora's dressing gowns.

"Do you realize that if you are caught—"

"Well, Helena, really!" Flora popped out of her side of the narrow bed. "How stupid do you imagine us to be? Of course we realize the consequences of being caught. That is why we traded rooms with you. Aunt Alfreda seldom visits me at night, but she would not be caught dead coming to a servant's room."

"And what was I to have said if she had appeared in your room and found me there?"

"You would have thought of something," Flora replied confidently.

Canny, Helena thought dazedly.

"Still, could you have not waited to . . . to . . . be with one another?" Helena asked. "Because Mr. Goodwin assured me that his boat, so to speak, is about to come in."

"Indeed, yes," Oswald said, smiling sunnily as he tied the dressing gown's pink satin sash into a bow. "That is why I sent Flora that message saying I would come to her last night. Things will be settled in two days, as a matter of fact."

"Two days," Helena repeated suspiciously.

"Yes. Well, that is the final round of competition for the International Dueling Tournament. The preliminary flights are held today and tomorrow."

"Flights?" Helena repeated in confusion. Why were they talking about the tournament unless . . . *Oh, no. Oh, please. No.*

"Yes," Flora nodded sagely. Apparently, over the course of her evening with Oswald, amongst other things she had become proficient at swordfight tournament terminology. "The flights are the divisions of competitors ranked by their previous wins *or* their reputations. Some gentlemen haven't had to fight in the preliminary rounds. Like Count Winebarger and Michel St. Joan."

Oswald winked at Flora. "And do not forget Mr. Munro."

Helena's heart trip-hammered in her chest. "Mr. Munro?"

"Yes!" Flora said excitedly. "Mr. Ramsey Munro. The gentleman at Aunt Alfreda's ball, and do not pretend you do not know who I am talking about, because the tittle-tattle is that he could not be kept away from you and that you sat for twenty minutes in the garden together."

"What about Mr. Munro?" she asked.

"He is the reason that Ossie and I shall be able to be reunited."

"*What?*"

"It is true, Miss Nash." Oswald came round the bed to stand next to Flora, seated at the end. He took her hand, and Flora, with a sigh of contentment, rested her cheek against the back of his. Rather like a spaniel leaning into her master's side. "I have studied the field for months, and after speaking to everyone who is anyone in the sport, it became clear to me that, though the tournament boasts the most celebrated names in the field of dueling, Munro will prevail."

Helena regarded him with dawning horror. "You are betting that Ramsey Munro will win the dueling tournament?"

"Yes!"

But Ramsey was withdrawing. "You can't," she said faintly.

"Oh, there's no 'can't' about it," Oswald said, rocking back on his heels. "Believe me, Miss Nash. I know what I'm doing. Munro is as nerveless a fellow as God ever made."

"What has *nerve* to do with anything?"

Oswald leaned forward, his glance darting left and right as if he suspected someone was eavesdropping. "Few people know this—if they did I wouldn't be on the way to making nearly so much money—but Munro was held in a French dungeon for *over two years.*" He nodded sententiously.

"*Everyone* knows that."

He straightened, blustered a bit, and finally nodded

his concession. "Well, *that*, yes. But what they don't know is that during those two years he was forced to fight duels with the guards."

That she hadn't known.

"Duels in which if he injured the guard, he would pay with the loss of some piece of his anatomy. So he had to hone his skill to a perfect pitch, winning without harming his opponent; or losing, somehow, without being griev-ously injured himself." Helena's hand moved over her belly, sickened. Oswald might have been discussing a cockfight, not a living man.

"He had to learn to separate emotion from talent, something few men, even the best, have ever been able to do. Can you imagine what a great advantage that must be in a tournament? But not many know about that. And thus the odds do not reflect it."

"He is not favored to win?"

"Oh, no. He's a relative newcomer to the sport, having been in London fewer than four years. He has a reputa-tion, but not nearly so great as that of others. I have begged, pleaded, borrowed from everyone I know, and have managed to accrue *fifty-three thousand, four hundred and eighty-eight pounds*, which I have wagered at the rate of twelve to one in his favor."

"You can't. Give it back."

"Too late for that," Oswald said happily. "Already made the bet."

"But what if he doesn't fight? They'd give you back your money then, wouldn't they?" she asked desperately.

Both Flora and Oswald were regarding her mournful-ly, trading glances that clearly bespoke their disap-pointment in her. "These aren't men who give back money. Might shift the wager to another player. But, frankly, I would be terrified to do that. Don't know the rest of the field from a hill of beans."

"But you said you'd studied it!"

"Well, studied in a sort of relative way. It's Munro I've been studying. Why do you think I had you meet me at that, er, rather risqué entertainment in White Friars? Don't go to those sorts of places myself. I'm a married man! I went because I heard Munro was giving a demonstration."

"And if Munro loses?"

Oswald bounced on his toes. "Ain't going to."

"But what if he does?" she demanded and wondered why Flora wasn't asking these questions instead of just sitting there staring up at Oswald as if he was Apollo come in his sun chariot to take her away.

"Have to slit my throat, I suppose," he finally said, sighing heavily. "Only honorable thing to do."

At this, Flora blanched, clutched her heart, and surged upright, throwing her arms around Oswald and sobbing into the shoulder of her pink dressing gown.

Mr. Oswald patted her on the back and looked balefully over her head at Helena. "How could you, Miss Nash? And her breeding and all?"

"I have to go," she said slowly.

He smiled a little tightly. "That might be for the best."

She backed out of her room, closing the door behind her. She moved as if in a dream. She could see no choice in what she intended to do. She would dress in one of Flora's gowns, greet Lady Tilpot at breakfast, and tell her that Flora was in the throes of yet another megrim. She would listen to Lady Tilpot's penny-by-penny account of last night's whist game, and then, afterwards, give the boy who swept the street crossing six pence to carry a note to Ram Munro.

And with it a golden rose.

TWENTY-SIX

REDOUBLEMENT:
*a new action that follows an attack
that missed or was parried*

THE ROYAL AMPHITHEATRE was filled to capacity. Though generally reserved for equestrian demonstrations, the auditorium had been resurfaced with fresh sawdust for this, the last day of the International Dueling Tournament. Nervous contestants, awaiting their turn to be disqualified from the competition or to go forth to the next round, milled about the perimeter of the arena, while inside the marked areas pairs of gentlemen matched their talent against one another until one of them was the first to score five hits against his opponent. If he succeeded, he went on in the competition.

Each battle tested not only skill but spirit as well, for even though the rules strictly denounced the drawing of blood, blood was often drawn. Consequently, as the tournament progressed each bout grew more fierce as exhaustion and nerves overtook the contestants.

It was early in the evening still and another three rounds to go before the championship was held. The ton, finally bored with the season's passion for masquerades, attended the event in full force, galvanized by a fantastical and unimaginable rumor that had leaked out of the amphitheater and raced like wildfire through Society: An Englishman, Cottrell's bastard grandson—who was a bastard no more, but that was another story—was marching through the ranks of competitors with a determination that seemed to suggest that he actually meant to win the damn thing!

The three levels of balconies surrounding the arena already teemed with spectators, and yet each moment more and more people arrived, ladies as well as gentlemen standing four deep, crowding every available box and doorway. Having made a substantial loan to the amphitheatre's owners for rebuilding the venue last year, Lady Tilpot had managed to secure a prime box.

"Milford is coming on next," Lady Tilpot confided to the party of social luminaries she hosted. She had taken to calling Ram by his courtesy title, Earl of Milford, with a familiarity that set Helena's teeth on edge. "Don't know who he's up against. Don't 'spect it will matter. He will win, of course."

"I'd heard he was withdrawing," said one of the swarm of young blades.

"I, also," said Lord Figburt. Figgy, too, had entered the competition as an unranked entrant. He'd made it to the third round yesterday before losing and was feeling quite pleased with himself. "I wonder what happened."

I happened, Helena thought, still amazed by her own

audacity. The words she had written Ram had taken a long time to compose, and yet they had been so few:

You must win the dueling tournament.
Helena

With the note she had sent the gold rose.

There had been no reply. Not a word. But he'd arrived at the competition yesterday morning and had set about mowing down his competition like a dark scythe.

"Pride," Lady Tilpot sniffed. "National pride. Something other young men would do well to emulate." She twisted her bulky form around and gave a dour stare to her niece tucked well back in the box with that unfortunate hanger-on, Oswald Goodfin? Goodriddance?

Flora returned her stare with an apologetic smile, giving a slight shrug, as if to ask what she could do without being unspeakably rude. And what could she do? Lady Tilpot wondered balefully. The other seats were all occupied. Flora could hardly ask him to move and make way for a more desirable potential mate. Or could she—

"Ah! There he is!" Mrs. Winebarger, seated behind Helena, pointed her fan toward the far side of the arena. Helena stretched up in her seat to see Ram's dark head moving through a sea of gentlemen. They parted before his smooth, purposeful stride as he stepped over the raised curb that delineated the ring.

The English crowd roared with approval, stamping their feet and shouting their approval. For decades the French, Prussians, and Italians had dominated the art of swordsmanship. Ramsey was their native son, come to champion them.

For a champion he seemed woefully unaware of his status. He did not acknowledge the crowd. His face was set, stern and cold, eons away from the dashing, knowing sophisticate those in Society who knew him had expected. He lifted his sword from the table where the combatants' weapons had been brought prior to the duel, and lowered it to his side. In contrast, his opponent, a tall, barrel-chested Spaniard, seized his blade and executed several sweeping slashes through the air.

"Señor Calvino is very good," Mrs. Winebarger murmured. "Aggressive and decisive. Or so says my husband."

"Yes," Lady Tilpot drawled insincerely, pivoting on her rump to eye Mrs. Winebarger. "Too bad about your husband. Pity. I'm sure he would have deported himself well."

Mrs. Winebarger had sadly informed them that her husband had been injured yesterday when his opponent had skewered his thigh a second or so after time had been called. While he was lucky no arteries or tendons had been cut, he would be unable to continue in the competition. He could, she told them, barely walk. "Yes," she said sadly, "he would have done well."

"I am surprised you left him alone in his defeat. Though of course we are delighted you felt able to do so."

"I felt strongly that I had to be here," Mrs. Winebarger replied, but her cheeks carried little flags of color.

Below, the duel had begun. Ram's focus was the first thing one noticed. He moved with restrained calm, his stillness in direct contrast to the Spaniard's seemingly uncontainable vigor. The Spaniard did not lunge, he *bounded* in on the attack, his long sword arm stretched to the limit. But every attack Ram deflected; every line, he somehow turned; and at the end of each of Calvino's assaults, the tip of Ram's blade darted in to score a point, and then two, and then a third.

The Spaniard, realizing he would lose the match if he did not take command, utilized his greater size and mass, bludgeoning his way through Ram's guard to score twice in quick succession. Bolstered by his success, he lunged again.

But Ram had learned his opponent's tactics quickly and just as quickly adjusted for them. He stepped in, bringing the action close. The blades flashed and darted, striking with deadly precision.

"Four!" the referee shouted, pointing at Ram. And then, "Five!"

The crowd went mad as the Spaniard, panting and red faced, snapped forward at the waist, bowing deeply in Ram's direction. Ram returned his bow with seeming impatience and then, ignoring the wild cheers and whistles that hailed his victory, disappeared into the crowd.

"Good. Fast and effective. I approve," Lady Tilpot declared. "When will he fight next?"

"He'll have about an hour's rest, then he'll fight the winner of this round for the final bout."

"Ah. Excellent. And who would that be?"

"The Frenchman St. George or the Italian Il Cavaliere, Vettori."

"Well," Lady Tilpot said, "it should prove a very entertaining spectacle then. And I don't suppose we have time to go in search of some little comestible while we wait? No." She answered her own question dolefully, but then her expression lightened.

"But you, Miss Nash, whatever do you care about dueling and fencing and such? You don't. So do make yourself useful and go fetch some cakes and berries and some lemonade. Cheese would be nice. And if there's butter and honey for the cakes, all the better."

She could hardly refuse. Which meant she must hurry. She stood up at once and was surprised when Mrs. Winebarger rose beside her. "I will help you, my dear. Doubtless it will take more than one person to transport all of that."

Lady Tilpot didn't even pretend to object. Mrs. Winebarger's usefulness to her had come to an abrupt end with her husband's incapacitation.

"Thank you," Helena murmured, following her into the corridor.

Once outside, Mrs. Winebarger linked her arm through Helena's and purposefully led her toward one of the niches lining the outer wall. "I have been looking for an opportunity to talk to you all day," Mrs. Winebarger said urgently, taking a seat and indicating that Helena should do likewise. Reluctantly, Helena did so.

"Please, Mrs. Winebarger, I do not want to miss Mr. Munro's—"

"Miss Nash." Page held up her hand. Her blue-green eyes were strained, and lines of tension bracketed her mouth, *"You* are the reason I have left my Robert this day."

"What?" Helena asked. "I don't understand."

"My dear, you must promise to listen to everything I have to tell you. You must promise not to walk away from me after my first sentence. Can you promise me this?"

Helena regarded her in consternation. "Yes, ma'am."

Mrs. Winebarger took a deep breath. "*I* am the woman who came to Ram's house two nights ago. The night you were there."

Helena stared, stunned beyond words, suddenly hating this lovely woman, hating the easy familiarity with which she said Ram's name, hating the sympathy in her pretty eyes. It all made sense: the lovely Prussian's intimate knowledge of him and his family, her familiarity with his salle, the always conveniently absent husband. *This* was the woman Ram had said was to be shown in no matter what his state or whom he was with.

Worse, though, even more devastating a blow than the revelation of Mrs. Winebarger's relationship with Ram, was the implicit knowledge that he had told Page about her. About them.

"He told you about me?" she said hollowly. She stood up. Why hadn't he protected her dignity, or rather what little he'd left her?

Mrs. Winebarger nodded. "*Yes.* A long time ago. Before we even met. That is in part why I accepted Lady Tilpot's invitations—because I was curious about this young woman with whom Ramsey was so smitten. Especially as I don't even think he realized it himself."

Helena's heart skittered into an anguished rapid beat.

"You were afraid you would be replaced?" she asked.

"Replaced?" The lovely aqua-green eyes widened. "Oh, my dear. No! I came to Ramsey's house to tell him I had lost you!"

"What?"

The woman was clearly stricken with embarrassment. Her cheeks were pink with it. "Ram asked me to watch out for you. To befriend you."

"Why?" Helena sank back down onto the settee, bemused. "I don't understand."

"My husband and Ram share a love of fencing," she said, her gaze somber, "but they also shared a French prison cell. The English are not the only ones with whom France is, or has been, at war.

"Ram helped my Robert escape. A few years later, when he heard of Ram's own release, we came to England. I wanted to meet the man who had saved my Robert. We became fast friends, the three of us, and have kept in touch through the years." She smiled tenderly.

"Then when Robert entered this tournament we took the opportunity to renew our friendship. In the course of our conversations, I mentioned that I had met you, whom he had spoken of in the past. It was clear to me that Ram worried about you, something you had done, some risk he perceived you to be in. I asked what I could do to help." She lifted her shoulder as if the rest was a matter of course.

"But why? Why would he—"

Page shook her head. "My dear, he loves you. Didn't you know that?"

Helena stilled. *Loved her?* No. It wasn't possible. He had never come close to making such a declaration. He felt responsible for her. He wanted her. He had an obligation to her family.

"No." She shook her head, refusing to believe this siren's song. "He is perhaps infatuated. But as soon as he tires of me, there will be another to take my place. Why, all of London," she repeated Jolly Milar's words bitterly, "is littered with Ram Munro's past lovers."

Page hesitated. "If Ram knew I was telling you

this . . ." She trailed off, troubled and uneasy, but then took a deep breath and began. "Let me tell you about a young man who was raised by loving parents to believe that despite his illegitimacy he was as good as anyone else on God's earth.

"But when he is nine his parents die, and he is sent to a workhouse where, for a few terrible weeks, the brutal reality of his situation is born in him with unerring efficacy. Then, almost miraculously, or so it would seem, he is rescued from the workhouse by a priest and brought to a tiny abbey secluded deep in the Scottish Highlands, where he is given a reprieve from the life that awaits orphan bastards without friends or recourse. There he finds a new family, loving guidance, and brothers of the heart, and is reassured of his value, his worthiness. He begins to believe in it again.

"This boy grows into a young man of surpassing masculine beauty, but not so beautiful as his spirit, which is generous and noble and brave. So noble and brave that he and his comrades agree to go on a dangerous mission at the behest of his benefactor, the abbot."

"The French debacle," as Ram had called it, Helena realized.

"But they are caught, the boy is tortured and branded and forced to fight in duels. Then he watches a beloved friend executed, knowing that one of those whom he trusted and loved had betrayed them.

"After a near-miraculous release, he is freed and travels to London. And there he is, twenty-three years old, haunted, beautiful, and experienced in ways no young man ought to be, and inexperienced in ways no young man ought to be."

Warmth spread in Helena's cheeks. She understood: Ramsey had been a virgin. Mrs. Winebarger's next words confirmed it. "He was primed to fall in love. She was a baronet's daughter. Pretty, captivating, headstrong. Amoral. She wanted Ram. She wanted him, and she set out to get him, and this young woman always got what she wanted."

"And Ram?" Helena asked softly.

"Ram fell madly in love with her. And he thought she loved him, too."

Helena's eyes fell.

"He asked her to marry him." Mrs. Winebarger's eyes grew flinty. "Well, you can imagine her surprise and amusement at that. Ram was very handsome, yes, and a grand and ardent lover, but she was not going to marry a bastard Scot. She would, however, keep him for her lover after she wed the neighboring earl's rich, corpulent, middle-aged nephew.

"As you can well imagine, Ram declined her proposal very politely, and told her they would not be seeing each other again. And then he went a little mad. He did, indeed, cut a wide swathe through the rows of eligible and willing young ladies who flung themselves at him. If he was to be used, he might as well enjoy it."

Helena looked away, hating to hear the confirmation of all she feared, all she had heard.

"Except," Mrs. Winebarger's voice softened, "he *didn't* enjoy it. He quit debauching rather soon after he began, a little ashamed of himself, I think. A little disgusted.

"And then one night at Vauxhall, he encountered you.

It wasn't the first time. He'd watched over you for years. Ah? I see you know that. I wonder how. He told us how circumspect and discreet he was in his observance. Nothing untoward or disreputable must attach itself to the fine Miss Helena Nash's good name, and what could be more disreputable than Ram Munro?

"He had half fallen in love with you already, watching you, I think. You seemed to him perfect. Serene and detached—untouched by your fall in the world. Uncorrupted by the base passions that had for a short time swallowed him."

"It is all a fake," Helena murmured. "A sham. A mask."

"Some," Mrs. Winebarger agreed. "But not all. He didn't know that. All he knew is that you suddenly appeared at Vauxhall in boy's clothes, telling him you were meeting a married man, saying you wanted an adventure.

"Given his history, is it any wonder he distrusted you or the feelings you awoke in him? No. What is a wonder is that he ignored all the evidence of his eyes and ears and fell in love with you despite the fact that you seemed cut from the same cloth as the young woman who'd broken his heart."

Helena looked up. "You make me sound small and wretched, and him noble and munificent. But *he knew who I was*. He made a decision to keep me ignorant while he *judged* me."

Mrs. Winebarger nodded sadly. "Yes. He was wrong. But maybe he wanted you to prove yourself by your willingness to reveal your identity to him without being asked."

"To test me," Helena stated baldly. "Because he did

not trust me. I do not say I was right to keep my identity from him, but at least I did not ask him to prove himself to me."

"But he *has* proven himself. Time and again," Mrs. Winebarger answered quietly. "He had me watch out for you. He asked the marquis, whom he has always held accountable for his parents' deaths, to go with him to Lady Tilpot's so he could see for himself what danger you stood in. Can you imagine how bitter that request must have been for him to make? Yet he did so without hesitation. What more can he do?"

But he had done more! Helena realized, staring at her interlocked hands. He had done everything for her. Everything! Why, he was here, fighting a duel he was not in the least interested in, believing they had no future, *simply because she had asked it of him.*

And she? She had been too stupid, too blind, to see it, because of *rumors*. Because she had believed that any man so perfect, so handsome, could not own a true and faithful heart. Because she had judged him by appearances just as she herself had so often been judged. Because she had wanted him to trust her when she had never trusted him. She'd been so wrong. God, she deserved to lose him!

Dear God, she could not!

"I must find him."

Page Winebarger smiled. "Yes."

"I must—"

A small, grubby hand suddenly appeared on her sleeve and tugged. Helena looked up into the grimy, grinning face of an eight-year-old boy. "Bloke said as to find the prettiest blonde lady I could and I'd be speaking to Miss Nash. That right? That be you?"

"Yes?" Helena said distractedly. She must write a letter. No, she must seek Ram out at once. As soon as the tournament ended—

"Then here." The boy pushed a rose into her hand. A beautiful yellow rose.

She leapt to her feet, spinning around, her gaze searching through the crowd. "Where is he?"

"He said you was to meet him behind the amphitheatre, in the alley by the stables. Now."

"But." She looked to Mrs. Winebarger.

The Prussian lady nodded. "I'll take care of Lady Tilpot. Go."

Helena pushed her way through the dense crowd of spectators, lifting her skirts and dashing down the wide staircase to the main floor, but there traffic choked the front foyer. She wheeled around, slapped open a servants' door, and found herself in a kitchen surrounded by the startled staff, ankle deep in vegetable parings and chicken feathers.

"I have to get to the stable alley. Which way is quickest?" she demanded.

Mutely, one of the girls stirring a pot lifted her spoon and pointed at a back doorway.

"Thank you!" Helena breathed. She needed to see Ram. She needed to tell him she loved him, that she was a blind prig of a woman who'd only seen the situation from one vantage, and never his. That she wanted very much to marry him if he could still want her. And then to beg him to please, *please* still want her.

She raced through the door and, true to the girl's word, found herself in a fast-darkening alley, the walls of the amphitheatre separated from the neighboring buildings by a narrow lane that ended a short distance away in a stable yard.

"Ram?" she called. "Ram!"

A figure stepped out into the dim light spilling from the tall windows overhead. It shone on a guinea-gold head.

"Not Ram, my love," said Forrester DeMarc. "Not ever again."

TWENTY-SEVEN

FORTE:
the lower, strongest third of the blade

The devil is here. He has seen me. If we are to meet it must be in the stables behind the amphitheatre in one hour's time. I will stay no longer. Bring with you the money.
   Arnoux

Ram cursed roundly, crumpling the note in his fist. An hour? In an hour he would be fighting a duel, most probably with that damnably good Italian, Vettori. But how could he turn his back on Kit, on Douglas? He clenched his teeth in frustration, torn by the thrice-cursed choice he must make. Helena or the past? Helena, whose image burned like acid in his heart? Or the companions of his youth, his brothers?

"Mr. Munro?"

Ram turned. A dirty street urchin stood just inside the door of the small chamber reserved for the duelists. "What do you want, son?"

"I got a message for you," the boy said, screwing up his face.

"Yes?"

Lord Figburt's fresh face suddenly appeared behind the lad. "Ah! Here you are, sir!"

Ram regarded him in exasperation, thrusting the crumpled note into his pocket. Young Figburt was in the throes of an exalted case of hero-worship and Ram was in no mood to be idolized. "Come in, Figburt. Anyone else hiding out in the hall? Might as well let them all in. Make a regular party of it."

Figburt blushed furiously but nonetheless stepped inside. "No. Just me, Mr. Mun—, er, milord. Thought you might want someone to rewrap the hilt of your sword."

"No, thank you," Ram said and turned back to the boy, who shuffled uneasily in place. "Now, you, young sir. What is this message?"

"You're to meet direct in the alley behind the amphitheatre."

Ram's spirits lifted. If he met Arnoux now he would still have time to fight in the final bout. He reached for his coat. "With whom am I to meet?"

"The pretty blonde lady."

Ram whirled around. "Miss Nash?"

The boy's face cleared. "Aye. That's her. Miss Nash. Right proper eyeful, eh, guv?"

Ram wasn't listening. He'd already brushed by the boy and Figburt and disappeared into the outer hall. Lord Figburt and the urchin eyed each other a second before simultaneously shrugging.

"Women'll do that to you," the lad said in patent disgust. "Hope he keeps a weather eye on the time, though that ain't likely."

"How's that?" Figburt asked.

"When me pa gets that look in his eye, he's like to spend all night out with his doxy, and milord is got a duel to fight shortly, don't he?"

"Yes," Lord Figburt said, his gaze falling on the sword Ramsey had left behind. "Yes. He does."

Making a sudden decision, he picked it up and headed after his hero.

"Where you going?" the boy asked curiously.

"To make sure England's victory is assured."

The boy watched him go, shrugged, took out the jar of ointment the other gentleman had given him, and went to work.

"I thought you were different. A lady. And you were. *My* lady." DeMarc's voice echoed down the alley. Ram slowed, fear tightening in a fist around his gut as he slipped forward amidst the shadows. "We were happy together, weren't we? *Weren't* we?"

"Yes, milord." He closed his eyes, cursing inwardly as his fears were all realized. It was Helena. She sounded calm, but her breathing was rapid, nervous.

"But he despoiled you. He stained you." DeMarc's

voice lowered, grew dark and angry. "A man has his pride, Helena. A man, a *real* man, does not stand for another man poaching on his land, does he?"

"Am I a parcel of land, milord?"

"What?" DeMarc sounded confused. An excellent feint, Ram thought. Keep him distracted, off balance. He had reached a point where could see them now. DeMarc's sword pointed at Helena's heart as he slowly backed her into a corner of the twisting alley.

"How much land?" Helena asked. "An acre? A hectare? Or more of a kitchen garden plot?"

"You are mocking me!"

"You are insulting me."

"You can't insult a slut."

Ram slipped along the shadows in the alley, looking around desperately for something to use as a weapon. There was nothing.

"I am surprised a man of your discrimination should have been inveigled by the likes of me."

"You weren't always a slut," DeMarc said sullenly. "But just like Sarah Sweet, you thought you could leave me. Throw me over for that black-haired bastard. Why?" His voice rose, shrill and infuriated.

Helena blanched. *Damn it!* Ram thought. Still too far away. DeMarc might lunge at Helena before he could get to him.

"Don't worry. I know what to do," the viscount said. "I know how to save you. We discussed it. You must die."

"How will that save me?" She had no bluster left. Ram could see it in her eyes. Her momentary hubris had died, leaving only fear.

"You won't be able to sin against me anymore. No

more betrayal. No more lies. Just like Sarah." His voice had grown gentle, almost musing. He reached out with the tip of his blade and let it flirt with her décolletage. She closed her eyes and trembled. "You were so perfect. I shall weep for you, my dear."

"Save your tears for yourself, Viscount," Ram said, stepping into the light.

DeMarc spun away from Helena, his sword's tip grazing her bosom. Ramsey stood with customary poise, bare headed, sans coat, sans waistcoat, sans gloves. Sans sword.

"Munro!" DeMarc exclaimed. "How kind of you to join us."

"How could I refuse such a charming invitation, Viscount?" Ramsey countered.

"What? What nonsense are you talking, Munro? No matter. You are here. Just in time to die."

"I had rather hoped that that time would prove later rather than sooner."

DeMarc shrugged, trying to adopt Ramsey's supercilious ease. "You are doomed for disappointment."

"As opposed to you, Viscount, who are simply doomed."

"Am I?"

"Indeed, yes. You injured Miss Nash, and that I will not tolerate. How seriously are you wounded, Miss Nash?"

" 'Tis a scratch," Helena called out hastily. Despite his seeming insouciance, Ram's concern for her might distract him. "I swear it."

"Thank you, my dear," he said quietly, and now the expression he turned on DeMarc was enough to make her blood run cold. "I think Miss Nash ought to leave now. I do not think it necessary that she witness this next bit of nonsense."

"What's that? Your death?" DeMarc replied, smiling with terrible confidence. "But I would rather she stay. Indeed, if she moves; I shall skewer her straight through her heart. Then I will kill you." His gaze flicked for a second toward her.

"You get back in that corner. Now! Or die," he told her, and because she must pass within the striking range of his sword to do otherwise, she edged back toward the corner.

"Now, Munro, 'tis time to make a pretty farewell and die."

He advanced toward Munro with his sword held slightly down, palm up, as if in invitation. Munro did not move. With the speed of a striking snake, DeMarc lashed out, and Munro arched away just in time.

"Very good, Munro. One would think you'd been used for target practice before. But then, if the rumors are true, you have!" He chuckled, the tip of his blade describing little circles in the air.

He struck again. This time Ram could not completely avoid the lethal tip. It slipped through his shirt, laying it open along his ribs and exposing a welling red line.

Helena bit down on her lip until she tasted blood. She mustn't make the slightest sound or smallest movement or do anything that would distract him.

"What?" DeMarc sneered. "Nothing to say?"

Ram looked down and up, angling a black brow insouciantly. "Why do people keep insisting upon ruining my perfectly good shirts?"

"Munro!" The sudden shout caused both men to look around. Lord Figburt stood in the alley a half-dozen yards away, clutching a sword. "Your weapon!" he called as he flung it forward.

The blade flashed in the air, glinting in the half-light. Ramsey caught it by the hilt, the blade making a sweet whooshing sound as he wheeled back and around. "Ah," he said with gentle pleasure. "Just what I was looking for. My thanks, Figburt."

The boy blustered, backpedaling quickly. But Ram was not looking at him. His gaze was fixed with lethal calm upon DeMarc. "Viscount. Make your pretty farewells."

With a roar, DeMarc charged, his attack striking Ram's blade. The sound rang out sharply in the closed confines of the alley.

Ram parried the attack, but DeMarc's strength obviously surprised him. DeMarc's footwork carried him in close. His blade flashed and darted, making little glyphs in the air. But no matter what line he sought, Ram closed it off; no matter what attack he made, Ram parried it.

She should have run, Helena knew. DeMarc was far too occupied now to heed her. But she stood frozen, afraid that any movement she made would catch Ram's eyes and allow DeMarc's gleaming point the sheath it sought.

"My God!" she heard a voice say from down the alley. "It's DeMarc! And it looks as if his point is bare!"

The unknown man was right. The thick wad of bunting that cushioned the sharp tip of competitors' swords was missing from DeMarc's blade. She looked around at a small group of young men gathering in the doorway that led to the alley. She wanted to shout, to scream at them to get help, to stop this madness before Ram was hurt, but once more the thought of distracting Ram muted her.

"Who's that he's fighting?" one of them asked.

"It's Munro!"

"But Munro is set to fight the final bout!"

"It's Munro, I tell you! Go get the others!"

Please, God. Keep him safe, she prayed as the battle continued. This was no orchestrated match. It was ugly, deadly, and in earnest. DeMarc fought like a madman, passion and vitriol lending his usual skill uncanny strength and force. Ram's counters, in contrast, were light, almost delicate, a hissing displacement of DeMarc's killing line, a feint that led DeMarc's attack an inch wide. His movements were economical, but he did not press for openings, he did not follow DeMarc's retreats.

"The same low line again, DeMarc? How many times is this? Five? Six? That was ever your weakness, all technique and no artistry."

"I'll promise to paint a picture with your heart's blood if you like."

"Ah, subtle. Like your change of engagement. You *have* tried a change of engagement, haven't you? I can't quite tell."

A moment of silence as the blades clattered, and then both duelists dropped back, eyeing each other warily.

"My God! It *is* Munro and DeMarc!" More voices, this time from the windows overlooking the alley from the second floor of the amphitheatre.

Helena glanced up. Men and women crowded several of the windows. As she watched, more were flung wide. She glanced around and saw that people filled the end of the alley now, shifting and craning their necks to see better. Two middle-aged ladies had managed to climb a loaded dray wagon to sit atop the crates in their silk gowns and feathered headdresses as if they were still in their box seats.

By God, didn't they understand what was happening? That Ram's life was at stake?

"Bastard!" Her head snapped round at DeMarc's frustrated cry of fury. He'd marched Ram down the alley, trying to corner him behind a row of barrels. But Ram had defeated his intent by springing atop one of them and kicking over its companion, sending it careening toward DeMarc. The viscount swore viciously as he dodged out of its path.

With a cavalier laugh, Ram leapt to the ground.

"Why don't you just let me kill you, Munro?" DeMarc demanded, striving to regain his aplomb.

"Now where would the art in that be? And without art, what satisfaction in the win?"

"Your concern for me is most touching."

"I swear, Viscount," Ram said conversationally as his blade slipped along the length of DeMarc's, "you have improved since last we exchanged pleasantries. Whatever have you been doing?"

DeMarc, his arm supple and wicked, executed a short, rapid series of flicks that landed on Ram's forearms, tearing open the skin. "Practicing for your death!"

Ram retreated, making a quarter turn away from DeMarc's attack, exposing his side, inviting a hit. DeMarc accepted. He lunged forward, but at the last moment Ram twisted, plunging the point of his sword into the viscount's extended bicep.

"Ah!" The viscount jumped back.

Ram smiled grimly. "Your time would have been better served practicing your remiss."

"I'll feast on your grave," DeMarc swore.

"So morbid, Viscount. You used to have more pleasant manners. Like all those roses you showered on Miss Nash. I own I was surprised at so romantic a gesture."

"What roses?" DeMarc snarled impatiently. "I gave her no roses. I gave her my *heart!* But she would rather have your—"

"Now, Viscount," Ram chided, but his gaze was hard. "If that is an example of your address, 'tis no wonder Miss Nash would not have you."

At the sound of Helena's name, the viscount's eyes narrowed. "Oh, I shall have her, Munro. Then I shall kill her. Like I did Sarah Sweet."

"Viscount," Ram said, falling back and taking his stance, "that was most decidedly the wrong thing to say. *En garde.*"

And now, finally, Helena realized what Ram had been doing these long minutes. Not only had he been allowing the viscount to exhaust himself with his lunges and heavy, bludgeoning attacks, but he'd been watching him, studying him, mentally critiquing DeMarc's skills.

And now he knew them.

His attack was swift and lethal, so quick the eye could barely register it. DeMarc at once fell back before the initial assault. Ram followed him with supple, graceful footwork, taking advantage of his momentary imbalance, forcing DeMarc to give ground even as his blade beat away DeMarc's increasingly agitated barrage.

It was over as swiftly as it had begun. One minute, De-Marc was lunging forward; the next, with lightning speed Ram's tip circled round the viscount's blade, sliding down it as he did so. The force of the move wrenched the blade clear of DeMarc's hand, and the sword clattered to the ground. Nonchalantly, Ram kicked it away.

DeMarc crouched where he'd been when his sword left his hand. His eyes darted back and forth, like a rat looking for an escape from the dog pits.

Ram looked down at him. "I commend you, Viscount, on finally finding your focus."

"What?"

Ram turned away from him, facing the massive crowd that surrounded them. There must have been three hundred people filling the alley and hanging from the windows overhead. "You all heard Lord DeMarc confess to the murder of one Sarah Sweet and his intention of doing the same to Miss Helena Nash, did you not?" he called out.

Angry sounds of assent and outrage rose from the sophisticated throng. Someone shouted for the constabulary. Another voice called out for someone to seize DeMarc.

Ram's gaze turned toward Helena and his sangfroid vanished. She saw, as clearly as the light of the morning star, the relaxation of a terrible and desperate fear. "Helena," he called softly and took a step toward her.

But as he came forward she saw DeMarc rise up behind him, his face twisted with hatred, his hand clenching the hilt of his recovered sword. With a snarl he plunged it toward Ram's unprotected back.

"*No!*"

Ram wheeled around, dropping into an instantaneous lunge, his sword hitting DeMarc's bellguard with the impact of a striking piston, shattering the tip and forcing the jagged end hard against the polished guard, the rest of his blade bowing under the pressure. DeMarc could not stand his ground against the force of the blow. He fell back and with the release of the pressure holding the jagged end in place, the bowed blade sprang free, whipping across DeMarc's shoulder and slicing it to the bone.

With a look of stunned surprise, DeMarc collapsed. Ram kicked his blade away, but it was already clear that DeMarc would not be lifting a blade now or ever again.

"Someone get a surgeon," Ram called. "And the magistrate."

"But . . . 'twas an accident!" someone called.

"Clear as day, 'twas an accident!" another voice added, and another and another. Ram looked around. "We all saw it!"

"By God, man, you have to fight in fifteen minutes. For the championship!" someone called out. "For England!"

"Best hurry." A dignified older man followed by two tall young men in footmen's livery approached DeMarc. "We'll take care of this."

Comprehension filled his face and, at the same time, Helena understood. England had never had its own great fencing master. This was its chance. And, Helena realized with a sickening lurch of her stomach, it was Flora's only chance, too.

The crowd bustled out of the alley, leaving as quickly as it had arrived, hurrying to take seats for the final attraction. In a matter of minutes the alley was nearly empty except for the old gentleman, his servants carrying DeMarc from the alley, and Lord Figburt milling uncertainly halfway up the alley. And Ram.

Ram's brows were locked together in a frown. "I can't, Helena."

"No," she agreed. "Of course not. You're exhausted and hurt and— You wouldn't be able to win, anyway, would you?"

He frowned down at her, alerted by something in her voice. Something she could not mask from him. Then she realized that she had no desire to hide anything from him. Nor any need. He knew her, knew her as well as she knew herself.

She was sick unto death of masks. She only wanted to be with him.

"Why did you ask me to fight, Helena? What is it to you whether I win or lose?"

She looked up into his eyes, clear, concerned, without a trace of suspicion or mistrust. "Flora, Lady Tilpot's niece. She secretly married a wastrel and a pauper and a fool named Oswald Goodwin. I have been acting as a courier between the two of them. That is why I was at Vauxhall.

"But Flora loves him. She loves him, and she is carrying his child, and Oswald, the idiot, has gone and borrowed a small fortune and wagered it all that you will win this tournament so that he can claim Flora as his bride. Otherwise, Flora fears her aunt will have the marriage annulled and the baby taken from her and Oswald will be sent to debtor's prison for the rest of his life."

He regarded her soberly. "And what do you think?"

Helena smiled apologetically. "I think she is correct."

"And this is important to you?" he asked quietly.

"Yes," she said.

He grazed her cheeks with a feather-soft touch. "Then I had best go win this bloody tournament, hadn't I?"

TWENTY-EIGHT

SUPINATION:
a hand with the palm facing up

"MILORD!" Figgy Figburt shouted anxiously. "Please!"

"I have to go now," Ram said, his gaze concerned and his touch a caress. "I have to get ready."

"I know," Helena said. He hesitated again, but at Figburt's impatient plea finally swung around with a muttered curse and strode away down the alley.

Helena hesitated, uncertain from where she would watch the duel. By now Lady Tilpot would be considering the most brutal and public manner in which to humiliate Helena and send her packing. Helena no longer cared, but she certainly wasn't going to give Lady Tilpot the satisfaction of dismissing her. Which meant she would likely have to stand at the door of the kitchen if she was to see anything of the final bout.

She had no regrets. She had done what she could for Flora and Oswald. Whatever fate awaited them, she would no longer be involved in trying to control it.

She started down the alley. A crumpled piece of paper caught her eye. It lay near where Ram had been when DeMarc had sliced open his shirt. She retrieved it, glancing down at the signature. *Arnoux.* That was the name of the man Ram had been going to meet tomorrow night. With a twinge of guilt, she read the note, at once realizing the implications.

This is what Ram had meant when he'd said he couldn't fight. It had nothing to do with wounds or exhaustion. He'd meant he couldn't fight because he had to meet Arnoux. Because this would be his one chance to learn the name of the man who'd betrayed him and his companions in LeMons dungeon. Instead, he'd elected to fight.

Because it had been important to her.

My God, what had she done? Years of searching come to naught so Flora and Oswald could have their happily-ever-after. And what about Ram? What about his need for a finish to *his* story, begun years ago with four lads bonding together as a brotherhood? What of his need for understanding, for answers?

She looked down at the note. It said the meeting was to take place in an hour. It must be nearing that now. There was no time to find Ram and release him from his pledge. She must go in his stead.

She headed toward the stables and went inside. It

was quiet, vacant of the workers who'd snuck into the amphitheatre for the final bout, most of the lanterns dimmed. The soft nickering of horses greeted her alongside the sweet smell of fresh hay and well-oiled leather.

She moved deeper inside, passing the shifting, shadowy forms of horses in their rows of stalls, chance light glinting on polished harnesses and metal bits. Someone was here. She could feel him.

"Arnoux?" she called softly. "Monsieur Arnoux?"

"Here!" a low voice whispered. "Back here!"

She hurried toward the voice, wanting to be done with her business so she could return to Ram. At the far end of the stable she saw a figure sitting on the ground, leaning against the door of a stall.

"Monsieur?"

A shadow moved just beyond where the man sat with his head on his chest, as if asleep.

"Monsieur?"

The shadowy figure materialized out of the gloom, medium tall, lean, and graceful in an oddly familiar way. He moved like Ram, she realized. He came closer, and she saw that he was dressed all in black, his face concealed by one of those basket masks duelists used to protect themselves in practice. In his hand he held a smallsword. With a dawning sense of horror, she realized that blood dripped from its edge.

"Ah, Miss Nash," the man purred. "Such a stalwart lass. I never imagined you would come in his place. I suppose I should have. Your sense of duty is all sorts of impressive. But then, 'twas that quality I have played upon from the beginning."

She took a step back.

"Please. Do not run. It will only make things messy, and I like you. I really do. Almost as much as I hate you."

"Hate me?" She took another step back and another. He followed her, but casually, as if he had long ago anticipated her every movement. "Why? Who are you?"

"Don't you recognize me? I'm hurt. But then"—a low chuckle emerged from behind the mask—"I admit I am somewhat gratified, too. I own I feel sinfully proud of my talents at masquerading. But I'm sure you are just as proud of yours."

"Who are you?" She edged her way toward the door.

"I know. We'll play a game. I was always good at games. Here's a clue: 'My dear Miss Nash, would you be so kind as to fetch me another sweet? I am entirely fond of sugarplums!' "

"Mr. Tawster," she whispered.

He laughed and pulled off the mask, revealing the bald pate and benign features of the vicar. Only he didn't look so benign now. Animation revealed a vitality and handsomeness she'd missed when his mouth had been pursed and his eyes lowered humbly or squinting worriedly.

"Yes, the *Reverend* Mr. Tawster. Quite amusing, that, but I don't suppose you could appreciate the irony. No? Ah, well. You know," he leaned forward confidingly, "I don't even like sugarplums."

"But your figure, your voice!"

"Padding and mimicry."

"I don't understand."

"Of course you don't. But I shall tell you because I truly do think highly of you, and I think to die without understanding is a terrible thing. I shouldn't want it to happen to me, and, as they say, do unto others . . ."

She was at the door now, moving through it into the yard. Still he kept stalking toward her, slowly, unconcernedly. "Tell me."

"If you stop trying to escape for a minute, I will. It's too good a story to relate while stomping about."

He's mad, she thought, but kept retreating. It was darker out here. And empty.

"Let me put it this way," he said, a touch of steel entering his subtly accented voice. French? "If you don't halt I shall kill you at once. Now."

She stopped, her heart pounding in her throat.

"There, that's better. Now, where were we? Ah, yes. Why I hate you. Because you are the whelp of the terribly untimely Colonel Nash. If he hadn't barged into LeMons ten times heroic and insisted on trading his life for . . . well, I'm sure you know who"—his eyes twinkled—"I wouldn't have to conspire at their deaths now."

Even terrified, Helena noted the odd choice of words.

"Why do you want to kill them?"

"I would *never* kill them." His voice had gone from playful to deadly serious in a heartbeat, and the look he bent on her now was filled with loathing, as if she had said something depraved. "I love them. Like brothers. Like sons. Even though they always set me apart." He grinned.

"But I won't kill them. No. They'd win then, you see. They'd be better than me. That *would* be a sin. But that doesn't mean I won't *arrange* for their deaths as I have already arranged a very nice death for Ram."

"How?" Helena asked, her focus at once honed.

He looked gratified by her question. "I knew about the pledge to your family. I knew you were alone in the world, without protection or friends. So I put you in danger, suggested that you find someone to extradite you from that danger, and let matters play out.

"Of course, I encouraged the danger," he smiled modestly, "well, rather a lot."

"I don't understand."

"Of course you don't," he said. "The entire point of the orchestration was that no one was supposed to know of my involvement. You see, I met DeMarc upon my arrival in London and realized early on his predilection for obsessions. The viscount was really quite unbalanced by the unfortunate episode with his former fixation, Sarah Sweet. He came to me for absolution. I gave him something else: you."

"You encouraged him?" Helena repeated, amazed that one man could set out to manipulate another to such dire purposes.

"Oh, yes. Often and strongly. I was the one who encouraged his belief that you reciprocated his rather nasty feelings. Then, I told him you 'betrayed him.' 'Twas I who sent him to Vauxhall after telling him you went there looking for men to seduce.

"He wasn't the perfect dupe, of course. They never are." He sighed heavily. "Ram listed the viscount's failings to a nicety: 'No creativity. No imagination. No *style*.' So sometimes I helped matters along.

"Who do you think accosted you in the rain in White Friars? DeMarc?" He scoffed. "As if DeMarc would be caught dead in a mask.

"And the roses? A nice touch, that, don't you think? And Lady Tilpot even gave me a key to the house . . ."

"You are mad."

Tawster pondered her words. "No. I am clever. I set DeMarc on a collision course with Ram. He was supposed to have killed him tonight. I sent you the flower, then I sent Ram word that you wanted to meet him here. But first I sent DeMarc word that Ram and you were meeting here for an assignation. But then that wretched boy—Figburt?—arrived with Ram's sword and . . . Well, you were here, weren't you?"

He sighed and then, as if recalling something delightful, said, "Happily, I am a man who always prepares a contingency plan. But until all of them are dead, I shall, at least for a while, have to stay in one disguise or another.

"Mustn't let the boys know whom they're dealing with, eh? Which is why, of course, I had to kill old Arnoux back there. And, of course, why I have to kill you. Sorry."

"What do you mean, a contingency plan?"

He pursed his face up in lines of concern that recalled Reverend Tawster's worried mien. "It is disgusting, the degree of poverty and desperation in which we allow the citizens of this great city to live. Why, that young boy I sent to you and Ram—do you know he lives in a room with eight other people? It's appalling, isn't it?"

"What are you saying?"

"For half a crown, he was willing to loosen the button protecting the tip of the sword Vettori was, or rather"—he glanced at the night sky—"*is* using, and spread an ointment I gave him on it. It's poison. Not that the boy knows this. But then, for a half crown, he wasn't asking many questions."

Oh, no! Realization of what he'd done swept over her. The button loosened, the final bout, heated and violent. The smallest cut—

She turned and ran.

He was after her at once. She lifted her skirts, stumbling down the dark alley, knowing she could not outdistance him, waiting to feel the bite of his blade in her back, and then she saw it, still lying glinting on the ground: DeMarc's sword.

With a sob she threw herself down and seized it by the hilt, swiveling as she rose to face her pursuer. He was trotting after her without any real haste, and his face, dear God! His face was filled with a near-blissful relief.

"Thank you, my dear! I was hoping you would do that. Brave, lass! Brava!"

Her hands were shaking so hard she needed both of them to lift the weapon, and when she did the point bobbed and dipped erratically.

His smile was kindly, even sympathetic. "As illogical as it is, I really was having a hard time bringing myself to kill you when you were so absolutely defenseless."

He walked up to her, easily within striking distance, and with terrible gravity, took the *en garde* position. "After you, my dear."

With a sob she swung the blade two-handed, trying to find her nerve. Her bowels felt on the verge of loosening, her vision danced, and her arms felt heavy and weak.

He knocked away her feeble blow and sighed. "Please. Can you do no better? You don't know the first thing about swordsmanship, do you?"

The only advantage you have, young sir, is your apparent unfamiliarity with your weapon. No one who sees you thus could take you seriously. Ram's words, spoken to Figburt that first night in Vauxhall, whispered like a calming wind through her chaotic thoughts.

*The only advantage a vulnerable person has when being at-
tacked is that he is vulnerable. His attacker will not expect him
to fight.*

Tawster regarded her in disappointment. "Well, I
don't suppose I can stand here all night hoping you'll
suddenly develop some skill." With a sigh, he stepped
forward—

"Bastard!" She lunged, twisting, her hand slamming
into the ground, body stretching, her arm extending in
one smooth motion up and out— And felt the point
plunge into a dense, heavy substance, felt the end snag on
something hard buried therein. With a cry she let go of
the sword and fell back, scrambling away on her hands
and feet.

Tawster stared down at the blade protruding from his
ribs. "Begad," he said faintly, the color leaching from his
face. *"Passata sotto."*

He looked at her, quaking just out of reach. "Damn
you."

He took a step forward, but the unexpected pain
caused him to falter, to look down again, this time in real
fear. His gaze swung around and he dropped his own
sword. He clasped the embedded blade with both his
hands and yanked. "Ah!" His stricken gaze rose to hers,
and his lips curled back in a hideous smile. "Tell Ram that
Dand sends his regards!"

Helena did not wait to see what would happen next.
She shot to her feet, her mind already set on Ram. She
had to get to him, warn him! She had to get to him before
it was too late!

Desperately she ran down the alley, plunged through
the door to the amphitheatre, and flew along the corridor

to the entrance to the main arena. A roar rose from within. A roar of pandemonium. Dear God! No!

Terrified, she pushed her way through the howling crowd overwhelming the center arena.

"Have you ever seen anything like it?"

"My God, the poor bastard never saw it coming!"

"He still doesn't understand what's happened to him!"

No. No. No. She shoved and pushed her way through the mill, desperate to get to him and then, suddenly, she was through and she saw him. Ram. Standing.

She forgot everything then, Tawster and DeMarc, the murder of Arnoux, the poisoned sword. All that mattered was that Ram was alive. Unharmed. Whole.

"Thank you," she breathed, barely aware of the tears streaming down her face, the smile trembling on her lips. She grabbed hold of a nearby sleeve and tugged at it until a round-faced man looked at her, beaming with pride. "What happened?" she asked.

"Not one touch. The Italian did not score *one* touch!" he shouted over the riotous crowd. "Never seen anything like it. 'Spect I never will again! Uncanny skill! Uncanny!"

Ramsey was turning now, his blue gaze sweeping over the crowd, as hands clapped him on the back and arms waved wildly.

Then he saw her. And the crowd, locating the object of that blistering gaze, miraculously parted, creating a corridor between them. As in a dream, Helena followed it.

She heard someone call out, "What prize for England's champion? What would you like, sir? What reward can we offer you?"

Ram's gaze locked with hers. "There is only one thing

I want," he said. He stood stiffly, this incredible, honorable, noble man, fearful of her answer, uncertain but willing to abdicate his pride by publicly declaring himself.

Pride. She had too full a measure of that trait. She'd once thought it was the only thing that the world could not strip away from her. She had clung to it. Hidden behind it. Grown suspicious in maintaining it. But what was pride without an equal measure of humility? Without trust? Without love.

"Miss Nash," Ram began, his voice rough. "Miss Nash, would you—"

Her fingers flew to his lips, silencing him. He misunderstood. His eyes shut briefly against what he assumed was her effort to stave off his public embarrassment. He swallowed and opened his eyes. They were tortured, longing, damned. He started to turn away.

"Marry me, Ramsey Munro," she said. He stopped. All around them everything stopped. Every voice dwindled away, the cheers died, the claps and handshakes ended.

"What?" He stopped, his back stiff, shoulders tense, bewilderment filling his voice.

"Marry me because when I close my eyes at night every dream that calls me back to wakefulness, every image that inspires anticipation in another day, is filled with you. I see your arms opening to embrace me and I want to feel their strength. I see your smile, and I want to smile too. I hear your voice and I want to answer. Because I love you."

He turned around, Hope and caution warred in his eyes.

She looked at him, trying to find the words that would

make him understand, and found inspiration. He would ever appreciate irony, her bastard marquis.

"And if you will not marry me because of that, then marry me because you will be a marquis and I would make a fine marchioness. Marry me because I will never bore you. Marry me because our children would be surpassingly gorgeous. Marry me so that I can become the finest female swordswoman in the world." Her eyes fell. "Marry me because I want you. Just marry me, Ram. I *most* ardently beseech—"

He snatched her up, crushing her in his arms that trembled.

"Enough, lass!" he said against her lips. "I'm yours!"

TWENTY-NINE

DISPLACEMENT:
moving the target to avoid attack

AND WHEN THEY SENT the Watch to look for Tawster's body . . . it was gone.

EPILOGUE

"Why don't we just change St. Bride's name to Gretna Green," grumbled Brother Martin, the abbey's cantankerous apothecary.

"I do like a wedding," replied his companion, round and benevolent Brother Fidelis, who as head gardener of the abbey had been given the task of bedizening the chapel with flowers and was now, the day after the ceremony, wistfully taking them down. "And was there ever a prettier bride?"

"Mrs. Blackburn was every bit as handsome," Brother Martin sniffed. He had developed a tendre for Helena's sister, Kate, during her stay with them, and no one was allowed to criticize her by word or inference.

"Oh, yes. She's a very handsome woman. But Miss Nash!" Brother Fidelis smiled dreamily. "She looked like an angel, what with all that silvery hair and in that pretty white frock."

"An angel given in marriage to Lucifer," Brother Martin said darkly. "What Father Tarkin ever saw in that black-haired whelp, I will never understand. Always was too canny by half, if you ask me, and more airs than the Prince of Darkness himself."

"He never made me uncomfortable."

"I didn't say he made me uncomfortable!" exclaimed Martin grumpily. "I said he had airs."

"Well, he's going to be a marquis. A marquis's got to have a few airs."

"Yes," Brother Fidelis said thoughtfully. "And that's odd, don't you think? Him being made a marquis? Especially seeing how last time I checked England didn't recognize a Catholic marriage with an underage bride."

"Hm," Brother Martin said with little interest. "Well, I never have understood how these things work."

"It doesn't work that way, I can assure—"

"Come on!" One of the younger monks poked his head into the chapel, bobbed a quick genuflection toward the altar, and gestured them out. "They're leaving!"

" 'Bout time," Brother Fidelis grumbled, bowing toward the altar before scurrying to catch up with Fidelis, who was trotting out ahead of him. "Next thing you know, we'll be having christenings."

His gaze fell darkly on the very pregnant figure of very young Flora Goodwin, who smiled beatifically from her seat beside her dull-witted but very prosperous-looking husband. Behind them sat a sour-faced dumpling of a woman in black. For whom she was in mourning, Martin did not care to guess. But had he asked, Lady Tilpot would have pronounced with sepulchral coldness, "My niece."

Not that Flora cared. She had her Ossie, and Ossie had a fortune, and soon the two of them would have a little Goodwin. If it was a boy, they would name him Oswald. If it was girl, Alfreda. Because Flora, despite having made some choices in the past that would lead one to suppose the contrary, was no one's fool.

The ginger-haired young lady heading for the trio of monks with far too easy a stride and far too knowing a smile for her tender years was clearly no one's fool, either. Charlotte Nash had neither her sister Kate's dark handsomeness nor Helena's ethereal beauty. Tip-tilted hazel eyes, a mouth some would call generous but more would declare too large, a stubborn jaw, and honey-tinted skin had firmly denied her the celebrated beauty of her sisters. No one, least of all Charlotte, seemed to care. She was reckless, ungoverned, and impolitic, with a growing reputation as a romp and a flirt, with a disastrous tongue and unrestrained wit.

It was a reputation she went lengths to foster.

"He is simply the most delicious man in England," she informed Brother Fidelis. Brother Fidelis blushed.

"What are you talking about, young lady?" Brother Martin crabbed.

"Ramsey. Simply hateful that he's now my brother. But," she laughed, "so gratifying that he's to be a marquis. Should afford me any number more degrees of latitude in my behavior."

At Brother Martin's shocked expression, she arched a gleaming brow.

"Someone should have taken a switch to you years ago," Brother Martin declared.

"Oh?" Her eyes opened, twinkling merrily. "I've never been switched. Hm. It might prove exhilarating."

Brother Martin sucked in a hissing breath and stomped away.

"Well, that was entirely too easy," Charlotte proclaimed, disappointed.

"My dear," Brother Fidelis said, his kindly round face troubled. "This is no way to go on. You must look to the future, to the family you will one day want, the husband whom you will want to respect and be respected by, the home and hearth you desire."

"Ew! Hearths require cleaning, husbands are entirely too possessive, and as for families, well," she shrugged, a little wistfully, "here today, gone tomorrow. Now, don't look like that, Brother Fidelis, and don't you worry. I have my future all planned out, and it will be a corker."

"It will?" Brother Fidelis said hopefully. "But . . . what will you do if not marry?"

"Become infamous," she said simply, and this time she did not look like she was teasing.

"You're certain he told your wife 'Dand'?" Father Tarkin, seated behind the big, scarred desk in his private apartments, furrowed his brow. He bent his white head over the rosary clasped in his hand before looking across the surface littered with correspondence, maps, and books to where Ramsey Munro stood.

"Yes," Ram replied. "But I never saw the man. Or rather, if I did, I didn't notice him. Helena said the only noteworthy thing about him was his baldness."

"Hm. Then we don't even know the color of his hair."

"We don't even know what the man was laying claim to. He told Helena, 'Tell Ramsey that Dand sends his regards.' He may have been intimating that he killed Dand."

The abbot shook his head as if trying to clear his thoughts. He was a straight-backed old man. When he'd been a boy, Ramsey had tried to emulate that intractably erect posture. "You must be careful, Ramsey."

"I intend to be, though I doubt it necessary. From Helena's description of his injury, he was pierced through the lung. He may have had enough time to crawl away. But he has most probably died from the wound."

"You cannot take that for granted."

"Father Abbot," Ram said, regarding him soberly, "I can assure you, since my release from LeMons I have taken nothing for granted, and now, with Helena . . ." He lifted his hand. He needn't say anything else. The abbot had seen them together: how he looked at her, how she awoke to his presence whenever he came near, how he warded over her, even from across a room, and above all the tenderness and amazed joy they shared.

"We will wait, then." The abbot pushed his chair back, satisfied. There were things he could do, measures he could take to ascertain the truth of what was going on. Measures that did not require Ram's involvement. He smiled. "I hear you have lately discovered your legitimacy."

At this Ram had the grace to look troubled. "I felt I made the right choice, Father. The marquis offered me the wherewithal to discover the traitor. The price, though a blow to the pride, did not seem too great."

"No, son. It was not. And God knows the truth. So, what now?"

Ram gave a lopsided smile. "Back to London. Find a house. Helena is trying to convince me to write a treatise on swordplay. I may do so. I may even teach. Apparently, if one becomes a national hero one can do whatever one da—whatever one pleases."

"You will offer Charlotte Nash a place in your new family?"

Ram frowned. "Helena already offered, and Charlotte declined. She said she'd had enough changes of address, and as the Weltons wanted her company, it would be discourteous to deprive them of it."

"She sounds a formidable young lady."

"Yes."

"And how does your wife feel about this?"

Ram's expression became a little puzzled. "Surpassingly well. She says Charlotte 'will triumph,' whatever that means, and as a newly minted husband I of course agree.

"Besides," he went on, "she has informed me that her concerns for the immediate future lay elsewhere. She is determined to play matchmaker."

"Really. For whom?"

"My grandfather and Lady Tilpot. She is convinced they deserve one another." His blue eyes gleamed appreciatively.

The abbot, having met Lady Tilpot and having heard much about the marquis over the decades, stared owlishly at Ram. "Your wife has a decidedly Jesuitical bent of mind."

"I know," he said proudly. "Delicious, is it not?" He looked down at the clock on the abbot's table. "And speaking of wives, I would like very much to stay, but I would like even more to join Helena. I am sure she is in the carriage already. Very punctual, my wife." He smiled more broadly. "I do like saying that. 'My wife.' "

"Of course." The abbot rose to his feet. "God be with you and yours, Ramsey."

"Apparently so, Father," Ramsey said with a return of his dry humor. "And right thankful I am."

● ● ●

Helena, having said her goodbyes to the wedding party, entered the richly lacquered carriage the marquis had insisted on sending to the abbey—though nothing could induce him to attend the papist ceremony Ramsey had insisted upon. A smile of anticipation on her lips, she settled back against the soft velvet cushions.

A moment later the door opened and Ram climbed in, giving a sharp rap to the roof before taking the seat across from her. At once the carriage rolled forward. "We'll be in Sterling by nightfall," he said conversationally.

"That's nice," she said and yawned delicately.

"You're tired," Ram said, immediately consolatory.

"A little," she confessed. The hours of their wedding night had been well filled, but not with sleep.

"Let me draw the curtains. I'll wake you when we stop for supper."

"Would you? Thank you," she said, smiling sweetly as Ram suited deed to word. At once the carriage interior was steeped in darkness, warm and enveloping. Helena waited, counting the minutes until they had driven out of the abbey yard and were on the long road heading south, and then very slowly, very quietly slipped from her side of the carriage to Ram's. She reached out and found his chest. She heard his breath catch, but he did not move. With nimble fingers she plucked the rose pin from his cravat and slipped it into her pocket. Then, while he silently acquiesced, she eased his jacket from his shoulder and over his long arms.

With lingering touches, she unwound the silk cravat and, finding the little pearl buttons of his shirt, popped them free one by one. Slowly, incrementally, she peeled back the linen and was rewarded by the feel of the crisp, silky curls that covered his muscular chest. She pressed her lips into that light furring and felt his heart drum thickly in response.

Her fingers traveled a sensuous trail down his chest, rolling over each velvety rib to his hard belly and stopping at the waistband of his trousers. She trailed her lips across his chest, nipping lightly, pausing at his flat, leathery male nipple to touch her tongue experimentally to the hard kernel at its center. His body jerked. His hand came up and clasped her wrist hard, but neither urging nor restraining, simply holding her. She smiled against his warm, dense body.

He was a very stalwart man, her husband. He could withstand much. He had withstood much, she thought as her free hand brushed over the thick, smooth ridges of his brand.

She crept closer, nuzzling him as she rained light kisses down his chest to the denser line of hair that disappeared beneath his waistband.

His hand came down and captured her chin, lifting her face to his. His eyes glittered in the half-light, passion darkened, adoring her. "I thought you were going to rest." His voice was amused and breathless.

She reached up, linking her hand behind his neck and pulling his eager mouth down to hers.

"I had a better idea," she whispered as his mouth closed on hers.

And she did.

AUTHOR'S NOTE

I OWE A GREAT DEBT of thanks to Cliff and Missy Iverson, the extremely knowledgeable and gracious coaches of the University of Minnesota's fencing team. Not only did they lend me their expertise, they gave me the opportunity to "fence." Any errors in this book involving the description of the dueling sequences are the result of my having taken poetic license, and any failure to properly explain certain terms are my fault alone. Thank you, Cliff and Missy.

As for the International Dueling Tournament, I have found no evidence that anything resembling such a competition ever existed in the Regency period, though certainly exhibitions were held between famous duelists in all the great capitals of Europe. Additionally, many lesser bouts were indeed held under the circumstances I outlined, with the winner's take a part of the gate. I see no reason to doubt that should someone have come up with the idea of an "international invitational," so to speak, it might well have been implemented. Even during times of war, the aristocracy in Napoleon's France and England found ways to interact.

As a final aside, I found it fascinating that one of Josephine's most trusted rose experts (an Englishman) was given diplomatic immunity to travel back and forth between France and his native England during the entire war.

A lady will have her garden.

Enjoy the following preview of the next novel in
Connie Brockway's The Rose Hunters trilogy,

MY SURRENDER

Now Available from Pocket Books

Charlotte paused on the threshold of the ballroom,
hanging back a little, fighting a nervousness she could not
ignore. Inside, the sparkle of a thousand candles ric-
ocheted against a hundred mirrors, throwing light like
confetti, sparking on diamante spangled bodices and
winking in diamond stickpins, glossing ropes of pearls
and shimmering in pomaded hair and satin waistcoats,
here picking out the tip of a tongue surreptitiously wet-
ting lips, there catching the glimmer of teeth flashing in
a smile.

She knew these people. She'd known some of them
since her arrival in London nearly six years before when
she'd been unofficially launched into society by her sur-
rogate family, the Weltons. Most were kindly if slightly
ramshackle types, no more likely to judge their fellows
than themselves. There was kindly Lady Bucklewaite,
concern over which sweetmeat to eat puckering her
face, the perpetually befogged Mrs. Hull, and sweet Lord
Mayhughe.

But there were also less friendly faces. Juliette Tupstone, née Bogh, her one-time schoolmate and eternal
enemy, and George Ravenscroft, whom she'd sent packing for being fresh five years ago when *fresh* had meant

stealing a kiss and she had thought it mattered, and Lord Bylespot, who had given her a far deeper understanding of *fresh* and to whom she'd given a far greater understanding of the word no.

Those were people she'd always been wary of alienating, those who with a word could annihilate a woman's social status and condemn her to a life in the gray half-world on the fringe of society. They and their ilk roosted like carrion eaters about the edges of the ballroom, waiting for her to fall and shatter so that they might swoop in and pick her bones clean.

Well, tonight they would have a feast. After tonight, if all went according to plan, she would be a Fallen Woman. The news would reach her would-be seducer the Comte St. Lyon within a week. She didn't care so awfully for herself. But she could not help but imagine her sisters' shock when they heard. Yet what other choice was there? Too much was at stake. Too many lives.

Once more she glanced toward Juliette Tupstone, her gaze scavenging through the crowd, searching for some misdemeanor to snack on. *Bon appétit*, Julie, she thought and, taking a deep breath, stepped through the door into the ballroom, her head held high, a coquettish smile on her lips, her eyes sparkling with feigned expectation.

At once she was surrounded by admirers, both men she knew and men tugging at the sleeves of their companions begging for an introduction. She enjoined the game as the expert she knew herself to be, smiling, casting sidelong glances like lures amongst the stream of men and reeling them in with a toss of her head, a winsome trill of laughter, a playful tap on an arm.

Within a very short time her fan was scribbled over

with the names of men who she had given a dance. But beneath the familiar banter and teasing bon mots, her nerves drew tighter and tighter. *When would he come? Where was he?*

"I believe this is my dance, Miss Nash?" A young lieutenant who been introduced to her at an art exhibition last week stood at her side.

She glanced down at her fan. Ah, yes. Albright, Matthew. "So, it is!"

Gaily she took his arm and let him lead her through the throng of admirers to be absorbed into the line of dancers. Lieutenant Albright held her gingerly, his gloved hand barely touching hers. His admiration, so candid and clean, was like a balm. "You are charming."

Charming. The simple compliment brought an unanticipated frisson of distress. Would ever another man find her charming after this evening? Or would the appellations hitherto attached to her name be ones no man would tolerate being associated with his daughter, his sister, let alone his wife?

"Thank you," she answered. "You are too kind."

"You little baggage," a male voice said from behind her.

She spun around. A tall, broad-shouldered man in exquisitely tailored evening dress stood before her. He was dark-visaged, with brilliant amber-colored eyes and thick brown hair clipped short. His hard jaw had been scraped smooth revealing a pale white scar on his tanned cheek. Dand Ross. Relief washed through her.

"You promised me this dance." His gaze locked on hers.

"I say, sir, you are mistaken," Albright stepped forward and pointed at the fan in Charlotte's hand. "You need only look to see that it is my name writ upon her fan. Not yours."

"Is it?" Dand asked, his gaze moving reluctantly from Charlotte to the young lieutenant. With a smile that just missed being friendly, he wrested the fan from her grip and with the same dangerous smile, crumpled it into a ball and dropped the mangled mass to the floor.

"Alas, Miss Nash has lost her fan. But I am certain she will recall that I, and not you, have claim of this dance. And the next." His gaze returned to her, possessive and fierce. "And the next." His voice was low and dark. "And the one after that. You remember, don't you, Lottie?"

Her heart pattered in her chest.

Playacting, she told herself firmly. She had never given him proper credit for being such a good actor. She must remember to commend him.

"She wouldn't ever dance so many times with one partner!" declared Albright, ruddy faced. "You are insulting a lady, sir. And as a gentleman, I demand satisfaction."

Dand turned from her to Albright, his expression lazily interested. A tomcat, Charlotte thought breathlessly, playing with a mouse.

"Before you go off doing something your father—assuming your father holds you in affection—will regret, why don't we ask the lady if she feels insulted? Well, Miss Nash?"

There would be no going back from her answer. She didn't hesitate. "No."

The lieutenant stared at her, a dark stain mounting his downy cheeks. Albright had set her on a pedestal and now she had plummeted from it and he was angry at her.

"I'm sorry," she said softly.

"I see," he said stiffly. He bowed toward Dand. "I wish you joy of her."

His words caused the blood to drain from Charlotte's face. The lieutenant began to turn on his heels, but Dand's hand shot out, spinning him back around.

"I don't think I heard you properly, son," Dand said, his voice light but his eyes narrowed. "For your sake, I hope so."

The young officer scowled, self-preservation warring with pride. Impulsively Charlotte laid her hand on Dand's arm. This was ridiculous. How could he harm this young man for believing what they had purposely led him to believe? "Dand . . ."

He ignored her. "Now. *What* did you say?"

Self-preservation won. The boy's eyes fell away. "I wish you joy of the evening," he muttered angrily and swung around again, stomping away through the crush of dancers. Charlotte watched him go, imagining the interested questions, the condemning replies.

"I'm sorry."

She looked back. Dand was regarding her gravely.

"Not on my account, I hope," she said with a lightness she was far from feeling. "We have achieved what we set out to achieve. My reputation is in shreds."

"Not yet." With unexpected gentleness, he secured her hand and pulled her into his arms and began to dance.

He was unexpectedly adept, a natural grace to his movements, an unself-conscious surety in the skill with which he guided her down the long line of dancers that made up the country set. He didn't speak, though when the steps of the lively dance brought them together, he watched her face with an intentness that any spectator could not fail to note. Like a lover, hungry and yearning . . .

Nonsense. He was just doing what his role demanded. She didn't know what was wrong with her, entertaining such notions.

"You look all at sixes and sevens, my dear," Dand said as he led her down the line.

"With some reason," she answered, finding the reason a second later. "You didn't have to ruin my fan."

"I'll buy you another," he answered in amused tones, catching hold of both her hands and swinging her lightly to the outside of the figure being executed. "It provided a nice little spectacle for our audience. Very manly of me, laying territorial claims and all that."

"By breaking a perfectly nice fan?" she asked doubtfully as he set his hand lightly on her waist.

He laughed, bringing several heads swinging about. "Indeed, yes. The boy understood at once that if I risked breaking your fan I must be *very* certain of your affection. But I don't expect you to understand. Women never appreciate such subtle signals."

His nonsense returned her humor to her. "You are right," she answered. "Far too subtle. I would have better understood what you were trying to convey if you had thrown me over your shoulder and carried me from the room."

He didn't answer. Instead, his lids slipped lazily over his eyes. The dance ended but he held on to her hand, drawing startled, offended looks from those nearby. And when the orchestra began another tune, he did not wait or ask permission, but pulled her back into his arms. This time the orchestra played a cotillion, an intricate French import. Within minutes she realized that he was more than an adept dancer, he was superb.

"Where did you learn to dance?" she asked wonderingly. "I cannot imagine there were many opportunities at the abbey."

"One picks up things here and there," he replied. His gaze flickered down to her face, an unreadable expression on his countenance.

"What is wrong?" she asked.

"Nothing," he said sharply. "It is just . . ." He abruptly stopped dancing, taking hold of her hand and pulling her out of the set. Wordlessly he headed for the pair of French doors standing open at the end of the ballroom. The other dancers scooted out of their way, eyes wide at the interruption, heads swinging to follow their departure.

At the end of the room he didn't stop, but instead led her through the open doors onto the bright, moonlit flagstones beyond. He stopped a few yards outside. "What are you doing?" she asked in a low voice.

"You suggested it yourself." He sounded a bit testy.

"Pray illuminate me," she said, trying to tease him out of this uncharacteristic tenseness. "What are you talking about?"

"Why spend the night dancing as I attempt to scowl down every one of your poor swains when we could far more easily and effectively secure the desired result?"

"I don't understand."

"God." He raked his hair back, ruining his carefully groomed locks and turning him once more into the disheveled, slightly disreputable blackguard she'd known. "I can't believe anyone could think you could succeed in this. This is madness!"

His irritation struck a spark. She didn't know precisely why, but that he questioned her ability to playact was all too clear. "It may be madness, but madness is, I believe, our only option," she retorted. "Now did you drag me out here to bolster my confidence or do you have something else to say?"

He regarded her with a tight jaw. "No."

"Then what are we doing out here? It is not dark, you know. People can see us quite clearly. And several are looking."

"That is precisely why we are out here," he said grimly. "That and this."

And without warning he caught her up in his arms, crushing her ruthlessly to him, his mouth descending on hers in a bruising kiss.

She headed toward the stables and went inside. It